PRAISE F

LONGLISTED FOR THE MCILVANNE
SCOTTISH CRIME BOOK OF THE

rilliant new talent for the lover of crime…a vibrant crime nership and sound forensic expertise." SUE BLACK, DBE, ENSIC ANTHROPOLOGIST

refreshingly different approach to the private investigator re… a fast-paced tale." – SHIRLEY WHITESIDE, *HERALD*

unflinching, often funny and yet ultimately tender portrayal ife on the margins of society…a lively debut, with a fresh, erent vibe." CRIME FICTION LOVER

"[A] fantastic new crime novel…a gritty book with a surprisingly m theme of female friendship." *THE LIST*

cLeary's prose is assured and engaging, bursting with the iness of the Aberdonian vernacular… an impressive debut." EN CRIME READS

oof that good things come to those who wait." *NDEE COURIER*

me fiction has a new stellar voice in Claire MacLeary. *Cross ose* is feisty, funny and darkly delicious." MICHAEL J MALONE

rrific crime debut with an unlikely crime-fighting partner-hat sets it apart from the rest…compelling to the end." ESA TALBOT

y and thought-provoking… With lashings of authentic leen and a fast paced plot keeping the pages turning. Highly mended." GRAB THIS BOOK

prising read with dialogue so salty and a plot so gritty that d keep a Highland road clear all winter." LAS SKELTON

Also by Claire MacLeary

Cross Purpose

Burnout

Claire MacLeary

CONTRABAND

Contraband is an imprint of Saraband

Published by Saraband,
Suite 202, 98 Woodlands Road
Glasgow, G3 6HB

and

Digital World Centre, 1 Lowry Plaza
The Quays, Salford, M50 3UB

www.saraband.net

ISBN: 9781912235117
ebook: 9781912235124

10 9 8 7 6 5 4 3 2 1

Printed and bound in Great Britain by Clays Ltd, St Ives plc.

burnout n. *physical, emotional, and mental exhaustion, caused by long-term involvement in situations that are emotionally demanding*

I

Maggie

The woman leaned in. 'I'll get straight to the point. I think my husband is trying to kill me.'

Wow! Maggie jolted upright. *That's a first!*

She struggled to maintain eye contact whilst her mind worked overtime. If their initial telephone conversation was anything to go by, this Mrs Struthers promised to be a profitable new client for the agency. But a threat on her life? That was a whole new ball game.

Maggie re-lived the dressing-down she'd had from DI Chisolm earlier that year when she got herself involved in an active murder investigation. What on earth was she going to do now?

'Mrs Laird?'

'Yes?'

'Did you hear what I said?'

'Oh, yes.' She drew a steadying breath. 'I did.'

Maggie took another squint at Sheena Struthers. Small-boned. Short hair. Good skin. Not much make-up. Pretty in an old-fashioned sort of way. And ages with herself, she reckoned, or thereabouts. In short, the realisation hit home, like Maggie in another life.

Poor woman looked a bag of nerves: eyes staring, fingers picking relentlessly at her cuticles. Almost as fraught as Maggie had been when she'd first picked up the reins of her husband's private investigation business. Still, the woman would be frightened, wouldn't she, if someone really was trying to top her?

'That's a very serious allegation, Mrs Struthers,' Maggie continued.

'Sheena, please.' The woman opposite pushed her cappuccino to one side.

They'd met in Patisserie Valerie in Union Square. Maggie had passed it often enough but never been inside. In her straitened position, she couldn't afford to stump up nearly three pounds for a cup of something and the same again for a pastry. But the easy parking suited both her and her prospective client, and the cafe was low-key, more private than Costa Coffee or Starbucks.

'Sheena.' Maggie started to smile, then, remembering the subject matter, hastily rearranged her face. 'On what grounds, might I ask, is this allegation based?'

Lord, would you listen to yourself? Since becoming a PI, Maggie had schooled herself to think like a detective. Now she was beginning to talk like one.

'Just a feeling, really. It's hard to explain, but...'

'It's this time of year.' She cut the woman off mid-flow. 'The run-up to Christmas puts a strain on the most solid of marriages.' What she wouldn't give, now, to have a man at her side, strain or no.

'You're so wrong.' Sheena Struthers looked her straight in the eye. 'But before we go any further...' She rummaged in what looked, to Maggie, like a designer handbag, drew out a snakeskin-covered notebook and slender silver pen. 'May I put a few questions to you?'

'Of course.' Relief flooded through Maggie's veins. That would buy her time to devise an exit. She took a judicious sip of her tea.

'I understand you haven't been a private investigator for long. Am I right in saying that your husband...?'

Is dead, Maggie finished the sentence in her head. Then, 'Let me stop you there.' She put down her cup. This was going nowhere. 'I'm afraid...' Frantically, she framed excuses in her head: inexperience, pressure of work, conflict of interest. No matter they weren't entirely true, they'd do the job.

Sheena Struthers ignored this. 'I've done my homework, Mrs Laird. Looked into other agencies, in Aberdeen and further afield. For one thing they're much too big. You'll appreciate that in my situation...' She cast a furtive glance around the cafe. 'Discretion is paramount. With companies that size, one can never be sure.'

'But the police,' Maggie interjected. 'Shouldn't you...?'

'My dear...' Keen brown eyes gazed into Maggie's own. 'One gets the impression they're stretched enough, don't you agree?'

Maggie offered a non-committal, 'Mmm.' No way was she going down that road.

'And besides,' Mrs Struthers insisted, 'you must realise that any police involvement could endanger my marriage.'

For the second time that afternoon Maggie was caught on the back foot. *Make your mind up, woman: your marriage or your life?* 'Oh, yes,' she murmured, 'I see what you mean,' though she was at a loss to follow this line of reasoning.

'Nor could I take the matter to a solicitor,' Sheena Struthers continued. She leaned in close, dropped her voice. 'My husband is an accountant, you see. Moves in rather a closed circle. And Aberdeen, it's small enough, still. Word gets around,' she looked to Maggie for reassurance. 'Doesn't it?'

'It certainly does.' Maggie buried her nose in her cup. She knew only too well what the woman was alluding to. The police were as much a closed circle as any other professional body. Because of one man's perjured testimony and another's breach of interview protocol her detective husband had been forced out of a career to which he had devoted his life.

'From what I've read in the papers, your late husband was an experienced detective.'

Maggie abandoned the tepid tea. 'That is correct.'

'So I assume the business has some standing. And you, from what I've heard, are a person of some integrity. And operate outwith,' she raised a questioning eyebrow, 'what one might loosely call "the establishment". In short, Mrs Laird, your firm seems the perfect fit.'

Oh, to Hell! Maggie had intended to bring the meeting to a close. Now she'd let this Struthers woman take control.

She straightened in her seat. 'It's kind of you to say so, but I really don't think I'm the right person.' Her mouth turned down. Wasn't that how she'd reacted when Wilma Harcus had urged her to take on George's business? *A daft idea*, she'd called the proposal from her gallus new neighbour. And it was. But Maggie had yielded in the end, in part as a conduit to clear her mounting debts, but primarily as a means to clearing her husband's sullied name, a quest for justice that was still ongoing.

'You will help me, won't you?' Sheena reached across the table, clutched at her arm. 'Please?'

Maggie played for time. 'Well, I...' She asked herself why she was still sitting here. Wilma wouldn't give this woman the time of day.

Sheena Struthers' eyes brimmed with tears. 'You're going to say no. I can tell.'

Here we go! Maggie couldn't count how often she'd had to harden herself to situations like this. But it had to be done.

'I'm sorry to disappoint you.' She assumed an expression of sincere regret. 'But I'm afraid I must.'

Wilma

'You did what?' In the conservatory to the rear of her bungalow, Wilma nearly jumped out of her chair.

'Took on that Mrs Struthers I told you about.'

'Maggie Laird!' She lapsed into the vernacular. 'Will ye no learn?'

'Yes, yes.' From the fat cushions of the cane chair opposite, Maggie held her hands up in a show of surrender. 'I know you're going to throw that Argo case at me again, but this is different.'

'Different? How? Tell me that, will you?'

'Mrs Argo was sick.'

'I'll give you "sick". She was a bloody head-banger!'

'That's unfair, Wilma, and you know it.'

'Unfair, now, is it? Pesky creature wasted hours of our time. And this Struthers woman sounds to me like more of the same. I'd put money on it she's shooting you a line.'

'Sheena Struthers is scared,' Maggie insisted. 'I could see it in her eyes.'

'Why doesn't she go to the police, then?'

'Moves in exalted circles. Wants to keep it quiet.'

'She could divorce the bastard.' Stage wink. 'On the quiet, like.'

Maggie shrugged. 'Loves him, by all accounts.'

'Och,' Wilma snorted. 'They all say that, leastwise till they're lyin up at ARI wi muckle tubes runnin out of them. Anyhow, did we no agree we were tae phase out the domestic stuff?'

'You're right, Wilma. We did, only…'

Wilma cut her short. 'An did we no mak that decision for a reason?'

'Yes, but…'

'A good reason. And that reason was, them cases take up too much fuckin time,' Wilma was pink in the face, 'for all they fuckin bring in. Ye're a grown wumman,' she wagged a fat finger, 'but ah wonder, sometimes, what's atween yer ears.'

Maggie stiffened. 'There's no need to be insulting.'

'None intended. Dae ye no see?' Wilma leaned across the coffee table, took hold of Maggie's hand. 'Ah'm only tryin tae protect you, ya feal quine.'

Maggie snatched her hand away. 'I'm perfectly capable of managing a case on my own, thank you. As you'll concede I've been doing for some time now.'

'*Perfectly capable*,' Wilma mimicked.

'Now you're being facetious.'

'Fac-ee whit? Fur fuck's sake, Maggie, cut it wi the lang words. All ah'm sayin is ye're a soft touch.'

'I am not.'

'No? Dae ye mind thon bodybuilder?' Wilma sat back, folded her arms. '*He was desperate,* says she. An that pair at Westhill? An the woman out Sheddocksley way? An...'

'Point taken. I might have been a bit gullible then, but if I've learned one thing from my experience as a private investigator it's to trust my instincts.'

'Well,' Wilma reverted to business mode. She unfolded her arms and raised a finger to her face. 'My nose is telling me this Struthers thing is a bit whiffy.'

'You're wrong,' Maggie remonstrated. 'Sheena Struthers comes across as perfectly straight. She's genuinely apprehensive, otherwise why would she go to the trouble of approaching us? And despite what you say, I warmed to her. She's a nice woman.'

'Nice, is it? You're too easily taken in by appearances, Maggie Laird. Just because she lives in Milltimber and the husband doesn't get his hands dirty doesn't stop her taking you for a mug.'

Since she'd moved to Mannofield, Wilma couldn't credit how easy folk made a crust. Back in Torry you'd be on a building site in all weathers, or standing in a fish processing factory on a wet concrete floor.

Maggie sighed inwardly. *Right again!* She could still remember her reaction when Wilma had rolled up on her doorstep: how she'd shrunk from the sheer vulgarity of the woman. Then that first time she'd been invited into Wilma's home: how gob-smacked she'd been at the over-the-top furnishings, how she couldn't stop herself from mentally totting up the cost.

'If you must know, I did turn her down.'

Wilma calmed down. 'There you are.'

'But in the end she managed to convince me.'

'Christ!' She bristled again. 'Didn't I say you were a soft touch?'

'It wasn't only that. If you must know, I fancy a challenge. When we started out, we were only going to pick up a bit of this and a bit of that. Basically, what the big players didn't want. We've been all over the place. It's time we moved on.'

Wilma grinned. 'I'm up for that.'

'Be serious! I know the bread and butter stuff is the backbone of the business, but it would be nice, just once in a while, to tackle something really meaty.'

'Do you not think we've challenge enough, Maggie, taking the business forward and still holding down our jobs? You've two kids and all to think of.'

'Agreed.' Maggie recalled, with a pang of guilt, the number of times she'd made it to school by a whisker, the duties she'd skimmed over, the ready-meals she'd dished up. 'But it's such a grind, this endless round of witness statements and credit checks.'

'Get you! It's me does the bulk of the checks.'

'I know.' Shamed look. Though Maggie had worked to improve her IT skills, Wilma was more clued up, her fingers nimbler on the keyboard. 'All the same, it would be good to focus on something that would tax my brain cells.'

'You could take up crosswords.'

'As if.'

Wilma stroked her chin. 'If you're having second thoughts, you could still back out.'

'How can I?'

'Give the Struthers dame a ring. Say something's come up.'

'I couldn't do that.' Indignant voice.

'Why not?' Wilma's blue eyes widened. 'You haven't gone and given her our terms of business, have you?'

'No.'

'Well, then, you're not committed.'

'But how could I…?'

'If you don't want to ring and tell her yourself, just don't accept her calls. She'll get the message soon enough.'

'Wil-ma, that would be a dreadful thing to do.'

'I don't doubt it, but a whole lot better than landing yourself in it.'

Pursed lips. 'Sheena Struthers is the real deal.'

'So you say.'

Maggie turned on her friend. 'If you're so sure she's a phoney, why don't you sit in on our next meeting and judge for yourself?'

Wilma squared up. 'I might just do that.'

Brian

Brian Burnett sat on his sofa bed. He flicked through the TV channels. On the coffee table in front of him, the remains of that evening's takeaway – sweet and sour pork and egg fried rice – congealed in glutinous lumps in their silver foil containers. He looked around. In one corner of the cramped bedsit, an airing rack draped with washing sagged alongside an ancient night storage heater. Beneath his feet, the carpet hadn't seen a Hoover in months. Behind thin curtains that barely met, the single window onto Urquhart Road dripped with condensation. He killed the TV, chucked the remote. *Christ, what a fucking way to live!*

From the flat upstairs came the dull *thump-thump* of bass, overlaid with heavy footsteps clumping back and forth. He sat back, let his eyelids droop. His student neighbours were decent enough lads, but laminate flooring and sporadic horseplay were no recipe for a quiet life.

In his job as a Detective Sergeant at Aberdeen Police HQ, Brian had spent an arid few weeks either on duty or steadfastly avoiding eye contact with those well-meaning colleagues who, he feared, might invite him to join in their pre-Christmas celebrations. And all the while obsessing about his soon-to-be ex-wife Bev: Bev whom he'd doted on, Bev who'd cheated on him, Bev who even as he sat there was most likely out on the razzle with one or other of her toy-boys.

There was a crash from upstairs, closely followed by hoots of laughter. Brian's head jerked up. Above him, the light fitting, with its nicotine-stained shade, swung alarmingly. That was all he needed, the bloody ceiling coming down. What the hell were they doing up there?

He jumped to his feet. He'd better go up and have a word. There had to be more than two of them in the flat to make that sort of racket. Come to think on it, he *had* noticed a couple of new faces on the stair. Brian wondered how many students were actually dossing in the property. One way to find out. He took a step towards the door. Turned. He really ought to go up, but he couldn't be arsed. He sat down again.

If he could only move on. Maggie Laird for a start. Brian's shoulders drooped as he recalled his tentative overtures to the widow of George Laird, his long-term buddy. Brian had carried a torch for years, ever since he and George trained together at Tulliallan. He'd never made a move, not until George was dead and buried.

The meetings Maggie had set up – assignations in the art gallery and the Wild Boar – Brian had read as a desire for male company. She'd been lonely, he assumed, after George died, just as he, Brian, had been lonely these past months. Then there was the night Maggie had rolled up at his place. He'd thought all his Christmases had come at once until he saw the carload of kids. How they'd managed to get embroiled in that student's murder – and her along with them – still flummoxed him. In all his years in the force, he'd never encountered a case so convoluted.

When, after the round of statements had been taken at Queen Street and he'd finally hit the sack, Brian resolved he'd not be taken for a mug again. He'd draw a line under Maggie Laird. Keep his distance. No more cosy chats. She'd milked his long friendship with George, no two ways about it. Bev had been the same, only she'd screwed him for money. Both ways it had ended in tears.

Not that he could blame Maggie Laird. Not entirely. Woman must have been desperate, what with the debts and the pension cock-up. Still and all, a bloke would have been upfront about it. No, Brian had jumped in too soon, he saw, now. Been too compliant. They took advantage of that, women, and Maggie Laird had been no exception. She'd played him, right from the start. Wangled information out of him: stuff he should never have divulged. He'd been lucky to get off with a verbal warning from his inspector. All because he'd let his feelings get the better of him, allowed himself to be sweet-talked into letting out more than he should. Less than was culpable, he consoled himself, now. As if he, Brian Burnett, would bring the police service into disrepute, and him with twenty-odd years of faultless service…

There was an almighty clatter from upstairs, followed by total silence. Maybe one of the buggers had got knocked out. Then again it might have been a piece of furniture. *Fuckit!* he mouthed. Why in Christ should he care? The skanky bedsit he occupied had never been intended as more than a short-term fix.

Now, Brian resolved, the time had come to gee himself up, make a start on the next chapter of his life. The New Year would herald a fresh beginning, his first priority to get himself out of this miserable howff he'd never managed to call home. Then he'd be able to invite folk back. He'd become something of a social leper this past while, so much so the invites had dried up.

Hell, he might even find himself a woman. That wee DC Strachan seemed to be unattached. He could ask her out for a meal. No strings. Take it from there.

Seaton School

The dinner hall was festooned with festive cardboard cut-outs and gaudy crepe paper chains. Maggie surveyed the detritus of that day's Christmas party. The kids had been even more hyper than usual, wound up by the prospect of a fortnight's holiday and a bumper haul from Santa. She thought back to her own two: the pleasure she and George had derived from seeing their wee faces on Christmas mornings as they ripped wrapping paper from their presents beneath the tree.

No point going down that road! The memories were still too raw. She banished the thought.

Staff and guests stood in awkward groups around the buffet. Well, 'buffet' was stretching it. In reality they were mopping up the leftovers from the kids' Christmas do. Padded out by bog-standard nibbles from the local Spar shop and a couple of bottles of wine, the congealed squares of pizza and curling sandwiches were an unappetising sight. The far from festive atmosphere wasn't helped by the liberal dose of scented air freshener somebody had scooshed to mask the lingering smell of steamed vegetables and bleach.

Wondering who'd come up with the idea – to invite partners to their end-of-term get-together – Maggie made a beeline for the only unaccompanied person in the room: Ros Prentice, a young teacher who'd moved up from Edinburgh the previous year. Back then, what with the few hours Maggie worked and her spell of compassionate leave, they hadn't had much opportunity to get to know each other. But, although a few years apart in age, they'd been drawn together by the hostile attitude of some of the older teachers: Maggie on account of her lowly status – learning support was resented as an intrusion – and Ros on account of her progressive teaching methods. Over the past months the two had developed a close rapport.

'Nic not able to make it?' Ros was wife to a senior lecturer at the university and mother to a small son.

'Yes.' Ros turned, an anxious look on her face. 'He said he'd come, but…' An awkward silence ensued.

Maggie filled the gap. 'He's likely just running late.'

'I suppose.' Ros didn't look too convinced.

'It's this time of year,' Maggie reassured her. 'Folk get caught up. Throws you off kilter, doesn't it?' Her smile masked the loneliness she felt.

'You can say that again,' Ros concurred. 'It has been a madhouse here today. I expect it's near as bad in Nic's department. And it's no better at home. What with the job, the housekeeping and Max, I've been toiling just trying to stay on top of things.'

'Has the wee one settled at nursery?'

'Loves it. The Rocking Horse is so handy. Nic says…'

'Do I hear my name taken in vain?' A voice at Ros's back.

She whirled. 'Nic!' A crimson flush rose in her neck and suffused her face.

'And you are?' he demanded of Maggie.

'Maggie Laird.' She'd heard plenty about Nic, but they'd never met. With a practised eye she filed a description: six-foot-two, slim build, fair hair, blue eyes. Handsome, in an effete sort of way.

She stuck out her hand.

'A colleague,' Ros added.

'You teach here?' Nic ignored Maggie's outstretched hand.

'I wish,' she quipped, letting it fall to her side. 'I'm only a classroom assistant.'

'That right?' Dismissive voice.

Despite herself, Maggie bristled. She'd barely exchanged two words with Nic Prentice and already she disliked the man. It's the posh accent, she told herself, that and the supercilious manner.

Don't be in such a rush to judge. She scolded herself. Wasn't it her own hoity-toity attitude that had landed her in trouble? Insisting on sending her kids to private schools, pressing George to take early retirement rather than risk a disciplinary hearing. She snapped back to the present. Ros's husband is young, she reminded herself. Maybe he's nervous in company. Overcompensates. She allowed herself a wry smile. We all do.

'Maggie runs her own business.' Ros rushed to her friend's defence. 'She only does a few hours here because she loves being around the kids.'

'Well, I...' Maggie began. That was only partly true. She did, indeed, love the kids, even the toe-rags. Her mind jumped to Willie Meston. Willie and his gang had led her such a dance when she'd become embroiled in Lucy Simmons' murder. She gave a small sigh. But the principal reason she clung to her Seaton job was to bring in some much-needed cash.

'Rather you than me.' Nic interrupted her train of thought. 'I couldn't stand it: brats misbehaving, peeing their pants.' He pulled a face. 'Students are bad enough.'

Maggie forced a smile. 'I daresay.'

'I don't know how Ros stands it,' he ran on. 'She's wasting her time,' he cast his eyes around the disordered space, 'in a dump like this.'

Ros threw him an anguished look.

Maggie willed herself not to respond.

'Anyhow, mustn't keep you talking.' Nic flashed a set of perfect teeth. 'Lead on,' he gripped Ros by the elbow. 'You'd best introduce me to your Head.'

Smoke and Mirrors

'*A feeling*, you said, last time we met.' Maggie eyed the woman opposite. 'I'm afraid we'll need something more solid than that if we're to progress with your case.'

This was her second visit to Patisserie Valerie, and Wilma's first. They'd been ahead of the game: getting to the meeting place early, securing a secluded table at the rear, observing the woman's approach. It was astonishing how much you could learn just from watching and waiting – standard stuff for a private investigator and second nature to them, now.

Sheena squirmed in her seat. 'I don't know how to answer you.'

'Well?' Maggie prompted. They'd agreed she should lead the interview. 'Has your husband done anything specific to give you cause for concern?'

'Nothing major.' Sheena drew a deep breath, exhaled at length. 'More, lots of little things, I suppose.'

'Such as?' Maggie pressed.

Sheena's eyes flicked from Maggie to Wilma, vibrant in sky-blue eyeshadow and shocking-pink lipstick. An embarrassed silence ensued before they slid back again.

Finally, she spoke. 'The way I catch him looking at me, sometimes.'

'And what way is that?

'Cold. No love there at all. Like he could see me dead and buried.'

Out of the corner of her eye, Maggie noticed Wilma's lips were twitching. 'Oh,' she rushed on, 'I'm sure we've all looked daggers at our spouse at some time or other.'

'Point taken. But there have been other things.'

'Can you give me some examples?'

'He snapped at me the other day because I creased his morning paper.'

'You don't say!' The words were out of Wilma's mouth before Maggie could silence her.

Maggie shot her partner a filthy look. 'Anything else?' she asked.

'He refuses to switch off his phone at night. I don't sleep well as it is, then it pings and wakes me up.'

'Mmm.' Maggie made a show of stirring her latte.

Wilma inspected her nails.

'He won't let me open his mail, and...'

'Let me stop you there.' Maggie had a growing feeling Wilma was right about Sheena Struthers, but wasn't ready to admit it. 'Has anyone else noticed anything amiss?' She pressed on in desperation. 'Your kids, for example?'

'Gordon and I, we don't have any children.'

'Oh.' Small voice. She'd dug another hole for herself.

'No.' A shadow crossed Sheena's face. 'When it wasn't happening, I wanted to get us both checked out, but he wouldn't agree to it. Male pride, I suppose.'

Wilma let out a loud snort.

'And, then, well, we were both working. Gordon was still studying for his professional exams and I was teaching. Time runs away, doesn't it?' She looked to Maggie for confirmation.

'Doesn't it just!' Maggie could barely believe that this time last year she'd been happily married. Well, perhaps not so happily given the nightmare George had been through. But they were together, still, a family unit. Maybe this Struthers woman should be thankful for what she'd got.

'His behaviour has been so out of character. That's what first alerted me. Gordon's so considerate, normally. So...equable, I think, is the right word.'

'Sounds like my Ian,' Wilma chipped in. 'Right pussy, he is.'

'At least he was, until...' Sheena eyed Wilma like a scared rabbit.

'Still,' Maggie continued, 'singularly or taken together, what you've described hardly constitutes a threat.'

'I know it doesn't sound much. But there have been other things.'

Sheena engaged both women in turn with a beseeching look. 'Incidents.' She looked around, checking she wouldn't be overheard.

A clear case of paranoia was what was running through Maggie's head. She wondered what Wilma was thinking. She needn't have worried. Her companion was hungrily eyeing the tempting display of cream cakes on the counter.

'Fill me in on the background, will you?' She'd give it one last go. 'How long have you and Gordon been married?'

'Twenty-five years, give or take.'

Much like herself. Maggie raised the mug to her lips. Only what she wouldn't give to have her husband back.

She set the mug down. 'How did the two of you meet?'

'At school. Cults Academy,' Sheena clarified. 'His folks moved up from Fife. Dad worked offshore. It was the end of fourth year, as I recall, and in comes this new boy, all plooks and prescription glasses.'

Maggie smiled. 'Sounds a bit of a geek.'

'He was. Right swot, we all thought, so much so we called him "Inky Fingers". Not that I was the class pin-up,' Sheena hastened to add. 'I was spotty too. A vision in puppy fat. Wore glasses as well.'

'So you felt sorry for him?'

Wilma shot her a warning look. *Shut up, Maggie. Don't go putting words in the client's mouth.*

'Not at all.' Coy smile. 'If anything, it was the other way around. I used to take it to heart, you see. Being left out of things: sports fixtures, not being asked up at school dances. But Gordon seemed impervious to what other people thought. Maybe that's what drew me to him. He might not have been a hunk like some of the rugby players, but he was funny. Had a quick mind and...' Wry face. 'A savage tongue. Anyhow, we started going out, stuck together right through uni, and, as they say, the rest is history.'

'Is he still like that, your husband?' Maggie fished.

'Oh, yes.' Fond look. 'Sharp as a tack. Maybe that's what makes him such a good accountant. I retired some years ago from my teaching post. Not that I'd lost interest. But Gordon didn't want his wife going out to work, not when he became senior partner. Argued it could harm his...' She hesitated. 'Connections. I didn't mind, not at the time. The discipline – or lack of it – at school was getting to me. I understand you work in education, so you'll know.'

'I'm only a teaching assistant,' Maggie responded. 'And the job's just a few hours a week. But, yes, it's an uphill struggle, some days, getting the kids to settle.'

'All the same...' Wistful look. 'I came to regret my decision. It's lonely being at home on your own all day. You lose your confidence.'

'Mmm.' Maggie could identify with that.

'Don't get me wrong,' Sheena continued. 'Gordon and I have a good life: bridge, golf, foreign holidays. We're comfortable. More than comfortable. We own a lovely home. Move in rather an elevated circle.' Knowing look. 'Our friends would say we're a solid team.'

'Can't be all bad, then,' Wilma offered with a curled lip.

Maggie ignored this. 'And you?' she pressed. 'What would you say?'

'I'd say,' Sheena chose her words with care, 'we have a marriage that's traditional, some might say old-fashioned.'

Like Maggie's own had been. 'I see.'

'Not perfect. But it has worked for me. Us,' she corrected. Her brow furrowed. 'Until now, that is.'

'Then why,' Maggie persisted, 'if your marriage has endured and your husband still demonstrates the same qualities that attracted you in the first place, would you want to rock the boat?'

Sheena looked puzzled. 'I don't. That's why, as I said at our first meeting, discretion is paramount.'

'You're still of a mind, then, that your husband has designs on you?'

'I'm convinced of it.'

'Oh, come on.' Wilma could contain herself no longer. 'You're telling us he wants to kill you, but you've no evidence to support this, only vague "feelings" and trivial incidents. Not one single concrete fact. When it all boils down, there's nothing there but smoke and mirrors.'

Sheena's eyes welled. 'You don't need to be so hurtful. I know it doesn't sound like much, the things Gordon has done, but you weren't there. And now you're going to send me packing,' she sniffed. 'I feel so alone.' Her voice tailed off.

'Then why don't you go to the police?' Wilma pressed on, relentless. 'That's what they're there for.'

'I can't. The publicity...'

That, Maggie could understand. During the long months between George's suspension and his eventual resignation, her hitherto tight family unit had been subjected to horrendous strain: her husband the subject of false rumour and innuendo, her children in distress, the Laird name making lurid press headlines.

'Better that than being dead,' Wilma snapped.

This provoked such an anguished sob that other customers eyed the trio with some asperity.

'Perhaps it would move us forward if you were to jot down these "incidents" as they happen,' Maggie sought to calm the situation. 'Then, next time we meet...'

Viciously, Wilma dug her in the ribs.

'...we can work through them, decide where to go from there. Is that a good idea, do you think?' She engaged Sheena with a questioning look.

'Yes.' There was silence, then: 'Thank you.' The woman's eyes shone through her tears. Ignoring Wilma, she rose to her feet. 'I'll be in touch.'

*

'I don't bloody believe you did that,' Wilma hissed when Sheena Struthers was safely out of sight.

'Did what?' Maggie played dumb.

'Let the bugger off the hook.'

'Don't know what you mean.'

'Christ,' Wilma spluttered. 'I set you up with an exit plan and you fuckin blew it.'

'If you mean I was supportive of another woman in distress?' Maggie recalled her own sense of isolation and helplessness after her husband's sudden death. 'Then I'm not going to apologise.'

Wilma eased herself out of the confines of the red tub chair. 'Don't give me that crap, Maggie Laird. Some days you really are up yourself. Admit it, you fucked up, instead of killing the thing stone dead.'

Maggie ducked her chin.

'We're supposed to be partners, remember?' Wilma wasn't going to let her off the hook. 'And you pulled rank on me.'

'I did not.'

'You did so.'

'Well,' Maggie retorted, 'if I did, that's us just about even.'

'What are you trying to say?'

'Serves you right for snooping on me when I was investigating the Seaton drugs business.'

'I was watching your back, I told you.'

'That's one way of putting it.'

Wilma pulled a face. 'Whatever! That aside, have you forgotten what we agreed? If I still had my doubts about your Mrs Struthers after meeting her face-to-face, you'd show her the door.'

'And do you?'

'Too bloody right I do. From what I've seen, she's just another menopausal woman having a loopy moment.'

'Who said she was menopausal?'

'Isn't she? She's about the right age.'

'She's only a few years older than we are.'

'Aye.' Wilma grinned. 'We've that to look forward to.'

She was met with a grimace.

The grin vanished from Wilma's face. 'Ah'll tell ye one thing, Maggie, and that's for nothing. If this Sheena Struthers lands you in the shit, dinna come runnin tae me.'

Maggie set her jaw. 'She won't land me in trouble.'

'So you're hell-bent…'

'As I've said already, I've agreed to take on the case.'

'Well, it's your business.'

'Ours.'

'Aye,' Wilma sneered. 'Some days.'

'Oh, Wilma…' Remorseful look. 'Don't be like that.'

'I'll tell you this, pal, and that's for nothing. If you go ahead with this Struthers thing…' Wilma looked Maggie straight in the eye. 'Make no mistake, you'll be on your own.'

Chisolm

Rain streaked the window as Allan Chisolm power-napped at his desk. After a couple of hours battling with paperwork, his neck and shoulders had seized up. That morning's gold meeting with strategic command had been a mixed bag: his squad had failed to secure the result they wanted in the Seaton case. Who'd have credited Christopher Gilruth would escape jail? Talk about one law for the rich? The DI let out a derisive snort. If his daddy hadn't rolled out the big guns in the shape of Louis Valentine, young Christopher – aka Fatboy – would be safely banged up right now.

The inspector had to hand it to his fellow Weegie, Valentine might be a total wanker but he got results. Not that it had been too hard on this occasion: the evidence led by a couple of fledgling female PIs and a bunch of wee boys. Talk about unreliable witnesses! One of the kids was soft in the head, a second denied all knowledge, the third wouldn't open his mouth at all. As to the tenant of the flat where the alleged criminality took place, Kym whatever-her-name-was had appeared in the witness box so out of it she could hardly tell the time of day.

Valentine had run rings round Maggie Laird as well. Still, it was her own fault for going where she had no business to be. Chisolm hoped she'd learned her lesson and would steer clear of what was, rightly, police business from now on. Mind you… Chisolm stroked his chin. The woman had balls: the way she'd squared up to all the shite that had been thrown at her, and her the size of nothing.

You're getting soft in your old age, he chided himself. *Don't even think of–*

'Sir?' A voice broke his train of thought. The door edged open. 'Got a minute?' DS Brian Burnett peeked into the room.

Chisolm shoved the budgetary reports to one side. In his

opinion, all the flow charts and projections and value assessments in the world were worthless without the manpower vital to effective policing. He straightened in his seat. 'I can give you ten.'

'Thanks, sir.' Brian approached the desk, sat down.

For a few moments there was a strained silence, then: 'Spill.'

'It's about my rank, sir.'

'What about it?'

'I wondered…' Brian twisted his hands in his lap. 'That is, I was thinking…'

'Spit it out, Burnett.'

'Would you be willing to put my application forward to the review panel for inspector?'

Chisolm leaned forward. 'What brought this on?'

'I've been marking time this past while. My wife and I…you might have heard…?'

Chisolm nodded acknowledgement.

'And I've been thinking – over Christmas and that – it's time I moved on.'

'You think going for inspector will help you do that?'

'Yes, sir.' Brian did his best to sound positive. 'I do.'

'What makes you think there's a vacancy? Detective inspectors' jobs aren't ten a penny, Burnett. Particularly in these times of budget constraints.

'I heard on the grapevine, sir, you were being tipped for DCI.'

Chisolm grimaced. 'Did you, now?'

'It's not true, then?'

'Might be.' Guarded voice. 'Though the outcome of the Seaton drugs business was less than satisfactory. Could go against me.'

'Maybe so, sir. But that was only one part of the picture. You surely scored brownie points with the powers that be over your handling of that student's death. And the university mummies and daddies will be mighty happy if the council clean up Seaton Park. Whatever, if you were to move up, it would create an opening.'

'Which a number of candidates could apply for.'

Brian's face flushed crimson. 'I realise that, sir. But we all know Wood's marking time, and I doubt Duffy would be bothered. He's got his hands full at home.'

'Yes, yes.' Chisolm drummed his fingers on the desktop. 'I know. How about Dunn, though?'

Brian eyed his superior. 'Lad's ambitious.' Did he detect the hint of a smirk? 'He'll want to go for sergeant.' Smarmy little bastard, he thought. 'But it's mebbe a bit early.' He wasn't going to diss the guy. Brian knew Douglas had rubbed enough noses in it to queer his own pitch.

'If I were to put you forward, Burnett,' Chisolm fixed him with a hard stare, 'what, do you think, are your chances of success?'

'I've done my time as sergeant, sir, got a solid track record. Plus...' he broke off.

'Go on.'

'I'm an all-rounder: good in the field, on top of the admin, well-developed social skills...'

'I hear you.'

'So if there are any,' he cleared his throat, 'developments, I'd appreciate if you'd give me the nod.'

'I'll do that.' Chisolm looked at his watch. 'But for now...'

'Sir.' Brian took the hint. He rose to his feet and hurried from the room.

Siblings

Colin, Maggie's teenage son, was sitting in front of his computer monitor reading articles on Reddit when: 'Have you seen my pen?' His sister Kirsty burst through the door.

'No.' He swivelled in his seat. 'Why would I?'

'Because you're always nicking my stuff.' She advanced on him. 'That's why.'

'And I suppose you never "borrow" anything of mine?'

'I most certainly do not.'

'Liar. What about the time you…?'

She back-tracked. 'Not lately anyhow.'

'That's because you're never here.'

'And that doesn't alter the fact my pen's gone missing.'

Colin unfolded himself from his seat. 'What's the big deal, anyway?' He looked down, a full head taller, now, than his sister.

'It's the one Dad gave me.' There was a catch in Kirsty's voice. 'When I got into uni.'

Her brother shrugged. 'Don't remember.'

'You *must* remember. We went out for dinner at Gerard's, the four of us, and Dad produced it at the end of the meal. It's a Parker, slim, silver-coloured…'

'Whatever.' Sarky face. 'Haven't seen it.'

'That's typical of you.' Kirsty faced him down. 'Forever ducking responsibility: the way you closet yourself up here, shy away from interaction with other people. You did the exact same thing when there was all that trouble over Dad.'

Colin held up his hands. 'If I did come up here, it was most likely to give him space.'

'Space?' Kirsty spat. 'Who are you kidding? You were up here so you didn't get nabbed by the reporters.'

'Look who's talking.' There was a smirk on her brother's face. 'Who was it did a runner but Daddy's Little Darling? If my memory serves me right, the minute it went pear-shaped you were out of here like a bat out of hell. It was me that got lumbered with the crap: the drawn curtains, the phone ringing off the hook. Not to mention the olds: Dad's nerve was shot, Mum was in total denial.'

'She was not.'

'How would you know?' he sneered. 'You weren't here.'

Kirsty gave him a sideways look. 'I know a lot more than you think.'

'Like what, for instance?'

'Kirsty?' There was a shout from downstairs. 'Food's ready.'

She half turned, called over her shoulder, 'Okay.' She turned back. 'Before we go down, I have to say it really pisses Mum off, the way you behave.'

'Me? How? You've just given me stick for keeping out of her road.'

'This room, for instance. Look at it.' With distaste, she surveyed the dog-eared posters covering the walls, the rumpled single bed, the clothes strewn on the floor. 'It's a pigsty. Plus,' she wrinkled her nose, 'it stinks.'

'Oh, yeah?' Colin's lip curled. 'And I don't suppose yours stinks? All that perfume and hairspray and stuff you can't do without?'

'Kir-sty.' The call came again.

She took a breath. 'Coming.'

'And how do you think it makes Mum feel,' Colin pressed, 'when you have a go at her? Since you went to uni you're forever doing that: sniping at her down the phone from Dundee. She comes off really upset. She tries to hide it, but I've caught her. You're so self-obsessed, I don't suppose that even occurs to you.'

'I don't "snipe" as you call it. Mum and me, we may not always see eye to eye, but…'

He rolled his eyes. 'That's the understatement of all time.'

'Regardless, Mum's got enough on her plate with this house

and her Seaton job without you making extra work for her. Then there's Dad's business…'

Colin cut in. 'It's her business, now.'

Filthy look. 'Hers and that big slapper next door.'

'If she didn't have the support of "that big slapper" as you call her, Mum would still be trying to clear Dad's name all by herself. You do know she went to see that thug James Gilruth?'

Kirsty shrugged. 'I didn't. But that's beside the point. If Mum has a score to settle with Gilruth, I can't see that Wilma Harcus will make a bit of difference.'

'Whatever,' Colin retorted. 'Anyhow, if Mum can't get back at the bastard, with or without the help of Wilma, I will.'

'How do you plan to do that?'

Colin shrugged. 'I'll think of something.'

Kirsty ignored this. 'As I was saying, as if it isn't bad enough…'

'Having her hook up with the riff-raff,' Colin supplied. 'Mix with low-life? You're such a snob, Kirsty Laird.'

'That isn't the worst thing you could call me, little brother,' she came back. 'But at least I haven't resorted to drugs.'

His eyes slid away. 'Don't know what you mean.'

'Oh, no? How about getting smashed out of your skull? Not to mention the spliffs?'

He reddened. 'It was only the once.'

'Come off it.' Kirsty stuck her face in his. 'It's splashed all over Facebook, Col – you and your mates getting wasted, making rude gestures, acting the clown. You know what? You're so immature it's pathetic.'

'I'd rather be immature than self-righteous.'

'Seriously, bro,' Kirsty lowered her voice, 'You want to be careful what you post. Once you're in the job market, prospective employers pick up on that sort of thing.'

Colin snorted. 'Just because you're doing law, doesn't give you the right to judge other people.'

'I'm only offering some sisterly advice.'

'Well, I don't need advice from you, so the sooner you go back to…'

'Do you two want to eat?' Maggie bawled. 'Or will I throw the whole lot in the bin?'

'Coming, Mum,' Kirsty responded.

'If you're done.' Colin took a step forward.

Kirsty turned. 'Don't worry, I'm going.'

On the threshold, she hesitated. 'About my pen?'

'I told you, I haven't seen it,' Colin spat. 'Now, get out. And,' he followed her down the stairs, 'next time you want to come into my room, knock first.'

A New Year

The peal of bells and the explosion of fireworks echoed from the television.

Ian raised a toast. 'Happy New Year!'

Maggie slid from the leather settee. 'And to you!' They clinked glasses.

'Hope it's a good one!' Wilma added her champagne flute to the mix.

'Yes, well...' Maggie broke off.

They were in Wilma's front room. Lowered window blinds and a hissing gas fire kept the space snug against the wintry weather outside. On the giant wall-mounted television, STV's Hogmanay party was in full swing.

'You'll be pleased to see the back of the aul year,' Ian said, cheerily. 'Everything that's happened, like.'

Wilma threw him a warning look.

Maggie buried her nose in her glass, affecting not to notice. She let the effervescent bubbles prick her nostrils, savoured the honeyed aroma. Ian was right, though. She was thankful to draw a line under the year past: a year in which George, her devoted husband of more than twenty years had died, her children been in crisis and she, Maggie Laird, rudely plucked from her cocoon of domesticity to embark on a career as a private detective.

She thought back to their first New Year together, she and George, in that poky rented flat in Ferryhill: top floor, two rooms, kitchen and bathroom. How, when the ships' hooters sounded, they'd rushed to the window and thrown up the sash. They'd rested their elbows on the sill and watched, transfixed, as crimson flares lit up the sky, all thoughts of toasts and TV abandoned. It was only when the harbour fell silent, and chill air nibbled at their elbows, that they'd lowered the window and crept through to their sagging three-quarter bed to spoon in the dark.

Tears welled in her eyes.

'Come for a bosie.' Wilma threw her arms wide.

Grateful, Maggie allowed herself to be enfolded in her friend's embrace. Changed days, she reflected, since Wilma had first moved into the douce West End suburb of Mannofield. It seemed no time since she'd first appeared on Maggie's doorstep, all Ten Ton Tessie in her sprayed-on leggings and fake tan. Then, Maggie had been a bit sniffy, she had to admit. But now look at the pair of them: so attuned to one another they could almost read each other's thoughts.

'You okay?' Wilma relaxed her hold.

'Yes.' Maggie wiped the tears away. 'Thanks for that.'

'No worries.' Wilma grinned. She turned to her husband. 'Top us up, will you? My pal here's needing a bittie cheering up.'

'I'm fine. Really,' Maggie protested, as Ian trickled fizz into her glass. 'Thanks! It's great just to have company.' She toasted them both. 'Cheery company,' she added, smiling.

She looked around. Wilma's house was ablaze – candles lit, chandelier twinkling, silver baubles glittering on a huge, fake tree. And that was just the inside. Maggie shuddered as she recalled her reaction to the curtain of LED lights dripping from the front of the adjacent bungalow, the giant illuminated reindeer standing by the front door. Made her own, dark house look like an old folks' home. Time was, her family would have driven out to Tyrebagger, the four of them, and picked a real tree from the Forestry Commission's site. Maggie hadn't had the heart, not this year. Instead, she'd unearthed the small fake tree that usually sat on the dining-room sideboard. A forlorn sight it looked, too, marooned as it was now in the sitting room bay window alongside George's empty chair.

'Where are they, your kids?' Wilma's voice brought Maggie back to the present.

'Colin's at a sleepover out at Cults. Kirsty's on the razzle with her pals. So I'm glad to be here with you guys, especially after the Christmas I've had.'

'That bad?' Wilma had been embroiled with her own extended family over the festive season, so there hadn't been time for small talk.

Maggie made a face. 'Nightmare! My folks meant well, inviting us out for Christmas lunch, but it was hard going, I can tell you. My dad sat slumped in his chair, hardly said a word. As for Mum, I scarcely saw her. She spent half the time in the kitchen, wouldn't let me do a thing. I don't doubt she was fretting over me the whole darned time, whilst I sat next door with dad and the kids worrying about her.'

Wilma chortled. 'I can just see it.'

'We had to sit all the way through the Queen. The kids were bored witless: Kirsty making eye signals at me, Colin thumbing his phone. Then, by the time we finally made it to the table, Col was so famished he stuck his head in his plate and wolfed every last thing that was put in front of him. If my mum wasn't biting her tongue at his total absence of table manners, she was sneaking horrified looks at Kirsty's navy-blue nail varnish. My dad, God bless him, was totally oblivious. It's sad, really, the way he's retreated into himself. Mum's the exact opposite. Once she'd had her annual ration of sweet sherry, she couldn't hold back from giving me the third degree.'

'Like?'

'The usual: didn't I think running a detective agency was an unsuitable occupation for a woman?'

Wilma rolled her eyes. 'Sounds familiar.'

'How was I getting along with my "friend"? That's you.' She gave Wilma a gentle nudge. 'Weren't there any "proper" jobs I could get? It was all I could do not to run screaming into the snow.'

'Ah, weel,' Wilma assumed a grave expression. 'That's a big hurdle over, Maggie – your first Christmas on your own. And your ma will come around. Just like Ian,' she joked, unable to stay serious for long.

'What about me?' Her husband turned his head from the television.

'I was just saying,' Wilma teased. 'You're okay now. With the agency, I mean.' *End of.* She could still recall how dogmatic he'd been, way back, when it was just a notion in her head.

His face darkened. '"Okay" just about covers it.'

'Oh, don't be like that,' Wilma pouted. 'We're celebrating.'

He drew his brows together, pursed his lips in a thin line. 'If you say so.'

She cosied up. Smiling, she tickled him under the arms.

'Steady on.' He backed off, balancing his drink so it didn't spill. His face bore a troubled expression, Maggie saw. Still and all, his eyes were twinkling.

In that moment, she envied her neighbours their moment of intimacy, wondered if she'd ever have that again.

II

Justice for George

'Right.' Maggie cast an eye over the files stacked on the table. 'Now we've got Christmas and New Year out of the way, let's see where we're at.'

'Fair, fat and forty,' Wilma joshed, thrusting out her boobs. 'Time I was back at the gym for starters. The pounds have been fair piling back on.' She grabbed a handful of flesh from the waistband of her jeans. 'All them feckin mince pies.'

'I know,' Maggie agreed. 'Not to mention the booze. It's high time we sobered up.' She threw a stern look in Wilma's direction. 'Got back to concentrating on the job in hand.'

'Don't give me that look.'

'What look?'

'The *I'm-Head-Girl-and-you're-only primary-one* look.'

Maggie drew herself up. 'Don't know what you're talking about.'

'Force of habit,' Wilma muttered.

'What did you say?'

Innocent face. 'How are the financials?'

'Ticking over. Apart from a couple of late payers, the bread and butter stuff is doing away. And,' she brightened, 'the Innes Crombie account has given us a bit of wiggle room. If business slows down, that should see us through January and February.'

'Things okay on the domestic front?' Wilma asked guilelessly. She knew how proud Maggie was, grabbed the chance to slip the question in.

Maggie seemed not to notice. 'The mortgage is less of a worry since I made the arrangement. I've managed to keep up the payments. Not that it isn't a struggle, what with Colin's school fees and Kirsty's uni accommodation, and that's before the household expenses. But,' she made a face, 'I manage.'

'At least *your* kids don't give you any grief.'

'No.' Colin's last school report showed a marked improvement in his grades and a near-perfect attendance record. Kirsty, too, was keeping her head down. There had been no more dramas, no repeat of the cutting episode. 'But, back to business.' She rubbed her hands together. 'To kick off, looks like we can firmly close the door on the Seaton business.'

Wilma sniffed. 'Was that no meaty enough for you, then? A murder in a graveyard, a bunch of schoolkids at the back of it? And that's before the drugs and thon alkie childminder.'

Maggie had the grace to blush.

'Bugger all we got out of it too. All the hours you spent checking out them kids.'

'It was useful surveillance practice.'

'Fair dos. But what about your face-off in that flat with thon maniac, Fatboy? You could have got yourself killed, Maggie.'

She shrugged. 'Don't exaggerate.'

'At the very least got your face disfigured.'

Maggie grimaced. 'To go with my skelly eye, you mean?'

'It's not skelly, just a bit on the lazy side. And you ken fine folk only notice when you're stressed.'

'That's pretty much all the time these days,' Maggie joked.

'Regardless, we got nothing out the end of it. No money, and that Weegie bastard took all the credit.'

'If you're referring to Inspector Chisolm...'

'Och.' Sly grin. 'You're his number one fan now, are you?'

'Not at all. But you've got to give the man credit. It was Chisolm took the case forward.'

'It was you did all the work.'

'Not all, exactly.'

'Near as.'

'No matter. For the time being we need to keep a low profile.'

'How? I thought we were meant to be promoting the agency.'

'We are. Only that whole saga resulted in adverse publicity.'

Maggie was still smarting from her ordeal in the witness box when Fatboy came to trial for dealing drugs. 'We don't want to attract any further attention.'

'Like what, for instance?'

'Well, it wouldn't look good if the details came out. Having my,' Maggie cleared her throat, 'unorthodox methodology splashed all over the papers. I mean, running surveillance on a bunch of wee boys, and me charged with their care. Detaining them in my car without parental authority. Gaining entry by subterfuge to that flat in Esplanade Court. I could lose my Seaton job for less.'

'Well, it's not as if you did anything illegal.' Arch look. 'You didn't, did you?'

'Not like you, is that what you mean?'

Wilma responded with a mischievous grin.

'Wil-ma...' Exasperated voice. 'I can't stress enough that private investigation isn't a game. If anyone gets wind of your escapades, we can wave goodbye to our licence.'

'Come off it, Maggie. The SIA have their work cut out policing them heavies call themselves doormen to be bothered about two wee wifies like us.'

'That's as may be, but we've served our apprenticeship now. It's time for the agency to begin a new chapter. A strictly professional one.'

Oops! Wilma turned her head away. She'd been going to fess up to the GPS tracker she'd recently ordered online. It might prove useful to them both, after all. Now, she thought better of it. Turned back. 'There you go again,' she chided, 'on your high horse. You've a face on you like a slapped arse. Thought you were going to lighten up.'

'And I thought *you* were going to stop treating the investigation business like a...a...TV game show.'

'Ooh,' Wilma rolled her eyes. 'Get you! Did you have a particular one in mind?'

'Yes. No.' She was so tired tears swam in front of Maggie's eyes.

'Forget I said that. Only our results are based on hard slog: hours spent sitting at a computer, fact-checking, taking down witness statements, you name it. A bit like police work. And that demands a rigorous approach. I know you're doing your best, Wilma, but I worry that one of these days those shortcuts of yours will sink the ship. And that would be a tragedy, don't you see? For you. For me. But more importantly, for George.'

'I get that.' Stricken face. 'Only...'

'You're doing great,' Maggie moved to reassure her friend. '*We're* doing great. Overall, we're more incisive in tackling our caseload, quicker to tie things up.'

'And get the invoices out,' Wilma came in like a flash.

'That too.' Wry smile. 'We've demonstrated we're learning our craft. The agency's grown from a struggling start-up to a sound enterprise. And it has every chance of continued growth. But, Wilma,' Maggie extended a hand. 'In our efforts to grow the business we mustn't lose sight of the bigger picture. We're doing all this for a reason.' Her face clouded. 'A very serious reason. A man has been gravely wronged. And none of this will have been worthwhile if we don't achieve our primary goal. And that's justice.' Tears welled in Maggie's eyes. 'Justice for George.'

Get Them Off

The Bide-a-Wee in Bucksburn was Aberdeen's go-to venue for strippers. The management brought them up from Newcastle, Wilma had been soberly informed when she'd made discreet enquiries of a local entertainment agency. Strippers in latex, strippers with snakes... You name it, they could source them. *Sexy girls*, the promoter said. *Best in the business.*

But it wasn't girls Wilma was interested in. Wednesday was ladies' night at the Bide-a-Wee. Her quest that evening was for something more, shall we say, macho.

Now, the compère – a Slick Willie in a too-tight tuxedo – flashed his toothpaste smile. 'Tonight, ladies,' emotionless blue eyes swept the audience, 'we have a mega treat in store. Straight from the London Palladium...' Pregnant pause to let this sink in, '...the Bide-a-Wee brings you the Biggie Boys!'

Aye, right, Wilma thought. For 'Biggie' read 'Mr Average'. As for the London Palladium, the 'Hull Hippodrome' more like.

'But before the boys strut their stuff...'

Wilma's ears pricked. The main attraction would be scheduled last, that was the way it worked: a big name to draw in the crowds, the programme padded out with a comedy act to warm up the audience, a bit of local talent – whoever was available. And cheap. Wilma said a silent prayer this would include her man.

Her mouth puckered into a peeved *moue*. Here she was working her socks off while Maggie wasted time on that nutter from Milltimber. Once a snob, always a snob, she thought sourly.

The agency's workload was supposed to be split down the middle. As the more academic of the two, Maggie would concentrate on their corporate clients: business that demanded scrupulous attention to detail and, above all, consistency. Wilma, with her gung-ho personality and short attention span, was happy to take on whatever else came their way. *Pick and mix*, she jokingly called this scatter-gun approach, but if she was honest, she enjoyed the variety.

After some early setbacks, mostly involving divorce cases, she'd opted to concentrate on fraud. The market was large, and growing. Time was, you wanted something, you earned the money to pay for it. Not anymore. This night's subject was a case in point. Wilma had heard word that the claimant – a wannabe professional footballer feigning an ankle injury – had turned to stripping. She'd already drawn a blank in several pubs, hoped tonight she might get lucky. Wasn't worth putting in more man hours if she drew a blank.

Listen to you, she chuckled inwardly. *Proper pro!*

Sure enough, on came the warm-up guy. Talk about warm! The weather outside wasn't bad for mid-January but, packed solid with under-dressed women, the function room was like a sauna. Wilma could feel perspiration pooling in her armpits and between her thighs. A jaded sixty-something in a shiny tuxedo and patent leather shoes, the comedian cracked a quick-fire burst of old jokes and lewd remarks, his delivery so un-nuanced he might as well have been reciting the ten times table. Between knocking back their vodkas and Bacardis, the audience heckled and jeered.

Michelin Mike was introduced next. Mike was a roly-poly, as the name implied. Wilma knew all the jargon. She eyed his trembling layers of fat. They overhung a pair of tiny scarlet Speedos and two stocky corned-beef legs. *Christ*, she marvelled, the fella would have to be hung like a donkey for his equipment to be visible under that lot. Not that Wilma could talk about weight, not these days. She'd been that pushed this last while, her gym sessions had gone to the wall.

'Show us yer willy!' The trio at the next table could have been triplets, kitted out as they were in matching lurex tank tops.

'Naw.' The hen party behind her had already drunk a bucketful, the pink marabou trim of their costumes sticky with spilled Baileys, gauzy angel wings askew. 'Fuck aff an bring on some real cock.'

With a nervous backward smile, Michelin Mike scuttled off.

Wilma yawned her way through a drag act. She'd had two late nights already that week, and the atmosphere in the function room wasn't helping: a fetid amalgam of cheap scent, alcohol and sweat. Plus, she was bursting for a pee. That was the problem with drinking sparkling water with ice and lemon and kidding yourself it was vodka and tonic. She'd have liked to nip to the ladies' but, sure as shit, if she did that she'd miss out on the action. Resolutely, she crossed her legs.

The drag act was followed by Tyrone, a triangulated bodybuilder with biceps so exaggerated he was a walking advert for steroids. Despite the promising bulge in his posing pouch, Wilma's eyelids wilted.

'And now,' the slime-bag compère was back. 'It is my great pleasure to introduce…' Roll of drums.

Wilma's eyes jolted open.

'Aberdeen's answer to *The Full Monty*. Our home-grown… Our very own…*Ding-a-Lings!*'

She strained forward in her seat. Watched as, one by one, five scruffy blokes shuffled onto the stage. Kitted out in jeans, ripped T-shirts and builders' boots, they sported enough tattoos to camouflage an elephant. With bashful faces, they formed an untidy line.

Wilma fished in her handbag, checked out a photo. *Bingo!* Her guy was second from the left. She snorted. Puny specimen he was too.

For long moments the five stood, stealing sideways glances at one another.

From the audience there were wolf whistles, shouts of 'Jordan' and 'Shane'.

The latter nodded acknowledgement. The former scratched his balls.

The music started up. The line lurched into a too-predictable routine. There were titters, the occasional catcall: 'Give us the fuckin Chippendales.'

The women waited, inebriated and restive. Then, 'Get them off!' a voice screeched.

Off came the T-shirts.

Wilma reached for her camera. Leapt to her feet. Dashed off a few shots.

'Off! Off!' The audience rose as one.

With a series of staccato rips, the Velcro fastenings gave and five pairs of customised jeans fell to the floor.

All around, over-excited women were jumping up and down, screaming at the top of their voices. Wilma tried to get a clear sight of her quarry, but the crowd obstructed her view.

Dammit! She clambered onto her chair.

'Christ's sake!' All around her, women jostled for a clear view.

The music grew louder.

The Ding-a-Lings were down to their Y-fronts now. Correction: Y-fronts and footwear.

Wilma sensed a stirring in her groin. Way before Uggs came into fashion, she'd had a proper fetish for big calfskin builders' boots.

With a nicotine-stained forefinger the nonagenarian seated at the table to Wilma's left adjusted her false teeth. 'Poofters,' she spat.

A gob of mucus traced a trajectory through the fetid air and landed on Wilma's shoe. Distracted, she paused mid-shot, lost her balance and toppled sideways. There was a loud crash as the table tipped, sending drinks glasses flying.

To a chorus of four-letter words, Wilma struggled to her feet.

She looked towards the stage.

The Ding-a-Lings stood, open-mouthed, legs spread, hands cupping their privates.

She ventured a quick shufti over her shoulder.

Two beefy bouncers were threading their way through the throng.

Bugger! It was yonks since she'd been to a ladies' night and she'd grudged the hefty entrance fee. Now it looked like she'd miss the main attraction.

Still, she rationalised, as she dusted herself down, she'd put in a good night's work: that Ding-a-Ling bastard wouldn't be pursuing his disability claim for much longer.

Ros

In Old Aberdeen, two couples sat around a dinner table.

'Happy Birthday!' Smiling, Ros raised her glass.

'Cheers!' Nic joined in the toast, his voice flat.

'Thanks.' Cath Munro, his mother-in-law, beamed from ear to ear. 'It was lovely of you both,' her glance flicked from one to the other, 'to invite us.'

'Lovely of you guys to come. Bearing gifts to boot. I thought the catering was our prerogative. Not that I'm objecting.' Ros took a sip of her wine, swirled the liquid around her mouth. 'This is delicious. And two bottles?' She rolled her eyes. 'Way too generous.'

Cath shrugged. 'Don't look at me. That's your dad's department.'

'Pushing the boat out, aren't you?' Nic reached for the bottle. He scrutinised the label. 'There must be a tenner's worth here, at least. I don't know how you can afford...'

'On a pension?' Phil Munro quipped. 'An old stick like me?' He grinned. 'I've a few years to go yet. But you're right, Nic, I can't afford this, not for everyday drinking. Usually make do with a four quid bottle of Chilean Merlot from Aldi. But this is a special occasion and,' he cast a loving look at his wife then turned to Ros, 'your mum is worth every penny, don't you agree?'

'Absolutely,' Ros concurred. She lifted the lid off a casserole, releasing a steaming cloud of herb-scented sauce. 'Now dig in.' She gestured to the serving dishes of vegetables. 'It's not like you don't know us well enough.'

I wish! As she watched her father carefully fill her mother's plate, Ros reflected on the lead-up to their visit. It was November. She and Nic had been ensconced in their old Ikea sofa, dinner digested, dishes washed, baby bedded, when:

'I was wondering...' Tentative voice. 'It's Mum's birthday next

month and, given we didn't see them at Christmas, I thought it might be an idea to invite her and dad.'

Nic's head had shot up from the car magazine he'd been leafing through. 'To stay over, do you mean?'

'It wouldn't be for long. Just the birthday, perhaps a day either side.'

'That's what you said last time, and they were dug in for over a week.'

Her cheeks flamed. 'That's not fair. Last time was different. They were doing us a favour, if you remember.'

'So they were. I'm sorry.' Playfully, he chucked her chin.

'Me, too. I shouldn't have disturbed you while you were trying to read.'

'Doesn't matter.' He let the magazine slip through his fingers. 'Not that I'd have got peace for long. Not with your wee man upstairs.'

My wee man? She was getting the blame for the baby, now. Or becoming paranoid, the thought occurred.

'Fancy a beer?' His voice broke her reverie. 'It is Friday after all.'

'Cheers.' She smiled. 'That would be great. And my folks, what do you think? It's months since they've seen Max, and he's shooting up. Grawin awa like a wee mushroom, one of the nursery staff said today.'

'Let's leave it for a week or so. See how the calendar's looking.'

'But...'

'It won't be too late.' He shot a warning glance. 'It's not as if they have a full diary.'

'I suppose.'

He stood. 'I'll fetch us that beer.'

Ros smiled to herself. So much for never asking a man for anything until you've fed him. Still, it had all come right, this birthday celebration, and it would come right with Nic as well. Once he was on top of the job. Once Max was that wee bit older. Once she wasn't so tired.

She gazed fondly across at her mum and dad. They were so comfortable in their own skins, so at ease with one another. A warm glow engulfed her. Talk about role models!

'Let me top you up.' Nic was in expansive mood. He circled the table, poured an inch of wine into each of their glasses, filled his own to the brim.

Ros caught her dad's eye. Winced. Why did her husband have to behave like such a dick? It's not as if he wasn't brought up to have good manners. On that first visit to her prospective in-laws – their only visit, now she came to think on it – they'd gone out for a meal one evening. But other than that…

A fleeting thought crossed her mind. She'd never observed Nic's family sit down to a meal together. From what she'd gathered, his parents seemed to follow their own pursuits. Unlike her own, who were a picture of togetherness. The very thought brought a smile to her lips. It dropped when she remembered how her own parents had reacted to Nic. They hadn't taken to him, either of them. Not that anything was said, but Ros knew. She'd hoped, over time, they'd warm to him. After all, she consoled herself, it wasn't as if he constantly behaved with such ill grace.

She looked across the table. Nic's glass was already half empty. Her heart sank. She hoped he didn't push for opening the second bottle. If his mood were to change… She knew all too well what that could mean. Her dad's head was bowed, her mum patently enjoying the food in front of her. *Such a treat to have something set down to you,* wasn't that what she always said? Inwardly, she sighed. If they only lived closer, she'd have help with the baby. Someone to confide in, at least, instead of letting her anxieties get out of hand.

Ros took another sip of her wine, happy that – despite the undercurrents in the room – her mum, at least, seemed blissfully unaware.

Craigmyle

'I miss them so much,' George's former partner in the police, Jimmy Craigmyle, sobbed. 'It's like someone cut off my right arm.'

'There.' Maggie grasped hold of said arm in a fruitless attempt at comfort. 'There.' Her New Year's resolution had been to believe – both in herself and the worthiness of her cause. To that end, although she'd never entirely trusted Craigmyle, she'd set up an early meeting.

They were back in the Hollywood Cafe in Holburn Street. It hadn't improved since their last meeting. If anything, the red leatherette booths were tattier, the Formica tables grimier, the ancient Italian waitress more decrepit than before.

'It'll all work out, Jimmy, I'm sure of it.' Maggie said with forced confidence.

He shook himself free. 'You don't know what it's like.' Drool slobbered down his chin and onto his crumpled shirt front. 'Living on my own. Eating on my own. Going to bed on my own…'

Yes, I bloody do! Maggie bit back on the bile that surged in her throat. This man didn't have sole ownership of loss. And he was alive, wasn't he, with his future in his own hands? Unlike her George, who'd never again face her across a table or lie with her through the night.

'And all the while,' Craigmyle ran on, 'knowing my kids are growing, changing. If this stand-off goes on much longer, they'll have forgotten what I bloody look like.' He snatched a pink paper napkin from a chrome stand on the table and noisily blew his nose.

'Oh, come on,' Maggie soothed. 'It's only been a few months. And the children are young yet. There's time.' Not like her own two, she thought with a sharp twinge of regret. Day by day, Maggie could feel them slipping away.

'But that's just it,' Craigmyle sniffed. 'We're into another year.'

'I know you've got your own agenda,' Maggie conceded. 'Nailing James Gilruth.'

'And I reckoned I was making progress – real progress – in flushing out one of Gilruth's money-laundering operations. Now, after all these months, I've had to duck my head under the parapet again. And as if that isn't bad enough, my wife's digging her heels in. Christ.' He balled up the damp napkin and worked it between cupped hands. 'It feels like I'm back to square one. Worse. Next thing she'll have some other bastard in my bed and divorce papers through my letterbox.'

'Vera's not like that,' Maggie retorted, 'and you know it. Hasn't she stood by you, Jimmy Craigmyle, through…?' Her words tailed off as she re-lived the trial, the false accusations, the fall-out that had ended in her own husband's disgrace and untimely death.

Enough! She pulled herself together. 'We both have regrets, but it's time to put them behind us, look to the future. Yours,' there was a catch in her voice, 'and mine. You're doing great.' She injected false enthusiasm into her voice. 'You're dug in there now: the club, the management, Gilruth's empire by extension…'

'Bloody long extension, if you ask me. There's been damn all activity in that back room since the Fatboy business, and he's been spirited away God knows where.'

'Fair enough. But that last raid has put down a marker. And Fatboy turning out to be Gilruth Junior has put James under the spotlight. Trust me, Jimmy, we'll achieve our objectives – yours and mine. It's only a matter of time.'

He stuffed the shredded napkin into a trouser pocket. 'Do you have anything in mind?'

She took a breath, her expression serious all of a sudden. 'I've had this plan. Right from the start when Wilma was telling me how we could be private investigators.'

'Oh, aye?' Doubtful look.

'It's not rocket science, Jimmy,' she retorted, riled. 'If you can run a home, you can run a business.'

Sheepish grin. 'I'll take your word for it.'

'It's a matter of logistics. Building blocks. Bit like Lego, really – if you get the base right, the rest will fit.'

He scratched his chin. 'I'm not following.'

'We know that George's drugs case fell apart for two reasons. Two principal reasons. Bobby Brannigan's perjured evidence and the interview room balls-up. So I've set three clear objectives: to get Brannigan to admit to perjury. To verify who turned off that tape.'

'Three objectives, you said.'

'Yes. Once I've achieved the first two, I have to persuade the fifth floor.'

'Peezers,' he said, his voice heavy with sarcasm.

'Well,' Maggie insisted, 'I'm almost there with the first two. I've got Brannigan's admission on tape.'

'A tape that's inadmissible in court.'

She squared her shoulders. 'I can build on that. Second, I've got you willing to hold your hands up to the tape.'

'Agreed.' He qualified. 'When the time is right. How about the powers-that-be, though?'

'They weren't against it, not in principle, when Allan Chisolm took it upstairs. My worry, now, is timing. If I can't pull this together soon, they might lose interest. You know how it is in Queen Street, policy blows with the wind.'

'Aye,' he sneered. 'Do I not?'

'We know the end game, Jimmy: put the record straight, for George's sake, and yours. I can't bring George back.' Her voice faltered. 'But I can restore his good name.' She composed herself. 'I will clear his name, if it's the last thing I do.'

Craigmyle shrugged. 'Whatever you say.'

'We just have to keep the end game in sight, Jimmy. Chip away. And then…' She broke off, uncertain.

'Then what?'

'Who knows,' she added lamely.

'But that's just it,' her companion came right back. '*If* this. *Maybe* that. There are too many imponderables, Maggie. When it comes to the crunch, we don't have enough.'

'That's not true. Well,' she conceded, 'it's partly true. 'But I've got Chisolm onside, and if I can put more pressure on Brannigan…'

Craigmyle smirked. 'You and your pal, Big Wilma.'

'Don't call her that.'

'I won't.' Bashful look. 'Not to her face, anyhow.'

'Yes, well…' Maggie felt an uncomfortable stirring in the pit of her stomach. Where she viewed the agency as a means to an end, Wilma held a glamourised view of the PI business. Her antics were an ongoing worry. And those were just the ones Maggie knew about. She'd never got the full story of how Bobby Brannigan's confession had been extracted, nor had she yet encountered Wilma's two sons, Wayne and Kevin, who'd played a pivotal role. 'Anyhow,' she continued, 'if we pull together we're bound to get there in the end.'

'Wish I had your confidence,' Craigmyle retorted sourly.

That was a joke. Although she'd come a long road since the day she'd argued her corner with George about going back to work, Maggie was still plagued by self-doubt.

String of Pearls

His legs are splayed. She kneels between them, both hands circling his cock. Only the tip is visible. It glistens fuchsia in the glow from the bedside lamp.

Her eyes stray to the lampshade. It looks dated. She decides a change would lift the room.

Don't let your mind wander, she tells herself. If you do this right it will be over soon.

She feels his member engorge.

Sits back on her heels.

Concentrate! She lets her eyes droop shut, works to maintain a steady rhythm.

He's panting, now, hips arcing off the mattress.

Not too fast or he'll come before he wants to.

She doesn't want to contemplate the repercussions from that. Tries to slow down, ease off.

Her left calf is starting to tingle. Not the best time to get pins and needles. She shifts position, leans forward again.

Suddenly, his cock spasms.

Her eyes open in alarm as an arc of sperm spits hot gobbets onto her chest. Dammit! She catches her breath. He won't be best pleased. Likes to finish in her mouth.

He lifts his head from the pillow.

She waits for what's coming.

Then, 'String of pearls!' he exclaims, a gleeful grin on his face.

'Wha-a...?' Confused look.

'That's what it's called when, you know...'

News to her. She squints downwards. Gobs of semen draw an untidy necklace on her breast.

Yuk! Her stomach heaves. She reaches for a tissue.

'Don't.' He stays her hand. 'Suits you.'

She pulls a face, turns her head away.

He laughs. 'You're such a prude.'

She doesn't respond.

'Well, aren't you?'

She turns back. 'I suppose.'

'You should count yourself lucky.'

'For this?' She tries to make light of it, though the viscous mess sits heavy on her skin.

He puffs out his chest. 'For a husband with imagination when it comes to lovemaking.'

'Is that what you'd call it?' Teasing voice. God, he can be such a pompous bastard at times. Still, he's right, she supposes. She should give him credit for trying to gee up their lovemaking, moribund this past while.

'Now, if you're done...'

He frowns. 'Don't you want me to...?'

She feels bad, then. He's only thinking of her.

'No.' She smiles an apology. 'Too tired.'

Sighs. 'Oh, well, if you're sure. Let me look at you, though. Just for a moment.' He traces a finger round her throat.

She kneels there, rigid. Feels his spunk spread sideways, tepid now. Shudders as she catches the sour whiff of it.

'I'm going to take a shower,' she says.

Something Needs to Change

Wilma's key rasped as it turned in the front door. *Shite!* She'd been that careful: cutting the car engine before she slid into the drive, leaving the driver's door a fraction ajar. No danger – not in Mannofield – of some toe-rag hot-wiring it.

In the pocket-sized porch she kicked off her shoes. Ian was an early bedder. She crept into the hall. For a moment she stood, swithering. Her undignified exit from the Bide-a-Wee had given her a thirst. It would only take ten minutes to sneak a beer from the fridge, have a sittie-doon in one of the conservatory's comfy chairs. Mebbe even, if she caught her second wind, put in an hour on the computer.

She was heading for the kitchen when a noise made her start. She froze. It came from behind. Could someone have followed her? No way. She wasn't so bloody tired she wouldn't have spotted a tail. Plus, she was stone cold sober. Wilma ran her tongue around a dry and fetid mouth. Now she stopped to think on it she was gasping.

It came again. From the direction of the lounge, she was pretty sure. Gingerly, she pushed the door open with one stockinged foot. In the dim sodium light from the street-lamp outside, she could make out a body.

Ian lay on the leather sofa, fully dressed, knees drawn up. One arm drooped to the carpet, where an empty mug lay on its side.

Wilma moved to stand over him.

'Ian?' She bent to the reclining form. 'Pet?' Gently, she shook him by the shoulder.

'Wha-at?' He started, straightening his legs.

'Don't tell me you dropped off watching telly again,' Wilma teased.

Ian sat up. 'What time is it?' He rubbed sleep from his eyes.

'Gone midnight,' she answered. 'Away to your bed. The alarm goes off at six.'

His jaw set. 'Never you mind the alarm. What time do you call this to come swanning in?'

Wilma squared up. 'Don't you use that tone of voice wi me.'

'I'll use whatever tone I want. Where the hell have you been?'

'Working.'

'Working where?'

'Bucksburn, if you must know.'

'Doing what?'

'Following up a fraud claim,' she dissembled.

'Till midnight?'

'Fella was in a pub.'

'What pub?'

Wilma's mind worked at the speed of light. The Bide-a-Wee was known throughout Grampian as a strippers haunt.

She dropped to her knees. 'You're nippy tonight.' Cosying up. 'Hiv ye no got yer beauty sleep?' Her hand strayed to his crotch. 'Or...' Stroking. 'Yer mebbe jist horny.'

'Don't you "horny" me.' Ian batted her hand away. 'There's no wife of mine is going to be out till all hours cavorting God knows where with...'

'Now we're getting to it.' Wilma sat back on her heels. 'I knew this place was too effing precious for the likes of me.' She struggled to her feet. 'But nobody told me there was a fucking curfew.'

Ian stood to face her. 'Don't get clever with me.'

'Clever, now, is it? One minute you're telling me how smart I am, Ian Harcus, the next you're complaining.'

'With good reason.'

'Jist because I come in late one night?'

He brushed a weary hand across his brow. 'It's not one night, Wilma, it's dozens of nights. If you're not out on the ran-dan you're sitting up at that computer.'

'So?'

'So I never expected this…business of yours to take over your life.'

'And I never expected, when I married you, that Mannofield would be so effin…' She struggled for the word. 'Suffocating.'

'Well, I'll tell you one thing.' Ian turned on his heel and made for the door. 'There's something needs to change.'

And Pigs Might Fly

'There's not a lot here.' Maggie frowned as she scanned the sheet of blue vellum Sheena Struthers had pulled from her handbag.

Sheena laid a hand on her arm. 'I know it doesn't look much on paper, but if you'll just let me explain.'

They were back in Valerie's. *This is getting to be a habit*, Maggie thought. *A bad habit.*

You'll be on your own, Wilma's words rang in her ears. She pushed them to the back of her mind. Her instincts were sound. Wilma was wrong.

Maggie ran a finger down the list. 'Let's go through these one by one, shall we?' Her brow crinkled. 'Mower? Can you elaborate on that?'

Sheena looked Maggie in the eye. 'Last summer my husband almost ran me down with the lawnmower.'

How could you run someone down with a lawnmower? Maggie's mind jumped to the rickety old thing George kept stored in their shed. *Bloody head-banger!* The words ricocheted around her head. She could just picture Wilma's face.

'It's four times the size of me,' Sheena persisted. 'A ride-on. We have several acres, you see.'

'Oh,' Maggie said, without enthusiasm. 'Right. But what makes you think…'

'I was sitting there on a garden chair reading a book. Gordon was going up and down. He likes the stripes to be even.'

'Yes?' Maggie wondered where this was going.

'He must have turned. It was the noise of the motor that alerted me. I looked up. And there was the mower, charging towards me full tilt.'

'So what did you do?'

'Dropped the book. Ran for my life.'

'And afterwards?'

'Gordon must have cut the engine, jumped off, because he came running after me. Full of apologies, he was. Said it must have been a malfunction.'

'Mmm,' Maggie offered. 'Seems a reasonable explanation to me.'

Sheena's lip curled. 'Plausible, more like.'

'What makes you say that?'

'The look in his eyes when he was coming at me. Wild. Like a mad thing. I was terrified, I can tell you. I've never seen my husband look like that.'

'And the mower?'

'He had the service people uplift it for an overhaul that very same day.'

So, Maggie thought, *another flight of fancy.*

'Let's move on.' Her eyes darted back to Sheena's list.

'Then there was my car.'

'Right. Brakes failed, you say.'

'Another malfunction. Wasted clevis pins, according to Gordon. Fancies himself as a car buff. Except...'

'Yes?' Maggie waited for the next *bon mot.*

'The garage said they'd never seen pins so badly worn. Asked if someone had been tinkering with the car?'

'Let me be clear...' Incredulous voice. 'You're implying your husband may have tampered with the brakes?'

'I didn't know what to think, not at the time. But that was before,' Sheena's eyes flashed, 'he tried to poison me.'

Under the table, Maggie's fingers drummed on her thigh. She'd had her misgivings where Sheena Struthers was concerned, but been persuaded by the woman's sincerity. Now, she could feel the situation developing from the questionable to the farcical.

'Gordon had been away on a business trip to London,' Sheena explained. 'He always brings me back a little gift, wherever he goes.' She smiled. 'He's romantic that way.'

'And?' Maggie was fast losing patience.

'This time it was a china hare. My husband bought it in Fortnum & Mason. Never been there, but I'm told it's wonderful. Anyway,' catching Maggie's irritated look, she moved swiftly on, 'I thought it was an ornament. Pretty thing.' Her eyes took on a dreamy quality. 'But turned out it had game pâté inside.'

Maggie's stomach growled. She'd skipped breakfast. Greedily, she eyed the counter display.

'Except I wasn't to know that,' Sheena rabbited on. 'Gave me acute food poisoning. Laid me low for a week.'

'Wasn't your husband affected?' Maggie enquired.

'No.' Wry face. 'Gordon doesn't like pâté. But it was his fault,' she added stubbornly.

'How so?'

'He'd removed the label before he gave it to me.'

'Perhaps he didn't want you to see the price.'

'Possibly. But he could have told me about the pâté.'

'Maybe he didn't know.'

'Oh, he knew alright. Then by the time I discovered…' She broke off. 'It should have been refrigerated.'

'That's not entirely your husband's fault.' Maggie resisted the urge to laugh. Compared to some of the sad cases she'd dealt with over the past year, this was bordering on the absurd.

Sheena jutted her chin. 'It was mainly his fault. And another thing…'

Maggie raised a questioning eyebrow.

'He destroyed my hydrangeas. You'll think me a silly woman, but they produced such a lovely show last year. Then Gordon…'

Maggie's heart sank to her stomach. She held up a hand. 'Let me stop you there.' Wilma *was* right. The woman was deluded. And Maggie had been well warned. What to do? Her head buzzed. Loth as she was to lose face with her business partner, she'd heard little to substantiate Sheena Struthers' claims. Mentally, she totted up the time she'd spent with the client, cursing her own credibility.

Although her pride would be dented by withdrawing from the case, she'd have to call it a day. She'd pass the buck, she decided. Suggest counselling, whatever. That would be the least awkward solution.

'Has it occurred to you,' Maggie moved to bring the conversation to an end, 'that you may be unwell?'

'If, Mrs Laird, you're implying I'm unhinged,' Sheena's face was a mask, 'let me disabuse you of the notion.'

'I didn't mean…' Maggie stuttered, embarrassed, now. 'Perhaps your marriage is just going through a bad patch,' she improvised. As she uttered the words, Maggie couldn't help but recall some of the ups and downs of her own marriage: her insistence on getting on the mortgage ladder when George would have been happy to carry on renting, arguing the case for their children's private schooling, his reluctance to see her go back to work. And that was without re-visiting the question of George's so-called 'retirement', a topic that had caused Maggie such soul-searching ever since.

'It's not that.' Sheena's voice brought Maggie back to the present.

'You're quite sure? Most long relationships have their fair share of these.'

'Yes.' Firm voice. 'I'm sure. That's why I need you to check up on him.'

Sod it! Maggie swept her scruples aside. She'd invested precious time on this client. Why not string the woman along, for a little while at least? The agency needed the money and Sheena Struthers, from what Maggie had heard, could well afford to pay.

She resolved to check out the husband as instructed. No harm in that. It would keep her hand in. Maggie hadn't done surveillance for a while, and it would make a change from the endless round of meetings and precognitions that formed the basis of her workload. Maybe she'd even get lucky, and Gordon Struthers would turn out to be up to something after all.

And pigs might fly, a small voice echoed inside her head.

Stinky Cheese

'What's all this?' Nic surveyed the bulging plastic bags forming a loose pyramid on the floor.

'Asda shop. Looks worse than it is.' Ros fought to keep her voice light. 'Stuart and Fiona are coming for supper on Saturday. You hadn't forgotten?'

'Totally. What a pain.' Nic rolled his eyes. 'We've only just got rid of your folks.'

Ros bit her lip. Best not rise to the bait.

'I take it they invited themselves.'

'No,' Ros answered, her voice quavering. She'd been looking forward to seeing the only real friend she'd made since they'd moved to Aberdeen. 'You did.'

'Oh, well.' He crooked a finger. 'Let's have it?'

Inwardly, Ros quailed. More than two years into her marriage she still hadn't got used to this. She dug into her handbag, fished out her purse, and extracted a folded supermarket receipt. Tentatively, she held it out.

Her husband snatched the narrow ribbon of paper, smoothed it between long fingers. 'Now, then…' He ran a practised eye down the column of type.

Ros felt her heartbeat flutter in her chest. Why did he always make her feel so guilty? It was only a bloody supermarket receipt.

'What have we here?' he pounced. 'Camembert?' Arch look. 'You know I don't like stinky cheese.'

'Fiona does. I bought it for her.'

'She's not going to eat the whole thing, is she?'

'No, but…'

He brushed this aside. 'Money isn't made on trees.'

She turned her head away. No point in making a fuss. It would only wind him up. Wouldn't happen at home, she thought mutinously. The very idea that her father – big, solid, manly Dad – might carp over such a trivial matter brought a sudden smile to her lips.

She turned back. 'I just thought...'

'That's the problem.' He waved the receipt under her nose. 'You don't think, do you?'

With his free hand he chucked her under the chin. Rather too hard. She resisted an urge to rub at the sore bit.

'You know we have to watch the pennies. And Max's nursery fees...'

'But my salary covers that.'

'Might as well not. You're way over-qualified for that scummy primary school.'

She set her jaw. 'I like it. And, besides, it was the only job...'

'If you'd set your sights higher...'

Like you? she wanted to scream. Nic sure wasn't lacking in the ambition stakes. But wasn't that what had attracted her to him in the first place? It seemed light years, now, since they'd met at that conference – the young Edinburgh graduate and the self-assured junior lecturer from Hampshire. He'd planned a career in law, he confided, then. Had set his sights on a Russell Group university. But he hadn't achieved the grades. Had settled for history. He had great plans, though: a senior lectureship by thirty-five, a chair by forty.

'But, the baby,' she managed, before he launched forth again.

'...held out for a decent job, you could have been earning...'

Here we go again! Ros drew a steadying breath. 'We've been through all that. It's not just about the money, Nic. It's quality of life we're talking. And didn't we agree I should settle for something less demanding, at least until Max starts school?'

'In theory,' he seethed. 'But that's not how it has turned out, is it? Seems to me this Seaton job's full-on. And it pays bugger-all.'

'I've got company, at least. People to talk to.'

'Like that sad, squinty-eyed little classroom assistant.'

'Maggie Laird isn't sad.' Defensive voice. 'She's a very able woman.'

'Come off it. I've seen firsthand. There's not a soul in that place you'd mix with socially. And it's not as if you're making a difference, Ros, not with the amount of social deprivation or whatever they call it these days. You'd be far better off at home. Save us a fortune in...'

Camembert?

Instead: 'I'm sorry.' She extended a conciliatory hand. 'That was silly of me. I won't do it again.'

Second Time Around

Wilma watched as the man approached the row of lock-ups. He fumbled in his trouser pocket, mouthed a curse. Tapping numbers into his phone, he turned on his heel and legged it. From her first-floor vantage point in the stairwell of a nearby block of flats, Wilma sent up a silent prayer of thanks. This was unfinished business. And Wilma didn't like loose ends.

'Second time around,' she muttered darkly, for they had form: the small-time fraudster and the wannabe PI. They'd crossed swords the previous year – a year when Wilma, in her headlong rush to learn her craft, had been dead keen but equally green. She'd fingered the bugger for car fraud: reporting a vehicle stolen and obtaining a pay-out before selling it on to a suspect body shop to be cut up for parts. He'd got one over on her, then. In her mind, Wilma could still see the look of triumph on the bastard's face as his souped-up vehicle outran her old Fiesta, his V-sign framed in the driver's window. But that was before she'd invested in a GPS tracking device. Wilma grinned. He wouldn't escape her twice.

She'd thought the deception to be an isolated instance. Learnt since that it was part of a wider fraud, her quarry acting as runner for a large-scale operation, a succession of supposedly 'stolen' vehicles passing through his hands. A source had told her that he was based in Torry. But where to begin? The district on the south side of the River Dee where Wilma had been raised was extensive, stretching from the historic fishing settlement at the river mouth all the way to the Brig o' Dee.

Footdee – pronounced 'Fitty' by the locals – was a favourite stomping-ground when she was a kid. Most summer evenings during the long school holidays, she and her pals repaired to the warren of tiny fishermen's cottages. To kids reared in tenement flats, it was a magical place: a huddle of houses and wash-houses hugging close behind the sea wall. There were smokehouses, too, for the fish – little more than wooden huts – and a sturdy Fishermen's Mission in the middle.

They'd play games of tag, and hide-and-seek. Pretend to be housewives, or fisher-folk, or spies. Not that different from what she was doing now, Wilma allowed a wry smile, as she shot down the stairs, lock-picks at the ready. She'd have started with keys, but that would have taken more time, and she had no more than a few minutes, she reckoned.

Now, she focussed on the job. Her hands shook as she inserted the picks into the lock.

Calm down! she told herself, as she tried one after the other. *This type of lock should be a doddle.* If you weren't peeing yourself, that is. Wilma wiped sweating palms on her thighs.

Finally, success. The handle turned. The garage door swung up.

She left it at an angle and ducked underneath, reading off the number plate as she went.

For a moment, she hesitated, unsure, then read it again. She'd have been gutted if, after all this time, she'd got it wrong. But, no.

Wilma fished in her pocket, stooped to the rear wheel arch, attached the GPS. The device, together with the small arsenal of other gizmos she'd already built up, fair helped to oil the wheels.

You wee darling! She grinned with satisfaction. Of all the accoutrements, this had been one of her better investments. It would buy her time. On this occasion, when she tailed the subject to the breaker's yard – Wilma said a silent prayer this was the plan, for why else would he visit a lock-up so far from home – she'd be able to sit well back. Colour rose in her face. What a rage she'd been in when he'd given her two fingers all those months before! Then all she had to do was get a few happy snaps.

If she got lucky, she'd mebbe even manage to hang around till the fucker had taken his lift home. She could shoot the breaker a line about scrapping her own car. Christ knows it wasn't worth a helluva lot more. Say she was feeling faint. Have a sittie-down in the Portakabin he called an office. Take a wee shuftie at the paperwork. In her head, she'd got it all planned out.

Wilma backed out of the lock-up and lowered the door. With a glance over her shoulder, she flicked through a set of keys and secured the lock, double-checking that it was secure. Then, like a bat out of hell, she made a beeline for her car. This time there would be no giving her the slip.

Talking Dirty

'Say it!' The face is inches from hers, the voice insistent.

She opens her mouth to speak, but no words come.

'Go on,' he urges.

She tries again. 'I'm a…a…' Her lips open and close like a fish coming up for air.

'A…?' he prompts.

She summons a breath. 'A dirty…'

'A dirty what?' He has that look on his face.

She screws her eyes shut against him.

'Look at me.' He shakes her by the shoulders.

With an effort, she blinks her eyes open.

'You were about to say…'

I was? She knows it pleases him: to talk dirty, act dirty. Turns him on.

She steels herself. 'I'm a dirty little…' But she can't finish. Can't say the word.

He's heavy, now, on top of her. 'Come on,' he coaxes. 'You know you like it.'

I bloody don't! She wants to scream, but her chest is constricted. It does nothing for her – talking dirty. Never has.

'It's not that hard.'

That's not true. She'd gone along with it. Thought it was normal, the things he did. The things he asked her to do. But their relationship has changed. She's changed.

'Is it?'

Spit it out, she tells herself. Then it will be done.

'I'm a dirty little c…' Curly 'c' or kicking 'k'? The image presents itself as she tries to frame the word.

She feels a sudden urge to laugh.

Then: 'Cunt,' he spits, with such force she can feel a spray of spittle on her face. 'You're a cunt.' He looms over her. 'What are you?'

'A c-c-cunt,' she manages.

'That's it. You're a dirty little cunt.' His face carries an expression of affection mingled with distaste.

Gordon

The grand former merchant's house that fronted the Queen's Road was set back from the pavement behind a low stone wall and a sweep of gravel, now largely given over to parking.

From the safety of her car, Maggie kept watch as a succession of sober-suited figures came and went through the imposing glass doors. She'd found a space directly opposite.

She checked the time on her phone. 12.45. On Fridays, she'd learned from Sheena, Gordon Struthers lunched at his club, the Royal Northern and University. Founded in 1854 and given its 'royal' status following a visit by Queen Victoria, it was not only home to the city's great and good, but located close to Holburn Junction, a short stroll from Gordon's office. Maggie had heard mention of the place. Knew it was a dining and social club, that you had to be someone in Aberdeen society to be proposed for membership. But she'd never been inside. She didn't even know if the club admitted women members, though she had a hazy recollection of a piece in the P&J: the old guard digging their heels in and refusing to bow to pressure. Typical!

Ten to one, Sheena had said. *Regular as clockwork.* That was an unexpected bonus. Since she'd taken on the business, Maggie had spent too many long hours sitting in her car, stiff, hungry and chilled to the bone. A creature of habit, as Gordon Struthers had been described, would make surveillance a whole lot easier.

Minutes later, a man emerged. He was short: no more than five-foot-eight, and slight. Reddish hair, round spectacles, was all Maggie could manage to make out from her viewpoint across the street, but she had little doubt she'd got her man.

He stood for some moments at the top of the shallow flight of steps, casting his eyes skywards as if checking for impending rain.

Then he straightened the knot of his tie, tweaked the velvet collar of his tailored camel overcoat and made his way down the steps.

She watched as he threaded through the cars that were shoe-horned into the front drive. There was a car park at the rear, she'd established, but parking in the city centre was at a premium, even since the price of a barrel of oil had nose-dived into the North Sea. At the entrance he paused. Maggie took note of a striped shirt and what looked like a school tie. The hair was carefully combed, she saw, in a neat side-parting, the complexion chalky. Behind the thick, horn-rimmed glasses she couldn't make out the eyes. The man reminded her of someone, she couldn't quite think who.

Then it came to her: James Gilruth.

Despite her warm coat, Maggie shivered as she brought to mind the past year's abortive visit to Rubislaw Den. What a manic creature she'd been, those first few weeks after George's death, and what a long road she'd travelled since.

Struthers turned right towards Queen's Cross.

Maggie turned the key in the ignition. *Don't make assumptions!* She turned it off again.

Swiftly, she checked a file that lay open on the passenger seat, punched a number into her phone.

'Ross and Struthers. How can I help you?'

'Is Mr Struthers free to speak?'

'I'm sorry, you've just missed him. Can anyone else help?'

'Thanks. I'll ring back.' Maggie cut the call.

She switched on the engine, signalled, and pulled out from the kerb.

He was strolling at a leisurely pace. Small steps – for a man – Maggie noted as she followed him with her eyes. Like David Suchet's Poirot, and, by the looks of him, equally fastidious.

Maggie hung back as he crossed St Swithin Street to the old Royal Bank building on the corner and continued along Albyn Place. At the roundabout, she waited in line as a stream of cars and vans crossed in front of her, proceeding up Fountainhall Road or turning right into Carden Place.

Among them, a blue Vauxhall Corsa bore the insignia of a driving school. The young female under instruction sat, rigid, in the driver's seat, neck craned stiffly forward, eyes glued on the road ahead.

Poor soul! Maggie watched as the car crawled at a snail's pace all the way around the crowned statue of Queen Victoria on its polished pink marble plinth to the last exit, Albyn Place. Then her eyes scoured the pavement. There was no sign of Gordon Struthers.

Dammit! She cursed her momentary lapse of attention. He wouldn't have had time to reach his club, and he couldn't have just disappeared. Ignoring the toots and hand gestures of the encroaching traffic, Maggie shot across the roundabout. She passed by a succession of substantial granite mansions: Ryden, Albyn Hospital – now, like Gordon Struthers' own business premises in commercial use. When she was halfway along she drew into the kerb.

Were it not January, the trees that graced Rubislaw Gardens would have rendered her surveillance less obvious. Now, they stood stark and bare. She peered ahead. Among the pedestrians heading for Holburn Junction there was no trace of her target. She checked her rear-view mirror: no joy.

Maggie took stock. Should she sit and wait? It was unlikely – on a Friday – that Gordon Struthers would rush back to his office. So should she cut her losses? She was weighing her options when, in her nearside wing mirror, she spied a trim figure emerge from the gardens and walk towards her.

Her mind worked overtime. Did Gordon Struthers suspect his wife was having him followed? Had he deliberately given Maggie the slip? And was he now about to confront her? Heart racing, she ducked into the passenger footwell, just in time to see a shadow pass by the car's window. Cautiously raising herself to the level of the dashboard, she watched the man proceed a dozen paces towards the junction. He stopped. Looked right, left, and right again and crossed the road.

Slumping back into her seat, she observed Gordon Struthers turn in the entrance of the Northern Club at No 9. Maggie had staked out the building the previous day, sneaking in through the rear car park. The dining room, she'd established, was accessed off the front reception hallway or through the Garden Room extension at the back, so she'd scant hope of achieving more than timing her quarry in and out. She settled down to wait. Still, *Inky Fingers!* Giddy with relief, *she* suppressed a giggle. For all Sheena's protestations, Gordon Struthers looked, to Maggie, more like a boy wizard than a murderer-in-waiting.

III

Seaton School

'You okay?'

Ros was sitting on a corner of the AstroTurf, head bent, knees drawn up to her chin. She looked up, nodded.

'What are you doing out here?' Maggie addressed her friend. 'You're not on playground duty, are you?'

'No.' Ros looked up. 'I just needed space to think. Staffroom's a bit stuffy.'

'In more ways than one.' Maggie joked. 'The old guard getting to you?'

'No. I'm glad to be back.'

Maggie smiled. 'I know the feeling.' After the Christmas holiday, it had been a relief to return to her wee job at Seaton School. 'Still...' She hugged her chest. 'It's perishing out here, and you look done in.'

'Bit tired, that's all.'

'Join the club.' It had been an effort getting out of bed that morning. 'Anything I can do to help?' She squatted down, the artificial grass pricking at her hands.

'Not really. Just feeling sorry for myself.'

'Job getting on top of you?'

'No. I mean it's a hard slog, sometimes, but I count myself lucky to have landed something full-time. It's all supply and maternity cover these days. Oh!' Ros put a hand to her mouth. 'I'd forgotten you were only part-time. Anyhow, it's good to have the income coming in, plus...' Her face lit up. 'I love the kids.'

'Me, too,' Maggie enthused. 'They fair take me out of myself.'

'Must be a help, especially now...' Ros broke off, embarrassed.

'Now I'm on my own, do you mean?'

'Well, that,' she conceded, 'and the other thing – the one that got you written up in the newspapers.'

Maggie pulled a face. 'Don't even go there.' She'd been keeping a low profile since Fatboy's trial. 'But, seriously, if it's not the job…' She hesitated. Wasn't it in this same playground she'd elicited a clue from a member of the Meston gang: a snippet of information that had set in train seismic events? 'Is it your wee boy you're worried about?'

'No. Not at all.'

'Everything alright at home?' Maggie was treading on dangerous ground now, she was all too aware, but she'd become so adept at posing leading questions she found it hard to stop.

'Yes. Well…' Ros presented a wretched face. 'Sort of.'

'Nic?' Maggie's mind went to fast-forward. She bet the self-satisfied bastard was having a fling. Just as quickly she dismissed the thought. The downside of working as a PI was looking for an agenda.

'Want to talk?' Maggie asked softly.

Ros nodded, mute.

For long moments the two sat in silence, then: 'It's not Nic,' Ros whispered. 'It's me.'

'You?' Maggie echoed. 'In what way?'

'Oh, just, I feel so inadequate. I don't seem to do anything right, not since…' She broke off, her voice cracking.

Post-natal depression, Maggie decided. She'd been there, could still recall that feeling of being in a long black tunnel, a tunnel with nary a chink of light at the end. Then, *pack it in!* Wasn't she forever telling Wilma off for jumping to conclusions? 'Go on,' she encouraged.

'I didn't feel that great after Max was born. Put it down to baby blues. Then I was at home with him for the first six months. Nic wanted me to breastfeed. I wanted that, too, of course. But it didn't go away, that feeling of helplessness. It was as if everything I'd built up over the years – my skills, my self-confidence – had been swamped in a sea of Babygros and nappies and cuddly toys.'

Maggie extended a comforting hand. 'It's not uncommon, you know. I can remember, right after Kirsty was born: the four-hour feeds, the lack of sleep. I could have cut my throat.' She grimaced. 'Hormones!'

'That's what I told myself,' Ros replied. 'They say pregnancy plays havoc with them. Affects your mood. God only knows what else? But it's been over a year, now, and I'm not making any progress. I'd put it down to exhaustion, but it can't just be that. I mean…' She appealed to Maggie. 'Other women cope, don't they? Women with far more on their plate than me. How come I'm forever getting things so wrong?'

'It takes two, you know,' Maggie said softly.

Ros shook her head. 'I can't put it on Nic, not when he has lectures to write and meetings to attend and research papers to produce. If anything, he should be more stressed than me. No, he's not the cause.' She gave a rueful smile. 'I tried to find the answer. Read up on post-partum depression. It affects one in seven women, apparently. Can even manifest as psychosis: paranoia, hallucinations, the works. I wondered, then, if that was me.' Her voice wavered. 'Still do.'

'Did you take any steps to…?'

'Of course,' Ros cut in. 'Ate healthily, took more exercise. Then, when none of that seemed to be working, I made an appointment with our GP. The minute we moved up here, a few weeks before Max was even born, Nic registered us with a wonderful chap who's red-hot on paediatrics.'

Bloody lot of use to a depressed new mother, sang a small voice inside Maggie's head. Instead she asked, 'What did the doctor have to say?'

'He said,' the corners of Ros's mouth turned down, '"Wait till you have three".'

'There's Aberdeen for you,' Maggie joked. 'He didn't prescribe anything? A mild anti-depressant? That can sometimes help.'

'No. He was much more interested in Max. I had to take him with me, you see. We'd not long moved up here before the birth. I didn't know anybody, and it's not as if Nic could take time out from the department…'

Not to support a wife who was in dire need, by the sounds of it. Maggie seethed inside. 'Oh.' She assumed a knowing expression. 'Right.'

'After that, I told myself I was being a wimp. Made a huge effort to pull myself together. Decided it might help to be more sociable. I joined a babysitting circle. Though,' she grimaced, 'that didn't last long. Nic had too much on for us to get out much, plus he didn't like the idea of me looking after other people's kids. Still, I showed willing: invited the university ladies in for coffee, had Nic's colleagues round for supper. I thought things were looking up, especially after I went back to work. It's been a long haul. Max is nearly walking, now.' Fond look. 'And I love this job. But, still...'

Maggie's heart went out to the girl. 'Your family, you don't see them that often I've heard you say.'

Ros shrugged. 'Birthdays and Christmas.'

'That's a shame. They're in Edinburgh, aren't they?'

Nods.

'That's no distance.'

A long pause, then: 'No.'

Maggie heard warning bells, changed tack. 'How about friends?' With a pang of loss she pictured her own friend, Val, still out in Dubai nursing her ailing mother. 'You've often mentioned Fiona. Doesn't she...?'

'Fiona's been a tower of strength. Other than Fi, though, it's people from school.' She smiled, suddenly. 'People like you.'

'If there's ever anything...' Maggie began.

'Thanks.' Ros glanced at her watch. 'Yikes,' she struggled to her feet. 'Got to go. I've a class in five minutes.'

'Too bad,' Maggie said lightly, cursing the timetabling system. She had the feeling Ros had been trying to tell her something. Something more troubling than the physical symptoms she'd described. 'I won't be far behind.'

Maggie watched as, head bowed, Ros made her way towards the school entrance.

A Private Matter

'Grumpian Police, Moira speaking.' The voice on the other end of the phone bore the unmistakable vowels of Aberdeenshire. There was a pause, then, 'Sorry, caller.' Suppressed giggle. 'Police Scotland Aberdeen. I keep forgetting.'

The absorption of the Grampian police force into Police Scotland hasn't made a whit of difference! Maggie thought, with some rancour. She took a breath. 'Maggie Laird here.'

Another pause, then: 'I'm sorry?'

Maggie was sorry too. Sorry that the civilian in the comms office hadn't the foggiest who she was. Sorry that she had speak to Force HQ ever again. Sorry for herself.

'Maggie Laird,' she repeated. 'George Laird's…' She couldn't bring herself to say the word 'widow'.

'Oh!' She could picture the girl's confusion, the frantic signals to whoever else was on duty. 'Mrs Laird. How can I help you?'

'I want' – Maggie corrected – '*need* to speak to Detective Inspector Chisolm.'

'May I ask what it's in connection with?'

None of your bloody business!

'It's a private matter.'

There was silence at the other end of the line.

'Hello?' Maggie's voice rose. 'Are you still there?'

'Yes.'

She'd imagined she detected a hint of embarrassment in Moira's tone. *Pack it in*, she said to herself. *You're becoming paranoid.*

'If you'd like to hold the line, Mrs Laird,' the girl hesitated for a moment, 'I'll check if he's available. Or perhaps it would be more convenient if he called you back.'

'I'll hold.' In her mind, Maggie had rehearsed what she was going to say. She'd no intention of being fobbed off.

The background music on the line – Mozart's *Eine Kleine Nachtmusik* – played over and over. Played for so long that it began to scramble Maggie's brain. She looked at her watch. Who on earth chose these tunes in the first place, she wondered? And why didn't it occur to them to change the track every now and again? She'd give it another two minutes, she decided. Perhaps the music was chosen on purpose to wear people down, lower their resistance. Like some form of psychological torture.

Calm down! If the girl had asked her to hold, Chisolm must be on duty. And at least Maggie hadn't been told the inspector was in a meeting. In her experience, men were always 'in a meeting', when they were simply bunking off.

She was just about to hang up when there was a click.

'Mrs Laird?' Detective Inspector Allan Chisolm's deep voice spoke her name. 'To what do I owe the pleasure?'

'It's...' A shiver ran down Maggie's spine. 'About the case.'

'The Seaton case?' he cut her short. 'I thought that was done and dusted.'

'No, not that.' She hadn't spoken to Allan Chisolm since the Seaton debacle. 'The other one.'

'Lucy Simmons?'

'No.' Maggie was becoming increasingly agitated. What was it about this man that so unnerved her?

There was a long silence, then: 'Which is it?' Could she detect a hint of amusement in the inspector's tone?

'My husband,' she managed. 'I wondered...' Small voice. 'If you'd heard anything from upstairs?'

'On re-opening your husband's case? Not a dickey bird. Though I have to hold my hands up. What with one thing and another I haven't made any moves on that front, I'm sorry.'

'Oh.' Maggie couldn't mask her disappointment. 'But you said...' For the second time that day Maggie felt stung. She'd committed everything in her – admittedly restricted – armoury to vindicating her husband, only to be let down.

'That I'd take your case forward, Mrs Laird? Yes, I did. And I've kept my word. Passed the information you provided together with the,' he paused, cleared his throat, 'tape recording to the fifth floor.'

'But you haven't heard anything back?'

'No. Not that that's necessarily a bad thing.' The inspector's tone was reassuring. 'At least they haven't rejected the new evidence out of hand.'

'But I thought...'

'The information obtained under duress? You're right. That does present a problem. It may be, though, that Mr Brannigan can be persuaded to ratify that with a voluntary statement. Last I heard we were working towards that outcome. But it all takes time, as I'm sure you appreciate, and with resources stretched as they are...'

'I understand.'

'All the same, I'll chase it up and let you know.'

'Would you? I'd be grateful.'

'My pleasure.'

Did Maggie detect real warmth in Chisolm's voice? She couldn't be sure.

'Is there anything else?'

Back to business, then. 'N-no.' He had her on the back foot again.

'You haven't stumbled across any bodies lately?'

Typical, Maggie seethed: the put-down to the little woman. Didn't merit a response.

'Mrs Laird? You still there?'

'I'm still here.' Frosty voice.

'I gather you didn't appreciate my joke,' Chisolm offered.

Silence.

'I'll take it that's a "no", then.'

Maggie took a deep breath. If her quest for justice were to succeed she had to keep this man onside. But, still, she had her pride.

'Thank you for your time,' she answered stiffly. Then she cut the call.

Fish Fingers

He raises a hand to his nose, takes a deep sniff. 'Fish fingers!' he exclaims.

'Don't be so vulgar,' she retorts. Moments earlier those same fingers had been inside her, trying to make her wet.

The smile vanishes from his face. 'Where's your sense of humour?' he demands, wiping his hand on the sheet.

She doesn't answer. He's been rubbing away forever and still she hasn't come. No surprises there, not these days. She wonders when marital relations – she can no longer think of it as lovemaking – became a duty rather than a joy. Speculates as to what happened to her libido, if she ever had one. She questions most things these days.

'Let me have another go.' His hand strays back.

She bats it away. 'I'm sore now.' And cross. It's not that she doesn't enjoy sex. Didn't. There was nothing to beat a straight fuck in the missionary position: the comfort of a male body – on her, in her – the loosing of tension from her limbs. She combs her mind, trying to recall the last time it had been like that. Can't. No matter. It's irrelevant now.

'Turn over, then. We can…'

'No.' The vehemence in her voice surprises her. She'd always acceded to his requests: wanting to pleasure him in the beginning, then anything for a quiet life.

'Go on,' he coaxes. 'We haven't done…that…in a while.'

And I know the reason why, she thinks, obdurate. 'That' will make me even sorer. She doesn't respond.

'You're so narrow-minded,' he sighs, rolling onto his back.

'If you say so.' She knows better than to argue, but it's not true. She doesn't mind a change of position once in a while: her going down on him, or him on her.

It's the other things that bother her.

Pillow Talk

'There's been another incident.' The words were out before Maggie had even sat down. She dropped onto a spindly bentwood chair. She was out of breath. Sheena Struthers had been quiet for a week or two. That morning's phone call, requesting an urgent meeting, had caught Maggie on the hop.

She'd been tempted to make an excuse. Wilma's reading of Sheena Struthers as 'just another menopausal woman' had caused Maggie considerable disquiet. She bitterly regretted their falling-out. In all the time she and Wilma had worked together, they'd never exchanged such harsh words.

Maggie would be able to bill for the time she'd spent on meetings and surveillance, so maybe it was time for her to swallow her pride and call it quits with the Struthers woman. It would be easily enough achieved. Hadn't Wilma schooled her well in the usefulness of the glib lie?

'You'd better tell me about it.' She dreaded what was coming. If it was up to the standard of what she'd heard previously it would be one giant yawn.

'This morning,' Sheena said, keeping her voice low, 'when I woke up, there was a pillow over my face. That's why I asked you to come out here at such short notice.'

Maggie looked around before she spoke. *Terroir*, a French bistro and deli on the main drag in Cults, was exposed to passing traffic through a large picture window. That and the open-plan interior weren't conducive to discreet conversation. She noted, with some dismay, a posse of young mums with buggies in the rear and an elderly woman with a large dog sitting at the next table.

'I'm not quite with you.'

Sheena's face was drawn, and there were dark circles under her eyes. 'I'm convinced Gordon was about to smother me.'

'Where was your husband at the time?'

'In bed beside me. No...' Sheena corrected. 'He was actually kneeling over me.'

'What did he have to say?'

'Laughed it off. Said I must have moved the pillow myself. I haven't been sleeping, you see.'

'How many pillows do you normally sleep on?'

'Two.'

'Don't you think, if you had a restless night, one of them might have come adrift?'

'Definitely not. And there's another thing. We went down the coast for lunch last week and took a stroll along the cliff path afterwards. I took a bad stumble. Didn't think much of it until today.' Sheena broke off, wild-eyed. 'But after this morning's incident, I'm pretty sure Gordon pushed me.'

'Oh, come on,' Maggie responded. The woman really was trying her patience. 'It's been so wet this past while, you probably slipped.'

Sheena's voice rose. 'I did not.'

Maggie struggled to find something more to say. Failed.

Sheena filled the silence. 'Mrs Laird. Maggie.' Her eyes flashed mute appeal. 'You have to believe me.'

Maggie wrestled with her conscience. On the one hand, she felt some affinity with Sheena Struthers, recognised in the woman aspects of her past life. On the other, Sheena was a mass of contradictions: the husband is devoted to her, next thing he's trying to kill her. She says she loves him, but she endangers the marriage by putting a private detective onto him.

Best be done with it, she decided. She drew a breath. Was just about to give Sheena the 'I'm sorry, but I'm unable to take your case further' spiel, when there was a commotion. The dog had slipped its leash and made a beeline for the back.

The mums made a dive for the buggies.

The babies emitted a concerted howl.

When the fuss had died down, Sheena changed tack. 'Did you check up on him – Gordon – like I asked?'

'Yes, I made some discreet enquiries.'

'And?' Sheena Struthers sat forward. 'How did you get on?'

'Your husband is where he says he is.'

'You're sure?'

'Absolutely. I've observed him going to and from his office, at his club, on the golf course. Though at this early stage, you'll appreciate I've only clocked him in and out. Otherwise...' Mentally, Maggie totted up the hours she could bill, despised herself for doing so.

'That's all I needed to know.' Sheena smiled encouragement.

'The rest of the time, as I understand it, you're together either at home or on social engagements.'

'Quite so. But Gordon is up to something, I'm sure of it.'

'An affair, is that what you're hinting at?' *Don't put words in the client's mouth!*

'No!' Sheena Struthers appeared genuinely horror-stricken.

'It's the most common reason by far for someone like yourself to call on my services.'

'That's as may be,' Sheena drew herself up. 'But my husband is devoted to me. Or was, and...' There was a catch in her voice. 'I love him very much.'

Then what are you doing here, silly woman? At that moment, Maggie would have given her eye teeth to have a husband to go home to, faithful or no. Instead: 'He hasn't taken extra care with his appearance lately, for instance?'

'Gordon is always particular about looking well turned out.'

'What about phone calls?'

Puzzled face. 'What about them?'

'You mentioned he won't turn his phone off at night. Has he made any covert calls? Broken off, perhaps, when you've come into the room?'

'No,' Sheena insisted. 'He gets a fair number of calls at home – business and social. Texts too. But I can't say I've noticed anything untoward.'

'You mentioned he makes trips to London. Could…'

Sheena cut her short. 'He sleeps at his club – the Caledonian in Belgravia – I've checked. No.' She compressed her lips. 'I think we can rule out an affair. It's something else entirely.'

'How about money?' Maggie was running out of options now. 'Has there been any change in his spending pattern?'

Sheena gave a small shrug. 'I wouldn't know. Gordon handles all our finances.'

'Is he secretive?' Maggie fished.

'You could say that.' Sheena picked nervously at her nail varnish. 'More careful than secretive, I would say.' Apologetic look. 'He is an accountant after all.'

'In short,' Maggie was running out of steam, 'your husband of over twenty years goes about his business as normal, does not appear to be conducting an affair and is not profligate with money. Would that be a fair summary of the situation, would you say?'

Sheena Struthers blushed crimson. 'When you put it like that. Yes, I suppose.'

'But these are the facts,' Maggie said gently. 'At least as you've described them. And yet you maintain that your husband is "up to something".'

Stubborn look. 'That's right.'

'You said, last time we met, that your marriage is "traditional".' Maggie was clutching at straws now. 'Could you elaborate on that?'

'My husband likes to be the man, if you know what I mean.'

Maggie played dumb. 'Not really.'

'Gordon wants to make the decisions, call the shots.'

Small men! She'd lay odds on he was a bully.

'And he's a bit of a perfectionist. Likes things just so. Goes with the job, I suppose, being meticulous. Plus, he's a creature of habit. Follows his little routines.'

'Your husband is the dominant partner in the marriage, then, would you say?'

'Yes.'

'What happens when things don't go his way?'

'He gets a bit,' Sheena Struthers chewed on her bottom lip, 'het up, I suppose you would call it.'

'And do you get het up?'

That stubborn face again. 'Sometimes.'

'Might I suggest,' Maggie fixed her companion with an earnest look, 'that the problem – if there is one – may lie with you?'

Sheena rallied. 'You've asked me that before. I don't have mental health issues, if that's what you're getting at.'

'Not at all.' In her dealings with Mrs Argo, Maggie had encountered acute psychiatric problems. 'But I've noticed, during our conversations, a level of anxiety that…' She decided to improvise. 'Let me be frank. Is it possible you're suffering from mild depression? In a long marriage like yours, one sometimes becomes uncertain, wonders what it's all…' She broke off suddenly. How did she know? She'd never have that now.

'Everybody does that,' Sheena retorted.

Maggie let that pass. 'From what you've told me, and the limited activities I've managed to observe, your husband doesn't appear to be undergoing a mid-life crisis. Might it be possible that you yourself are going through a period of…?' She struggled to find a tactful expression. 'Emotional flux?'

'Well, I…' Sheena Struthers fiddled with her teaspoon. She couldn't meet Maggie's eye.

'You mentioned you haven't been sleeping. That can have a knock-on effect on your health. Might it not be worth paying a visit to your GP?' she suggested. 'Just to rule out anything medical.' She reached for her coat. 'Then we can take it from there.'

Playing Away

The red Fiesta sped through Banchory Devenick and hurtled past the pillared entrance to Ardoe House Hotel. Wilma sat forward in the driver's seat, but she wasn't admiring the scenery. She was a woman on a mission. And she'd been thwarted more than once already.

It was the old story: the client suspected her husband of having an affair. Although, officially, the agency had sworn off matrimonial cases, February had been a slow month, cash flow helped not one bit by the hours Maggie had been putting in on the Struthers case. Having failed to dissuade Maggie from her cause, Wilma had resigned herself to playing a waiting game. In the meantime, she'd resolved to pick up whatever additional business came their way.

Waste of time, had been Wilma's reaction when she'd rolled up to the house: a whacking great ranch-style bungalow that would put the Ponderosa to shame.

Mark Rowland, devoted father of four children, had started acting completely out of character.

He's become obsessed with his body, Tina Rowland had told Wilma. *Last week I caught him doing press-ups in the bathroom. He hasn't taken exercise in years.*

Wife had done the usual: riffled through his receipts, emptied his pockets, checked his phone. Nothing. Then she'd called Harcus & Laird.

By the sound of things, the husband was having a wee mid-life crisis. Wilma had seen it many a time: a fella suddenly dressing half his age, trying to screw everything in sight. Last one she'd come across had cashed in his pension, bought a red Ferrari, cruised up and down Union Street until he was taken to task.

The wife had let herself go, that much was obvious. Woman

would be better off spending the money she was paying the agency on an exotic holiday – Wilma reckoned more middle-aged blokes went ape out of sheer bloody boredom than lack of sex – either that or some judicious Juvederm filler. Still, when it came to marriage, who was she to judge, especially in the light of Ian's recent moodiness? And it's not as if the client was short of cash, if appearances were anything to go by.

Mark Rowland worked in the oil industry, had always kept long hours, so no surprises there. For weeks Wilma had tailed him from his place of work to a series of restaurants and bars. He was a good-looking guy: tall, dark, still had all his hair. And trim enough, regardless of what the wife said, not soft in the belly like older men tend to go. Rowland tended to frequent quiet venues, not the trendy bars that were popular with his younger colleagues. But she'd never spotted him with another woman, or at least always in a crowd, never alone.

The breakthrough came when she'd followed him to a flat in Prospect Terrace. Sitting high above the harbour at the back of Crown Street, the Victorian terraced cottages would have had a view, once, out over the old railway terminus at Ferryhill to the harbour. Now the intervening space was largely occupied by office blocks and the Union Square shopping centre, the cottages divided into flats.

Her quarry was only there for a short time. It took Wilma till the following evening to find out why. The flat had been let on a short-term lease. After an elderly upstairs neighbour had repeatedly complained about sounds of sexual activity – *like animals*, she'd told the landlord – and the tenant had failed to respond, the locks on the interior door had been changed.

Nosy cow, Wilma's teenage informant snivelled, *the way she's aye at the window. Like living with your granny.* Then, the teenager had helpfully supplied her with the details of the caravan park he'd offered to the forlorn Mark Rowland as a stop-gap.

Switching the heater up full blast – there hadn't been snow, but it was bitterly cold – Wilma shot past the turn-off for Milltimber. Not that she was pushed. The text the GPS had sent confirmed the locus. But the days drew in early at this time of year and Wilma was anxious to get the job done. Besides which, she supposed caravans would have blinds these days: proper, fitted blinds, not scaffy old curtains like in the draughty residential homes she'd shared with Darren. If she landed lucky, she'd get some decent photos.

Must be nearly there. She kept her eyes peeled for the sign. *This should be good*, she had a quiet chortle to herself. She'd checked out the holiday park online, knew there was a mix of lodges, caravans and camping pods. Pods? That was a new one. Kids were that pampered these days. What was wrong with a bloody tent? She speculated as to how many units would be occupied in the winter months. She could ask at reception, if it was manned, but that would be giving the game away. And, besides, Rowland might have booked under an assumed name. She'd start with a recce for his car, she resolved. Shouldn't be too hard. There couldn't be that many 7 Series Beamers on a bloody camping site in January, now could there?

The sign sprang into view. Wilma flicked her indicator and turned off the B9077.

As she'd expected, the accommodation was set out in rows. For a moment she hesitated. If there were only two of them, they'd rent one of the smaller units, wouldn't they? Plus, although price probably wasn't a factor, in this icy weather a small unit would be cosier.

She crawled forward, parked the Fiesta behind a toilet block. And then she spotted it. The BMW was slotted neatly between two caravans.

Bingo! Wilma delved for her camera, turned up her collar and slid out of the driving seat, closing the door part-way so as to make no sound. Crouched low, she crept forward until she was level with the suspect's car.

No lights were showing from either caravan, but there were no blinds drawn either. She was debating which to try first when she heard a noise. Not a loud noise. More of a muffled gasp.

She turned. That caravan couldn't be rocking, could it? Wilma stifled a giggle. Took her back to those early days of PI work: thon couple in the car at Nigg. She pressed her body against the side of the caravan. Calves aching, she raised herself inch by painful inch till her eyes were level with the underside of the window.

There were two people on the bed, both stark naked. The errant husband was on all fours, pumping away. Beneath him a figure knelt, blonde head half buried in the pillow. That must have been the noise she'd heard, Wilma reckoned: the smothered panting.

She readied her camera. It was only as the subject climaxed and the partner's head jerked back that she was knocked off her stotter. *Boys Own!* she marvelled as she rattled off a few shots.

The glare bounced back at her off the window.

Christ! In the waning light Wilma hadn't dared disable the flash.

The subject's head swivelled.

From inside the caravan, there was an outraged roar.

Wilma legged it as two burly men tried to hurriedly dress themselves in a confined space.

Treats Shelf

'It's my fault,' Ros confided, as she whisked the salad dressing. 'I know I should give him time to clear his head, but when he walks through the door I just sort of jump on him.'

'What's wrong with that?' Fiona leaned against the sink. Fiona was the partner of Nic's junior lecturer, and Ros's best friend. She and Ros were enjoying a glass of wine in the kitchen, the boys demolishing a beer in the next door sitting room whilst they watched the end of a noisy football game on TV. 'Isn't he pleased to see you?'

'I suppose.' Ros beat the emulsion furiously. 'But it makes him cross all the same.'

'Cross? How?'

'Snappy. Irritable.' She set the salad dressing aside. 'He'll grab a drink from the fridge and a packet of crisps or something from his treats shelf and shut himself in the study till supper.'

'*Treats shelf?*' Fiona scoffed. She wondered what that was all about.

'Loads of people do that.' Ros rose to her husband's defence. 'Parents. Hide things from their kids. My mum used to keep cake under the bed.'

'Cake?'

'Walnut cake. With royal icing. Came from a shop called Fuller's in Buchanan Street. Cost a bomb, probably.'

'That I can understand,' Fiona pulled a wry face. 'But crisps. I mean...' She took a sip of her wine, decided to leave it for now. 'And when he does that, how do you feel?'

'Small.' Ros signalled with a finger and thumb. 'Shut out. Angry.'

'With Nic?'

'With myself, for not having the wit to go about it the right way.' She grimaced. 'Fish the salad spoons out of that drawer, will you?'

Fiona rummaged in the cutlery drawer, extracted a pair of lime green plastic salad servers, handed them over. 'You think there is a "right way"?'

'Oh.' Ros brushed a hand across her brow. 'I don't know. It's like…you see in old movies how the little woman welcomes the guy home, all prettied up, hanging on his every word.'

'A woman who's been home all day,' Fiona interrupted. 'Not knocking her pan out with a class of manic seven-year-olds, then haring around the supermarket before she picks up a fractious baby from nursery.'

'That's what my friend Maggie says.' Wry smile. 'Just wait till you and Stuart have kids.'

Fiona grinned. 'We're in no hurry.'

Ros reached for her glass. 'Maybe that's where I went wrong.' She eyed the contents contemplatively. 'Had a rush of blood when I turned thirty. Saw my chances narrowing by the minute. Grabbed the first guy with prospects that came along. And Nic was…is…the blond Adonis, all blue eyes and boyish looks. Plus, he stood out.' She twiddled with a strand of her hair. 'Shone, is the best way I can describe it. It wasn't swagger so much as innate self-confidence. As if he knew exactly where he was going. I envied him that, Fi, I must confess. I've always felt at a disadvantage.'

'But you look so…together.'

'I do my best. But for us Scots it's difficult, don't you think, to shake off all the stuff that's been drummed into you: speak when you're spoken to, don't get above your station, all that. It was only much later, after we'd been living together for a while, that I realised how different our values were…' Her voice trailed off. 'The rest,' she cast a rueful glance over the baby bowls and beakers lined up on the windowsill, 'is history.'

'Serves you right,' Fiona countered, with a cheeky look. 'Hooking up with anything from south of the border.'

Ros sprang to Nic's defence. 'Now you're being racist.'

'I'm not. All I'm saying is…talk of the devil!' She clasped a hand to her mouth when Nic stuck his head through the door.

'What are you two cooking up? Mayhem and sedition?' He took a step forward.

Instinctively, Ros stiffened. She turned her head away. 'Supper's almost ready,' she said with forced brightness. 'You guys could help by opening the wine that's through there on the table. And Fiona,' her eyes flashed warning signs, 'if you'd like to fill this water jug and dress the salad, we can eat in a few minutes.'

Fiona flapped her hands. 'You heard her. Open the wine, then get back to your football. We're having a private conversation.'

'What about?'

'None of your business.' She challenged him with a hard stare. 'It's private. Didn't you hear me?'

Nic threw her a look. 'I heard you.' He retreated into the living room.

'What was I saying? Oh, yes. In addition to his obvious...' Stage wink. '...attributes, your dear husband does embody some of the worse aspects of the south-east.'

'Such as?'

'His obsession with money. Look at the way he's always hacking on about his father.'

'He's proud of his dad, that's all.'

'Is it?' Thoughtful face. 'Seems to me it's a bit more than that. Bordering on the unhealthy, if you ask me.'

Ros crooked an eyebrow. 'D'you think?' She'd little doubt Nic's character had been shaped by his father. But 'unhealthy'? The thought had never crossed her mind.

Ros had only met the man on that single visit, in those heady days before she and Nic got engaged. Harold Prentice had been a taciturn sixty-something with a sharp turn of phrase. A self-made man, he'd sold his company and taken early retirement. There was an older brother in Australia. Nic's mum, Jill, did her own thing. From what Ros had gleaned, she and Harold seemed barely to communicate.

'You could be right. He didn't even come to our wedding. Jill flew up on her own. Harold,' her mouth twisted, 'sent a cheque.'

'Well,' Fiona countered, 'at least he made a contribution.'

'You're wrong there. My folks stumped up for every last thing.'

'But, I thought you said...'

'Harold sent Nic a cheque. I wouldn't have known, except I was there when he opened it. Went straight into his bank account. Weird, now I look back on it. But I was so caught up in the wedding preparations,' she pulled a face. 'You know how it is.'

'I do have a hazy recollection,' Fiona chuckled. 'Heavily fuelled by alcohol.' She took a slurp of her wine. 'But didn't you ask his folks to contribute? I mean, it's standard practice, isn't it, these days?'

'I didn't have the nerve. I'd only met them once, you see. And they were so different. Even their house was different – a great red brick pile on the outskirts of a village. I sort of went into blushing bride mode.'

'What about your folks? Didn't they bring it up?'

'No. Mum and Dad, bless their hearts, scrupulously avoided comment. Still...' She changed the subject. 'I know I should give Nic space when he comes in from work. He'll have had a full day too, shoe-horning in lectures and meetings and research and whatever. Plus...' Apologetic look. 'Anything I have to say could easily wait until supper time. It's just, there's precious little opportunity in our staffroom to talk about anything but schoolwork, and by the time it gets to four o'clock I'm screaming for adult conversation.'

'You and me both,' Fiona chuckled. "The chitchat in my office is pretty inconsequential. But at least I don't go home to a round of feeds and trainer pants.'

'And this?' Ros waved an arm around the cramped kitchen. Their rented nineteenth-century cottage in College Bounds was charming, but tight for space. 'I envy you your big kitchen-diner.'

'Minimalist living is all very well,' Fiona quipped, 'but where would you hide the toys?'

'I know. And this place is handy for Max's nursery. For Seaton, too, so I shouldn't complain.'

'Getting back to Nic,' Fiona's face took on a serious expression. 'Have you told him how you feel?'

Shocked voice. 'No.'

'Why not?'

'It would only make things worse.'

'I can understand that, if you brought it up when he'd just got in. But couldn't you wait till you've put the baby to bed? Or you've gone to bed yourselves. That way, you'll have all his attention. Speaking of which…' She reached out a hand. 'Don't say if you don't want to, but are things alright in that department?'

'Fine.' Ros brightened. 'That's the one thing that hasn't suffered. At least only for a short while after the baby…' She broke off. 'We're back to normal, now. The only thing is…' She pulled a face. 'As in everything else, Nic does like to call the shots.'

Fiona grinned. 'Don't they all? But, as I was saying, try to have it out with him, the other thing. But hold off till he's more relaxed.'

'You know him well enough by now,' Ros let out a long sigh. 'Nic doesn't do "relaxed".'

Peace of Mind

'We met through the internet,' the woman seated across the table from Maggie confided. 'Ralph…' Coy smile. 'He was my fourth match.'

'Mmm,' Maggie murmured, non-committal. They'd agreed to meet in a hotel lounge on Great Western Road. It wasn't far from Maggie to walk and, besides, she'd had a bellyful of Patisserie Valerie.

The case – a prenuptial background vetting check – had come to Harcus & Laird by way of Sheena Struthers. The client was an acquaintance of Sheena's, one of a coterie of middle-class ladies who lunched and played bridge together. Maggie had accepted Helen Cruickshank's business with alacrity. Verification in these sorts of cases was a growing, and lucrative, field. And easy money, an internet search often all that was required to achieve a satisfactory outcome. More important, Maggie hoped the extra income would go some way towards thawing her strained relations with her friend and colleague.

By rights, the case had fallen to Wilma, who had already run a background check. But this particular evening, big-hearted Wilma was doing emergency sickness cover at her Torry pub and had asked Maggie to present the agency's report.

I've done all the work. You only have to wind things up, Wilma insisted. *Piece of cake!*

Maggie had been reluctant, but in the circumstances felt she could hardly refuse. Still, she said a silent prayer that Helen Cruickshank wasn't going to turn out to be another Sheena Struthers.

'I'd been a bit depressed,' the client volunteered. 'After Christmas, when the family went home and the decorations came down…' She leaned forward. 'You know how it is.'

Maggie knew only too well. Bad enough she'd to go on living without George, day by day, week by week. But the holiday period had hammered home that not only was she without a husband, her parents had become strangers, her children increasingly out of reach.

'I was drinking too much,' Mrs Cruickshank went on. 'A gin and tonic on the dot of six – gave me an instant lift – then I'd tipple away till bedtime. If I'd still had company…' Apologetic look. 'I'd have stuck to wine. Good wine at that. Tony prided himself on his cellar. But there's no point in opening a bottle, is there, to drink on my own?'

Doesn't stop Wilma, Maggie thought wryly. Me neither, not these days. Since she'd teamed up with Wilma Harcus, Maggie's tastes – in all manner of things – had undergone a rapid re-jig.

'Quite so,' she murmured. She took a squint at the woman sitting opposite. Dissolute or not, Helen Cruickshank looked like a forties movie star, all smokey eyes and serious lipstick. Maggie made a mental note to ask Kirsty for make-up advice next time she was home.

'And besides,' her companion ran on, 'spirits are cleaner, sharper. Don't dehydrate you. I told myself once the cold weather eased I'd cut down, but then…'

'You were going to tell me about Ralph.' Gently, Maggie interrupted the torrent of words. She'd come across this many times: a client happy to talk about anything but the reason for their meeting.

'Oh.' Mrs Cruickshank twisted an embroidered hankie between her hands. 'So I was. My first match…'

Dammit! Maggie wished she hadn't put the question. She already knew the answer, so there was no need to pick through the sordid details. All the same, the knowledge she gained she could put to good use in future cases.

Cynical bitch! You're getting as bad as Wilma.

'Bit touchy-feely.' Sideways look. 'If you know what I mean.'

Maggie gave a small nod.

'Number two was in sales. I couldn't get a word in.'

Nor me! Maggie kept her counsel.

'Match number three was an academic. Decent enough, but on the nervy side. Problem was, I couldn't help but compare those men with Tony. He's been dead three years now.' There was a wobble in her voice. 'And they didn't measure up.'

'What about Ralph?' Maggie steered the conversation back.

'Took me by storm. Like my late husband, he's a public schoolboy. And dishy with it. Presented himself for our first dinner date impeccably groomed. And bearing a nosegay of snowdrops, would you believe? I've no idea how he knew I love snowdrops.'

Classic, Maggie thought. From her research, she'd learned that sociopaths tend to target lonely women, use the information they post online to tell them what they want to hear.

'I was charmed, my dear,' Mrs Cruickshank rattled on. 'My Tony, for all his virtues, was a sloppy dresser, happiest in old cords and a shapeless sweater,' she grimaced. 'Invariably with a trail of spills down the front.'

'And Ralph? What happened next?'

'Took me home. Said his farewells at the front door. Then…'

Maggie sneaked a quick peek at her phone. When she'd posed the question, she'd meant how had the relationship developed. She prayed she wasn't in for a blow-by-blow account of heavy sex.

'I've had such a lovely time these past few weeks,' her companion offered. 'Dinner, theatre, country drives…' She broke off.

Maggie waited for the 'but'. There was always a 'but'. It never came.

'You must be very happy then,' she prompted.

'Oh, yes.' Fond smile. 'But, as I told you on the telephone, the children aren't. At least, not since Ralph asked me to marry him.'

'Why is that?' Maggie dissembled.

'They're worried about my well-being. That and…' Strained smile. '…their inheritance. We were well set up, you see, before Tony's sudden death. The sale of the business, well, it brought the fruits of thirty years of hard work, something we'd been looking to enjoy before…' Her voice hitched. 'I was left on my own. And there are other investments. If I were to marry…' She battled to regain her composure. 'Anyhow, they tell me it's standard practice, these days, to run a check like I asked you to.'

'Yes,' Maggie concurred. 'The internet is a minefield these days. Better,' she hesitated, 'to have peace of mind.'

Peace of mind! She felt like a snake-oil salesman as she uttered the words. She was about to ruin this lonely woman's day. Plus, she'd long since accepted that it would be years yet – if ever – before she herself achieved a state of mental equilibrium.

She composed herself. It was high time she broke the news.

'My report,' she slid a slim folder across the table.

Helen Cruickshank brightened. 'So soon? Your firm is very efficient, Mrs Laird.'

And thorough!

Wilma's internet trawl had thrown up the subject's registration on multiple dating sites. Ralph's real name was Mark Rowland. Maggie hadn't had the nerve to ask Wilma how she'd found out. Nor had he attended public school. He'd claimed to be a widower, his wife having died of ovarian cancer. Not only was the wife very much alive, but 'Ralph' was still married with four dependent children.

Bastard!

Maggie watched as Helen Cruickshank opened the folder and started to read, as the colour drained from her face.

Time of the Month

Through the thin fabric of her nightie she can feel the movement.

His cock bobs up. Like one of those fairground skittles. Comic, really. Well, it would be, only she's not in the mood.

'Mmm.' He nuzzles her neck.

She shrugs one shoulder, sending a signal. Or so she hopes. She's been feeling lousy all day: flu-ish, headache-y. Told herself, as she struggled through the motions, it would pass. It hasn't, stomach cramps stopping her mid-chore. Goes with the territory when it's that time of the month. You'd think, by now, she'd be used to them, those sharp muscle-clenching pains. But, no, they invariably catch her unawares. This time they've been more painful, violent almost, the blood darker when she goes to the bathroom. She wonders what's going on…

His penis is rod-hard, now, poking into the small of her back.

She tries to ignore it, but it persists, nagging like a toothache. Or period pain, come to that.

With a wry smile, she reaches a hand between her legs, checks the tampon is still in place. Between her fingers, the string tail is dripping wet. Dammit! She snatches her hand away. She'd better get up before…

He likes to fuck her when she's bleeding. Seems to turn him on: her look of distaste as he penetrates, his cock dripping scarlet when he withdraws, the tang of iron on his fingers. Once, she'd even caught him at the laundry basket, his nose buried in a pair of soiled knickers.

'Don't be disgusting,' she'd exclaimed, then.

He'd laughed. 'It's perfectly normal,' he said.

Then, she had believed him. Now, she's not so sure.

The prodding at her back is insistent.

She squeezes her eyes shut, tries to ignore it.

A hand snakes around her waist.

'Don't.' She pushes it away.

'Come on,' he wheedles. 'You can tell I'm horny.'

'I'm not feeling up for it tonight. I've got my period.'

'So?' The hand strays downwards.

Sod it! She shouldn't have let on.

She feels strong fingers between her thighs.

They tug at the tampon. 'What have we here?'

A sudden movement.

She turns.

He dangles the tampon over his face, sniffs appreciatively, then drops it onto the bed.

'Don't worry.' He moves to mount her. 'I'll be quick.'

It'll Sort

Wilma stood on Maggie's doorstep. 'Well?' she challenged with a hostile stare.

'What's up?' Maggie drew her dressing-gown tighter across her chest. 'Do you have any idea what time it is?' She took in Wilma's dishevelled state: bird's nest hair, skimpy jacket over leopard-print pyjamas, bare feet protruding from an outsize pair of fluffy mules.

'Aye. Time ah wisna standin here,' Wilma shivered. 'Can ah come in?'

'Of course.' Maggie took a step back. 'Come away through.'

Wilma shot down the hallway, switched on the dining-room light, parked herself on a chair.

Maggie shut the front door and followed. 'You look perished. Can I get you something? Cup of tea?'

'It's a bloody drink ah'm needin.' Wilma stamped her feet. 'Brandy, if ye've got it.' She rubbed the circulation back into her hands. 'An mak it a big one.'

Maggie sank to her knees and rummaged in the back of the side-board. 'I'm sure I had some left,' she called over her shoulder. 'From the Christmas cake.'

'Which Christmas was that?' Wilma muttered *sotto voce*.

'I can hear you, madam.' Maggie didn't turn. 'Here it is,' she unearthed a dumpy bottle. Half-turning, she held it up to the light.

'Christ,' Wilma eyed the inch of amber liquid in the bottom. 'That wouldn't last a minute in my house.'

Clutching her trailing housecoat in one hand, Maggie struggled to her feet. 'Do you want it or not?'

'Give it here.' Wilma stuck out a blue-tinged hand. 'Dinna bother wi a glass.'

'So.' Maggie sat facing her friend. 'What's this all this about?'

'What?' Wilma's face and hands had resumed a pinkish tinge, which was more than could be said for Maggie who, roused from sleep, was chalk white.

'This nocturnal...' She fought for clarity. 'Visitation.'

Wilma made a face. 'Ye couldna use jist the one syllable when four would do?'

'Wilma Harcus, if you think you're going to come knocking on my door at,' she checked her watch, 'two in the morning. And then take the piss, you've got another think...' She broke off as a fat tear slid down Wilma's cheek.

'Wilma.' Maggie shoved the empty bottle aside, grasped her friend's hand. 'What's the matter?'

'H-here,' Wilma hiccupped. 'H-him.' She brushed a sleeve across her dripping nose.

'Ian?'

'Aye.'

'Have you two had a row?'

'Ah'd say,' Wilma produced a sheepish grin, 'that was a fuckin understatement.'

Inwardly, Maggie sighed. If the pair of them had had a set-to, she'd have put money on Wilma coming out on top, especially now she had her boxing gym training behind her. Covertly, she checked her neighbour's knuckles for signs of injury. Found none.

'What brought that on?' she asked.

'Och,' Wilma muttered into her chest, 'he wis kickin up.'

'What about?'

'Us.'

'The agency?'

'Aye. Wettin hisself on account of the hours ah've been puttin in. Says it's one thing you knockin yer pan oot, it's anither me daein the same.'

'Well.' Maggie stroked Wilma's hand. 'He's right, you know.'

Wilma shook her off. 'That's as may be, but the stushie wisna on account of agency business. It's been brewin for a while. What finally got his goat wis ma extra wee shift at the pub. Anyhow,' she set her chin. 'It's nae up tae him. He disna own me.'

'No.' Maggie's heart tugged as she recalled the row she'd had with George over the Seaton job. 'He doesn't.'

'An we're no goin tae make a success of things sittin on oor fat arses. Oh.' Wilma put a hand to her mouth. 'Didna mean that whit div ye say…?'

'Literally,' Maggie finished the sentence.

The doorbell chimed.

'Shush,' Wilma put a finger to her lips. 'Switch the light off.'

'Why?' Maggie protested. 'Nobody can see us.'

'It'll be Ian. He might go round the back.'

It rang again.

Oh to hell! Maggie cursed. All she needed was for Colin to waken.

Wilma leapt to her feet and made a dive for the light switch, plunging the room into darkness. She tiptoed back across and sat down.

The two sat in silence for what seemed like an eternity before they heard footsteps receding, a door slam shut.

'You'll think ah'm a daft cow.' Loud whisper. 'Divorcin wan bugger an then fallin oot wi the next.'

'You don't need to whisper, Wilma. He's gone. But from what you've told me, Darren was a different kettle of fish altogether.

'Ye can say that again. I've still got the marks.'

Maggie chose not to go there. 'But,' she probed, 'Ian seems so easy-going.'

'He is.' Wilma sounded shame-faced. 'It's jist, ah used tae think – when Ian an me met up first – folk were better over here than in Torry. An men were better than women, wherever. But since you and me got together, well…ah reckon now ah've a career,' she paused. 'A proper business career,' she enunciated carefully. 'Not a bunch of low-paid skivvying jobs. He should give my opinions the time of day.'

Lord! Maggie thought she had a lot to answer for as it was. Now she was turning Wilma into a feminist. Come to think on it, she'd become much more vocal herself since she'd taken on the agency. She smiled as she recalled the tongue-lashing she'd given Detective Inspector Chisolm the first time he'd called.

'So,' she continued, 'how did it end up?'

'Told him to stuff his effin bungalow up his effin arse.'

Maggie burst out laughing. 'You never did.'

'Aye.' Outraged voice. 'And I meant it.'

'Which is why we're sitting here in the dark in the middle of the night.'

'Aye,' Wilma mumbled. 'Sorry to wake you, Maggie. And you needing all the rest ye can get.'

'Doesn't matter. Just as long as Colin doesn't decide to join us,' Maggie stifled a yawn. 'Now why don't I put the kettle on?'

'I'll not be needing tea.'

'No.' Maggie rose. 'But I could use something warm in my stomach to send me back to sleep. And while I'm at it I'll fill you a hot water bottle.' She crossed to switch on the light. 'Then you can cosy up in Kirsty's bed.'

'Thanks pal.'

'And Wilma...'

From beneath heavy eyelids Wilma peered up.

'It'll sort.'

IV

A Fly Cup

The body lay, half in half out of the bed, one hand clutching at the counterpane. As if the woman had decided to get up. Changed her mind. Tried to climb back in again.

That's women for you, was PC Ian Souter's first reaction. His mind jumped to the last female corpse he'd attended: student Lucy Simmons spread-eagled on a cold, hard tombstone in a dank, dark kirk-yard. Briskly, he dismissed the thought.

The bedside light was on. He looked around. The room was large, big enough to fit in the entire first floor of his chalet bungalow in Bridge of Don, he thought covetously. And well-furnished, in a dated sort of a way: embossed wallpaper, velvet pile carpet, heavy brocade curtains over delicate voile blinds. The fitted oak wardrobes looked bespoke, even to his untrained eye. A pair of matching, solid wood cabinets framed the sumptuously dressed king-size bed. Like the downstairs – what little Souter had seen as he and Miller charged through the front door – it all screamed money.

The woman was small, slight, her short dark hair tousled from sleep. And of a certain age. Souter wasn't great at judging, but he reckoned mid-forties. She was wearing a nightgown: pink satin edged with lace. One shoestring strap had slipped from her shoulder, the hem ridden up to her thighs. Probably cost a bomb, though the thing would hardly have covered her at the best of times. Not like the passion-killer his own wife had sported throughout the winter. Shirley felt the cold, and their house had been Baltic since they'd turned the heating down. This place, on the other hand, was toasty. He pictured the energy reminder sitting in his hall. Pulled a face.

He squatted by the woman's side. Grasped hold of one limp wrist, searched for the radial pulse. No joy. He looked up. Atop the bedside cabinet, a bookmark peeped from a paperback book: *Lie With*

Me. Souter wondered if it was steamy. A china cup and saucer held the remains of what looked like tea. He noted a box of tissues – one of those cube things, flowery – halfway down the bed. On the far side, the pillow held the shape of what might be a male head. The woman's nightie looked damp. Souter speculated whether they still had sex. A crumpled tissue lay on the floor. He resisted the urge to pick it up, take a sniff.

They'd been attending an incident at Bridge of Dee when they got the shout. Shot out South Deeside Road on blues. Hit a snarl-up at Ardoe House – one of them posh weddings, most like. Murtle Den Road, when they finally got there, had been a bummer: muckle big houses surrounded by trees and nary a number in sight.

It was Miller spotted the cleaner screaming blue murder at the gate. They'd made her stay outside while they checked the locus. His partner was downstairs, now, trying to get a statement out of her. Souter hoped he'd make it good, otherwise the desk sergeant would have their guts for garters.

Souter let go of the woman's wrist. Touched two fingertips to the soft groove beside her windpipe, reckoned he felt a fluttering there. *Sod it!* His youngest had a birthday that day and he'd promised to be home by lunchtime. Now he'd likely have to follow the ambulance to ARI, and God knows how long he'd get stuck there. He could always send Miller, but what help would that be? One or other of them was required to stay at the locus till they got the all clear.

He heard a vehicle screech to a halt. Doors slammed. A bell pealed. Running footsteps on the stairs. And the paramedics were by his side. Gratefully, Souter removed his fingers from the woman's neck.

'Absent pulse.' He nodded to the lead. 'Maybe you'll have better luck.'

The man nodded. 'Leave it to us.'

'Okay.'

Souter got to his feet. He took another, cursory, look around the room. Half hidden under the quilt, he spied a pair of spectacles, legs askew. Woman must have been reading in bed when she…

There were no outward signs of a stroke. Most likely had a seizure, he concluded. He'd seen too many heart attacks strike down apparently healthy people. Young folk, even, like that student at St Machar. Poor bairn. Can't have been long out of school. Souter grimaced. He knew how unpredictable the human heart could be.

He hurried out of the bedroom and headed down the stairs.

The cleaning woman was huddled in a cane chair, a wad of sodden tissues clutched in her fists. Her hair was in disarray, her eyes liquid from weeping, her nose red raw. Miller was crouched close on the floor at her feet. Too close, Souter reckoned. He'd caught a swift movement as he entered the room. Had his partner's hand been on the woman's knee? Souter couldn't be sure. He estimated her age to be mid-twenties. Wondered if Miller had ideas in that direction. *Wanker!* He'd chase anything in a skirt.

Souter turned to appraise the sleek fitted kitchen with its stainless steel appliances. His eyes lit on a state-of-the-art kitchen tap: one of those ones that dispensed boiling water like he'd seen on the telly. He grinned. *Good-oh!* There might even be decent biscuits.

I'll Be Fine

Maggie let herself into the conservatory.

'How's you?' She addressed the figure curled up in one of the chairs.

Wilma raised a miserable face. 'Not great.' She indicated a bottle on the glass table. 'Fancy a beer?'

'No thanks,' Maggie answered with a shudder. 'Bit early in the day for me.'

Wilma's mouth turned down even further.

'But don't let me stop you,' Maggie rushed to add, unwinding her scarf and plonking herself down opposite her friend.

Wilma reached for the bottle and took a hearty swig.

'Well…' Maggie couldn't wait a moment longer. 'Did you catch Ian before he left for work?'

'Aye. Sneaked in when he was shaving.'

'And?'

Wilma set her beer down. 'I wouldn't say he was pleased to see me, for all I had his breakfast laid out.'

'What did he have to say?'

'Said I could stuff the breakfast for starters. And that's not all. He told me he wished he'd never met me, and to pack my bags and be out of here before he got home. Said by all accounts that wouldn't be a problem, I was that used to moonlight flits when I was with Darren.'

Maggie's eyes widened. 'Oh, Wilma…'

'I've effing blown it.' Wilma's eyes welled with tears.

'Come on.' Maggie crossed to her side. She drew Wilma into her arms. 'I'm sure it's not that bad.'

Wilma pulled away. 'You don't know my Ian. Look at the way he dug his heels in over the agency.'

'Yes, but he came around.'

'Took him long enough. And he still isn't convinced. You should see the look I get, some nights, when I'm in late. Like he doesn't know if I've been out on the ran-dan or what.'

Maggie squatted at Wilma's feet. 'I'm sure you're imagining things. He must have heard my car at all hours too, the front door closing, whatever.'

'That's just it. He thinks you're a bad influence on me.'

That's rich coming from you, Maggie thought. 'Does he really?' was all she managed.

'Yes, and...' Wilma started to cry, '...I don't know what to do.'

'Well, if the agency's the root of the problem,' Maggie responded half-heartedly, 'I suppose you'd better give it up.'

'I don't want to give it up,' Wilma bleated. 'And besides, what will you do?'

'I'll be fine,' Maggie reassured her, heart pounding. She had a sudden urge to throw up.

'I love the bugger,' Wilma snivelled. 'That's the problem. Never met anyone like him – fella that would look up to a woman like she was a pop star or something. Doesn't force himself on her. Wants to look after her, instead of her seeing to him.'

Like George, Maggie thought with a pang. *Steady, thoughtful, loving George.*

'We didn't start out with much,' Wilma ran on, 'him and me. But we've been doing away. And now, with the agency and that... I had such plans, Maggie. Put a proper extension on the back instead of this DIY job.'

'I like your conservatory,' Maggie offered.

'Change my car, mebbe. How Ian's managed to keep it on the road this long's a fucking miracle.'

'He's an ace mechanic, that's for sure.'

'Aye. And now all that's out the window.'

'It will blow over.' Maggie cupped the big woman's face in her hands. 'Maybe Ian feels threatened by the agency, the fact you're doing your own thing might be a blow to his masculinity. Maybe he's feeling neglected, what with the hours you put in and…'

Wilma tossed her head. 'He's getting his load off, if that's what you're getting at.

'It isn't.' Maggie recoiled in shock, then mustered a smile. 'All I was going to say is keep a low profile for a bit, spoil him rotten. Nothing like a few good dinners.'

'And a bit of nookie,' Wilma cut in.

Maggie grimaced. 'I suppose.'

'That's all very well, what you're saying. But he's stubborn. What if he does throw me out? I've nowhere to go.'

'He won't throw you out. You've a good man there, Wilma. If you love him, hang onto him. Being on your own is no fun.' She worked to keep her voice steady. 'You only have to look at me.'

'Oh, pet.' Wilma scrubbed the tears from her eyes. 'Here's me sounding off and I haven't even offered you a cup of tea.'

'I'm fine. It doesn't…' She broke off as the back door swung open and Ian barged in.

His eyes swept the space: a tear-stained Wilma huddled in the chair, beer bottle in front of her, Maggie crouched by her side.

'What's cooking with you two?' he demanded.

'Nothing,' they answered in unison.

'I was just leaving.' Maggie jumped to her feet. She grabbed her scarf, and scuttled out the back door.

A Case Number

'Well, Souter?' The sergeant looked up. He peered over the rim of his reading glasses.

PC Ian Souter shuffled his size twelve feet. Willie Esson was a big man, with a temper to match, and Souter had been at the wrong end of it once too often.

'Reporting on the call-out to Murtle Den Road, Sergeant.'

'Ye-es?' Willie Esson removed his glasses and put them down on the desk in front of him.

'There was a shout for the nearest unit to Milltimber. PC Miller and me responded.'

'PC Miller and *I*, Souter.'

'PC Miller and *aye*, sir.'

Willie Esson ran his fingers through what was left of his hair. He didn't know where they got these young guys from. Some of them, even the university graduates, were barely literate these days.

'What did you find when you got there, Constable?'

'A body, sir.'

The sergeant sighed theatrically. 'What sort of a bloody body, Souter?'

'A female body.'

'Go on.'

Souter scratched the side of his nose, unsure quite how to respond.

'What about this body, Constable?' prompted the senior officer. 'Who found it? Where was it? Give me the facts.'

Forehead creased, Souter bent to consult his notebook. He straightened. 'Incident called in 09.02 to emergency services. PCs Souter and Miller first to respond. Arrived Murtle Den Road, Milltimber 09.16. Entry to property given by Zofia Wisniewski, cleaner. Body of unresponsive female found in first floor bedroom. Identified as householder Sheena Struthers. No other parties present. Ambulance services arrived 09.22. Patient transferred to ARI.'

'That's better, son,' Willie Esson leaned back in his chair. 'Did you establish if there is anyone else resident at the address?'

'Husband. Gordon Struthers.'

'Has anyone contacted him?'

'I left Miller to do that.'

'All the same.' The sergeant threw his constable an arch look. 'We'd better follow that up.' He scribbled a note. 'Now, I'd like you to tell me, in your own words, exactly what you saw at the scene.'

'Not a lot.' Souter couldn't meet his senior officer's eyes. He stood, rooted to the spot. 'It all happened in that much of a rush, sir: us gaining access, the ambulance arriving at our back.'

Behind the desk, his superior sat, anger seething out of every pore. 'You have to do better than that.'

Souter blushed from the base of his neck to the roots of his hair. Finally, he spoke. 'There were no obvious signs of injury, Sarge. Seems the woman suffered a heart attack, and...'

The sergeant cut him off mid-flow 'How did you establish that, Constable? No, on second thought, don't tell me.' He drew a breath. 'And don't go making bloody assumptions. You've obviously been watching too much shite on the telly, Souter. Stick to the fucking facts.'

'Yes, sir.'

'Where was Miller while this was happening?'

'Downstairs, sir, with the cleaner.'

'She gave you access?'

'Yes, sir.'

'Miller took a statement from the cleaner, then.'

'N-no, sir,' Souter stammered.

'Why the fuck not?'

'She doesn't speak English.'

'Christ Almighty.' The sergeant's face suffused with blood. 'Not one word?'

'Hardly any, sir. She's Polish. Miller got her to write down her name, then…'

'Never mind,' Esson cut him short. 'I hope you two wankers didn't disturb anything.'

'No, sir. That's one of the first things…'

'Right. And maybe one of the very few things you haven't forgotten.'

Souter stammered. 'S-sir.'

The older man sighed deeply. 'What happened then?'

'Well, me and Miller…'

'Miller and *I*,' thundered the sergeant.

'I followed the ambulance. Miller stayed at the house.'

'It's taken us fucking long enough to get to this stage.' Sergeant Esson let out a long sigh. 'Now, before we're done here, take a minute, son. Is there anything you've overlooked?'

Souter scrunched his eyes shut. He stood for a few moments, then opened them again. 'No, sir.'

'You're sure?'

'Yes, sir.'

'Then, away you go, and get the thing written up.'

'Right you are, sir.' Relief written all over his face, Souter turned away.

'And Souter…'

'Yes, Sarge?' He swivelled on his heel to face his boss again.

'Don't forget to put a fucking case number on it.'

A Decision

How r u? Maggie texted. She didn't dare go near Wilma's place until she knew the coast was clear.

Can u come round? A text pinged back.

Maggie thumbed a reply. She grabbed her phone and shot out the back door.

'How's you?' Wilma met her halfway. Dressed in baggy grey trackie bottoms and an equally shapeless hoodie, her hair straggled in limp strands to her shoulders. Grim-faced, she was, for once, devoid of make-up.

'Here.' Maggie threw her arms wide. 'Let me give you a hug.'

'It'll take more than a fucking hug.' Wilma let herself be comforted. 'Come in about.' She led the way through to the sitting room and flopped down on the settee. 'Cosy up.' She patted the space beside her.

'Well.' Maggie did as she was bid. 'What did Ian have to say?'

Wilma snorted. 'Said he'd been a bit hasty, nipped back from work to apologise. But…' The word hung in the air. 'He insisted that didn't change things.' She uttered a loud sniff. 'Told you he was a stubborn bugger.' Her stomach rumbled. She rubbed her belly. 'Now you're here, how's about I make us a spot of lunch?'

'Oh,' Maggie demurred, 'there's no need…' But Wilma was already on her feet.

'Cheese on toast do?' she yelled from the kitchen. 'I shouldn't, not when I'm supposed to be watching my carbs, but it's all I've got.'

'Fine by me.' Maggie followed her through.

'Stick the radio on, will you?'

Obediently, Maggie moved through to the conservatory. She twisted the radio's dial and was about to sit down, when:

A man has suffered a serious assault in the Torry district of the city.

'Turn that up.'

Maggie reached over to the windowsill and turned up the volume on the lunchtime news.

The man, who has not been named, was rushed by ambulance to Aberdeen Royal Infirmary. A hospital spokesperson described his injuries as serious, but declined to give further details. Police Scotland have issued a statement saying that enquiries into the incident are ongoing.

'Christ.' Wilma appeared in the doorway. 'What a fright that gave me.' She wiped her hands down the front of her tracksuit. 'I can never hear Torry but I think of trouble.'

'I'm sure,' Maggie empathised. 'Your two, have you heard from them lately?'

'Not a dickey bird. Oh, Maggie...' Wilma's eyes stood out on her cheeks. 'You don't think...'

'Wayne or Kevin? Don't be silly. I mean, what are the odds?'

Odds indeed. Maggie gave a rueful smile. Why hadn't she stopped to think before she'd gone chasing after James Gilruth? Or let her suspicions fester over Colin's possible involvement in poor Lucy Simmons' death?

'I know. Still, once you've got them.' She let out a sigh. 'You never stop worrying about your weans from the day they're born.'

Maggie's thoughts turned to Kirsty's cutting episode. Then Colin. He'd been acting cagey again. She nodded agreement. 'Tell me about it. But, your boys, don't you pay them the odd visit?'

Wilma shrugged. 'Haven't the time.'

'They could come to you.'

'To Mannofield?' She sniffed. 'Why would they? Torry's their world.' She looked wistful, all of a sudden.

'You don't think...' Maggie began, her mind jumping to

Brannigan. Last she'd heard he'd been cautioned by the police and told to stay out of trouble. He'd be keeping a low profile, so the incident wouldn't involve him.

Still, an anxious niggle tugged at the back of her mind. 'I was wondering…' Her words were drowned out by the shrill of a smoke alarm.

'Shite!' Wilma about-faced. 'The toasties!' She shot back through to the kitchen, Maggie at her heels.

Through a pall of smoke, Wilma grabbed a tea towel, groped for the grill tray and pulled it out. Two charred rectangles were all that remained of what should have been lunch.

'Fuckit!' She carried the tray to the sink and tipped the cinders into the waste bin.

'My fault,' Maggie volunteered, flapping smoke out of her eyes. Banishing all thoughts of Bobby Brannigan, she smiled in apology. 'That's what we get for obsessing over our kids. We shouldn't have been eating toasties anyway,' she added. 'Wasn't meant.'

'It's alright for you,' Wilma countered, 'wee skelf that you are. But there's not another thing in the fridge. And see me,' she rolled her eyes. 'Right this minute I could eat a fucking horse.'

'Never mind.' Maggie took her by the hand. 'We'll make do with a cuppa. But first, finish off what you were saying about Ian.'

Wilma settled herself in one of the big cane chairs. 'It's the agency,' she said miserably. 'I reckoned I had him talked round. We were doing away fine, the pair of us. Or so I thought. But it's obviously been eating away at him, the whole thing. Oh, Maggie.' Her chins wobbled. 'What am I going to do?'

'Go with your gut,' Maggie said decisively. 'If there's one thing I've learned…'

Wilma sniffed. 'Easier said than done. I'm in that deep. And…' Her eyes stood out on stalks as mentally she totted up the amount of money she'd spent on gizmos. 'There's no way I'd want to leave you in the lurch, especially not after…'

Impishly: 'Strong-arming me into it in the first place.'

Wilma sat up. 'I never did.'

'You most certainly did so. Back then, I'd never have had the nerve to do something so...' For a moment she hesitated. 'Out of character.'

'But it's come right?' Small voice. 'Hasn't it?'

'It has indeed.' Maggie's mind jumped back to the day she'd first confronted Wilma Harcus. Talk about role reversal! Who'd have thought that country mouse would now be offering moral support?

She reached across the coffee table and laid a hand on Wilma's arm. 'Trust me. It will all work out.'

Roughly, Wilma shook her off. 'You don't know my Ian. Once he sets his mind to something...' Her eyes brimmed with tears. 'It's all very well saying butter him up, but it's too late for that. I've been an eejit, Maggie, that's the beginning and end of it. Thinking I could rise above my station, become some big detective, sort out the... the...' Her voice shook with emotion. 'The fucking world.'

'You have.' Maggie, too, was on the verge of tears. 'You can.'

'No, I fucking can't.' The tears were streaming, now, down Wilma's cheeks. 'I have to make a decision: the agency or Ian. And I have to make it now.'

Back Burner

'Right, folks.' Allan Chisolm's eyes swept the room. 'Let's get started.'

From their work-stations, his squad ambled over and joined him for that morning's briefing.

'What have we got?' He addressed the expectant faces around the table.

Brian Burnett consulted his notes. 'One case of aggravated assault, couple of minor scraps, bank scams, break-ins. Oh, and a possible drug overdose,' he rattled off, anxious to sound on-the-ball.

'Let's start with the assault.'

Brian passed his superior a file.

Chisolm opened it, scanned the report inside. 'Mmm,' he murmured, knitting his brows. 'Keep me up to speed on this, Sergeant. We've had too many of these lately.'

'Sir.'

'And the break-ins?'

DS Dave Wood, his belly straining uncomfortably over the waistband of his pleated trousers, raised his head. In a world-weary voice, he answered, 'Usual suspects.'

Chisolm shot him a sharp look. Thought better of it. Wood was within a year of retirement. After all the changes he'd been forced to adapt to over the past few years, who could blame him for a spot of cynicism.

'Bank scams? Who's on that?'

Sergeant George Duffy sighed. 'Nowt to be done, not in these cases anyhow. Complainants instructed the transactions.'

'I take it you've advised them to follow the bank's complaints procedure as their first course of redress?' Douglas Dunn interjected. DC Dunn was a graduate recruit and an unending source of irritation to his senior officers.

Brown-arsed wee bastard, Duffy thought. 'I have, yes.' He nodded.

'And passed on details of the financial ombudsman,' Douglas prompted.

Duffy gritted his teeth. 'That too.'

'Let's move on.' Chisolm drummed his fingers on the table. 'This overdose? It's only a possible, you say?'

Brian again. 'Attending officers found the subject unresponsive. No apparent injuries.'

'Why are we classifying it as a drug overdose, tell me?'

'It was one of the paramedics found pills.'

Chisolm's eyebrows shot into his hairline. 'Attending officers?' he demanded.

'Souter and Miller.'

DC Susan Strachan, the only female in the company, shot Brian a sideways look. She couldn't believe the uniforms had missed such a crucial piece of evidence. Those two were in for a bollocking, that was for sure.

'Fatal?'

'No, sir. Leastways not yet. Victim's in intensive care. From what I can gather it's touch and go.'

'A druggie?'

'No, sir. Middle-aged wifie from out Milltimber. A Mrs Sheena Struthers.'

'Accidental?'

'Looks like it.'

Christ, Chisholm thought, a cushy life in Milltimber and it still wasn't enough. 'Nonetheless, make sure those pills have been dusted for fingerprints. There wasn't a note?'

'No, sir.'

'You sure?' Doubtful voice. If uniform could manage to miss a package of pills, Christ knows what else they'd overlooked.

Brian ducked. He didn't reply.

'I'll take that as affirmative. Witnesses?'

'Woman was alone in the house. Discovered by the cleaner.'

'I take it we have a statement.'

'Belatedly. Cleaner is Polish. Speaks very little English. Luckily, her partner is a builder working out at Peterculter this week. We managed to get hold of him and he translated. Cleaner said she wasn't due until 9.30, but got a lift with the boyfriend and arrived early. She rang the doorbell. Had her own key, but didn't use it in case her employer was in the shower or summat. When there was no response, she let herself in. Poor girl was in bits, rabbiting on if she'd been half an hour later, her boss could have been…'

'What's the current state of play?'

'Hospital's running tests. I've asked Souter to follow up on the results.'

Chisolm crooked an eyebrow. 'Double check. Given the…' he hesitated, '…circumstances, better not leave it to uniform.'

'Sir.'

'Right.' He shuffled his files together. 'If there's no evidence of criminality, we'll put that one on the back burner for now.'

The Inversnecky

Maggie looked up. 'You made it.'

'Yes,' Ros shrugged out of her coat and dropped onto the seat opposite. 'Didn't even have to make an excuse. When I checked my timetable, I saw the kids had PE last thing, so I did a runner.'

Following their conversation in the playground, they'd meant to meet for coffee, but one or other of them had been forced to call off. When, finally, they'd made a firm date, the Inversnecky, a short drive along the Esplanade from Seaton School, had seemed the ideal venue. Until, that is, Maggie recalled it was where she'd sat with a car-load of small boys on the fateful evening she'd learned of their involvement in the desecration of a corpse. She stowed the thought away. *That's ancient history!* Italian owned, the café was an Aberdeen institution, somewhere she and George had shared many a cuppa, a plate of fish and chips or, on a fine day, a dish of ice cream.

A young waitress approached, order pad at the ready. 'What can I get you?' She smiled.

'Pot of tea,' Maggie said decisively. 'I'm gasping.'

'For two?'

'Diet Coke for me,' Ros said.

'How are things?'

'Oh,' Ros breathed a sigh. 'Same old.'

'I'm sorry.'

'Don't be. It's not as if we have blazing rows. It's just,' she brushed a hand across her brow, 'this constant drip-drip of criticism. Seems no matter what I say or do I'm in the wrong.'

'Have you challenged him about it?'

'Yes. In the beginning, at least. Before Max was born, that is, I used to stand up to him, fight my corner. But he'd throw it back in my face, twist it round so I didn't know whether I was coming or going. Then, if that didn't work, he'd play the IQ card: how men are more logical, all that.'

'Has he ever been physically violent towards you?'

'Physical? Oh, he's physical alright. We used to have great sex. Sometimes I ask myself if that's the main reason I married Nic. But even that's gone downhill recently. But violent? No. Quite the reverse. He'll sulk, sometimes for days, but he's never lifted a finger to me,' Ros uttered a contemptuous laugh. 'Doesn't have to. He has such a way with words. He's so smart, Maggie. So quick, I gave up fighting in the end. After that, I decided everything probably was my fault: the cock-ups, the breakdowns in communication. I've been so tired, you see. Doesn't help when it comes to making rational decisions.'

'No.' Maggie extended a comforting hand. 'But you're not alone in that. We've all been there,' she offered, with a flutter of recognition: over the passage of time, she identified more and more with this troubled young woman. 'How about your friend Fiona? What does she have to say?'

'I get short shrift there.' Wry smile. 'Fiona doesn't see eye to eye with Nic. Nor he with her, come to that. He thinks she's a bad influence. A rabid feminist, he says.'

'And is she, do you think?'

'Not a bit. She's pretty forthright, though. Tells it like it is. Says he's a selfish prat. That I'm shouldering the heavier workload. But, then, she and Stuart don't have kids. Plus, there's the Scottish thing.'

Maggie raised a questioning eyebrow.

'Fiona says serves me right for marrying an English git.'

Maggie chuckled. 'That's not very PC.'

'I know. And I wouldn't have taken her remark on board, at first. But now...' She broke off, a look of misery on her face. 'Now I can see where she's coming from.'

'I gather they really don't get on.'

'No.' Ros made a face. 'You'd think Nic would listen to someone in his inner circle, wouldn't you? Stuart and Fiona are our closest friends. Our only friends, really, in Aberdeen. Other than you,' she quickly added. 'Nic and Stuart rub along well enough. But, then, they have to, they have work in common. And we get on fine as a foursome. We might not always agree, but it's just friendly banter. When it comes to me and Fiona on our own, though, Nic makes all sorts of excuses why we shouldn't meet up. So much so I'm beginning to think he doesn't want me to see her at all.'

'Sounds like he sees Fiona as a threat.'

'Well, they do seem a bit…' She struggled to find the word. 'Confrontational at times.'

'Don't you have other friends?'

Ros brightened. 'Of course. But the crowd from school and uni are all over the place now. Scattered to the winds, you might say.'

'How about here, in Aberdeen? Other mums?'

Ros rolled her eyes. 'I wish. There's a bunch of women at nursery, congregate in the family area. They seem a jolly lot, and not unfriendly. It's just I'm always in such a rush, trying to fit in a shop or whatever after school. I tend to cut it fine, and then I daren't hang about. Nic likes me to have Max fed and settled before he gets in.'

'What about your parents?' Maggie queried. 'Couldn't you take a break? It often helps to put some distance between…'

'Not a good time. Mum hasn't been well. I wouldn't want to bother her. Or Dad, especially since they weren't that hot on Nic in the first place. What I'm really saying, if I'm honest, is my pride won't let me. And it's not as if I'm nineteen. I'm a grown woman, Maggie. I have to sort this out for myself.'

'That's all very well,' Maggie said. 'But it seems to me you've become isolated, whether by accident or design. And that can't be healthy.' As she voiced the words, she thought of her own situation: a forty-something widow, struggling to construct a future, and all the while her kids drifting away.

'So true. I've gone from living in a city surrounded by family and friends to being stuck with a small child in an academic bubble. If I didn't have my Seaton job I think I'd have gone stark raving mad.'

Maggie nodded her understanding.

'But it's not Nic's fault, you know. He moved up here for a senior lectureship. And I was with him on that. Only...' Ros's voice wavered, 'I didn't think it would be this hard.'

'Has his behaviour changed, would you say, since the move?'

'Not really. He's always been...picky, I suppose you could call it. I'm not used to that in a man. I mean, my dad...'

'You don't have to explain.'

'I think I just didn't notice it so much, not till I was at home all day with Max. And since I've been back at work, well, I haven't had space in my head to think, never mind sit down and explain my feelings to him.'

'Could counselling be the answer?' Maggie ventured. 'If you were to meet with an independent third party, get the opportunity to open up. Do you think Nic would be willing to commit to that?'

'I doubt it. He doesn't see that there is a problem, that's the nub of it. In his mind any misunderstanding lies with me. I'm at my wit's end, Maggie,' Ros buried her face in her hands. 'It's like walking on eggshells. I try to anticipate his mood.' She raised her head a fraction. 'Avoid saying anything contentious. Massage his ego. All that. But no matter what I say or do, he twists it around. And I'm so worn out these days it doesn't seem worth arguing, so I just let it go.'

'If you ever need to talk,' Maggie volunteered, 'just pick up the phone.' Not that she had time to spare.

'Thanks.' Ros pushed her empty glass to one side. 'Today's been a big help, just offloading to someone. But I better be heading.' She rose to her feet. 'Or there will be hell to pay.'

'Off you go, then.' Maggie reached for Ros's coat, helped her into it. 'Better wrap up.' The weather had taken a turn for the better, but there was a stiff breeze, always, on the Esplanade.

'What about the bill?'

'Don't worry.' Maggie shooed her away. 'I'll get it.'

'Thanks.' Ros summoned a smile. 'You're a darling.'

Maggie watched as Ros threaded her way through the tables. Poor girl. If the unspoken signals she'd picked up were to be relied upon, Ros's marriage wasn't likely to survive.

End of Story

'Before you say a word,' Ian's face was tight with anger. 'It won't make a blind bit of difference.'

Maggie perched uncomfortably on the edge of the leather sofa. She'd put added pressure on Wilma, she was convinced, by her mishandling of the Struthers case. Why else would Wilma and the normally quiescent Ian be at loggerheads?

'I wasn't going to...' she began.

'Wilma and me have split. End of story.'

'She's gone?'

'Aye.'

'Can you tell me where?'

'Back to Torry.' His lip curled. 'Where she belongs.'

'Is she with her boys?'

Sharp look. 'Where else?'

Relief flooded through Maggie's small frame. She slumped back on the settee. It squeaked sharply behind her knees.

'She's safe, at least,' she ventured, at last.

'If that's what you'd call it,' he jeered. 'Pair of no good...'

Maggie's mind worked overtime. She'd hoped to catch Ian on a low, play the little woman, appeal to his softer side. But in this intransigent frame of mind... She could see, now, what Wilma meant when she said her husband was stubborn.

'All I came to say was, it's not Wilma's fault, this...' She struggled for the right word, settled for '...mess. It's mine.'

A muscle worked in Ian's jaw. 'Yours and hers both.'

'Mainly mine.'

Act humble! She changed tack. 'George's death came as a great shock. To me and the kids. So many things came at me,' she hazarded a covert glance. 'I was overwhelmed.'

'I believe you.'

Did she imagine his tone softened?

'And...' Her voice hitched as the memories came flooding back. 'Wilma saved my life.'

'She sure saved your bacon.' There was a hard note in the voice again.

'Yes,' she conceded. 'That, too.'

'And you've used her ever since.'

'No!' Maggie jumped forward in her seat. 'That's not true.'

'So how come Wilma gets to do all the dirty work?'

'She doesn't.' Maggie drew a calming breath. 'We each do what we feel capable of. Wilma has taken on some of the more...' she hesitated, 'colourful cases, I'll grant you. But it's been a two-way street. We've had to learn as we went along. We've helped one another to...'

Ian finished the sentence: 'Get up to God knows what? Cavort around the country? Stay out till all hours?'

'I'm sorry you feel that way,' Maggie responded in a quiet voice. 'I certainly never set out to take advantage of Wilma in any way.'

'You didn't need to. She has a good heart.'

'You don't have to tell me.'

'But since you teamed up together you've ploughed your own furrow. Without regard to your other responsibilities, seems to me.'

'We might have neglected things at home, I admit, but...'

Ian cut her short. 'That's the understatement of all time.'

Maggie's glance swept the room. She was tempted to argue the toss. Wilma kept her home spotless. The fragrance diffusers plugged into every other socket might be a bit OTT for Maggie's taste, but...

'I've hardly seen Wilma since you and her got in cahoots.' Ian interrupted her train of thought. 'As for what she gets up to when she's out and about, I don't know and,' he rolled his eyes, 'I don't want to know. One thing's for sure, though...' He broke off.

Maggie waited, heart in mouth.

'This business venture of yours has taught me a lesson. Wilma doesn't belong here.' That stubborn look again. 'Never did. Never will.'

'I don't accept that,' Maggie answered resolutely, though her heart was racing. This could be her chance – her only chance – to save her friend's marriage. 'Wilma's had a hard life, for sure, and she's a bit rough round the edges, but she has so many good qualities.' She met his gaze in mute appeal. 'She's positive, open-minded, practical, generous, funny…' She broke off. 'Brave, too.'

Ian didn't react.

'Whereas I,' she ran on in desperation, 'am negative, judgemental, gormless…'

'You make a bonny pair, that's for sure.'

Unsure whether this was said in earnest or jest, Maggie didn't respond.

'But that doesn't change anything.'

'That's just it, don't you see?' she blurted. 'Wilma's changed. I've changed.'

'Aye, and not for the better.'

'How can you say that?' Maggie rose to her friend's defence. 'Look at the ways Wilma's worked to better herself, as she puts it: honing her computer skills, boning up on business practice, even working out at that gym to improve her appearance.'

Ian came straight back. 'She was fine the way she was.'

'Plus, she was proud to bring in a bit extra, help with the mortgage…'

'I don't need any help.'

'No, of course.' Too late, Maggie realised she'd hit a nerve.

'But I've learned so much from her: self-confidence, to accept people for what they are, loads of things, really,' she broke off.

'All I'm saying is…Wilma's worked hard to be a better wife, a…a…better person.'

'Yes,' Ian responded wearily. 'She's a grafter, I'll grant you that.'

Pig-headed bugger! Maggie had to restrain herself from grabbing Ian by the collar and shaking sense into him. Instead she bit her lip and rose to leave.

Just the Thing

The upmarket jeweller on Union Bridge was close-carpeted, its walls lined with warm wood panelling. Into this were set a row of brightly illuminated display cases. They sparkled against their contrasting setting. Like those whopping diamonds in the window, Ros thought, as she sat alongside Nic at the high counter, a sober-suited sales assistant seated opposite.

'I've been neglecting you,' her husband had announced that Saturday morning. 'A treat, that's what you need. Put on your glad rags. We're going into town.'

'But, the baby...' she countered. 'He needs changed, and then...'

'Forget about Max.' Smug smile. 'Fiona's going to hold the fort.'

'What about breakfast?'

'Skip it. She knows the ropes. We can grab something in town. Go on.' He gave her a playful push. 'She'll be here in ten minutes.'

Excited, Ros ran upstairs, exchanged her baggy T-shirt for a Zara blouse, squeezed into her best jeans. She rummaged in the bottom of the wardrobe for a pair of high-heeled boots, slapped tinted moisturiser on her face, added two coats of mascara and a slick of lip gloss, ran a comb through her hair.

She'd protested when they stood outside. The over-sized watch that marked the establishment proclaimed ROLEX. Way too expensive for a university lecturer, she thought with a sinking heart. In the tiled arcade, she recognised more prestigious names: Omega, Longines. Zenith, the preserve of sports stars and glossy magazines. Revolving platforms displayed rings set with diamonds, emeralds, aquamarines. Swathes of coloured silk set off lustrous pearl ropes. Pendants and earrings dangled from miniature stands. Like Christmas come all at once, she couldn't help thinking. Even the vertical blinds that backed the displays gave the impression that these treasures were within reach.

For a few minutes they'd stood, faces pressed against the glass. Then: 'This is way beyond our budget, Nic,' she said. 'I'd be just as happy in John Lewis.'

He put a finger to her lips. 'Shush. For my girl it's nothing but the best.'

'But...'

'Look there,' he said, pointing downwards. Her eyes followed. Sure enough, displays at a lower level offered a range of modern jewellery in silver and semi-precious stones. Necklets, rings and cuffs gleamed against black or purple pads.

Ros squinted against the light, trying to establish prices.

'Come on,' Nic tugged at her arm. 'We haven't got all day.'

Now, she sat on an ivory leather stool, butterflies pinging their way around an empty stomach. On the console table, a swivel mirror threatened. Determinedly, Ros avoided catching her reflection.

Nic took the lead. 'I'm looking for a gift for my wife.'

'To mark a special occasion?' the salesman enquired. 'A birthday, perhaps? An anniversary?'

'Neither.' Nic smiled. He turned to Ros. 'To say thanks for putting up with me.'

She felt a glow of happiness. Beamed at both Nic and the salesman.

'Do you have a budget, may I ask?'

'Nothing too expensive,' Ros came back quickly. 'It's only a token, after all.'

'Did you have anything in mind?'

'Not really,' she answered. 'Something in silver, maybe. A ring would be nice.' Or perhaps not. She glanced down at her hands. Time was, her nails would have been manicured and polished, now they were ragged and stripped of varnish. 'Or earrings,' she added hastily. 'I saw a pair in the window that...'

'Something more substantial,' Nic cut her short. 'A necklace. Or a bracelet – one of those cuff things.'

'But…' Ros squirmed uncomfortably on the high stool. She felt conspicuous, sitting just inside the entrance in full view of the arcade, wished they'd opted for one of the display tables at the rear. She turned to her husband. 'Don't you think…?' A wash of colour crept up her neck as she tried to frame a face-saving excuse. Nic knew full well they couldn't afford to be buying expensive jewellery, not when they were supposed to be saving for a house.

'No arguments.' He clasped both her hands in his. 'Remember what I said.' He threw the salesman a conspiratorial smile. 'Nothing but the best for my girl.'

'If you'll give me a few moments…' The man rose, his face a study in discretion. 'I'm sure we'll have just the thing.'

Ward 201

Wilma pushed through the double doors. Was surprised to find the ward reception unmanned, for she'd identified herself on the intercom and been buzzed through just moments earlier. She could hear a commotion up ahead, assumed staff were attending to some emergency.

At the abandoned nurses station she scanned the roster on the wall. *Staff on duty: Charge Nurse Carol Fowlie* headed the list. Not a name she recognised. But she wouldn't, would she? For all the years she'd worked at ARI, Wilma's duties had been confined to the General Surgery or Gynae wards on the third and fourth floors. Either that, or Urology on the fifth. She'd rarely had occasion to venture downstairs to Level 1, which housed the main theatre suite and Ward 201/ITU, the intensive therapy unit.

It had been by sheer luck that she'd eavesdropped on a conversation – two nurses on their break. Overheard a familiar name. Despite the stand-off with Ian, Maggie and the agency were still uppermost in her mind. She'd abandoned her much-needed cup of coffee and clattered down the stairs.

Curtained bays were set along one wall. On the other, glass-fronted single rooms housed patients requiring isolation. Wilma took a chance, went in the other direction from the hubbub. Had only gone a few steps when a shrill voice echoed: 'What the hell do you think you're doing?'

Wilma whirled to face a dark-haired twenty-something. She stood, feet apart, face flushed with indignation. The uniform identified her as a charge nurse, the name badge as Carol Fowlie.

Wilma's mind went into overdrive. 'Ah wis jist…' she began.

'You can't just come crashing in here,' Fowlie said. 'This is a critical care area. These patients are very susceptible to infection.'

Snooty cow, Wilma thought. They were all the same, these young ones. Reckoned because they had a degree they were as well-qualified as the bloody consultants. Besides which, Wilma could tell the wee bitch something about infection. Hadn't she been cleaning for God knows how long?

'I was just,' she said, assuming her poshest accent, 'looking for a friend. I've only just heard she's been admitted.'

'A friend?' Fowlie looked her up and down.

Like she was dirt. Wilma was used to that. Her role as a healthcare support worker was only one notch up from the domestics. For a moment she wished she'd had the benefit of further education. Then, she had second thoughts. If it meant learning all those big words Maggie Laird kept coming out with, she was better off without.

Wilma stood up straight, pulled in her stomach. 'Sheena Struthers.'

'Ah!' Wary look. 'Mrs Struthers.'

'She here, then?'

Momentarily, Carol's eyes slid to her left. 'She is, yes. But before you ask, there's not a chance in hell of you getting anywhere near her.'

*

Wilma pressed her nose to the glass. The woman the charge nurse had unwittingly identified by her sideways eye movement as Sheena Struthers was lying on her back, her head propped against a bank of pillows. Her eyes were closed, her hands resting on the white sheet. There was no apparent sign of injury. In fact, from this distance you might have thought she was sleeping, until you registered the machines at the bedhead, the wires and tubes snaking from her nose and head and hands.

Wilma had lurked in a sluice room until she saw Carol Fowlie disappear down a corridor, mug in hand. Ten minutes, she reckoned. Apart from anything else, Wilma had gone AWOL from her own ward. She was way over her break time already. And there's no way she could afford to lose her job. Still…ten minutes. She could learn a lot in that time.

She narrowed her eyes, trying, in the dim light, to memorise what details she could. Sheena's notes were beyond her reach. And the chances of squeezing information out of Carol Fowlie – zilch.

It was difficult to suss Sheena's level of consciousness. She'd most likely be sedated, Wilma knew, perhaps even still in a coma.

She tried tapping on the glass to attract attention. The figure on the bed didn't stir. She called Sheena's name, all the while keeping a weather eye out for medical or nursing staff, to no avail.

Christ! Wilma racked her brains. How was she going to get around this one?

She heard the approaching squeak of rubber-soled shoes.

Took one last, lingering look at the body on the bed.

Did a runner.

An Ultimatum

'Thanks for coming,' Jimmy Craigmyle gave an embarrassed smile. 'My nerves are that shot, I didn't want to take another chance on being seen in town.'

'You're right.' Maggie regarded her late husband's former colleague. 'Holburn Street's too close to your place of work and,' she sat down opposite, 'we neither of us want to be caught in the other's company. Not until I've assembled all the evidence I need and George's case has been reopened.'

'That's why I asked for this meeting.'

'Oh.' Maggie's face lit up. 'Have you found something out?'

Craigmyle scowled. 'Nae chance. Since they re-branded the club, new management has been drafted in, procedures tightened up. There's no access, now, to that back room. Not for the likes of me, anyhow. Plus, I reckon Gilruth's moved his drugs operation elsewhere.' His mouth turned down. 'He'd be mad not to, not after…'

With a heavy heart, Maggie cut him off. 'I suppose.' She looked around. They were in a country restaurant on the back road to Banchory. Well, more of a tearoom, really. Renowned for its home baking, it was a popular stopping off point for commuters needing a reviving cuppa or families out for a weekend drive. On this late midweek afternoon, customers – one elderly couple sat by the window and what looked like a rep totting up his sales – were thin on the ground.

'No,' Craigmyle's voice broke her train of thought. 'It's the other thing I wanted to talk about: holding my hands up to the interview tape. Have you heard anything back on Brannigan from Queen Street?'

'Not a word. I chased it up with Chisolm the other day. All he could tell me was what we already know: that they're working towards getting a formal statement out of Bobby. But you know how it is: the wheels turn at a snail's pace.' She drew a deep breath. 'It might put a pin up their backsides if you were to come clean right now.'

'That's just it.' Craigmyle toyed with his teaspoon, wouldn't meet her eyes. 'For as long as I'm in James Gilruth's employ, there's no way I can give the police that statement. Bottom line is, if I help you out now, I can forget about Gilruth. For good and all.' Grim face. 'Man like that doesn't forget folk who grass.'

'But I thought you just said he'd shut down his drugs operation.'

'I said he'd moved it elsewhere. And it just so happens I've been offered a job at the "elsewhere", no doubt in consequence of keeping my nose clean all these months. And,' his face darkened, 'my mouth firmly shut.'

'So does that mean...?'

Craigmyle finished the sentence for her. 'I'd still be working on the inside, mebbe get closer to the action now I've served my apprenticeship, help nail the bugger for money-laundering if the police can't get him on drugs. But I'm between a rock and a hard place, Maggie. Either I take the job and get personal gratification by going after Gilruth, or I do as you ask.'

'Mmm,' Maggie's mind tumbled with conflicting thoughts: sympathy for Craigmyle, anger towards James Gilruth, frustration that her quest for justice was getting nowhere.

'Added to which,' Craigmyle ran on, 'I've had a call from the wife. Wants me to move back in. At least,' he set the spoon down, 'the kids are wanting their dad home. I guess Vera's fed up getting pestered. Anyhow,' he offered a shy grin, 'I'm hoping to move once we sort out the practicalities.'

'That's great news.' Maggie beamed. Although she'd never entirely trusted Jimmy Craigmyle, she was genuinely happy for the man.

'But that gives me another problem.'

Her brow puckered. 'I don't see why.'

He shifted uncomfortably. 'Vera's given me an ultimatum.'

'Oh?' Perplexed look.

'No unsocial hours or I can forget about the whole thing.'

'How does that…?' Maggie hesitated. Then, 'Oh, I get it. If you take up Gilruth's job, Vera will withdraw her offer.'

'Aye.' The man sitting opposite looked wistful all of a sudden. 'That's it in a nutshell.'

'What are you going to do, Jimmy?'

'I've been mulling it over all night, ever since the subject of the new job was raised. It would be a promotion. More money. Easier access to the inner circle.' He grimaced. 'Plus, I'm desperate to nail the bastard. Forget about George. I owe that to myself. And, besides, I can hold my hands up to that tape anytime. You said yourself the wheels turn slowly. But I have to let them know about the job by the end of the week. That's why I wanted to bounce it off you.'

Maggie's heart hung heavy in her chest. Jimmy Craigmyle's admission to turning off Bobby Brannigan's interview tape was integral to her campaign to vindicate her dead husband. If Craigmyle were to take Gilruth's job it could take months, even years, of working undercover before he achieved a result.

'Where does that leave your kids?' She felt bad playing that card, but bringing Gilruth to justice could wait, whereas clearing George's name… Too much time had already passed, and interest at force HQ was cooling, that's for sure.

Craigmyle scratched his head. 'There is that.'

'So…' Maggie braced herself. 'Which way are you going to jump?'

He grinned. 'What do you think?'

One Sentence

'Pete?'

The man straightened. Turned. 'I'm busy.' He ran his eyes from Wilma's extravagant blonde coif, to her mischievous blue eyes, to her full red lips. They travelled on down over her generous bosom to her shapely legs. Then they travelled all the way up again. 'But, for you, darlin…' His lips parted to show a handsome set of gnashers. 'I'll make an exception.'

She batted her false eyelashes. Not that she fancied the bugger. Except…he was showing enough muscle under that green jumpsuit to make any warm-blooded woman wilt. And a man in uniform, well, that was always a turn-on. Plus, she'd always been a sucker for guys with a cleft in their chin. Mind you, that baldy head…

Cut to the chase! 'I need some information.'

'What sort of information?'

'On a patient you brought in yesterday.'

'Oh.' The paramedic's face darkened. 'That's different, sunshine. Can't help you there.'

Wilma's heart plummeted into her high-heeled shoes. She'd scored a blank from the ITU, but this was too important to let go. If she was going to help Maggie, she had to get a head start on finding out what had happened to Sheena Struthers.

'You're not going to give me patient confidentiality?'

Pete grinned. 'For starters.'

'But…' She pouted. 'Sheena's a friend of mine.'

'Then you'll know the husband,' Pete came back. 'Why don't you ask him?'

'We don't get on.'

'That right?' Disbelieving voice. 'Still can't help you, darling.' Winks. 'Much as I'd like to.'

'All right.' Wilma was so close to him now, she could almost taste what he'd had for breakfast. 'I'll level with you, Pete. I'm a journalist.'

Suspicious look. 'What paper did you say you worked for?'

Wilma grinned. 'Good try! I didn't. I'm freelance. It's a bummer these days trying to scrape a living, I can tell you. There have been that many cuts. Look…' She made cow eyes at him. 'All I'm asking for is a few wee details. Just enough to get a heads-up on the big boys. Though I'll bet there's not many of the buggers…' Her eyes dropped to his crotch. 'As big as you.'

'We-ell.' A wash of colour rose in his face. 'I don't know.'

'Please?' Wilma herself was pretty hot by this time, what with running round to Ashgrove Road in double-quick time and turning it on for this wanker.

Close at hand, an alarm sounded.

Pete started. 'Gotta go,' he mouthed over his shoulder as he reached for his kit.

'No!' Wilma sensed her chances of helping Maggie disappear down a vast sinkhole. She clutched at Pete's arm. 'Come on, man. Two sentences.'

He shook from her grasp.

'One sentence.' She followed his receding back in the direction of the parked-up emergency vehicles.

He turned.

Whispered in her ear.

And then he was gone.

Something to Share

Maggie leaned on the kitchen worktop, nervously thumbing her phone. Although she'd sworn off all future contact with Queen Street, this was her second call to Force HQ within a matter of weeks.

The text from Wilma had come as a bolt from the blue. The news that Sheena Struthers – who Maggie had blithely seen off from the Cults cafe with advice to consult her GP – had been admitted to hospital shocked Maggie to the core. With Wilma out of circulation, Maggie struggled to formulate a plan. Not being a close relative of Sheena's, she'd get scant information out of ARI. She decided her best option was to act the daft housewife, see what some plod at Queen Street would let out of the bag.

When her call was answered – thankfully not by Moira – Maggie asked to speak to whoever answered the call-out to Sheena Struthers at Milltimber.

She'd only been on hold for a couple of minutes when a tetchy voice cut in. 'Chisolm.'

Damn! Maggie had expected to be put through to some anonymous uniform. Hadn't spoken to the inspector since New Year. Then, relations had been relatively cordial. Now, if the curtness of Chisolm's greeting was anything to go by, she'd get sod all out of him.

She came straight to the point. 'It's about a Mrs Struthers.'

There was silence, then: 'What about her?'

Maggie swallowed hard. She was right. Chisolm wasn't going to give anything away. 'The incident may have come to your attention. Mrs Struthers was admitted to ARI earlier this week.'

'Let me think…' The DI paused. 'Drug overdose, wasn't it?'

'That's right.'

'Accidental as far as we know.'

'Yes. Only...' Her voice tailed off. Why did this man always make her feel like a kid out of school? Still, she girded herself, now the inspector was on the line, she'd better own up to her own involvement. 'It may not have been an accident,' she whispered.

On the other end of the line there was a long silence, then: 'Is there something you wish to share with me?'

'We-ell...' Maggie's mind rewound to the dressing-down Chisolm had given her after the Seaton job. He'd come to her home. Quizzed her on the investigation, the standards of her agency work, and – most embarrassing – her relationship with his sergeant. She'd been humiliated, then. But this time, she summoned all her courage to stand up to him. 'You should know, Mrs Struthers is a client of mine.'

His voice rose. 'Is that so?'

'Yes. And...' Her nerve deserted her. 'She told me her husband has been trying to kill her.' The words came out in a rush. 'Or so she alleges,' Maggie added lamely.

'On what grounds did she...?' the inspector began.

She cut him off. 'That's just it.' The woman's claims were so far-fetched. And if they sounded fantastical to Maggie... She could just picture the scathing expression on the DI's face. 'Everything she's said, Sheena Struthers... And I've questioned her closely, honestly I have. But...well...none of it adds up.'

'With respect, Mrs Laird, I'll be the better judge of that.'

Maggie's ears were burning. She didn't reply.

'But it prompts the question,' Chisolm continued. 'If Mrs Struthers is so deluded, why did you take her on?'

'She seemed so genuine.' Maggie wasn't going to admit she'd cynically strung the woman along in an attempt to bump up the agency's fee. Instead she played the sympathy card. 'I felt sorry for her, I suppose.' That was partly true, at least.

'Ah.' Another silence, then: 'If the woman is genuine, why hasn't she brought her suspicions to us?'

'That's what I said.' Small voice. Viewed from this perspective, it sounded feeble. She felt a total fool.

'As by now you should be well aware, Mrs Laird,' the inspector's delivery was toneless, 'if there is criminality involved, this is a police matter.'

Maggie's mind whirled with flashes of past misdeeds. But why? She'd addressed Sheena's allegations and found them groundless. The woman was unbalanced. No fault of Maggie's.

'Leave it with me,' Chisolm filled the silence. 'And Mrs Laird…'

'Yes?'

'If this does turn into a criminal investigation, I'll expect your one hundred per cent co-operation, client or no.'

A New Development

'Listen up, folks.' Chisolm called his team to attention. 'We have a new development in the Struthers case.'

Around the room, there were blank faces.

'Let me jog your memories: Milltimber. Drug overdose.'

'Oh...right.' Gradually, recognition dawned.

'From information received, it seems Mrs Struthers has made a series of accusations against her husband.'

'What sort of accusations?' Douglas Dunn sat forward, eager as a schoolboy.

'Repeated attempts on her life.'

'Any grounds?' Brian beat Douglas to it this time. He'd need to show willing if he was to make inspector.

'Circumstantial, from what I can make out. Tampering with her car's brakes, trying to run her down...'

'With said car?' Douglas this time.

'With a lawnmower.'

'Christ.' George Duffy spat a wad of chewing-gum from his mouth, stuck it to the underside of the table. 'You couldn't make it up.'

'Agreed. Seems pretty far-fetched to me, too. Unfortunately, the lady in question is not, currently, in a position to substantiate those allegations. As you know, Mrs Struthers is in intensive care in a critical condition. The latest from the registrar is she's at level five on the Glasgow Coma Scale. To you and me, she's totally out of it, and likely to remain so for quite some time.'

'No hope of getting a statement, then,' Dave Wood said, gloomily.

'Not until she recovers.' Chisolm grimaced. 'If she recovers.'

'What do we know about the husband?' Susan enquired.

'Gordon Struthers, age forty-six, accountant. Partner in his firm.

That much,' wry look, 'Souter established when he attended the scene.'

'Has someone spoken to Mr Struthers?'

'Only to inform him of the situation.'

'Should we bring him in, do you think?' Thoughtfully, Susan chewed the end of her pen.

'What about the intel, though?' Brian again. 'Is it from a reliable source?'

'I'll leave you lot to be the judge of that,' Chisolm said, his face unreadable. 'I had a call late yesterday from a Mrs Laird...'

Christ! Brian thought he was going to throw up. Saw his chances of promotion going down the drain.

Around the table there were titters, hastily suppressed.

Then: '*That* Mrs Laird?' asked Douglas Dunn.

'Afraid so.'

There was an embarrassed silence. They all knew chapter and verse on Maggie Laird's involvement in the Simmons case. To Susan Strachan, the woman was a role model: the way she'd picked herself up and taken on the husband's business, how she'd stood up for those wee boys. To the others she was a thorn in their flesh.

'It appears Sheena Struthers retained the services of Harcus & Laird some weeks ago.'

'Why didn't the woman come to us?' Douglas demanded, his expression outraged.

Chisolm pursed his lips. 'Why indeed?'

'How old is this dame?'

'Forty-six. Same age as the husband.'

'I'd lay a tenner on it's the menopause. Sends them doolally,' Duffy came back in. 'When my missus hit the change...'

'Quite.' Chisolm silenced him with a look.

'Sounds like a case of paranoia,' Susan observed. 'Either that or a cry for help.'

'If she'd wanted help,' Douglas again, 'wouldn't she have seen her doctor?'

Susan eyed him balefully. 'Given she was in possession of sleeping pills, she most likely did.'

'She could have got them off the net.'

Dunn would argue with his bloody shadow, Susan thought. Still, he had a point.

'Some of these dames,' Duffy observed. 'Sitting out there in their big, detached houses. No kids to run after. No close neighbours. Nothing to do and all day to do it in. No bloody wonder they get depressed. If my missus…'

'Whatever,' Chisolm cut him off. 'After our last dalliance with the inimitable Mrs Laird, I can understand your concern. However, now these allegations have been brought to our attention, we have a duty to investigate. I'll instruct ARI to alert us when there's a change in the patient's condition. In the meantime, let's have a chat with the husband, fill in the background. See to it, will you, Burnett.'

'Sir.'

'But, remember, this guy's well-connected, so tread carefully. We wouldn't want to upset anybody,' he fixed Brian with a hard look, 'now would we?'

Shaz

'Mum, meet Shaz.'

Maggie's eyes travelled from the dishevelled dark head to the eyebrow piercing and settled on the stud embedded beneath the lad's lower lip.

'Hello.' She extended a hand.

Shaz appraised her coolly. 'Hi.' He didn't reciprocate.

Maggie's hand fell to her side. She looked to her daughter for guidance.

Kirsty shrugged. 'Can we have a drink of something? Bus was sweltering.'

'Of course. What can I get you?' Maggie addressed her guest. 'Tea? Coffee? Something cold?'

'A beer would be good,' Shaz grinned. 'And the lav. I'm bursting for a pee.'

'On the right down the hall,' Maggie muttered through clenched teeth. This hadn't got off to a good start.

Kirsty flopped down on the settee. 'First impressions?'

'He seems…' guarded voice, 'nice enough.'

'That all?'

'Well…' Maggie played for time. 'I've only just met your friend. I haven't had time to form an opinion.'

'You're quick enough on the draw when it comes to other people.'

Maggie had a mental vision of Wilma in all her glory that first time she'd called round. Resolutely, she erased it. 'I suppose.'

There was silence. Then: 'He's cute, though, don't you think?'

Quizzically, Maggie eyed her daughter. '"Wee" is the word I'd have used.'

'Mu-um!'

'Okay. Let me re-phrase that. He's a bit on the small side for my taste.'

Kirsty drew herself up. 'There's no accounting for...'

Maggie cut her off. 'Where did you say he was from?'

'I didn't. But Liverpool, since you ask.'

'Oh.'

'What does that mean?'

'Nothing.' Blank face. 'Never been there.'

'He's going to take me when uni breaks up. Meet the family.'

'Really?' Maggie fought to quell the alarm rising in her stomach.

'Yes. Big family. And, before you ask, they live in a Council house. Can you imagine? Eight of them in three bedrooms.'

Maggie could. 'Are his parents both...' she struggled for the right word, '...around?' she ended lamely.

'No. His mum's on her own. But you'd better stop giving me the third degree before he gets out of the loo.'

'How are you, pet?' Hastily, Maggie changed the subject.

'Oh, fine.'

'Working hard?'

'Give the girl a break,' Shaz sauntered into the room. 'All right?' He stooped. Pinched Kirsty's cheek so hard she flinched. 'We're here to chill. Ain't that right, Lardy?' He dropped onto the sofa beside her.

Lardy? Maggie's hackles rose. Her beautiful daughter embroiled with this...lout. And the way he treated her. Maggie eyed the red marks on her daughter's face.

In her role as a private investigator, she'd come across too many men who wielded control over women in myriad ways. Her thoughts jumped to Wilma. Hadn't she spent the best years of her life with an abusive partner? Wilma hadn't confided a great deal about her previous marriage, but from what Maggie had gleaned, Darren Fowlie was a bad lot.

Then, mindful of the hard lessons she'd learned, she quashed her snobbish instincts.

'I'll fetch you that drink.' With a forced smile, she stood and hurried from the room.

You Tell Me

Brian made a show of clearing his throat. 'Thanks for coming in.'

The man sitting stiffly in the seat opposite inclined his head. Didn't speak.

'Can I get you a tea or a coffee?' the sergeant offered, heedful of the warning from his superior officer to treat the subject with kid gloves.

This was met with a curt, 'No.'

'May I first say how sorry I am about your wife's...' Brian struggled for the right word. He'd been that pushed he hadn't had time to get up to speed. Didn't want to get off on the wrong foot. Settled for, 'mishap.'

'Thank you.'

'Let's get rid of the formalities first.' He drew a pen from his inside pocket. 'I need your signature.' He slid a form across the table. 'Just to confirm you've come in voluntarily.'

Tight-faced, Struthers scribbled his name.

'Now,' Brian continued, 'just to give me a clearer picture, could you talk me through your movements from the time you woke until the time you reached your office?'

'I got up, made my wife a cup of tea, went to work.'

'In more detail, Mr Struthers, if you would. What time did you rise?'

'6.45.' Firm voice.

'You sound very sure.'

Gordon Struthers pursed his lips. 'That's the time my alarm's set for.'

Figures, Brian thought. He bet this wee bastard accountant did everything by rote. Could picture him in his office, bent over columns of figures, specs on the end of his nose.

He jotted a note. 'And the tea?'

'Seven o'clock.' Again, there was no doubt in the man's voice.

'How does she take her tea, your wife?'

Sharp look. 'Is that pertinent?'

Brian summoned his sympathy face. 'Everything you can tell me at this stage is helpful.'

'Then, milk, no sugar. She uses sweetener instead. The powdered stuff, if that's your next question.'

Pompous little prick! Brian scribbled on his notepad. He looked up. 'What time did you leave for work?'

'7.30.'

'By car?'

'What do you think?' Behind the glasses, Struthers' eyes flashed with irritation.

Brian ducked. 'Quite.' He recovered. 'Do you always leave at that time?'

'I do.'

'Your office, it's on the Queens's Road, I understand.'

'Correct.'

This is going well, Brian mused. Talk about getting blood out of a stone. He wondered whether the wife wasn't better off up at ARI, chastised himself for his cynicism. Who knows what went on in other people's marriages? And who the hell was he to judge?

'What time do you reach your office, would you say?'

'Between 7.45 and 7.55. I like to be at my desk by eight o'clock.'

'And Mrs Struthers, she'd be doing what?' Brian left the question open-ended.

'Still in bed, I imagine. She likes to read while she's drinking her tea. Then she'll usually take a shower.'

'I see.' That would tally with the report, Brian noted. 'Does your wife have any medical conditions that you're aware of?'

'None.'

'Nothing physical, then?'

'I just told you, Sergeant…' That flash of temper again. 'And you'd think I'd know.' He puffed his chest. 'I'm her husband.'

Too right, Brian thought. And first in line when it comes to pointing the finger. He busied himself with his notebook, looked up. 'How about her mental state?'

The man bristled. 'What are you hinting at?'

'Women…' Brian broke off. He'd need to tread carefully. 'When they reach a certain age…'

'My wife is not menopausal. At least…' For the first time a flicker of doubt appeared in Gordon Struthers' face. 'She may be approaching that time of life…'

'What makes you say that?'

'Nothing, other than that Sheena has always been a sound sleeper, but she hasn't been sleeping well of late.'

'Ah,' Brian exhaled. Now we're getting to it. 'That might explain the pills,' he said.

'What pills?' Struthers started back in his seat.

Brian suppressed a grin. 'I was rather hoping you would tell me that.'

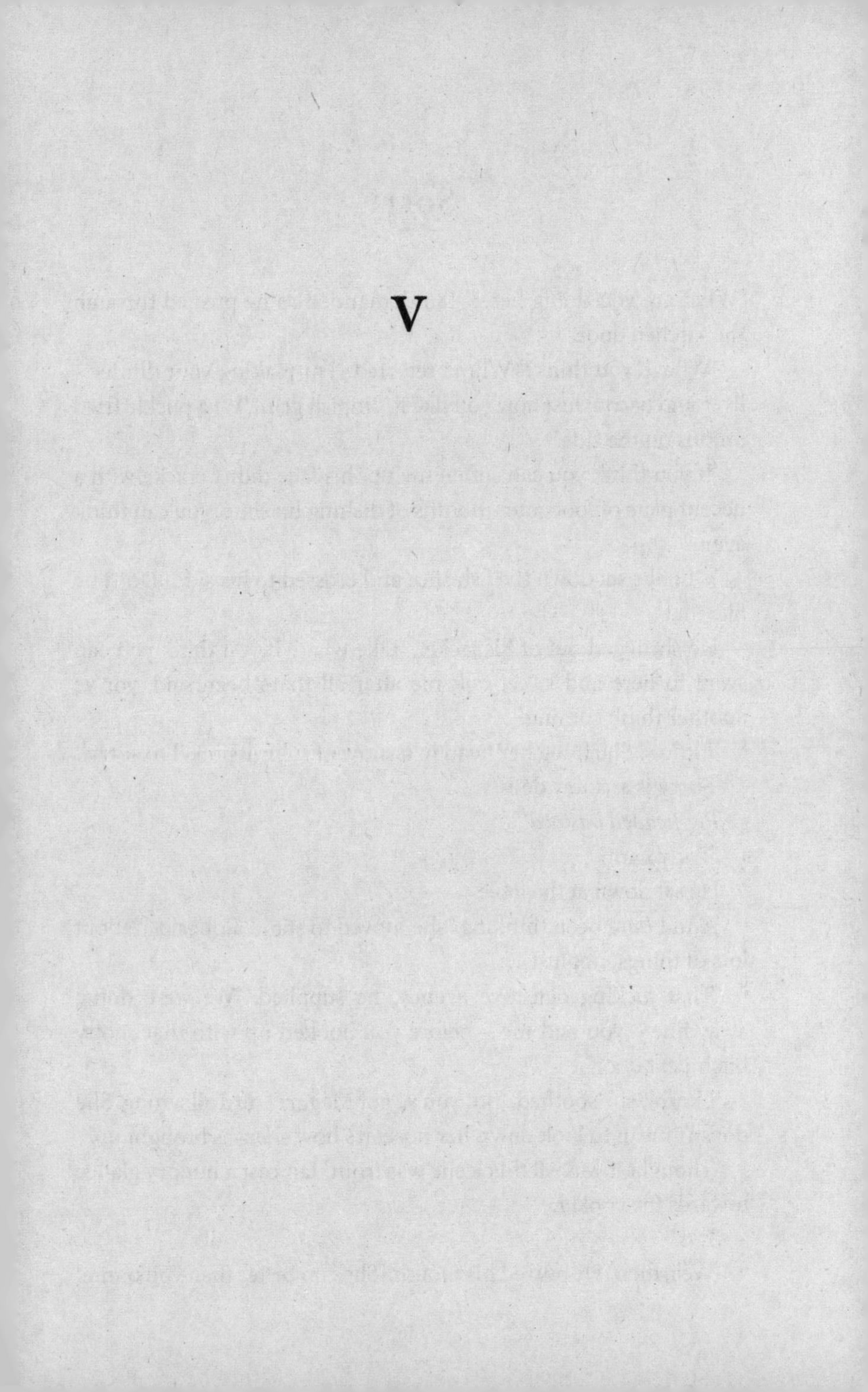

V

Sorry

'What are you doing here?' Ian demanded as he pushed through the kitchen door.

'What d'you think?' Wilma retorted. 'I'm making your dinner – liver and bacon, just how you like it.' Impish grin. 'Wi a puckle fried onions on the side.'

'If you think you can soften me up,' his face didn't crack, 'with a decent plate of food after months of dishing up shite, you can think again.'

'Oh.' She set down the fish slice and crossed to his side. 'Don't be like that.'

He shrugged out of his jacket. 'Like what? If you think you can swan in here and sweet-talk me after all that's been said, you've another think coming.'

'I know.' She hung her head in a show of submission. 'I'm sorry.'

'Sorry is as sorry does.'

Pig-headed bastard!

'Truly I am.'

He sat down at the table.

'And I *have* been thinking,' she moved to stand alongside, 'about lots of things, not just...'

'That fucking detective agency,' he supplied. 'We were doing away fine – you and me – before you hooked up with that snotty bitch next door.'

'I know,' she soothed. 'But you've got Maggie Laird all wrong. She doesn't mean to look down her nose. It's how she was brought up.'

'Thought it was Methlick she was from.' Ian cast a hungry glance towards the cooker.

'It is.'

'Well, then.' He pursed his mouth. 'She's no better than you or me.'

'Nobody ever said she was,' Wilma began. Then, realising she was in dangerous territory, changed tack. 'We thought we were doing good.' She batted her eyelashes, to no avail.

'Aye? Running around the country, neglecting your duties, out to all hours like a pair of...'

Hoors? Wilma stifled a chuckle.

'...tarts.'

'I'll give you we've been putting in long hours. But that's going to change. Once the money starts to come in regular from the corporate accounts, we...'

Ian raised a hand. 'Spare me the explanations. Too little, too late, Wilma. Now, if we're done...'

She swivelled on her heel and crossed to the cooker. 'You'll not be wanting your dinner, then,' she challenged, her back to him. Surreptitiously, she turned up the gas under the frying-pan.

'Well, I...'

The aroma of bacon and onions filled the room.

'Sit down.'

Turning the dial to its lowest setting, Wilma did as she was bid.

'I'm willing to give it another go,' Ian offered, grim-faced.

She met his eye. 'Thanks.'

'Under certain conditions.'

You're kidding!

'Name them,' she said.

You're Not Wearing That

The Vice-Principal's residence was cavernous and gloomy with an abundance of heavy furniture and florid stained glass. In the formal dining room, a two-bar electric fire sputtered in a Victorian tiled grate. Over the dining table, a neon-bright rise and fall light fitment swung hypnotically in the draught. The table was draped in a yellowing damask tablecloth, upon which sat a regiment of slightly tarnished silver-plated cutlery and a mismatched collection of cut-glass.

There were eight in the company. In an elbow chair at the table's head presided the Vice-Principal, a huge, bear-like shambles of a man in a shapeless tweed suit. His wife, a shrivelled stick of a woman with bad teeth and over-permed hair, fidgeted anxiously at the other end. Between them sat two professors and their spouses, along with Nic and Ros.

She'd already tiptoed her way through a pre-dinner round of drinks. If, she thought mutinously, you could actually call a glass of sweet sherry a drink. A vision of a long vodka floated tantalisingly in her head. Not that she was much of a drinker. But, still!

In the chill of the room, silence reigned. Ros sat stiffly on her high-backed Queen Anne chair. The control knickers she'd been forced to unearth were digging into her waist, and her breasts bulged from the plunging neckline of the black dress. *Like a brace of cantaloupe melons*, she thought miserably, as she eyed the dark veins threading the pallid skin. Why anyone would pay for breast augmentation was beyond her.

The hostess broke the silence. 'Mrs Prentice has a new baby,' she announced to the assembled company.

'Oh...' Ros felt her face flood with colour. 'Not that new. He's fifteen months now.'

'Correction. Sixteen,' Nic interjected. 'Isn't she lovely, though?' He cast a proud glance in Ros's direction. 'My girl.'

Around the table, all eyes turned to Ros. Self-conscious, she fingered the necklace at her throat. *A statement piece*, that's what the salesman had called it. And it was that, alright – a chunky semicircle of silver fastened at the back with a slender chain. Like an upmarket dog-collar, she'd thought at the time. Ros would have preferred something more delicate. And significantly less expensive. She'd quailed when she caught sight of the price tag. But Nic had more experience than she when it came to things like that. More experience, full stop. Plus, it pleased him, and that was what mattered. She smiled inwardly as she recalled the look on his face when he'd handed her the beautifully wrapped package. Unlike earlier. Her eyes travelled down to her left hand, where her wedding ring winked at her. The solitaire diamond engagement ring lay, these days, in its velvet-lined box in the top drawer of the dressing-table. She'd stowed it away that last time they'd rowed. Like tonight. In her mind, she replayed their earlier scene:

'You're not wearing that?' Nic's face was a picture.

'Why not?' Ros squinted at her reflection. The silvering of the wardrobe mirror was patchy with age. She thought she looked okay.

'It's too big.' He raked her body with forensic eyes. 'Makes you look like a sack of potatoes.'

Her mouth turned down, but she steeled herself not to answer back. She'd asked him to come home early so that she could have a bath, ease the tiredness in her limbs after the working day, take time to do her hair and nails, look her best. Nic had been late, abstracted, the bath forgotten. A babysitter had been hired for Max: one of the cooks from a nearby hall of residence. Ros had spent too long familiarising the girl with Max's routine. They'd ended up pushed for time.

She forced a smile. 'Hides a multitude of sins. And, besides, it's my favourite.' She'd picked up the cotton kaftan in India. Jewel-bright, it made her feel confident and cheerful. 'I'll feel more relaxed if I'm comfy.'

'Not nervous are you?' he jibed.

'Some. I'm a fair bit younger than the other wives who'll be there. Conversation might be a bit…well…hard-going. And the men, you'll have to remind me their subjects so I don't look a complete fool.'

'All the more reason to wear something glam, knock them for six.'

'Like what?'

'That black number you had on at the Principal's do.'

'That was yonks ago. It'll be way too tight.'

He grinned. 'Show off your boobs, then.'

'I don't want to show off my boobs. They're obscene.'

'Try it on,' he wheedled.

'No.'

'For me?' He slid an arm around her waist.

She spun to face him. 'I'm telling you, Nic, it's too tight for me now.'

His grip tightened. 'This dinner is important to me, Ros.'

She breathed a sigh. 'I know.'

'And you're not just doing it for me. We're a team, remember?' His fingertips made nascent bruises on her spine.

She nodded assent.

'So, be a good girl and try it on, then we'll see.'

And now, only a couple of hours later, there he was – charm personified – chatting animatedly to the lady on his left.

Ros was seated next to a small man, who she now knew to be a mathematician. He was almost completely bald, with a shiny round head and shiny round wire-framed glasses. He was wearing a rather shiny suit over a not-quite-white nylon shirt and an elaborate bow tie.

The soup course was served.

In between slurps, her neighbour attempted to make conversation. 'Your baby…boy or girl?'

'Boy.'

There was an awkward pause.

Ros attempted to fill it. 'Do you have children?'

'No.'

'You're a mathematician, aren't you?' She moved to safer ground.

He brightened. 'That's right… Statistics. Are you familiar with the subject?'

'Not really.' Behind the spectacles, his gaze dropped to her cleavage.

The mathematician took off his glasses, breathed on each lens in turn, polished them with his napkin, put them on again.

Ros challenged him with a look.

The man's eyes swivelled back to his soup plate.

She shifted in her seat, trying to blank out her discomfort and the sweat that was pooling between her constricted thighs.

The Vice-Principal's wife was flushed now, her complexion mottled as she dashed back and forth bearing steaming casserole dishes from the kitchen. Ros had offered to help, but been politely rebuffed. She marvelled that the woman – Norma was her name – was expected to entertain single-handed. Must be the cuts, she concluded. If Nic were to be believed, 'the cuts' insinuated themselves into every aspect of university life.

Norma fussed over the green beans, then: 'Hand round the potatoes, Daddy.'

The Vice-Principal, who seemed not to mind this form of address, rose from his seat. 'Yes, dear.' He moved around the table, dutifully attending to his guests, then dispensed, with meticulous care, from a single bottle of Liebfraumilch.

Ros took a judicious sip of the thimbleful of wine at the bottom of her glass. Too sweet. Her thoughts turned to Max, lying in his cot at home, tucked up and soporific. Inwardly, she sighed. She'd have given a case of bloody Liebfraumilch to have been back home in a comfy pair of pyjamas. Dutifully, she turned to the man on her left.

*

Pudding came and went. Coffee was served. The conversation was animated, now, with talk of departmental budgets and research papers. Nic caught her eye. Winked. He seemed in good form, at ease with these senior academics.

For a moment, there was a lull.

Ros made an effort to contribute. 'In my job…'

Nic cut her short. 'My wife is a primary school teacher. Not exactly taxing on the intellect, is it, darling?'

Stung, Ros scraped back her chair. 'The bathroom?' She turned to her hostess.

'Upstairs.'

Seething with resentment, Ros fled up the stairs. She came onto a pitch dark landing, off which led a number of doors. She tried the handle of one after another. Finally, she revealed a vast, tiled bathroom. Ros groped for the light switch, shut the door behind her and slid the door-snib to. Crossing her legs at the knee, she tugged the hem of the black dress up to her waist, tucked her thumbs into the waistband of the control knickers and eased them with her tights down her thighs. She lifted a towel from the side of the bath and spread it on the icy linoleum floor. Then she lay down, frock round her waist, knickers at her knees.

Ros closed her eyes. It was always the same, the way Nic put her down: clothed in endearments, but they were barbs just the same. Like acupuncture – the carefully selected puncture sites, the ultra-fine needles propelled from their sheaths, the precision timing. She wondered what she'd done to attract such vitriol. Nic surely hadn't always been like that, otherwise why would she have married him? She concentrated hard, trying to pinpoint when – and why – his behaviour had changed. Then she felt a rush of guilt. He couldn't help it. Poor soul was under constant pressure. And he was working towards a common goal, was he not? Why else would they be here in Aberdeen?

'You all right in there?' A woman's voice. 'Your husband is worried about you.'

With some reluctance, Ros raised her head from the floor. She looked down at her naked torso: the unkempt groin, the unshaven legs, the scruffy knickers. A tear slid down one cheek. Angrily, she brushed it away. If Nic hadn't taken exception to her kaftan… If, just this once, she'd stood her ground…

'I'm fine,' she shouted, trying desperately to manipulate herself back into the too-tight Lycra. 'I'll be right down.'

Never Better

'Wilma!'

Maggie spilled half a packet of bran flakes as Wilma stormed through the back door. She threw her arms around Wilma's neck. 'How are you? Where have you been?'

'Give me a minute, pal.' Beaming broadly, Wilma unhooked Maggie's arms and led her through to the dining room. She arranged herself on a chair. 'Christ, I'm gasping. Be a good soul and brew me a cuppa.'

Reluctantly, Maggie did as she was told, side-stepping the mess on the kitchen floor to fill the kettle at the sink. 'Are you okay?' she called, fetching down a couple of mugs and plopping in two teabags.

'I'm fine.'

'I was worried about you.' Maggie filled the mugs with boiling water, added milk from the fridge. 'Hope someone's been looking after you.'

'Chance would be a fine thing. My two saw it as an opportunity to get their dinner cooked and the house cleaned.'

'Poor you.' Maggie carried the mugs through, set them down on coasters. 'Still, you'll have had the chance to catch up. How are they doing, your lads?'

Wilma sniffed. 'Don't ask.'

Maggie changed the subject. 'Have you and Ian managed to sort out your differences yet?'

Shifty look. 'I'm working on it.'

'Poor man has a point, you know. He's had reservations right from the start.'

'Och,' Wilma scoffed, 'He's a right Aberdonian: feart to step outside his comfort zone.'

'I accept he's risk-averse, but...'

'Christ, there you go again. you wi your fancy phrases.'

'There's no need to jump down my throat.'

'Sorry, pal,' Wilma waved an imaginary white flag. 'I'm a bit touchy at the moment where he's concerned.'

'And with good reason. So...' Maggie fished, heart in mouth, 'if you're back in Mannofield, can I take it you've settled your differences?'

Wilma looked at her feet. 'You could say that.'

'What does that mean?'

'Seems someone,' Wilma threw Maggie an old-fashioned look, 'talked sense into him.'

'That right?' She looked the picture of innocence.

'Aye,' Wilma took a greedy slurp of her tea. 'Praised me to the heavens, by all accounts.'

'Oh,' Maggie said lamely. 'That's nice.'

'Not enough to change the bugger's mind, though.'

'Really?'

'No. He's only agreed to take me back under certain conditions.'

'Oh.' Maggie's heart plummeted into her shoes. She recalled Wilma's parting shot.

I have to make a decision: the agency or Ian.

'Does that mean...?' she began. Then the implication dawned.

Wilma had made her choice. And she'd chosen Ian.

Maggie's head spun. Months of hard work down the drain. More than that. Without Wilma's input, there's no way she could keep the business afloat. And without the business – mentally she calculated her meagre salary from Seaton – she couldn't pay the bills. As if that wasn't catastrophic enough, Maggie's quest for justice, which drew heavily not only Wilma's contacts but her moral support, might be compromised.

For some minutes the two sat in silence, then: 'Ian needs his sleep, what with the overtime he puts in and his early start.'

Maggie wondered where this was going.

'My late nights have been getting to him, so we've agreed a weekend curfew.

'Oh,' she murmured. 'That's sensible.'

'Also means regular nookie.' Wilma offered a lascivious grin. 'I reckon he's been missing that and all.'

'Mmm.' That was one place Maggie didn't want to go.

'And there's to be no more ready-meals.' Stage wink.

Maggie felt a pang of conscience. Colin ate everything she served up, processed or no. Still, she fretted about the additives. He was still developing. They couldn't be doing him a lot of good. 'So...' She didn't dare hope. 'The agency?'

Wilma reached across the table, took Maggie's hand in hers. 'You didn't think I'd leave you in the lurch, did you?' She smiled affectionately. 'Daft quine!'

How's Tricks?

'How's tricks?' Maggie smiled into Brian's eyes.

Tricks? he thought scornfully. They were back in the Wild Boar, scene of a previous meeting. Her suggestion this time. Brian hadn't been keen. The little bar was way too intimate for a casual coffee. The previous year, he'd chosen it with care in the hope of progressing the relationship. He still carried the open sores of Maggie Laird's rebuffs.

Now, he affected an upbeat tone. 'Busy-busy.'

As if. Chisolm hadn't revisited the subject of Brian's promotion prospects, and he'd got short shrift when he'd made a tentative pass at DC Strachan.

'That's good.'

Under the keen gaze of those hypnotic eyes, Brian could feel his temperature rise. Maggie's phone call that morning had roused mixed emotions: on the one hand, maybe she was ready to eat humble pie and start afresh. On the other – if her track record was anything to go by – she might well have another agenda. In his head, Brian did a quick recce of his caseload, but couldn't think of anything she could possibly have managed to get herself embroiled in.

She cut to the chase. 'What's the story on Sheena Struthers?'

So that was it. A rush of blood suffused his neck and threatened to engulf his face. *Chill*, he told himself. At least she'd been straight up about it this time.

'No idea.' He wasn't about to be drawn.

'Brian,' a girlish voice trilled. A pert blonde materialised out of the gloom.

'Oh.' Brian looked up, smiled broadly. 'Hello, Megan.'

'Didn't know you hung out here?' Coquettish look.

'I don't,' he said pointedly. 'Megan, meet Maggie Laird. Maggie's an old friend.' He sneaked a glance in her direction. 'A very old friend,' he added.

'Pleased to meet you.' Maggie offered a grudging smile.

'You too.' Megan returned the smile, displaying a set of sparkling white teeth.

'Megan's a civilian officer,' Brian explained. 'Just recently moved up from South Wales.'

He noted, with some satisfaction, Maggie giving Megan a covert once-over. Couldn't help but conclude that, weighed against Maggie's petite frame and unruly red curls, this svelte young blonde with her big blue eyes and milky skin looked a million dollars.

'Will I see you later?' Megan turned her attention back to Brian.

'Yes.' A blush spread from below his shirt collar to the tips of his ears. 'The Athenaeum?'

'Fine. Catch you then.'

'Good to meet you, Maggie.' Megan turned to go.

Brian squirmed in his seat. Wasn't it just his bloody luck to get caught in a compromising situation? Not that you could count Maggie as a love interest. Not now, anyway. But young Megan wasn't to know that. And he'd got good vibes there, reckoned he was onto something. *Bugger Maggie Laird*. He gripped the edge of his chair. The sooner he got to the bottom of what had prompted this meeting and got back to the station, the sooner he could make inroads with Megan. Before some other bastard beat him to it.

'Sorry about that.' He turned to Maggie. 'Where were we?'

'You were telling me about the Struthers case.' The words tripped off her tongue.

'I don't think so.' He caught her in the lie.

Her cheeks tinged with colour.

'What's your interest anyhow?' he demanded.

'Sheena Struthers is a client of mine,' Maggie said airily.

'Not for much longer, maybe.'

'What do you mean?'

Brian reminded himself of the promise he'd made to himself: to keep Maggie Laird at arm's length. 'Nothing.' He could have bitten his tongue.

'Brian?' She leaned into him.

He caught a whiff of her fragrance. That scent she used: lilac, freesia, whatever it was. Then shampoo. And something else. Something more. He felt a stirring in his crotch.

'I had the husband in to the station the other day,' he let out.

'Oh.' Her eyes flashed interest. 'Find out anything?'

Don't even go there! His resolve hardened along with the beginnings of an erection.

Maggie Laird had led him by the nose. He wouldn't give her tuppence, no matter he was soft on the woman. He willed the tumescence to subside.

She took his hand in hers. Clasped it tight.

'She might not make it, do you mean?' she persisted.

Brian crossed his legs, uncrossed them again. To hide the bulge in his trousers he cupped his free hand over his groin, feeling like a twelve-year-old.

'Brian?' He could feel her breath on his cheek.

Finally, he spoke. 'Looks like it.'

A Wee Posse

Ros turned, flushed with excitement, as Nic came through the door.

'You'll never guess…'

He tossed his satchel into a corner, shrugged off his jacket, dropped onto a chair. 'Guess what?'

'Sophie's just off the phone. She's coming up in a couple of weeks.'

'Here?'

'No, silly.' Ros wiped her hands on her apron, crossed to drop a kiss on top of his head. 'Edinburgh. Visit her folks. Amazing thing is, Louise is over then for a conference. And Sarah…well, Glasgow's not that far.'

'So?'

'She mooted a reunion, Sophie that is. If we went down…'

'No chance.' Nic's brows rearranged themselves into a frown. 'I've far too much on my plate.'

'But, Nic, I haven't seen her since we moved here. It must be two years, at least, since our wee posse had a real get together.'

'Posse,' Nic scoffed. 'Coven, more like, the way you lot huddle together, gossiping about God knows what.'

'We're not gossiping. We're catching up, that's all.'

He shrugged. 'Whatever. Anyhow, all that girls together stuff gives me a sore head.'

'Nobody's asking you to join in. Mark will be coming as well. The pair of you could…'

'Mark's a tosser.'

Ros winced. 'That's not true.'

'They're all tossers, those city types, living off the backs of…'

'Do I detect a note of jealousy?' Teasing voice.

He had the grace to look sheepish. 'Maybe. If we had their money…'

'Well, we don't, but we're none the worse for it.' She worked to keep her tone light.

Ros cursed herself for raising the subject. She should have known better than to broach it when he'd just got in from work. *Never ask a man for anything until you've fed him.* Wasn't that what her maternal granny used to say? Best drop it for now, she decided, bring it up another time.

She changed the subject. 'How was your day?'

He grimaced. 'Full morning of lectures. Departmental meeting in the afternoon. More cuts. Nightmare! Everyone at each other's throats.'

'Poor you.' Gently, her fingers kneaded the nape of his neck.

'How's Max?' He didn't ask about her day.

'He was shattered when I picked him up. I put him down for a nap before tea. It will be a while yet.' She broke off, crossed back to the sink. 'I was a bit pushed this afternoon. Can I get you something for now? Cup of tea?'

'It will take more than that.' Nic rose, made for the pantry.

Oh, hell! Ros could feel her chest constrict. Desperate for a sugar rush, she'd eaten one of his chocolate bars earlier. Heart thudding, she said a fervent prayer he wouldn't notice.

'Now, then,' his voice echoed from the recess of the cupboard. 'Who's been raiding my treats shelf?'

Better own up. 'Sorry.' She smiled an apology. 'I was desperate.' Her voice sounded far away.

Nic re-emerged, gnawing on a cereal bar. 'Thought you were desperate to lose weight?' He clutched a handful of spare flesh.

'Ow!' She pulled away. 'I was. Am.'

'Well, we won't lose weight stuffing ourselves with choccie bars, will we?'

That's the girls' reunion out the window, Ros thought, miserably.

There was a wail from upstairs, closely followed by another.

Dejected, she made for the stairs.

Loose Ends

Brian addressed the man sitting across the low table. 'I appreciate you coming in.'

'Did I have a choice?' Gordon Struthers asked, his face wooden.

Brian ignored this. 'There are some loose ends I need to tie up.'

'What do you mean, "loose ends"?' Struthers' eyes flashed a warning. 'Should I be calling my solicitor?'

Suit yourself, Brian thought. Instead, he summoned what he hoped was a reassuring smile. 'You're not under caution, Mr Struthers, so there's no need.' He paused. 'Not unless there's something you've been holding back.'

'Like what, for example?' Stony look.

'Like the Zopiclone I broached in our last meeting: pills which were found in your bedroom, and of which you claim to have had no knowledge.'

'I *have* no knowledge,' Struthers insisted.

Brian ignored this. 'A psychoactive drug which, we've established, your wife has been supplied with under prescription from her GP.'

'She has?' Behind the owlish spectacles, Struthers' eyes popped.

Brian leaned forward. 'You weren't aware?'

'No. I...'

He changed tack. 'How would you rate your marriage?'

'Do you expect me to score it out of ten?' Struthers retorted with a sneer. 'I thought they saved that sort of stuff for the tabloids.'

Brian was caught on the back foot. 'Generally, I mean.'

'Gen-er-ally.' Gordon Struthers accentuated each syllable, 'Affectionate. Enduring. Cordial.' His lip curled. 'Get the picture?'

'Thank you.' Brian responded politely, though he'd have liked to shove the bastard's spectacles up his arse.

'"Cordial", you said. Are you trying to tell me you and your wife don't have rows?'

'I'm not "trying" to tell you anything. I'm stating a fact.'

'So you don't have rows.'

'As in any long marriage, we have experienced occasional...' Struthers emitted an exaggerated sigh, '...difficulties.'

'Regarding?'

'Domestic matters. But I'm talking minor disagreements. I'd hardly class them as rows.'

'These "disagreements",' Brian pressed. 'Have they ever culminated in physical violence?'

Behind his glasses, Gordon Struthers' eyes narrowed. 'Certainly not.'

'Then,' Brian went for the jugular, 'how do you explain your wife's injury?'

'Injury?' The eyes popped. 'My wife isn't injured.'

'On the contrary. Tests have shown that Mrs Struthers sustained a recent injury to her right forearm.'

Struthers shook his head. 'That can't be right.'

'There's absolutely no doubt.' Brian was enjoying himself now. 'I've seen the X-rays. They clearly show a fractured greenstick.' He left a long silence, let it do its work. Then: 'Can you tell me how your wife might have sustained such an injury?'

'I have no idea.'

'None?'

'No. If my wife hurt herself, she didn't let on.'

'She didn't tell you about the sleeping pills, you say. And now she hasn't disclosed an injury – one that must have caused her considerable discomfort.' Brian engaged his interviewee with a steely gaze.

'My wife has a fear of needles. Even if she was hurt, she wouldn't rush to...'

Brian cut him short. 'You've just described your marriage as "affectionate". Doesn't that imply that you're close?'

'It does.'

'Doesn't it then follow that you might confide in one another?'

Struthers shifted in his seat. 'As I said…'

'Mr Struthers, I must press you on this.'

'I'm telling you…' There was a film of perspiration, now, on the pale brow.

'So you maintain…'

'I do.' He hesitated. 'Unless…'

Brian's ears pricked.

'A couple of weeks ago, my wife had a fall. More of a stumble, really. We'd gone out to lunch. A very *cordial* lunch.' He shot Brian a cutting look. 'Afterwards we went for a walk. The path was somewhat uneven and Sheena caught her toe. She pitched forward. She must have hurt her arm in an attempt to break her fall.'

Brian's lip curled. 'Is that so?'

'That's the only explanation I can think of.'

'This path, where was it exactly?'

'By the sea. Catterline's…'

'Yes,' he interrupted. 'I know it well.'

Brian had been there many a time. And he could just picture it: the row of whitewashed cottages, the towering cliffs, that dark, churning sea.

A Total Bog

'Didn't say a word.'

From the depths of the big chair, Maggie presented an ashen face. 'You didn't need to. Oh, Wilma, I've made a total bog of the Struthers case.'

'Shush,' Wilma soothed, from a comfy corner of the settee. 'It'll all work out.'

'No, it won't. A client comes to me saying her husband is trying to kill her. I can't find a shred of evidence. Next thing I know you're texting me she's in intensive care.'

Shrug. 'Thought you'd want to know.'

'Too right I would,' Maggie retorted. 'How did you find out? No, don't tell me. You heard it on the hospital radio at Foresterhill?'

'Pretty much. And there was me thinking I could give up the ARI job any day. But that was before Ian threw a wobbly over the agency.'

'He's okay with it now,' Maggie prompted, heart in mouth. 'He is, isn't he?'

'Perverse bugger won't commit himself either way. What I can say,' Wilma grinned wickedly, 'is his sex life has never been better.'

Maggie groaned. 'Too much information. But, to get back to Sheena Struthers, the latest is she's at death's door.'

Wilma crooked an eyebrow. 'Where did you get that from?'

'I had a coffee with Brian.'

'Did you, now? He still got the hots for you?'

'How would I know?' Maggie could feel her colour rise. Prayed it didn't show in her face.

'What's he saying, then?'

'Oh.' Maggie ran a distracted hand through her hair. 'Other than they think she's not going to make it, he wouldn't be drawn. Clammed up tighter than a…a…'

'Nun's arse?' Wilma completed the sentence.

'Wil-ma!' Maggie exclaimed. 'This is no time to be cracking jokes.'

'I wasn't,' she responded innocently. 'Just trying to be helpful.'

'Well, don't. Anyhow, as I said, Brian wouldn't offer another word on the subject. No doubt trying to keep his nose clean after the fall-out from the Simmons affair.'

'Can't blame the guy.'

'That's all very well, but where does that leave me?'

'Us.'

'This is *my* mess, Wilma. And it's all down to false pride. I hold my hands up to that. I thought I knew better than you, and I was wrong.'

Wilma leaned forward. 'You do know better than me. You're that smart, Maggie. It was you landed Innes Crombie, remember?'

'Yes,' she conceded with a wavering smile.

'And look at the business you've brought in since.'

'Nothing major.'

'Small cases, I grant you, but they're building. And these are corporate accounts, Maggie, companies like Harlaw Insurance. Once we have their confidence they'll grow even more. And they pay. That's a consideration. And more than can be said of some people.'

'Don't remind me.' Maggie blushed as she recalled one of her major boo-boos: a sweet-talking patter merchant who'd left them out of pocket to the tune of several hundred pounds.

'Do you remember thon day you said we'd to divvy-up?'

Maggie frowned. 'Vaguely.'

'Oh, come on, you gave me the full-on lecture on how we were to divide our workload according to our skill set.'

'Really? Did I do that?'

'Aye. And to anyone looking at us, it's pretty obvious. You're the brains and I'm the...' She affected a macho stance. 'Muscle.'

Maggie grimaced. 'Not where my kids are concerned.'

'How no?'

'Ever since Kirsty brought that boy home I've been worried sick.'

'Thought something was bothering you. You've had a face on you this past while like a bulldog chewing a wasp.'

Bristles. 'I have not.'

'Don't come the high horse wi' me, Maggie Laird. I ken you ower weel.' Wilma draped herself on the arm of Maggie's chair. 'What's the matter with him?'

'Oh.' Maggie shrugged. 'He's a bit on the brash side for my taste. And much too familiar: the way he comes up close, sticks his face in mine. And his accent. *Nice, is it?* or *Good, is it?*'

'What's wrong with that?'

'Nothing at all. It's just the way it comes out: the curled lip. Challenging, confrontational almost. That boy's too cocky for words.' She paused. 'If I'm honest, I think he's too working class for Kirsty.'

'You fucking snob!'

Maggie shrugged. 'I know. Blame it on my parents.' Who she hadn't seen for long enough, she reminded herself, neither her nor the kids.

'Och, dinna fash yourself. He's likely just her bit of rough.'

'That's precisely what's concerning me. The way he behaved in front of me, her own mother, I worry about what...'

'Chill, Maggie!' Wilma cut her short. 'Kirsty will be fine. It's a phase they all go through.'

'I didn't.'

'Aye, well, we know about you.'

'What about me?'

Wilma gave Maggie an affectionate nudge. 'Methlick's got a lot to answer for.'

Maggie brushed her off. 'Don't you start, Wilma Harcus.'

Grins. 'I'm not. Seriously, though, your Kirsty's got more sense than to get in the sack with some nutter.'

'Who said they were sleeping together?'

'Aren't they?'

'I sincerely hope not.'

'*I sincerely hope not*,' Wilma echoed. 'Seriously, though, I'll lay a tenner on it's just a passing fancy. '

'I'd like to think so. But I have my doubts. Usually, Kirsty gives as good as she gets. Not this time. I'm fearful she lets him push her around.' She hesitated for a moment. 'There's a fine line between horseplay and full-on abuse.'

'Relax,' Wilma urged. 'Kirsty can look after herself.'

'To get back to what we were talking about...' Maggie changed the subject. 'I've screwed up. Landed myself in another hole. And now I'll have to dig myself out of it.'

'No you don't.' Wilma stood up. 'We're partners, are we no'?'

'We are. And thank you.' Maggie blew a kiss. 'What are we going to do now, then, the two of us?'

'We're going to do what we always do.' Wilma advanced across the room. 'First, establish the facts.'

'How the hell are we going to do that,' Maggie countered, 'if Brian won't tell me anything and the client is quarantined in the ITU? Sheena Struthers might even be under police guard, for all we know.'

'She's not.' The words were out before Wilma could stop herself.

Maggie leapt out of the chair and squared up to her. 'How do you know?'

'Because I had a wee go at getting in there.'

'To the intensive therapy unit?'

'Aye.'

'I don't believe it.' Maggie's eyes were wide. 'First Seaton, now this. Have you been snooping on me again, Wilma Harcus?'

'No. All I was doing was taking a leaf out of your book: using my connections to move the agency forward. Plus, I still work at the infirmary, remember? Have a problem with that?'

'Of course not.' Maggie dropped back onto the chair. 'And I'm sorry, Wilma. I didn't mean to have a go at you. It's just, I feel such a fool. And never mind me, think of that poor woman.' She drew breath. 'How did you find her, anyway?'

Wilma perched on the arm. 'Horizontal.' She grinned.

'Wil-ma!' Maggie reached up, threw a mock punch. 'If you crack one more joke…'

'Didn't get much more than you got from Brian. Charge nurse threw me off the ward.'

'Oh,' Maggie's face fell. 'So…'

'Nearest I got was a look-see through the window. It was weird an all, being on the other side of the glass: her laid out wi muckle tubes runnin out o' her and close to death by all accounts. Bit like thon day I took you down the mortuary, only… Oh, Christ!' Her hand flew to her mouth. 'I'm sorry, Maggie, I didn't mean…'

'Doesn't matter.'

'You sure?'

'Yes. It was upsetting at the time, seeing George lying there dead: the way they'd combed his hair all wrong, things like that. But, now, what I remember is the weird stuff: the fake flowers in the viewing room, the sheet that covered him. Green, it was, not white like you see on TV. And there was this pillow. I hadn't expected a pillow. Not a pink one, anyhow. Creased to death, they were, too.' She looked embarrassed at the pun. 'I remember thinking – imagine the Council supplying a washing machine and no iron.'

'Oof!' Wilma exclaimed. 'Must have been a man.'

Maggie sighed. 'To get back to Sheena Struthers…'

'Stuck-up bitch of a charge nurse wouldn't tell me a thing.' Wilma wrinkled her nose. 'Not even who it was brought her in.'

'So what did you do?'

Grins. 'Used my detective skills. I've ways, you know. Hot-tailed it round to the ambulance station. Lucky our guy was on shift.'

'And?'

'Overdose.' Triumphant look. 'Official line is it was accidental, but between you, me and the gatepost,' Wilma tapped the side of her nose, 'they're treating it as a suicide attempt.'

'But…' Maggie struggled to compose herself. 'We both know it's not suicide.'

Wilma cocked her head. 'Do we?'

'Of course we do.' Irritated voice.

'What difference does it make?' Wilma shot back. 'It's two cheeks of the same arse.'

'Whatever.' Maggie wasn't going to argue.

She felt like a dead weight had been lodged in the pit of her stomach.

Sheena Struthers was going to die.

And if she did it would be all Maggie's fault.

An Unlikely Pairing

Allan Chisolm surveyed the mass of paperwork spread over his desk. Changed days. Talk about effective policing! He hardly made it out of the office any more. To add to his team's caseload, now there was this blessed Struthers case.

With a sigh, he pushed the file he'd been working on to one side and picked up the box of TicTacs he kept on his desktop. *Eeeny-meeny*, he juggled it back and forth between his hands. Could be something, could be nothing. Who knows? What he did know for sure was it had taken up far too much time – his and that of a load of overworked and underpaid detectives. Might be time to put some pressure on – he weighed the box in one hand – see what they could come up with before they called it a day.

There was a tentative tap on the door.

'Enter.'

The door opened. A young civilian officer crept into the room.

'Well?' Chisolm looked up.

'I've a message for you, sir. Call came in while you were upstairs. I didn't think you'd want to be interrupted.' Apologetic look.

'No.'

There was silence, then: 'Out with it.'

'It was from ARI, sir. To do with a Mrs Sheena Struthers,' the girl broke off, blushing to the roots of her hair.

'And?'

'They're saying she's regained consciousness.'

'Right.' Chisolm turned his attention back to the reports in front of him.

The officer stood, waiting for further instructions.

He looked up. 'Off you go then.'

'Sir.' She scuttled out of the room.

After the balls-up uniform had made of the call-out to Milltimber, he'd best send somebody sensible to take a statement from Sheena Struthers. If the husband was a big wheel in the city, upstairs wouldn't want the guy kicking up. He performed a mental head-count of his officers: Wood and Duffy he dismissed as being too old-school. When he'd first taken up his post, Chisolm had toyed with the idea of sending the pair on a Diversity Awareness Course, concluded it was way too late. Dunn, he decided, was a tad too brash to interview the older woman. That left Burnett and Strachan.

Flipping open the perspex lid with his thumb, Chisolm tipped a couple of mints into his mouth. It was over a year since he'd stopped smoking – just one of the things he'd sloughed off when he'd turned his back on Glasgow. Or had it turned its back on him? He uttered a rueful snort. Who knows?

Burnett would do the job, he chewed thoughtfully. Bit buttoned-up, but he'd get a result. Chisolm wondered if his sergeant had always been that unforthcoming, or whether the fallout from the marriage break-up – Chisolm had heard the stories – had caused the man to retreat into himself…

Chisolm swallowed down the last of the mints. That wee girl, Strachan, though… She might only be a DC, but she'd shown real insight since she joined his squad.

Wasn't it always the same? The female recruits were invariably more collected: didn't feel the need to strut their stuff, not like the blokes. Not unless…

His face creased into a grin, as he remembered the dyke from his last posting. Talk about gay pride! The woman was aggression writ large: tried at every turn to shove her sexuality down your throat. The complete opposite of that Laird woman.

Maggie Laird. The grin vanished from Chisolm's face. All that soft femininity. The last time he'd called on her, he thought she'd got the message: if she must play private detective, she'd have to confine herself to more mundane things in future. She'd taken it on the chin, and he'd warmed to her, then, even toyed with the idea of asking her out. Nothing heavy. A casual drink, maybe, just to break the ice. But that was before she turned up again like a bad penny, looking to gate-crash police enquiries at will.

Chisolm couldn't imagine anyone trying that sort of thing on in Glasgow, least of all some pint-sized female. As for the other dame? Jesus! She was a joke. The DI had only seen the neighbour in passing, but to say the two were an unlikely pairing was putting it mildly. Women! He stroked his chin.

Still…Strachan. She'd earned her credentials on the Seaton case, the insight she'd shown into that Fatboy bastard's make-up, her compassion towards those toe-rags. Maybe she'd be the one could get into Sheena Struthers' head.

He'd give the wee girl a chance.

He reached for the phone.

A New Friend

'Happy?' Nic broke off from nuzzling her neck.

'Ish,' she muttered, not turning.

'That all?'

Ros rolled over to face him. 'Sorry.' She wished she could sound more enthusiastic but, truth be told, all she felt was worn out.

'Still feeling low?' He stroked her cheek.

Her body went rigid. 'Don't give me that again.'

'Give you what?' He assumed that blond, blue-eyed, little-boy-lost look that had so captivated her, in the beginning.

'Oh.' She couldn't keep the irritation out of her voice. 'The mental health card.'

'Babe…'

'Don't you "babe" me, Nic Prentice. I'm not suffering from depression. I'm lonely, that's what it boils down to.'

'But…' Puzzled look. 'You've got Max.'

'Babies don't talk to you. Well…' she corrected. 'Maybe later on they do.'

Her mind ran back to that first six months she'd spent at home – those endless days when she'd seen no one, spoken to no one, and the phone didn't ring. Even when she'd girded herself to take a walk with the buggy up the Chanonry and through Seaton Park or down High Street and over the Spital into town, not a single person had exchanged a greeting. Ros sighed. She might as well have been invisible.

Nic interrupted her train of thought. 'How about the mums at nursery?'

'I've no time to sit around and chat, Nic. I'm always in such a rush.'

'Fiona, then.'

‘That’s rich coming from you.’ Ros spluttered. ‘You’ve done your best to drive Fiona away.’

‘Now you’re being paranoid.’

‘I’m not bloody paranoid. Maggie Laird says…’

He cut in. ‘Who’s Maggie Laird?’

‘We work together.’

‘You don’t mean that dame I met at the Christmas do?’ he sneered.

‘That’s exactly who I mean.’

‘Oh, come on. She’s just some sad divorcee.’

‘She’s a widow. And she says…’

‘You’ve found a new friend, have you?’ he spoke over her. ‘First it was Fiona – Fiona this, Fiona that. Now it’s Maggie Laird.’

‘I gather you don’t like her either.’

‘It’s not a question of “like”. What the hell does a nonentity like that know about anything?’

‘She’s…’

‘It’s not even Maggie Laird. It’s you, Ros. You can’t stand on your own two feet, can’t make a decision to save yourself, can’t…’

‘You don’t have to tell me, you’ve told me often enough.’ She broke down in tears. ‘All that’s wrong with me,’ she snivelled, ‘is I’m worn out trying to juggle a full-time job, a house and a baby all on my own.’

‘You’re not on your own.’

‘No? If you’re not in the department, you’re in Senior Common Room, either that or out running.’

‘I do help.’ Plaintive voice. ‘I’ve dropped Max off at nursery twice this week. Plus, I bathed him and unloaded the dishwasher and…’

‘It’s not that sort of help I had in mind. It’s…’ Noisily, she blew her nose. ‘Moral support.’

‘Don’t know what you’re getting at.’

She sighed. ‘What I’m saying is, for every practical thing you do to help… And don’t get me wrong, I do appreciate it. You come out with some niggle or other. If it’s not the house, it’s the nursery, or the shopping, or how often I use the car. And it's ground me down. I feel like I'm walking on eggshells all the time, and I can't take any more.'

'Whoa!' He caught hold of her wrist. 'What brought this on?'

She wrenched away. 'Your attitude.'

'*My* attitude?'

'Yes. You're so negative, Nic. The way you're forever finding fault. And it's not just me. It's my folks, my friends. Small wonder I hardly see them anymore.'

'How's about a night out?' He tickled her chin. 'That positive enough for you?'

She swatted his hand away. 'Be serious.'

Grins. 'I am being serious.'

Ros let out a long sigh. 'Nothing's ever your fault, is it, Nic? And whenever I try to have a serious conversation, all you do is duck and weave.'

'Ducking and weaving is my speciality.' He landed a kiss on the tip of her nose.

'Oh, for heaven's sake…' She turned her back on him.

'Love you, baby.' He ran his fingers up and down her naked spine.

Against all her inclinations she giggled.

'I'm sorry.' He spooned into her. 'Sounds like I've been a grouch.'

'Mega grouch!' she mumbled.

'Pressure of work.' He rolled her to face him. 'Poor baby. I'm really sorry I've been so tied up. But I'll make it up to you.' He kissed her, on the mouth this time. 'I promise.'

Women of a Certain Age

'Jump to it,' Allan Chisolm looked down the table. 'We've a ton of stuff to get through this morning.' He eyeballed Brian. 'Any movement on the Struthers thing, Burnett? Did you get any joy out of the husband?'

'Not a lot. Denies all knowledge of the medication we found at the scene.'

'Wife's gone behind his back, then?'

'Looks like it.'

'But why would she do that? I mean, sleeping pills, it's not as if they're uncommon, especially in...'

'Och.' Duffy stuck his oar in. 'I've told you. Women of a certain age.'

'Never mind "a certain age",' Wood's face bore a permanently sour expression. 'Women full stop.'

Brian ducked his head. *Amen to that.*

Susan glowered at them both. If anyone said 'a certain age' one more time she'd give them one in the nuts.

'She might have had suicidal thoughts. Got hold of the pills. Hidden them while...'

'Could be,' Chisolm cut her off. 'Anything from the hospital?' he queried.

Brian shuffled the papers in front of him, flipped open a file. 'Test results just came through this morning.' He scanned the print. 'Gist of it is...' His head shot up as a fire alarm rattled through the building.

'Christ Almighty!' Chisolm swore. 'That's all we bloody need.' That morning's fire drill had completely slipped his mind.

Untidily, the detectives seated around the table rose to their feet and made for the door.

Nice and orderly, guys, if you please,' their inspector chided. 'I'll see you downstairs.'

*

Susan hugged her arms to her chest as she slid back into her seat. When the alarm went off, she hadn't had time to grab her jacket, and the muster station in the rear podium car park was exposed to a biting wind off the North Sea, even on the balmiest of days. To cap it all, that dickhead Douglas Dunn had made a crude pass at her. Brian Burnett had been bad enough; stuttering and blushing like a teenager. But at least he was decent. A bit of a social misfit, maybe, but she felt sympathy for the guy. Unlike this creep, who she deemed a total wanker.

'Alright, darling?' Dunn occupied the chair next to her.

With a scowl, Susan scraped her seat sideways.

'Don't be like that,' Douglas wheedled.

'Fuck off,' she hissed, turning her back on him.

Douglas leaned in. 'You'll come round.' He smirked. 'They all do.'

She whirled to face him. 'Didn't you hear me? I said...'

'Cut it out, you two,' Chisolm entered the room. He sat down. 'Burnett, as you were saying before the meeting broke up...'

Brian cleared his throat. 'Drug screen states meds in the bloodstream weren't sufficient to put Sheena Struthers in a coma.'

'Well.' Duffy sat up. He flexed his shoulder muscles. 'How about that?'

Chisolm pursed his lips. 'How indeed?'

'That would square with the blister pack we...' Remembering Souter's cock-up, he corrected himself. 'That was found in the bedroom. There weren't that many pills missing, plus they were standard dose: 7.5 mg. She'd have had to take a fair few to put her in that state.'

Chisolm surveyed his squad. 'That throws up an interesting question: what else could have happened to produce that outcome?'

He looked down the table. 'Any suggestions?'

'Alcohol?' Susan Strachan offered. 'Could have interacted with the pills.'

'Good point,' Chisolm said. 'Any history there, do we know?' He looked pointedly at Brian.

'Not that I'm aware, sir.' Brian felt colour seep from under his collar. *Fuckit!* He should have asked. 'But,' he looked down at the file again, 'it says here no alcohol was present.'

Douglas added his tuppence-worth. 'Another substance, then?' he opined.

'Such as?' Duffy countered. Any opportunity to nail the twat.

'Oh.' Douglas ruffled his already artfully disordered hair. 'Too many variables. I'd have to confer with toxicology before I could give a definitive answer.'

'As fucking if!' Duffy fixed him with a withering stare.

'You two,' Chisolm barked. 'Enough. In short, we have only one valid suggestion: that another substance was ingested. And that begs what question?'

Susan broke the ensuing silence: 'Did Mrs Struthers take an additional substance of her own volition or...'

Anxious to put his oar in, Douglas piped up. 'Was it administered by another party? There was a half drunk cup of tea, if I'm not mistaken, on the bedside table.'

'Quite.' Chisolm acknowledged this contribution with a curt nod. 'But only one set of fingerprints on the pills.'

Brian attempted to interject. 'Can I just say...'

Chisolm ignored him. 'Before we go down that road, there's something else we have to consider.'

Around the table there were baffled faces. Then: 'A pre-existing medical condition?' Susan volunteered.

'Well done, Strachan.' Chisolm nodded his approval.

'There is one more thing, sir,' Brian coloured. He better get this in before their deliberations went down yet another channel. 'X-rays are showing an injury to Sheena Struthers' right arm.'

Chisolm scowled. 'Why didn't you raise this before?'

'I…' Christ, Brian thought, I've screwed up again. 'Tried,' he added lamely.

'Well, now you've finally got there,' Chisolm threw him a pointed look, 'are we agreed the Struthers case warrants further investigation?'

He was met by murmurs of assent.

'To summarise, we've a number of hypotheses: drugs – what we've found plus question mark something else – were self-administered, whether by accident or design; drugs were administered by another party; injury was accidental, or not. As to the actions, someone had better have another chat with Mrs Laird. No, not you, Burnett.' He eyeballed Brian. 'You've got form there. I'll do it myself. Haul Gordon Struthers back in here. Sounds like he's been less than forthcoming. If he's hiding something, we need to find out what. Strachan, I want you up at ARI. Establish the latest on Sheena Struthers' condition. And no visitors, not that ITU is likely to admit anyone. Well, nobody but the husband. We can't stop him, I suppose. But I don't want anyone else near her until we get a statement. And Duffy, ask their lab if they're willing to run more tests.'

Best Guess

'You'd news, you said,' Maggie blurted as she caught sight of Jimmy Craigmyle. They'd settled on Duthie Park for that morning's rendezvous. The show of spring bulbs was stunning, but it was nippy, still. The David Welch Winter Gardens afforded a secluded base away from the prying eyes of the public in general and Jimmy Craigmyle's wife, Vera, in particular.

'Yes,' he emerged from the shelter of a giant tree fern. 'I've decided to take up Gilruth's job offer.'

'Oh.' Maggie felt nauseous, suddenly, whether from the let-down or the humidity.

'In the short term, at least. Good news is I've landed another job altogether.'

Maggie's heart raced. 'Where?'

'Bridge of Don. Warehouse manager,' he elaborated. 'Pay's not that great, but all the security jobs I've gone after have been unsocial hours. At least this is eight to four.'

'But that's wonderful,' Maggie said without conviction, unsure whether this news was good or bad. 'When do you start?'

He shrugged. 'That's the downside. Current guy is working his notice. They don't need me for another month.' He grinned. 'Don't you see? That gives me a window of opportunity. I can start at the new venue. Play along. Stick my nose in. Now I'm off, it's not as if I have much to lose.'

'No, I suppose.' she conceded.

'And Vera's happy. Well,' he qualified, 'as happy as she's likely to be till the kids settle down and…' Stage wink. 'Her and me get lovey-dovey again.'

Lovey-dovey! Maggie's imagination ran ahead of her.

'Downside is,' Craigmyle's voice broke her train of thought, 'it'll take time. I mean, we've been separated for over a year now, Vera and me. You can't just walk back in and…'

'No, I can see that.'

'And I wouldn't want to rock the boat by dredging up that whole drugs business. I mean, no offence, Maggie, but it's ancient history, and Vera's touchy enough about the ignominious end to my police career…' His voice tailed off.

Maggie steadied herself against a banana tree. She closed her eyes. Seemed it was peppered with potholes, this unrelenting road to justice. Just when she thought she was making progress, something set her back. Take Bobby Brannigan. She'd had to muster all her courage to track him down, and Wilma had shown initiative and tenacity in obtaining his taped statement, only for it to be deemed inadmissible. Plus, the guy was slippery as an eel. Who knows what tactics he'll employ to wriggle out of ratifying his confession. She'd been banking on expediting Craigmyle's testimony. Mentally, Maggie calculated when she could reasonably ask Jimmy to proceed. Clearly, not whilst he was still in Gilruth's employ. In her mind, she substituted 'months' for the 'weeks' she'd estimated earlier.

'Then there's the money side of things,' he ran on. 'I've a six-month lease on my place. And there's the deposit to consider. I can't afford to lose that.'

'No.' Maggie went weak at the knees. She could see Jimmy Craigmyle's statement – admitting that it was he, not George, who'd turned off Brannigan's interview tape – vanishing into the ether. 'Is it hot in here or is it me?' She brushed a film of moisture from her forehead.

'Not hot, no. Temperature's fine for me.' He grinned. 'And them, obviously,' he gestured to the lush foliage that filled the space from ground level to the arched roof of the glasshouse.

Oh Lord! Maggie said a quiet prayer she hadn't been hit with her first hot flush. 'So, your statement, how long do you think until…?'

Craigmyle cut her short. 'Best guess? Tail-end of the year.'

One Less

'Well,' Dave Miller plonked his tray of tomato soup down on the canteen table. 'They cracked it yet?'

Ian Souter stopped chewing on his ham sandwich for a moment. 'What?' He spoke out of the side of his mouth.

Miller sat down. 'Thon Struthers case, ya moron.'

'Mebbe,' Souter masticated a few times more. 'Mebbe not.' He swallowed. 'Husband's been interviewed a couple of times.'

'Anything out of him?'

'Same old. Still maintaining total innocence.'

'Well…' Greedily, Miller slurped his soup. 'He would, wouldn't he?'

'But the evidence…'

'Circumstantial, from what I gather. Either the wife's havering,' he offered a knowing look, 'or the tox tests will give us something.'

'Them pills…' Souter broke off.

'Christ,' Miller wiped the back of his hand across his mouth. 'We screwed up there.'

Ian Souter bolted down the last of his sandwich and reached for a Tunnock's Caramel Wafer.

'We did that. Arse-licking in order, pal, eh no?'

His companion grunted. 'Too right.' He broke a chunk off his rowie, dipped it in his soup.

'Thought the test results were in.'

'The boss has requested more.'

Souter bit into his biscuit. 'Where d'you get that?'

'Jungle drums.' Miller spoke through a mouthful of soup and roll. 'Don't know what he's after, but you have to hand it to him,' he swallowed noisily. 'He's a fly bastard, our new man.'

'I wouldn't disagree with you. That Struthers is a sleekit wee cunt by all accounts. If he's hiding summat Chisolm will winkle it out of him.'

'Story goes…' Miller winked. 'Our suspect has a bidey-in.'

'Where d'you get that?'

'Down the pub.'

'You sure it was Struthers?'

Miller's voice faltered. 'Pretty sure.'

'Och,' Ian Souter scoffed, 'You don't want to believe the stuff you hear when folk are in their cups.' He lowered his voice. 'I wouldn't broadcast it either, if I were you. If you've heard wrong, the DI will have your guts for garters.'

Miller choked on his soup, sending gobbets of tomato-coloured dough into his partner's face.

'Chrissake,' Souter held up a defensive hand.

'Sorry, pal.'

'It's okay.' Souter wiped his face.

'All the same, the wife's at thon age.'

'And the fella's no getting his load away.' Souter made a lewd gesture.

'And she's that well set up I bet she wullna give him a divorce.'

'You reckon the husband done it, then?' Souter took a slurp of his tea.

'Who the fuck knows? Miller wiped his bowl clean with what was left of his rowie, stuffed it in his mouth. 'But I'll tell you one thing.'

Souter stifled a yawn. 'What's that?'

'Poncy wee prick like him,' Miller pushed his plate to one side. 'If we stick it on him he'll have a gey fine time in Peterhead.'

'You're right there. Remember that last perp,' Souter scratched his head. 'What was his name? Meechan? Michie? Something like that.'

'Mutch.'

'Mutch. Right. Got razored his second day. Hanged himself before the month was out.'

'Ah, weel.' Miller grinned. 'One less.'

Big Fat Zero

In the briefing room there was an air of high expectancy. They'd been called in at short notice: Strachan from filing a report, Dunn from a dental appointment, Duffy and Burnett from their respective actions, Wood from a quick snifter in the Athenaeum. Now, they sat around the table, Susan sipping from a styrofoam cup of coffee, Dunn doodling as usual, all of them quietly speculating on what had prompted the summons.

'Good evening.' Chisolm took his place at the head of the table.

'Evening, sir.' Four heads looked up.

'That includes you, Wood.'

Dave Wood raised his head, his expression careworn. He glanced in the direction of the window. The clocks hadn't yet gone forward. Outside, the sky was a uniform grey. 'Good, is it, sir?' His mouth turned down. 'Hadn't noticed.'

Chisolm let this go. 'I've called you in,' he waved an envelope in the air, 'because we've just received the results of the second round of toxicology tests on Sheena Struthers.'

From around the table there was a restless stir.

'What's the outcome, sir?' Douglas was always first off the mark.

'To summarise,' Chisolm held the report in front of his face.

Five pairs of eyes fixed on it.

'The tox screen shows no additional substances.'

'What about a pre-existing medical condition?'

'No joy. Other than that injury to her arm, Sheena Struthers was in perfect health.' He turned to Brian. 'What does the husband have to say about the injury?'

'Insists she had a fall.'

Duffy snorted. 'That's what they all say.'

'In the house?' Chisolm continued.

'Aye.' Wood's cynicism knew no bounds. 'Fell down the stairs.'

'Be serious,' Brian remonstrated. 'Struthers asserts they were out walking. The wife tripped, put an arm out to save herself. End of story.'

'And you believe him?'

'Hard to know. He's a bit of a stuffed shirt, Gordon Struthers. Doesn't give a lot away.'

'This walk, where did it take place?'

'Catterline.'

'Now,' Dunn said portentously, 'there's a thing.'

Chisolm cocked an eyebrow.

'Ex-fishing village, sir. Known for its views.' He smirked. 'Clifftop views.'

Chisolm frowned. 'You inferring this fall may not have been accidental?'

Hastily, Douglas rearranged his face. 'Just opening up the discussion, sir.'

'Christ.' Dave Wood's mouth turned down. 'Where does that leave us?'

'We need to look elsewhere. Establish the who, the what, the why. Then, and maybe only then, we'll find out the how. First off,' Chisolm engaged each of them in turn, 'we have to ask ourselves why Sheena Struthers would want to kill herself? Or why someone would want her dead?'

'I'm still with the change of life,' Duffy insisted. 'My Sadie's been…'

'Tell me about it,' Wood jumped in. 'They dry up.' He made a face. 'Down there. Talk about chucking a banana down Union Street?' He made a lewd gesture.

'I was going to say…' Duffy came back.

'Joking apart,' Susan intervened. 'The menopause may have significance here. You guys crack jokes about it, and women make light of it – the hot flushes, the night sweats – but there's more to it than that. A lot more. It's a seismic shock to a woman's body, both physical and mental. It changes everything: not just the ability to conceive, but her skin, hair, libido. Her entire function as a woman.'

'I'm with you there,' Duffy again. 'The wife, she's been solid all these years. No dramatics. But since the change set in she'll turn on the waterworks at the least thing. And it's not just tears. There's that much bottled up in there, it's like bloody Vesuvius erupting.'

'Thank you, Sergeant,' Chisolm said hastily. 'I'm sure we all found that very…' He paused. 'Instructive.'

'According to the feedback from your interview with Mrs Laird, sir,' Susan picked up the thread of her argument, 'Sheena Struthers, thoughout their interaction, was in a highly emotional state.'

'Well, she would be, wouldn't she,' Douglas responded, 'if her allegation the husband is trying to kill her has any substance.'

'So,' Chisolm stepped in. 'Other than the sleep disturbance she took to her GP and the demonstrable anxiety she exhibited to Mrs Laird, what do we know?'

'Big fat zero,' Dave Wood muttered. 'Woman had it all for Chrissake.'

'Not a suicide attempt, then?'

'Menopausal or not, there's no evidence Sheena Struthers' mind was unbalanced to that degree,' Brian concurred.

'Plus,' Susan continued, 'on a practical level, no woman I know would attempt suicide in a state of undress, with no makeup and bed hair.'

'Don't forget the specs,' Douglas added.

Susan threw him a withering look.

Chisolm took control. 'Then we'll have to start again. Pin down whatever's been ingested. Or administered, if Sheena Struthers didn't self-harm. Let's not rule that out. Whichever it is, what effected that outcome without leaving any trace?' He turned to Duffy. 'Sergeant, speak to Mrs Laird again. I want those incidents documented: exact dates, times. No woolly stuff, mind. On second thought,' he frowned. 'I'll do it myself. Burnett,' he turned back to Brian. 'You've got the measure of the man. Look at his firm. How sound is it? Would Gordon Struthers stand to benefit financially from his wife's death?' He paused. 'Now that the business side's taken care of, let's address the personal angle. Is there another woman in the frame? If the wife is, indeed, menopausal and the husband is sexually active, he may be on the lookout for – or have already found – a younger model.'

'Wouldn't the…?' Susan began. She'd have to choose her words carefully. It was a matter of record that Chisolm and Maggie Laird had crossed swords. She settled for, '…agency have checked that out?'

'Maybe.' Chisolm's voice was scathing. 'Maybe not. Douglas.' His voice rose.

'Sir.' Dunn's head shot up from the pad he was doodling on.

'You get onto that.'

'Yes, sir.'

'Wood, get yourself down to Catterline, see what you can find out.'

'Okey-dokey.' For the first time that day, Dave Wood's face brightened, probably at the prospect of a free lunch.

'Susan, you'll continue to monitor progress at ARI. Given Mrs Struthers' approach to the…ahem!' He cleared his throat. 'PI agency. When she's able to speak.' He hesitated. 'If she's able to speak, she's more likely to open up to another woman.'

'Right you are, sir.'

'And all of you,' Chisolm eyed each of his team in turn, 'make it quick. Pull in a couple of uniform if need be. And keep me in the loop. I've a gold meeting on the cards and, given our last saga with Harcus & Laird, I want this one out my hair.'

A Long Night

'DC Strachan.' Susan showed her card. 'To see Mrs Struthers.'

'Let me check with the charge nurse.' The fresh-faced girl at the nurse's station looked no more than eighteen. Made Susan, in her work outfit of grey trouser suit and serviceable white shirt, feel middle-aged. Like the woman she'd been sent to take a statement off. *Why me?* she thought wryly. For all the edicts on gender equality that emanated from on high, she still felt like the token tottie on the team.

'I'm afraid it's not convenient right now.' In what seemed like seconds the girl was back behind the desk.

Susan squared her shoulders. 'Says who?'

'Charge nurse.'

Frowning, Susan's eyes dropped to the girl's name badge. *Lauren Mitchell.*

'Well, Lauren, you go back and tell your charge nurse that someone rang police headquarters not an hour ago to say the patient had regained consciousness.'

'But...' The girl hesitated.

'Go on,' Susan urged.

With a look of abject terror, the nurse scuttled down the wide corridor, her white rubber clogs making small slurping sounds on the linoleum.

Susan waited, her fingers drumming impatiently on the desktop.

'How can I help?' The woman who returned with the girl was small, but had a steely glint in her eye.

'You can help,' Susan drew a steadying breath, 'by pointing me in the direction of your patient, Mrs Sheena Struthers.'

'Mrs Struthers is not able to speak right now.'

'But,' Susan eyed up the well-upholstered figure, the feet planted apart, the severe haircut, 'we've been advised otherwise.'

'Well, you've been advised wrong.'

Inwardly, Susan groaned. Another cock-up. And one, given the paucity of resources, the squad could well do without. 'She *has* recovered consciousness?'

'That's correct.'

'Then why…?'

'Mrs Struthers remains in a serious condition.'

How serious, Susan wondered? *Get me the facts,* she could hear her boss's voice. She debated asking, thought the better of it. Instead directed her gaze to the whiteboard on the wall listing the staff currently on duty. It was headed up by *Nurse in Charge: Vi Coutts.*

'Is your patient awake?' Susan asked pointedly.

Vi pursed her lips. 'I can't say.'

Well, what can you bloody say? Susan wanted to scream. Except there was no point taking the woman on. Susan knew she'd have to keep in Vi's good books if she was going to get a result.

She plastered a smile on her face. 'We need to take a statement from Mrs Struthers, and I'll get blue murder from my boss if I go back empty-handed.' Conspiratorial look. 'You know how it is. So would it be okay if I sit by the bed for a bit? Just on the off-chance?' Seeing the doubt on Vi's face: 'I'll be quiet,' she added.

'Doubt you'll get anything today,' the charge nurse insisted. 'Patient's heavily medicated.'

'All the same,' Susan hoisted her bag onto her shoulder, took a decisive step forward. 'If you'll lead the way.'

*

Susan perched on the edge of a high-backed blue vinyl chair. Alongside her, Sheena Struthers lay, arms tethered loosely to machines by transparent tubing, a catheter snaking from under the bedclothes. On a stand by the bed, the drip that fed her body with nutrients ran to the cannula that was secured by a square of pink plaster to the back of Sheena Struthers' left hand. It curled loosely on the tight-fitted sheet, the ring finger decked, still, with diamonds. *Funny, that.* Susan was used to seeing bodies devoid of ornament. Except this woman wasn't dead, the DC had to remind herself, whatever the intent that had landed her here.

She extended a tentative forefinger and stroked the woman's face. There was no response. She repeated the movement, running her finger from cheekbone to chin, like you would a tiny baby. Sheena Struthers' skin was soft under her touch, but tinged with grey. And not moist, as you might expect, but paper-dry, a consequence perhaps of the hospital's hothouse temperature. Other than small furrows between the brows and a light wrinkling of the forehead, her face exhibited scant signs of ageing. Comes of leading a pampered life, Susan judged. For the nth time she speculated as to what had rendered Sheena comatose, and why.

Still in her mid-twenties, it was hard for Susan to understand what could have driven the woman to such desperation, more so since she appeared to lead a charmed life. Susan had seen it often enough in her short career: women so tired or so desperate they'd do anything to achieve oblivion. Not women like this, though. She eyed the white gold band, the engagement ring with its fat solitaire, the eternity band studded with brilliants. Couldn't be short of a bob or two, yet Sheena Struthers' life was so empty she'd wanted to end it.

Once in a while, one of Sheena's limbs would twitch. Her mouth might work, perhaps, or her eyelids flutter. Then, Susan would rise from the chair. She'd bend low over the bed. *Sheena*, she'd mouth, her lips against the woman's ear. And again, louder, *Sheena*. With all her mental strength, Susan willed the woman on the bed to waken. God knew what that bloody Douglas was up to, out there in the middle of the action, while she was stuck with this dame in an overheated room. A private room at that. It's alright for some.

Susan wondered if the husband had pulled strings to secure this privacy. Then she revised her thoughts. It was probably standard practice to put someone in a private room once they'd been discharged from ITU until they were strong enough to be moved to a ward.

She glanced up at the oversized clock on the wall. In accordance with hospital policy, she'd turned off her phone. Susan's shift had ended, so she was on her own time. But, determined to prove herself to her inspector, she resolved to give it another couple of hours.

She tried to snuggle down into the high-backed chair, but the plastic upholstery was unyielding.

Above her head, the drip plopped hypnotically.

Susan yawned.

It was going to be a long night.

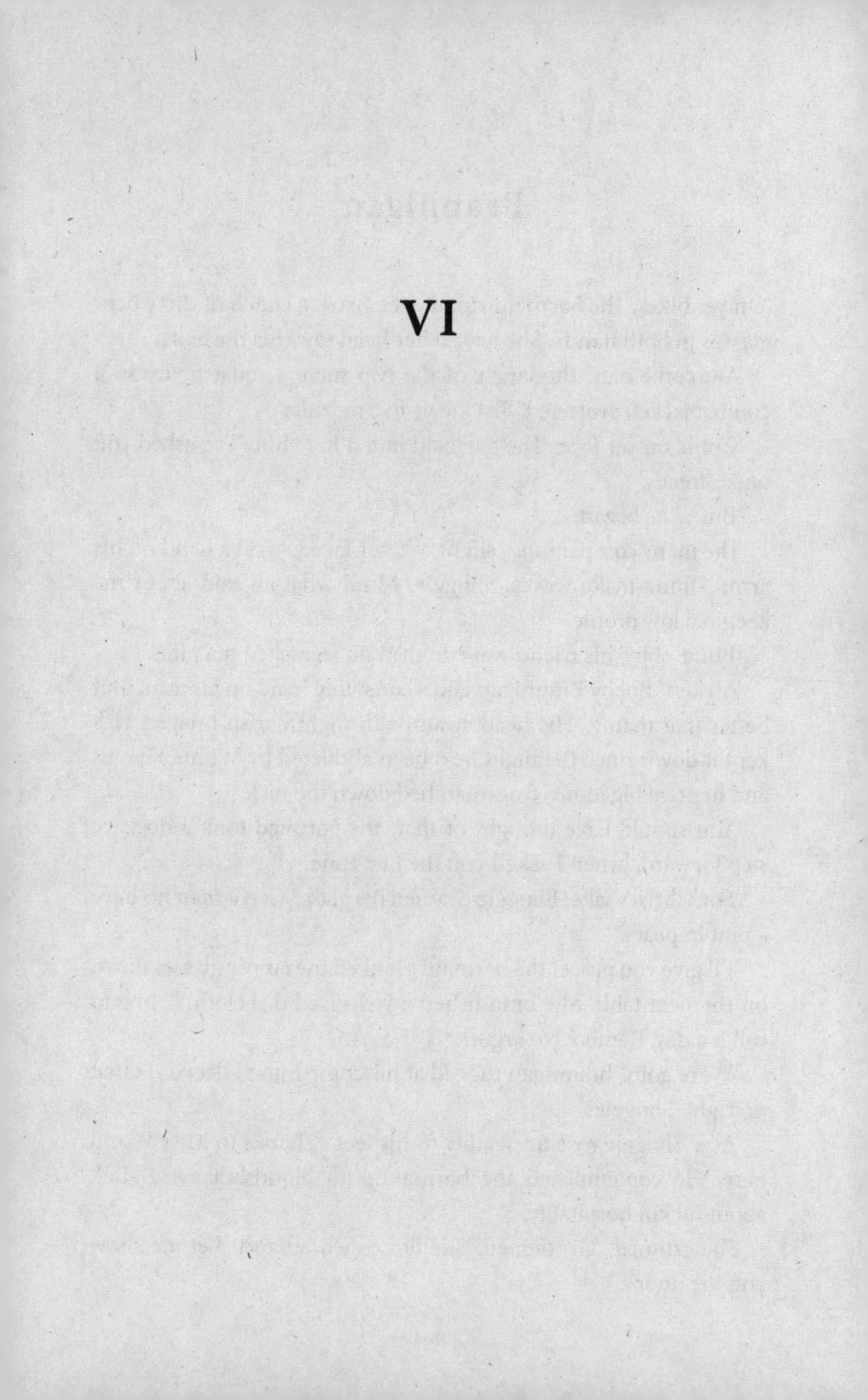

VI

Brannigan

'On yer bikes,' the barmaid stood, feet apart, a clutch of dirty beer glasses in both hands. She jerked her head towards the exit.

'Aw, come oan,' the larger of the two men, a squat figure in a combat jacket, protested. 'Jist gie us five meenits.'

'Come on yer face.' The barmaid jutted her chin. 'I've asked you once already.'

'But…' he began.

The man's companion – slight, weasel-faced – laid a hand on his arm. 'Dinna make waves, Shuggie. Mind what ah said aboot me keepin a low profile.'

'But, Bobby,' his friend wailed, 'ah'm no feenished ma pint.'

'Ah ken.' Bobby Brannigan laid a consoling hand on his arm. 'But better that than…' His head swam with nightmarish images. He's kept it down since the night he'd been abducted by Wilma Harcus and her two big loons, frog-marched down the nick.

'You should have thought of that,' the barmaid took a decisive step forward, 'when I asked you the first time.'

'For Christ's sake.' Shuggie drained his glass. 'Can a man no have a pint in peace?'

'I'll give you peace,' the barmaid plonked the empty glasses down on the next table. She brandished a well-used dishcloth. 'Time to call it a day, Rambo. No arguing.'

'We're goin.' Brannigan tugged at his companion's sleeve. 'Is that no right, Shuggie?'

'Aye.' Shuggie rose unsteadily to his feet. 'Thanks to Miss World here.' He contemplated the barmaid with bloodshot eyes. 'Talk about fuckin hospitality.'

She grinned. 'Gentlemen.' She flourished a hand. 'Let me show you the door.'

*

Eyes downcast, Bobby Brannigan weaved an uncertain path along the pavement. One outcome of consecutive years of Council cutbacks had been a rash of potholes and uneven paving slabs. Those, together with the hulking plastic refuse bins that sat abandoned at all angles and the black bin bags whose contents had been forensically dissected by marauding seagulls, made for slow progress.

Every few steps, he darted a nervous glance behind. Bobby had been on the point of asking Shuggie to chum him home, on the pretence of offering his pal a bevy. Thought better of it. Shuggie lived in the opposite direction. And, besides, it wouldn't do much for Bobby's reputation as a hard man. His bladder strained uncomfortably. He'd been caught short, was pissing in a shop doorway when the big private eye had nabbed him. He clenched his arse. Wouldn't make that mistake twice.

A haar had drifted in off the North Sea. It hung, heavy with moisture, blurring the outlines of the buildings, the kerb and the shop doorways. It smelled dank, raw, filling Bobby's nostrils and working its way under his shirt collar. Cursing, he hiked his jacket higher on his shoulders. Pinching his nostrils with the thumb and forefinger of one hand, he howked a gob of phlegm into the cupped palm of the other and wiped it on his trouser leg.

'Fucksake!' He tripped over a bag of takeaway cartons. Momentarily off-balance, he thrust out a hand to steady himself, hoping to find the wall. Instead, his fingers found something soft. Cloth, maybe. No, wool. Rough wool, like a…a…

'That yourself, Bobby?' A disembodied voice came out of the gloom.

'Wh-wha is it?' Bobby stuttered. His heart pounded. His mind ran like a steam train. He'd lain doggo since thon drugs trial. Seen no one. Said nothing to nobody. Well, no one except for thon fat cow with her dodgy recording gadget. And, he reassured himself, that was months ago.

'Never you mind.' The man in the balaclava took up position behind him. His words sounded ghostly, as if fragmented by the mist.

'Wh-what do you want?' Bobby stood stock still, literally petrified by fear.

'You, Bobby.' An arm locked around his throat. Before the blackness overwhelmed him, he glimpsed a flash of steel.

A Pro Job

'Jump to it.' Allan Chisolm drummed his fingers on the table. 'I haven't got all bloody day.'

From his workstation by the window, Douglas Dunn shot across the room. George Duffy followed at a more sedate pace. Chewing the last of his morning piece, Dave Wood lumbered to his feet. He joined Susan at the end of the table.

'Where's Burnett?'

'Said he had a meeting.'

'I'll *meeting* him,' Chisolm muttered. 'Whatever it is, this is way more important.'

His team waited, expectant.

Chisolm let them wait. After a few more moments, he spoke. 'By now, you'll all know that Bobby Brannigan was assaulted last night.'

There were nods and mutterings around the table.

'This was a life-threatening attack.'

'You thinking it was a hit, sir?' This from Dunn.

'It bears all the hallmarks: single wound to the throat…'

'Sounds like a pro job to me,' Wood interrupted.

Idle twat. Chisolm shot him a look. 'And you would know.'

'Can't have been that professional if the geezer's still in the land of the living.' This from Duffy.

'Could be the assailant was disturbed. From what I understand Brannigan had just come out the pub. Might have been other folk around.'

'Where's the motive?' Susan ventured in a small voice. As the most junior member of the team, she was still nervous about pushing herself forward.

Duffy snorted. 'He's a snitch.'

'Oh.' Susan's eyes widened. 'Whose?'

'Any bugger that will pay him,' Brian answered, coming into the room. 'Apologies, sir,' he directed to Chisolm. 'I was unavoidably detained.'

'You can explain later,' Chisolm snapped. 'Right now, I want you to fill DC Strachan in on our friend.'

Brian looked down the table. 'We reckon Brannigan was fingered by James Gilruth to throw a drugs trial. Happened before your time,' he elaborated, 'but the results were far-reaching: trial had to be abandoned at huge cost to the taxpayer, and two of our own,' he paused, 'including my best mate, were sent out into the cold.'

'Do you think Gilruth could have ordered a hit?' Susan asked, her eyes like saucers.

'It's not beyond the realms of possibility, though Brannigan hasn't been active, not for a long time.'

'So what could he have done,' she queried, 'to piss anyone off?'

'Except threaten to grass?' Douglas retorted. 'And re-open a can of worms some folk would rather leave shut.'

'Come on,' Brian interceded, 'Bobby Brannigan dropped totally below the radar until...'

'Your girlfriend outed him,' Dunn supplied.

Brian whirled in his seat. 'Don't you fucking dare.'

Douglas smirked. 'And from what I hear she's been turning the screw.'

'How would you...?' Brian started.

'Cut it,' Chisolm barked. 'What we do know is, these past few years, Mr Gilruth has been a picture of probity, his drug activities disguised behind a wall of respectability – a wall that he has defended with extreme care. Until, that is, his own son made a chink in that wall. It may be that the raid on his club was a wake-up call. All that adverse publicity.'

'And he knows we're frustrated that he's sent the son to the fucking Costa del Sol,' George Duffy added.

'He should be so lucky,' Dave Wood observed. 'Out of the frying-pan into the fire, I'd say.' The look on his face was more mournful than ever. 'They're nutcases, the most of them, down there.'

'Are you thinking that, combined with rumours of Brannigan's revised testimony, forced Gilruth's hand?' Duffy enquired.

'Doesn't sound sufficient reason to me,' Chisolm responded. 'But there's a lot we don't know where our friend Gilruth's concerned.'

'Has Bobby agreed to give a statement, then?' Wood asked. 'I thought we only had the tape recording them two wifies screwed out of him.' He chortled at his own joke.

'You're right.' Chisolm answered his question. 'We do, at present, only have a tape, improperly obtained. But I was on the cusp of bringing Brannigan in to try to get a formal statement out of him when the assault occurred.'

'With incentives, can we assume?' Douglas piped up.

Chisolm threw him an icy look. 'We can.'

'Bit of a coincidence,' Wood muttered darkly.

'Quite so. But, whatever the motive behind this attack, our first priority is to obtain that formal statement.'

'How do we manage that?' Douglas wanted to know. 'The guy's unconscious.'

'He might not make it,' Wood added, his expression glum.

'I have a twenty-four-hour guard on that man,' Chisolm pronounced, grim-faced. 'And I intend to get a statement out of him, come what may.'

A Farm Steading

The red Fiesta bumped its way down the rutted farm track. *Bastard!* Wilma swore under her breath as the undercarriage connected with something solid. She checked the rearview mirror as she changed down a gear. A large stone protruded from a tussock. Teeth clenched, Wilma scoured the way ahead. Ian had spent many of his days off doing running repairs. Clapped-out or no, he'd invested that much effort on keeping the vehicle roadworthy he'd kill her if she pranged it.

She'd had to take the assignment at short notice. In normal circumstances the case would have fallen to Maggie: the client a farmer who'd been defrauded in the sale of sheep. Maggie was familiar with farmers and their ways, unlike Wilma, a city girl born and bred. But early that morning Maggie had received a panicked phone call from that bloody Struthers woman. Wilma screwed up her nose in distaste. Another drama!

Wilma had hoped to get on the job at the double, catch the perp – a fellow farmer – before he was out and about. But the agency phone had rung off the hook and it was too early days, still, to let messages go unanswered for long. Then she'd decided she better stick on a washing. There couldn't have been any clean pants nor socks when Ian got up that morning. Not that he'd said, but she was on probation, still, after their estrangement.

Now, she negotiated a bend in the track. In a hollow stood a Victorian one-and-a-half storey cottage: four-paned sash windows either side of a deep-recessed door, two dormers jutting from a slate roof. No car, though it could be in the steading. Across a muddy yard, the outbuilding was in an advanced stage of dilapidation, doors hanging at an angle from rusted hinges, half the roof caved in. Wilma nosed the car into a corner and switched off the ignition.

Didn't bother to lock it in case she needed to make a rapid exit. Wrinkling her nose against the strong country smells, she crept across the yard, rapped smartly on the door. No answer. She peered in one window, then the other. Saw nothing other than cobwebs and an ancient chenille suite.

He might still be in bed. Unlikely, though, for a farmer. Or perhaps in the scullery. Cautiously, she made her way round the back. The kitchen was housed in a wooden extension, with a small window that offered sight of a red formica table and one of those 1950s cabinets with a pull-down zinc work surface. Wilma wondered if you'd get money for it. There was no sign of her man.

Wilma retraced her steps till she reached the steading. She pushed against one of the rickety doors. She half expected it to topple, but it swung open with a creak. The interior was in near darkness, the hole in the roof throwing the interior into shadowy relief. A tractor stood to one side. Even in the half light, Wilma could see it was decrepit. Alongside the vehicle, a range of implements lay scattered. There was nobody around. That much was obvious.

If you snooze you lose! Wilma cursed her tardiness. She turned to go. Then her curiosity got the better of her. If she'd wasted her morning, she might as well have a nosey before she headed home.

Through a carpet of matted straw, she picked her way towards the rear. She'd only advanced a few steps when she heard the noise: a soft snuffling at first, followed by a wet snort, then an angry bellow.

Christ! In a metal-railed pen, Wilma could just make out the haunches of a huge beast.

Fucking hell! She near shat herself, and that's before she clocked its big, hairy…

Heart racing, she backed away, tripped on the rusted blade of a scythe and toppled backwards onto the ground. For some moments she lay winded, thankful that her tumble had been cushioned by the straw.

Beneath her buttocks it felt reassuringly warm. And alarmingly wet.

She raised a hand to her face. Took a cautious sniff. Screwed up her nose. Sharn? Shite? No word could adequately describe the pungency of fresh manure.

Furious, she sat up.

Desperately, she beat at her back and thighs, trying to dislodge the gunk and straw that were clinging to her clothes. But that only seemed to make the mess worse.

Fuckit! She scrambled to her feet.

The beast – whatever it was – pawed the ground.

Wilma flinched as heavy hooves clattered against hard concrete, shrank from the sound of its heavy breath.

She turned and ran – out through the creaky door, across the muddy yard.

Bugger this! She vowed to stick to the city in future as, panting with exertion after her unaccustomed sprint, she reached the relative safety of her car.

Small Talk

'Mrs Gilruth?'

Yes?' The woman on the doorstep smiled, suggestively.

With a swift once-over, Brian took in the glossy black hair, the crimson lips, the hourglass figure. Not that this was necessary. Brian already knew Sharon Gilruth by sight. Christ, the whole of Aberdeen knew Sharon Gilruth by sight. If she wasn't strutting her stuff at some charity do or other, she was splashed all over the newspapers.

Sharon was a handsome woman. And sexy with it. He dragged his eyes away from her cleavage. 'DS Burnett and DC Dunn.' They showed their warrant cards. 'Is your husband at home?'

'Afraid not.' One knee bent, one hand on the door jamb, Sharon adjusted her pose.

Bloody hell! Brian's temperature soared. He'd never seen Sharon up close. This close. She was a hot piece of stuff, that's for sure.

His train of thought was broken by the sound of Dunn's voice. 'We're making enquiries about a serious assault that occurred last night in the Torry area of the city.'

Sharon's come-hither look morphed into one of acute suspicion. 'I don't see…'

'The victim has a connection to your husband,' Brian supplied.

Sharon's eyes narrowed. 'What sort of connection?'

'I'd rather not discuss it on the doorstep,' he parried. 'May we come in?'

'This isn't a good moment.' Sharon took a backward step and made to shut the door.

Dunn took a step forward. 'We won't take up much of your time.' He flashed a toothpaste smile. 'Save us disturbing you again.'

Brian followed his constable down the hallway, thankful, for once, of Dunn's forward nature. They were led into what Sharon described as 'the lounge', a vast space at the rear of the house decorated with enough braid and bullion fringe to stock a haberdashery store. Vast brocade sofas were heaped with plump cushions. An army of side tables twinkled with Swarovski crystal ornaments.

'Lovely room,' he lied, lowering himself onto one of the sofas.

'Thank you.' Sharon sat down opposite, crossing her legs provocatively. 'We like it.'

'Have you lived here long?' Dunn asked from his perch on a delicate side chair.

'A few years.' She smiled.

Brian cut to the chase. 'Does the name Brannigan mean anything to you?'

The smile turned to a frown. 'Should it?'

Brian pressed. 'You tell me.'

'I don't think so.' Defensive voice. 'Why?'

'We think Mr Brannigan may be on your husband's payroll.'

Sharon shrugged. 'My husband has loads of employees. Hundreds, in fact. I've never heard him mention anyone by that name.'

'Mrs Gilruth,' Dunn chipped in, 'am I right in thinking he works from home?'

'That's correct.'

'But he's not here at the minute?' He fixed Sharon with a searching look. The Rubislaw mansion was such that Gilruth could easily be closeted out of sight.

For an instant she hesitated, then: 'I thought you said you weren't going to be long.'

'We'll just be off,' Douglas responded smoothly, 'once you confirm Mr Gilruth is away from his office.'

Her eyes flashed. 'That's what I said.'

'When do you expect him home?' Brian enquired.

'Who knows?' She shrugged. 'He's away on business.'

'What did you say his business was?' Douglas Dunn jumped in.

Sharon shot him a hard look. 'I didn't.' Her expression softened a fraction. 'James has a wide range of business interests.'

'Would any of them be in Torry?' Brian insinuated.

'Definitely not,' she snapped.

'And you're positive you haven't heard the name Brannigan in connection with your husband?'

'Yes.' She faltered. Then: 'No.'

'Which is it?' Brian insisted.

'I'm not sure.' She turned her head away. 'Now you're confusing me.'

'Apologies for my colleague,' Douglas said, adopting his bedside voice.

Sharon turned back. 'That's okay. It's just, my husband doesn't like me getting involved in his business affairs.'

I'll bet! Brian had registered the way Sharon Gilruth clammed up the minute her husband's commercial enterprises were mentioned. I bet she has dirt on him, he mused, and plenty of it. Wouldn't like to be in his shoes if she ever takes umbrage. He suppressed a grin.

'We quite understand,' he said. 'This is a routine enquiry. No need for you to get upset.' He paused. 'I understand you do a lot of charity work.'

'Yes.' Sharon brightened. 'Not enough hours in the day.'

'And Mr Gilruth, does he have interests outside business? Golf? Shooting? That sort of thing?' Brian wondered if Gilruth kept guns in the house. And, if so, whether they were licensed…

'He doesn't have a lot of spare time but, yes, he plays the occasional round of golf.'

'Don't have the time myself,' Douglas quipped. 'Or the skill. I'd rather save my free days for a decent holiday.' He let the notion take seed, then: 'Do you have anything planned?' he asked.

Sharon took the bait. 'We're hoping to have a week in Spain sometime soon.' She smiled, coyly. 'That's if James can fit it in.'

'Will you be meeting up with your son?' Brian enquired, deadpan. 'Christopher, isn't it?'

Enough

'Sheena?'

The woman on the bed stirred. For a moment her eyes flickered, then half opened. She turned her head. Saw Susan. Frowned.

Susan leaned towards her. 'It's all right, Mrs Struthers,' she said in a soft voice. 'Don't be alarmed. My name's Susan. I'm a detective. I'd like to ask you a few questions.' She paused. 'If you feel up to it, that is.'

Slight nod.

'You know you're in hospital?'

Her eyes roamed the room. 'Yes.'

'Can you tell me how you came to be here?'

'No.' Sheena Struthers gave a small shrug. 'I've been trying to work it out in my head.' She squeezed her eyes shut, opened them again. 'But I can't remember.'

What's the last thing you recall, Sheena? Is it okay if I call you that?'

Another nod. 'Getting into bed.'

'On Thursday night, would that have been?'

Confused look. 'I don't know.'

'Well, just say it was, do you remember anything after that?'

Sheena yawned deeply. 'No.'

'What about waking up?' Susan prompted.

Shake of the head.

'Getting a cup of tea?'

'There's nothing.' She turned her back. 'Mind's a complete blank.'

Susan bunched her fists in frustration. This was going nowhere.

'Do you have any memory of coming to hospital?' She gave Sheena's shoulder a small shake.

There was no response.

'Sheena?' Susan stood up and leaned across the bed.

But Sheena Struthers had lapsed from consciousness.

*

The moment Sheena stirred, Susan leapt from her chair.

'You're awake,' she encouraged. 'That's good. I've just a couple of questions for you.'

Through filmy eyes, Sheena stared, uncomprehending.

'What's the first thing you saw after going to bed that night?'

Sheena scrunched her eyes shut. 'A doctor. He was changing the cannula to my other hand. It hurt.' She pulled a face. 'Must have woken me up.'

'Can we go back a little?' Susan asked. 'Your husband told us he usually brings you a cup of tea in the morning.'

'That's right.'

'And he must have done so on the morning of your accident, because our officers found a cup of tea by your bed. Thing is…' She watched Sheena Struthers keenly. 'The cup was half empty, so you must have drunk some of it.'

Sheena ruminated for a few moments, then: 'I suppose.'

'But you've no recollection of doing so, you say?'

'None at all.'

Susan changed tack. 'How would you describe your marriage?'

'We've been together over twenty years.' Sheena stated, her face devoid of expression.

Doesn't follow that the marriage is happy, Susan thought. She'd seen many a miserable pairing in the course of her work.

'Have you had any upsets lately?'

Evasive look. 'Don't know what you mean.'

'Rows? Hiccups?'

'Not that I can think of. Gordon's very even-tempered.'

'How about you?'

'I'm...' She hesitated. 'Pragmatic, I guess is the word. I tend to keep my own counsel. Like a lot of women, I suppose.'

Susan was wondering if this was a coded message, when: 'Is that all?' Sheena tugged the sheet up to her chin. 'I'd like to help you...' She broke off. 'What did you say your name was again?'

'Susan.'

'I'd like to help you, Susan, but I have absolutely no idea how I ended up here.' She grimaced. 'And I'm tired now, so...'

'I'll leave you to sleep.' Susan rose to her feet. 'Before I go, though, there's just one thing...'

Sheena lifted a drowsy face. 'Yes?'

'You came around earlier.'

'Did I? Don't remember.'

'And you said something.'

A look of utter panic swept over Sheena Struthers' face. Swiftly, she dispelled it. 'What might that be?' she queried.

'"Enough", you said.'

'Did I?'

'Yes. Can you tell me, Sheena, what you meant by that?'

Sheena's face darkened.

'Don't remember,' she muttered. 'I need to rest now.'

And she pulled the sheet up to cover her face.

Thainstone Mart

'Who'll give me two hundred? One hundred? Fifty, then, to get started? Fifty, I'm bid!' From his perch on the elevated metal dais, the white-coated auctioneer scanned the faces gathered around the ring. Behind him, an identically clad assistant kept a watchful eye. The two were flanked by a female clerk, her eyes glued to a computer screen.

With an annual turnover of over one hundred million, Thainstone Mart comprises a purpose-built complex of auction halls, stores and offices on the outskirts of Inverurie. With over five thousand members, the farmer-owned co-operative hosts a weekly Thursday sale of cast cows and bulls, prime cattle and sheep, and on Fridays, of young, store and breeding cattle and ewes. These are augmented by sales of fodder, plant and machinery, vehicles, furniture, and by farm displenish sales or roups.

Maggie had been to a fair few sales with her folks when they lived on the farm, though these had been at the old Kittybrewster Mart, a rather random collection of sheds on Aberdeen's Great Northern Road. The site had been redeveloped, now: new flats and neighbouring superstores. But she could still hear the scrunch of her dad's car tyres on gravel as they bumped over the unmade approach road, smell the two rank toilets that huddled in one corner, and taste the stovies that came, steaming, on a bendy paper plate from a makeshift kitchen.

Now, she sat in the tiered blue folding seats that rose behind the Thainstone auction ring. Following Wilma's unfortunate episode at Kemnay, Maggie had decided to resume control of the case. Farming was second nature to her, and she was determined to achieve a satisfactory outcome. One in the eye for Wilma; she wasn't the only one who could take on somebody bigger than herself and get a speedy result. Maggie allowed herself a quiet smile at the thought her business partner had been floored by a coo.

She'd decided the best way forward was to nail the subject on sale day. That way she was sure he'd be solvent. She scanned the rows of seats. Men of all ages, shapes and sizes, clad in quilted body-warmers, fleeces, Barbour jackets. A scattering of women. There was no sign of her man.

'Sold!' She was snapped out of her reverie by the crack of the auctioneer's gavel. Above his head, the screen flashed red, live-streaming details of the lot under the hammer: number, sex and age of the beasts, country of birth, breed of sire. Then the medical history and whether farm assured – this last, she knew, essential to meet supermarket criteria.

'Walk on!' She heard the familiar command of the yardsman in his blue coat and welly boots, as he brandished his stick at the sold beast's rump. On the other side of the dais, another beast snorted and nudged at the steel bars of the pen as it waited its turn to be led into the ring.

It was years since her dad had kept cattle, but it all came flooding back: the serene presence of the cows with their solid flanks and liquid brown eyes, the sweet smell of silage. With a pang, Maggie recalled the day her folks held their own roup: the household goods in the yard, the machinery laid out in rows in the field. The anticipation as the auctioneer sought a vantage point on a chair or tractor, the poignancy of dismantling a lifetime's toil.

How Maggie wished, now, she'd offered her mum and dad more support. Decisively, she dismissed the thought. Wasn't it always the same, the way a woman was pulled in two different directions – that constant tug-of-love between husband and child, parent and family, even one sibling and another?

Concentrate! Maggie turned her attention to the potential bidders. Perched on moulded blue plastic stools, the weather-reddened faces at the ringside were a study in fierce deliberation, broken only by the occasional quip out the side of a mouth. Bids were hard to spot: a raised eyebrow, a barely perceptible lift of the chin. Maggie indulged in a quiet chuckle. This lot could teach a poker school a thing or two.

She'd inveigled her way into the office, established her man's consignment was Lot No. 137. Now all she had to do was wait. Lot 100 came and went. 110. 120. The auctioneer rattled through the lots. Maggie followed with her eyes the new arrivals in the hall. Lot 130. 135. 137. She sat forward in her seat.

The bidding was sluggish at first: one man wearing a lovat green jersey with shoulder and elbow patches leaned on the ringside opposite, one hand on the railing, his little finger flicking bids. Another sat in the seats high up. He raised a catalogue to show intent. And then she saw him. He was standing just inside the doorway, his face partly obscured by a checked scarf.

The bids crept upwards, so slowly Maggie feared they wouldn't meet the reserve. And then what? She caught her breath. She'd have spent time and petrol for nothing.

A new bidder, this time on the seats below her, though Maggie could only see the back of his head and the auctioneer's acknowledgement. Her eyes glued to the action, she observed another couple of bids. Then they stalled.

'I'm sorry, that's a pass.' The auctioneer jotted a note.

Damn and blast! So much for the Mart's guaranteed same-day payment. Half Maggie's day had been wasted. In her head she totted up the cost to the agency. And that didn't factor in Wilma's wee adventure.

As the beasts were led out, Maggie caught a movement. Her man had turned and was pushing through the exit.

She leapt to her feet, skittered down the steps and followed. She was just in time to see him huddled in the near corner in conversation with another man.

There was a brief nod of the head, a shuffling of hands, a roll of banknotes. So her guy had done a deal on the side. Maggie cursed herself for being so slow on the uptake, for many a transaction was effected outside the sale hall to avoid paying the Mart's commission. For just a moment she felt sorry for the man. High levels of indebtedness among farmers were widespread, she knew, farm suicides not uncommon. Her man had likely been driven by financial difficulty to perpetrate the fraud she was investigating. He'd just sold his beasts for less than they were worth. And he wouldn't be alone.

Still, she reminded herself, fraud is fraud.

She watched as the two shook hands.

The target turned.

Made to walk away.

Maggie moved like a bullet.

'Got a minute.' She tugged at his sleeve. 'There's a wee something we have to discuss.'

Stay With It

'Get this midden cleared up,' Chisolm gestured to the half-finished coffee cups and empty water bottles that littered the table. 'No. Not you,' he growled as Susan stepped forward. 'Whoever made the fucking mess.' He eyed the male members of his squad.

Murmurs of dissatisfaction accompanied the men's reluctant movements.

When the table was cleared of debris, Chisolm sat down.

'Where are we at with Brannigan?'

'Not looking good, sir.' Douglas was first off the mark as usual. 'He's been in and out of theatre. They're not saying much. But what I can tell you,' he paused theatrically, for all the world like a seasoned politician, 'is that in the course of the attack his windpipe was severed.'

'Windpipe's repairable,' Duffy said with a satisfied smirk. 'Most times, anyhow.'

'I'll hand you that,' Douglas came back. 'But it still gives us a problem.'

'How's that?' Duffy walked right in.

Wood beat Douglas to it. 'Fucker canna speak,' he drawled, a look of grim satisfaction on his face.

'Bang goes our statement.' Chisolm slumped in his seat. 'I'll stand down the twenty-four-hour guard. But I want regular updates on Brannigan's condition.' He squared his shoulders. 'Make sure I get them, Burnett.'

'Sir.'

'Susan, what's the latest on Sheena Struthers?'

'Not much progress there, I'm afraid. So far, all I've managed to get out of her is general chat. Nothing specific, not even what she remembers of the hours leading up to her hospitalisation.'

'Which is?'

'Zilch, according to her. Insists she has no memory of events after she went to bed the previous night.'

'It might equally testify to the fact the woman is still heavily medicated.'

'Mmm.' Chisolm steepled his fingers. 'What about the husband? Has she said anything on that?'

'I've raised the question of the marriage, sir. She's pretty non-committal. Pleads exhaustion when I try to draw her out.'

'So we're still some way from a formal statement.'

'I'd say so.' Susan hung her head. She'd have given anything to shout success in front of these hard-nosed bastards. 'Sorry, sir,' she added, somewhat lamely.

'Stay with it, Strachan.' For once, Chisolm looked kindly. 'Get yourself up there when you get the chance. Sometimes, perseverance is all. However,' he looked down the table, 'seems like we're not going to get a result in either of these cases. Not anytime soon.'

'There is just one thing, sir,' Susan ventured. 'Sheena Struthers did say something. Patient was drowsy at the time so it could be nothing,' her voice tailed off.

'Out with it,' Chisolm encouraged.

'She said "enough".'

'Enough what?' Duffy demanded with a cheeky grin. 'Tea? Gin?'

'Mebbe she's had enough of marriage,' Dave Wood chipped in, his face dour. 'I know I fucking have.'

'Maybe it's her has a fancy man on the side.' Duffy again.

'As I said,' Susan rushed to defend her position, 'it could be nothing. Only...'

All eyes were upon her.

'When I pressed her about it she became quite defensive. Agitated, is the word I'd use.'

'Can you be more specific?' Chisolm asked.

Susan shrugged. 'Not really.'

'Oh, come on,' Douglas rounded on her. 'What sort of "agitated"?

Excited? Distressed? Scared?'

Inwardly, Susan cursed. Her chance to shine and she'd blown it. She drew a calming breath. 'All of those, I'd say.'

Time We Saw Someone

'Nic?' Ros sank onto the sofa and kicked off her shoes.

'Yup?' His eyes didn't move from the television.

'I've been thinking…'

His head swivelled.

'Don't you think it's time we saw someone?'

'What d'you mean?'

'Counselling.' Ros felt the colour start to rise to her face. She raised a hand to her cheek. Felt the heat. Wondered when she'd started blushing, something she never used to do. 'Doesn't have to be heavy. Just an informal chat.'

He took hold of her hand. 'You having me on?'

'I'm serious.' She pulled away.

'What brought this on?'

'Nothing.' She was flustered now. 'Not one thing, anyway. More a whole lot of little things.'

'Like?'

'Like, we seem to row all the time.'

'Darling.' He draped an arm around her shoulder. 'Don't exaggerate.'

She set her chin. 'I'm not.'

'Yes, you are. Tell me the last time we had a fight.'

'Last night.'

'That wasn't what I'd call a fight.'

Ros took a deep breath. 'I disagree.'

'So…' He removed his arm. 'We have a minor disagreement over a matter of domestic minutiae and you feel the need to involve a third party, am I right?'

'Don't make it sound so trivial,' she shot back.

Smug look. 'That's because it is.'

'It's not.' Her cheeks flamed. 'It's important. To me, anyhow.'

He smirked. 'So I see.'

'Why are you always putting me down, Nic?'

'Am I? Wasn't aware of it.'

'I don't believe you. Ever since…' She broke off. 'You're forever finding fault. I feel as if…' She struggled to make sense of the thoughts that were tumbling in her head. 'These days I can't seem to do anything right.'

'Ah…' He nodded sagely. 'Now we're getting to it.'

'Getting to what.'

'The real reason for this outburst.'

She sat back, perplexed. 'Are we?'

'Ever since Max was born, I think you were going to say. And you're right, Ros. Since the baby arrived you *have* been a bit unhinged.'

Her shoulders sagged. So it really was all her fault.

'But don't let it get to you,' he went on. 'I've talked to people…'

'What people?'

'Colleagues. Medical professionals. Seems it's pretty common, post-natal depression, especially with a first child.'

'It's been over a year, Nic.' She fought to keep her voice even. 'And, anyhow, what makes you think it's depression?'

'Well, you have been…are…a bit…' He considered for a moment. 'Paranoid.'

'Is that what you'd call it?' She uttered a shrill laugh. 'Well, you're not the only one who has colleagues to talk to. The people I've discussed it with put it down to exhaustion.'

'Ah.' He assumed a knowing look. 'Sounds like your new friend has been putting ideas in your head.'

'It's not that at all. If you must know, I went to see your precious GP. He said it was nervous exhaustion too.'

Nic patted her knee. 'We're both worn out, if the truth be told. Comes of trying to maintain full-time jobs whilst we're raising a child.'

'*We?*' she seethed. When had Nic ever put himself out in the nursery department?

Bang on cue, the baby alarm crackled into life.

Sod it! Ros dragged herself to her feet and trudged up the stairs in her stocking soles.

In his cot, Max struggled to free himself from the confines of his bedclothes, legs kicking, face purple with exertion.

'There.' She bent to pull back the covers. 'There.'

She picked him up, took a judicious sniff of his nappy, then clasped his hot little body to her breast. He smelled of vanilla, talcum powder. All things sweet. Ros remembered, then, a farmer friend of her father's, a man of few words. He'd been talking about silage. *So sweet you could eat it yourself,* he'd enthused. She'd been touched by the comment at the time. A man's man, but with a romantic streak. Like her dad. She wondered where that left Nic?

Ros carried the small bundle downstairs.

'What's up?'

'He's not long fed. Doesn't need changed.' She sat down again. 'Probably just looking for attention.'

'Bit like mum,' Nic observed. Then: 'Joke.'

She buried her head in the baby's neck.

'But, yes,' he added. 'To continue where we left off…'

Too tired to argue, Ros sat there, defeated.

'You're quite right. It probably is time we saw someone.'

Hardly daring to believe her ears, she raised her head.

Nic cupped her chin. 'A specialist, perhaps. After all, Ros, your mental health is every bit as important as your physical wellbeing.'

A Big Ask

Maggie wasn't long out the shower when the doorbell rang. Must be the window cleaner. This week, she'd finally squeezed time out of her jam-packed schedule to address domestic matters.

She scrambled into a torn pair of jeans she'd saved for doing housework and tugged a baggy jumper over her head. Grabbing her purse, she made a beeline for the front door.

Allan Chisolm stood on the doorstep. His eyes swept the dishevelled clothes, the tousled hair. 'Have I got you out of bed?' he asked, an amused look on his face.

Maggie bristled. 'No.' Instinctively, one hand reached up to smooth her curls. 'I've chores to tackle, that's all.'

His expression grew serious. 'I'm sorry to land on you like this, but I wondered if I could have a word?'

Not again! Maggie felt like a schoolgirl summoned to detention. What was it about the man that always had her on the back foot?

'Of course.' She composed herself. 'Come in.' She stepped aside to let him pass, shut the door and led him into the front room.

'May I?' Without waiting for an answer, Chisolm lowered himself onto the settee. 'It's about Sheena Struthers.'

'Oh.' Small voice. That was one place Maggie definitely didn't want to go.

'I'll be honest with you, Mrs Laird.' He made himself comfortable. 'We've reached something of an impasse in our investigation.' He looked for a reaction, found none. 'I rather hoped you might help us move forward.'

'In what way?' Maggie perched on the edge of the big chair in the window.

'Put some flesh on the bones of our findings. From the statement you gave at Queen Street, I understand you had several meetings with Mrs Struthers before she…' He eyed Maggie circumspectly. 'Before the incident.'

'I did, yes.'

'And at that time you stated you were of the opinion the lady was, shall we say, misguided?'

'I thought she was imagining things.'

'Did you at any point think her state of mind would lead her to attempt suicide?'

'No.'

'Turning to the husband, you also pursued enquiries there?'

'Yes. As I informed your officer, I ran what were fairly limited checks on Gordon Struthers' movements, but found nothing to substantiate his wife's claims.'

'In short, he had no reason to make an attempt on her life.'

'None that I could establish.'

'Nor was she, in your stated opinion, sufficiently distraught to make an attempt on her own?'

'Mrs Struthers exhibited varying levels of anxiety. I suggested she seek medical advice,' Maggie answered defensively. 'I understand she did so. I doubt this takes you forward, but…' She broke off.

'No matter.' Allan Chisolm made to rise. 'I'll let you get on.' There was a twinkle of merriment in the clear blue eyes. 'With whatever.'

'While you're here…' How Maggie wished, now, she was properly dressed and made up. 'Can I press you on George's…' She flushed. 'My husband's case?'

Chisholm leaned back again. 'I did raise it again only last week. I'm sorry to tell you the impression I got is they'd like it to go away. I'll be straight with you. When I first took it upstairs, they seemed amenable to the idea. Indeed, the ACC himself said if I could deliver the goods – in the shape of a formal, signed admission from Craigmyle that he'd turned off that tape recorder, and from Brannigan that he'd been coerced into giving perjured evidence – they'd be willing to re-examine the circumstances surrounding your husband's departure from the force. That case was a blot on

Aberdeen's resolution rate, after all, and it would be mighty satisfying to put the record straight. However...' He shifted uncomfortably. 'This last couple of meetings, I get the impression the thinking has changed. Too much time has passed, Mrs Laird. There's little appetite to reopen old wounds.'

'I know. Nonetheless...'

Chisolm cut her short. 'If I were to present them with a *fait accompli* in the form of Craigmyle's statement, that might concentrate minds. Are you in a position yet to obtain that?'

'No. There's been a development in that quarter. A setback actually.' She broke off, a defeated look on her face.

'Well, in that event...'

Maggie strained forward. 'If you could put some pressure on.' She looked into the inspector's eyes. 'Persuade the powers-that-be to pull Bobby Brannigan back in...' She held his gaze. 'That would get the ball rolling.'

'That's a big ask, Mrs Laird.' The blue eyes didn't waver. 'It had been my firm intention to do so. But that was before this latest turn of events.'

'I don't quite...' Maggie began.

'You haven't heard?' Chisolm's mind raced. He'd been under the impression Maggie Laird's business partner had her ear to the ground at Foresterhill. But he'd also heard a rumour that Big Wilma, as she was referred to at Queen Street, was back in Torry, and that the partnership had been dissolved.

He collected his thoughts. 'I'm sorry to be the bearer of bad tidings. Bobby Brannigan was attacked in the street earlier this week.'

'Oh!' Maggie put a hand to her mouth. She slumped back in her seat. 'How serious?'

'It's touch and go. He's out of surgery. They've put him in an induced coma. According to his consultant, he's likely to stay that way for quite some time.'

'Will he recover, do you think?'

Chisolm offered a grim smile. 'I hope so.'

'Me too.' Maggie offered up a silent prayer.

'I should warn you, Mrs Laird,' Chisolm added. 'There is extensive damage to Mr Brannigan's vocal chords.'

Maggie felt sick. She couldn't meet his eyes.

'Even if he does survive the attack, he may be unable to speak.'

A Mobile Phone

'What are you doing?' Ros stopped mid-stride as she came through the sitting room door.

'Nothing.' Nic dropped the phone as if it was red-hot. It fell with a clatter onto the coffee table.

Ros crossed the room, snatched it up. 'Have you been checking my mobile?' she demanded.

'No, of course not.'

'Then why is your face bright red?'

'Is it?' He checked his reflection in the mirror above the fireplace. 'Must have been from running at lunchtime.'

'You didn't say you were going running.'

'And you didn't ask.' Casually, he ambled to her side. 'What is this? The third degree?'

'Makes a change.' Sarky voice. 'It's usually the other way around.'

'Come on.' Reluctantly, she was pulled into an embrace. 'Just because I pick up your phone doesn't mean I'm checking up on you. If you must know, I had a meeting cancelled at the last minute. Thought I'd take a quick run to clear the cobwebs, then nip home and have a tidy round. Give you a surprise.'

'You did that, right enough,' she retorted. 'Just as well I came back for it.'

'Ros.' He gave a squeeze. 'Don't you think you're being a bit…?'

'If you say "paranoid" one more time…'

'Hasty,' he squeezed harder, 'was the word I had in mind.'

'As hasty as you jumping in that last time I was on the phone to Fi? Wanting me to switch to speakerphone so you could listen in?'

'Not listen in, silly. I thought you were arranging something – a jolly. I was keen to be part of the conversation, that's all.'

'Since when? You don't have a good word to say for Fiona. She's too bloody…' She groped for the right word. 'Self-sufficient for you.'

Nic grinned. 'She is a bit ballsy, agreed, but I like that in a woman.'

'Just not in this woman, is that it?'

Blank look. 'Don't know what you're talking about.'

'What I'm talking about…' She wriggled free of his embrace. 'Is…before we met…' She held his gaze. 'I *was* that woman. Not as bolshie as Fiona, I'll grant you, but strong and self-confident and independent-minded all the same. And since we married, I've lost all that. You've systematically ground me down, Nic, with your petty criticisms. Picked me apart.' She fought back tears. 'To the extent I've completely lost sight of who I am.'

'Oh, babes.' He reached for her hand. 'Don't take it to heart like that.'

She batted him away. 'How the hell do you expect me to take it when you put me down in front of our friends, my family, your colleagues even?'

'It's only meant as a bit of fun.'

'Fun?' she shrilled. 'Right. It's been a bundle of fun. Since we moved here. For as long as I can bloody remember.'

He shrugged. 'I didn't realise it made you that unhappy.'

'No? You only have to look at your own family: the way they live in their own little bubbles.'

'There's no need to bring my family into this.'

'No? They're dysfunctional, Nic. And you're the product of that, can't you see? It's history repeating itself. And it sure isn't the way I want to live my life, nor bring up my child.'

'Huh!' he sneered. 'Now you're playing the baby card.'

'Max!' Her eyes widened in alarm. 'What time do you make it?'

He glanced at his wrist. 'Oh, Christ! We're late.'

'I'll go.' Ros lunged for her bag.

'No, me. I'll be quicker.' He made a dash for the door.

A Misdemeanour

Maggie was working her way through a mound of ironing when her mobile rang. She scrabbled in a tangle of washing for her phone. 'Maggie Laird.'

'Bill Cowie here. I'm duty desk sergeant at Police Scotland Headquarters here in Aberdeen.'

'Oh.' She racked her brains, but couldn't conceive what could have prompted the call.

'Can you confirm Colin George Laird, a student at Robert Gordons, is your son?'

Maggie's knees buckled. Letting go of the iron, she sank to the floor.

'He is.' Disembodied voice.

'Then you'd better come down to the station. He's got himself in a bit of bother.'

She fought for breath. 'What sort of bother?'

'When my officer searched him, he was found to be in possession of a quantity of cannabis.'

'A quantity, you say?'

'Don't worry, it was a very small amount.'

'Then, surely…' Maggie began.

On the other end of the line she swore she could hear a chuckle. 'If you're going to tell me they've all tried a spliff at his age I'd have to agree with you.'

'In that case,' Maggie recovered herself, 'I take it you won't be charging him.' Livid as she was with Colin, she wouldn't give a single one of those bastards at Queen Street – with the possible exception of Brian – the satisfaction of further sullying the Laird name.

There was a long pause, then: 'It's not as straightforward as that.'

Her pulse raced. 'You've just said it was a small amount. And you've accepted it was for his own use. So what's the problem?'

'The problem...' Another silence ensued. 'Is that your son was apprehended in the perpetration of a theft.'

'A theft?' Maggie repeated, dumbfounded. Colin might try her patience, but he knew right from wrong. 'What of?'

'Centre caps from a car.' The sergeant cleared his throat. 'A very expensive car.'

'Where did this happen?'

'The West End.'

Little sod! Maggie made a point of giving Colin money for a hot meal at lunchtime, more so since she was often late home. The idea that he was roaming the city squandering her hard-earned cash on who-knows-what made her see red.

She tried to think straight. 'Was he alone when he committed this...'

Cowie came to her rescue. 'We'll call it a misdemeanour.' He added ominously, 'For now. And, no, your son wasn't alone. We've one of his pals here and all.'

Maggie closed her eyes.

If only George were alive, he'd know what to do.

There was a smell of burning.

She blinked her eyes open and dropped the phone, lunged for the iron and slid it safely into its holder. On the ironing board, a new Next blouse bore a large triangular singe mark.

Dammit to hell! She'd only bought the blouse a couple of weeks before, a treat to herself to glam up an old trouser suit.

'Sergeant Cowie?' She picked up her phone. 'Are you still there?'

'Aye.' Patient voice.

'What happens now?'

'Depends.'

'On what?'

'I doubt we'll take any action on the possession,' another chuckle, 'other than tear your lad off a strip. The vandalism, however...' He was serious, all of a sudden. 'That's another matter. Once we've spoken to the vehicle's owner...'

'How long will that take?'

'I can't say. They can sometimes be difficult to get hold of. But, after that, we'll establish if he wants to press charges.'

Maggie tried to make sense of it. 'Am I right in saying you've recovered these...caps?'

'Correct.'

'Then...'

'That makes no difference. At the end of the day, the charging decision's up to the owner. So, as I've said, best you get yourself down here, Mrs Laird. As you can imagine, your lad's in a bit of a state.'

He's in a state? Maggie raged. She was a quivering wreck.

Slipping into PI mode, she gave it one last go. 'The car owner, you said "he", so I take it we're talking about a gentleman?'

'We are.'

'Is he local, may I ask?' Long shot, but it might be somebody she knew. Knew of. Anything to get Colin out of this mess.

'He is.' The silence that followed was so prolonged Maggie thought she'd been disconnected. Finally, the sergeant's weary voice: 'Our records have identified him as Mr James Gilruth.'

Back to Square One

'Brannigan.' Chisolm scanned the room. 'Give me an update.'

'No change in his condition, sir,' Duffy answered. 'I checked with ARI first thing this morning.'

'Struthers case.' Chisolm moved swiftly on.

This was met by groans of dismay. His team had invested way too many man-hours on the bloody woman, their backlog of newer cases was building up, and there was no end in sight.

'Right, guys, what have we got that's new and exciting?'

'Fuck all.' Dave Wood was his usual cheery self.

'You first, DC Strachan. What's the latest? Is Sheena Struthers ready to give us a statement yet?'

'No, sir. Sorry. I've sat at the bedside for hours on end, but the patient is phasing in and out, only comes to for a few minutes at a time, so I haven't been able to do any real questioning. She's still hooked up to a whole load of stuff.' Her face was earnest. 'Plus, there's a real targer in charge of the ward.'

'Don't give us that po-face,' Douglas Dunn sneered. 'I'm sure there's charm lurking in there somewhere.'

Chisolm ignored this. 'Husband been in?'

'I'll say. He visits first thing in the morning, and comes back in after work.'

'First impressions?'

'Devoted. Sits holding her hand. Won't leave at night till they throw him out.'

'True love,' Wood muttered with a curl to his lip.

'Sounds like he's desperate to get her back,' Burnett observed. He knew only too well what it was like to live on one's own.

'Either that or terrified she'll come round and spill the beans,' George Duffy chipped in.

'Well, stay on it, Strachan.' Chisolm threw Susan an encouraging glance. To Douglas, he said only, 'DC Dunn, I have your report. I need nothing more from you.' Sharp look. 'For now. How did the interview go, Burnett?'

'Good, sir.' Brian swelled, seeing a chance to redeem himself in his superior's eyes. 'Struthers had his solicitor present. Savvy bugger. Up to all the tricks.'

'And?' Impatient voice.

'Dunn raised some financial question marks that might give Struthers a motive. Might be worth digging deeper.'

'We'll return to that. But first I want to discuss the latest from the lab. We asked ARI to test for a whole range of substances.' He consulted a folder. 'They've all tested negative.'

A ripple of disappointment ran round the table.

'Where do we go from here?' Susan asked.

'Back to square one,' Dave Wood muttered dolefully.

'You're a negative bastard, Wood, you know that?' Duffy nudged his colleague in the ribs.

He responded in kind. 'What do you suggest then, smartass?'

'We need to think outside the box, that's what.' Chisolm scraped back his chair. He rose to his feet. 'What do we know?' His arm shot out, finger pointing straight at Duffy.

Douglas pondered for a moment, then: 'Attempted suicide-slash-murder?'

'Before that?' Chisolm started pacing round the table.

'Susan?' he stopped behind his DC.

She craned her neck. 'An unconscious woman?'

Chisolm moved on. 'With what in her bloodstream? Wood?' He stopped again, tapped his sergeant on the shoulder.

'Zopiclone.'

'And?' Chisolm completed the circuit of his squad.

There was total silence.

'We know what isn't present.' He resumed his seat. 'This little lot.' He opened the topmost file and waved the test results in the air.

'The lab has screened for every common substance you can imagine. So now,' he stuffed the sheets back into the file, 'I'm asking you to address the uncommon, the esoteric…' He paused. 'The fucking obscure.'

Wood ducked his head, Duffy wrinkled his brow, Dunn doodled furiously on his notepad. Susan looked towards DS Burnett for inspiration. Brian looked away.

'Wake up!' Chisolm banged the flat of his hand on the table. 'What substance wouldn't you expect to find in the bloodstream of a middle-aged, middle-class married woman?'

Nobody answered.

'*Think*! Is there something we haven't tested for? Something we can't test for?' He scanned the bowed heads. 'DC Dunn?'

Douglas's head shot up.

'You're the one with the university degree. Put your tiny brain cells to work.'

For once Douglas was lost for words.

'Well?' A muscle worked in Chisolm's jaw.

Desperately, Douglas looked to his colleagues for support. One after another they averted their eyes.

Finally: 'Rohypnol?' The question in his voice suggested the answer was more in hope than expectation.

Dave Wood gave a hoot of derisive laughter. Duffy looked quickly away. The other two watched and waited for Chisolm's reaction.

'Don't mock,' he responded, to Dunn's audible sigh of relief. 'Flunitrazepam, also known as Rohypnol, is rapid onset and has a short half-life. It metabolizes rapidly, so is undetectable after a short period of time.'

'There's one problem, though.' Dunn moved to redeem himself. 'It has been banned for medical use in the UK since 2016.'

'Point taken. But it could have been illicitly sourced or old stock.'

'Even so,' Dunn persisted, 'the blue dye that's put into it now will appear if it's added to any drink. Unless the liquid is very dark in colour. If we're trying to stick this on the husband, that rules out the wife's morning cuppa.'

'If the drug was purchased on the internet,' Chisolm countered, 'generic versions don't necessarily have the dye.'

'True, sir.'

'Then again, he could have used GHB. That's colourless and odourless and has an even shorter half-life.' Chisolm steepled his fingers. 'So, humour me, you lot. If we run with this hypothesis, is it likely this outwardly respectable woman would have self-medicated such drugs?'

'Categorically not, sir.' Douglas was back on form. 'Sheena Struthers had the means, though I'd have to qualify that. A woman of her…' He hesitated. '…age group, almost certainly wouldn't have had the knowledge.'

'Five bags, full, sir,' Duffy muttered under his breath.

'What was that?'

'She could have Googled it, sir,' he said.

'I'll continue, then, if I may,' Douglas said portentously. 'She had the opportunity. Turning to the husband, Gordon Struthers had the means, he had the motive, and he had ample opportunity. He…'

Chisolm held up a hand. 'Let me stop you there.'

'Wh-what…?' Douglas's mouth turned down. He didn't relish being halted mid-flow.

'If we're pointing the finger at the husband, we'll need a lot more than that to build a case.'

There was a general murmur of assent.

'So. Actions. We have to look again at Gordon Struthers' movements that morning, see how far he can back them up. Burnett, I want you to go over his statement with a fine-tooth comb. Duffy, you talk to the lab, see what they can do. Strachan, get back up to the hospital. Use all your feminine skills to get into Sheena Struthers' head. Wood, get hold of that cleaner. Again, pin her movements down to the wire. Dunn, the financial irregularities Burnett flagged up, see what else you can find.'

'Bit difficult, sir, without a warrant.'

'We don't have a hope in hell of getting that,' Brian retorted. 'But Gordon Struthers is hiding something, I feel it in my bones.'

'Then apply some pressure,' Chisolm said briskly. 'Interview him again. Create a timeline of his movements. The time frame is critical if we're to make a case. Pin him down to the last second, if you can.'

'If we could only get into his computer,' Douglas mused. Brazenly, he eyed Brian. 'Fancy asking if he'd give us a look-see?'

Brian snorted. 'In your dreams.'

'Don't ask, don't get,' Duffy added. 'If he's nothing to hide, he might agree, just to get us off his back.'

'It's worth a go,' Chisolm decided. 'But, remember: kid gloves. We're talking voluntary surrender. It's critical we make the right call.'

'Sir.'

There was a stir in the room, as the team gathered papers together and made to leave.

'Before you leave.' Chisolm held up a hand. 'A word of caution. I know you're all frustrated that we've made so little progress on this one. But before you go rampaging, keep in mind that we're working on a hypothesis here. And that's all it is.' He ran a hand across his brow. 'Before I can take it upstairs, we need to be one hundred per cent sure there's criminal activity involved and, what's more, if Gordon Struthers is culpable, that the wife is not in any way implicated. Plus, we'll need a load of solid evidence before they'll sanction seizing mobile phones, what have you. You've already heard Struthers' solicitor is on the ball. So tread warily.' He broke off. 'It's important we're sure-footed around this one.'

A Different Complexion

'Brian.' Maggie dropped a kiss on his cheek. 'I'm so pleased to see you. Thanks for coming along at such short notice.'

They were in Marks & Spencer's cafe, the closest Maggie could get to Queen Street without risking contact with those senior officers who'd ended her husband's career.

'You said it was an emergency.' Sceptical, he rubbed at an imagined lipstick mark. 'I dropped everything. Nipped out as soon as I could.' He sat down beside her. 'What's this all about?'

'Haven't you heard?'

Frown. 'No. Should I?'

'It's Colin.'

'What about him?'

'He's been nicked.'

Brian's eyebrows shot up. 'What for?'

'Theft.' Her chin trembled. 'That, and possession.'

He cocked his head. 'You're having me on.'

'No.' Tears welled in her eyes. 'Wish I was.'

'Take deep breaths.' He extended a hand. 'In…out…and again.'

Maggie felt the thudding of her heart, the warmth of the strong hand pressed to her chest. Couldn't decide which disturbed her more.

'Now.' Brian's hand dropped to his side. 'Tell me, when did this happen?'

'Lunchtime today. It was your desk sergeant rang me, asked me to come in.'

'And did you?'

'Yes. Straight away. I asked Sergeant Cowie to ring upstairs, see if you were around…'

'Sorry.' He shrugged an apology. 'I was in a meeting. Only just got finished.'

'Anyhow, it transpires Colin and another boy were on their lunch break when one or other of them had the bright idea to nick some badges off a car.'

Brian grinned. 'Sounds familiar.'

'Don't laugh,' Maggie snapped. 'It's not funny.'

His face straightened. 'What happened then?'

'Uniform caught them red-handed. Then, when they emptied their pockets, didn't the eejits have the makings of a couple of spliffs?'

'Classic.' Brian smothered a smile. 'But you said Colin had been nicked. Have they actually laid charges?'

'No. Cowie said it was up to the car owner.'

'Well, then, you've nothing to worry about. There's no way that's going to happen.'

'That's just it.' The tears welled again. 'The car belongs to James Gilruth.'

'Christ!' Brian's eyes looked like they were going to pop out of their sockets. 'That puts a different complexion on the thing altogether.'

'I know. That's why I was so desperate to find you, Brian.' She clasped his hand in both her own. 'I knew, if anybody would be able to sort this out, it would be you.'

As she voiced the words, Maggie was overwhelmed by a tide of mixed emotions. She was hard-pressed to put a finger on what, exactly, they were. What she did know was that she'd seen another side to Brian. Over the years, she'd been careless of their friendship: taken his familiar presence for granted, been dismissive of his abilities. Worse, since George's death – guilty thought – she'd used Brian shamelessly in pursuit of her own ends. That afternoon, he'd demonstrated a positivity and incisiveness that she couldn't help but admire. Looking back, she realised how devoted he'd been, how steady.

'Don't worry.' He raised the hand she held, planted a soft kiss on the back of her own.

Maggie's pulse quickened. Could she have a future with Brian after all?

Don't get carried away! Her rational head kicked in. Just because you're in a pickle and he's come to the rescue doesn't mean you should start thinking about marriage. Soberly, Maggie weighed her options. What were her prospects – a forty-something mother of two with no money? And it's not as if she was pretty. Well, not seriously pretty. And there was the eye, still. She'd determined to do something about it once she'd succeeded in her quest for justice. But would Brian want her? She experienced a small shiver of fear. She'd repulsed him in the past.

For the first time, Maggie realised she had feelings for the man – witness how put out she'd been when he'd come on to that girl. Horrible thought. That was ages ago. They could be an item by now.

'I'd better go.' Brian freed his hand. 'Boss is waiting on a report.'

'But…'

'Leave it with me.' He looked into her eyes. 'I'll see what I can do.'

All Jumbled Up

In the rigid confines of the orthopaedic chair, Susan stirred. She stretched aching limbs, ground bunched fists into her eyes. In the half-light of the hospital room, she could make out the ghostly outline of the drip-stand, beyond that the small figure on the bed.

She'd called in earlier on her airwave radio, been told to stay put. Her stomach rumbled. *Oh, to hell!* Susan had sacrificed hours of her precious free time in the hope of getting a result. But for every brief moment of lucidity, Sheena Struthers seemed to spend an inordinate length of time in deep sleep. Susan didn't dare argue the toss lest she incur the wrath of her boss. She was scared to death of Inspector Chisolm. One angry look from him could send her scurrying for the sanctuary of the female toilets.

She'd dozed off again when the door swung open and a nurse bustled in. The woman's face didn't look familiar – an agency nurse perhaps – and the light was too dim to make out her name tag. She ignored Susan's presence, snapped on blue latex gloves from a dispenser and busied herself checking the patient's vital signs.

That's what I get for messing with the charge nurse, Susan thought, wryly. Her stomach growled again. She'd ask the nurse to keep an eye while she nipped down to the vending machines. It was hours since she'd last eaten, and that was only a Diet Coke and a two-finger KitKat. Plus, she was dying for a pee.

She eyed the figure bending over the bed. Hell, she might even have time to go down to the cafe on the second floor, stretch her legs, use the toilet while she was there.

'How are you doing?' She decided a charm offensive was in order.

'What's it to you?' came the retort.

'Just asking,' Susan tried to pass it off.

The nurse responded by turning her back.

Never mind, Susan rubbed scrunched fists into hollow eye sockets, she could always use the en-suite. Now she'd been sitting that long, it was sod's law that Sheena Struthers would wake up if she left the room.

*

As Sheena Struthers stirred, Susan shot out of her seat.

She stood by the bed. 'Sheena?'

'You again?' Drowsy voice.

She smiled. ''Fraid so. Is it okay if I put the light on?' In the gloom, Susan could barely make out Sheena's features, far less her expression. She reached to a switch above the bed.

'Don't!' Uttered with such vehemence, Susan started.

'Not a problem.' Hastily, Susan lowered her arm. She'd got off to a bad start. Still, at least the patient was awake.

Susan's eyes strayed to the window. The sky was streaked pink with the first glimmers of daylight. Beyond the window, birds were tweeting. Down the corridor a trolley clattered. Soft-soled shoes squeaked on polished floors. The sounds of the world waking up. She stifled a yawn. Please God, now the focus of the investigation seemed to be swinging back towards the husband, she wouldn't have to spend too much longer in this dreary room.

Sheena Struthers struggled to sit up. 'What is it this time?'

'Just a few more questions? I won't keep you long. I wonder if we could run over the events leading up to your admission?'

'But why? I already told you I can't remember anything about that day. I've been racking my brains, but I'm afraid, from the moment I got into bed until I woke up in here, there's nothing. Nothing at all.'

'You don't remember waking that morning?'

'No.'

'Or getting your morning tea?'

'No.'

'Or trying to get out of bed.'

In the orange glow of the rising sun, Susan's eyes flashed irritation. 'I already told you.'

Susan changed the subject. Wouldn't do to get the patient agitated. Susan had given Vi Coutts a body-swerve after that first, bruising, encounter. She was chary of a return match.

'Now I can see you properly, you're looking heaps better.'

'Am I?' Doubtful look.

'Definitely. Your eyes are clearer, and your skin's a better colour.'

'I wouldn't know. I haven't been allowed out of bed.'

'You don't have a handbag mirror?'

'The nurses comb my hair and, well,' Sheena cast a glance over the apparatus at the side of the bed, 'appearance has been the least of my concerns.'

'Your husband, hasn't he…?'

'Gordon's fetched bits and pieces from home, but as you know,' she clasped to her head the hand that wasn't attached to a tube, 'my head's been all over the place since my…' Pregnant pause. 'Accident.'

'You've had a bad time.' Susan's sympathy wasn't assumed. 'Little wonder you're feeling low.'

No response.

'What you've been through is enough to muddle anybody's head. So don't worry if you haven't been able to answer my questions up till now.' She took Sheena's hand in hers, gave it a little squeeze. 'I'm not trying to hassle you. As I told you before, I'm here to help.'

'Before I left you last time,' Susan tried to build on their small moment of intimacy, 'I asked you about something you said to me.'

'Oh?'

'"Enough", you said. What did you mean by that?'

'Nothing. I mean…' Flustered look. 'You must have misheard. I don't recall saying any such thing.'

Susan eyeballed her. 'I doubt that's the case.'

'Are you questioning my word?' Sheena snatched her hand away. 'My mind's all jumbled up, can't you understand?'

'Not at all. Just trying to clarify.' Susan leaned forward. 'I'm trying to help you, Sheena.'

Sheena's face set, her lips compressed in a thin line.

'Enough of what?' Susan pressed, heart thudding. Was this the clue that would unravel the puzzle, or the delirious ramblings of a troubled mind?'

Resolutely, Sheena Struthers turned her head away.

Bugger! She's clammed up now. But why?

Susan laid her hand on Sheena's shoulder. 'You have to trust me,' she said in a soft voice. 'Woman to woman. I'm telling the truth when I say I'm here to help you.'

Beneath the starched sheet, Sheena's body stiffened. 'Then why do you keep asking me the same questions over and over?'

'I'm trying to find out what happened to you, that's all.'

'Happened?' With a look of utter hopelessness, Sheena Struthers sank back onto the bank of pillows, her eyelids heavy, her mouth slack.

She's falling asleep again. For the second time, Susan cursed herself for not being quicker off the mark.

She bent over the bed. 'Can you remember what happened, Sheena?' Urgent whisper. 'Anything? Even the smallest detail?'

Sheena's eyelids fluttered. 'Gordon,' she whispered through lips that were dry and cracked.

Susan's pulse raced. 'What about Gordon?' This might be the breakthrough she'd been waiting for.

There was silence, then, save for the tick and wheeze of the machines.

A Bad Patch

'Maggie?' Ros raised her head from that day's newspaper. 'Can I ask you a question?'

'Ask away.' The two were alone in the staffroom of Seaton School.

'Did you ever think of leaving him? George, I mean.'

Maggie looked into the troubled face of the younger woman. 'I might have cursed him now and again.' She smiled with just a trace of sadness. 'But actually leaving? The answer's no.'

'Thought not.'

'Don't get me wrong,' Maggie hastened to add. 'George was no saint. Not that he ever cheated on me,' she added hastily. 'And in the police service, believe me, there's plenty opportunity for that. No, he was devoted, bless him, from the day we first met. It's just…' She broke off. 'Now he's gone I've made a saint out of him. For the kids' sake as well as my own. But when I cast my mind back, I feel, if I'm honest, he lacked ambition. Was content with a quiet life, whereas I…' She pulled a face. 'I've always wanted more, Ros. More than is good for me, my mum used to say.'

'Nothing wrong with that,' the younger woman remarked. 'Nic's ambitious too. Not just for himself,' she explained with a just a trace of embarrassment. 'For me too.'

'George was the opposite,' Maggie chuckled. 'Not that he was lazy. He put in the hours, rarely turned down an offer of overtime. But, deep down, I resented that he didn't try harder. To better himself, I mean. Sounds old-fashioned, when you put it like that, but he was satisfied with his lot, whereas other guys – men with less ability in my opinion – rose above him. That, I'm now ashamed to admit, stuck in my craw.'

'Well, if that's all…'

'That's just for starters. He was a thrawn bugger, my George. Say black and he'd tell you white. I could never win an argument.'

'You fought, then?'

'Some of the time. Goes with the territory.'

'Being married to a policeman?'

'Being married, full stop. If it's not about money, it's about the kids. And if it's not the kids, it's…' She frowned. 'Why do you ask?'

There was an awkward silence, then: 'I'm so unhappy.'

Maggie reached out to take her hand. 'I guessed as much. I'm really sorry, Ros. You've enough on your plate – juggling the job and the wee one – without trouble at home.'

'I keep telling myself we're going through a phase, the sort of thing that happens in every marriage, especially when…' Ros pulled away. She brushed a tear from one eye. 'There's a small child in the mix. But I've been kidding myself. It's more than that: something deep-seated, something I'm not able to fix for myself. Nic tries to dominate every aspect of my life, Maggie. Everything's alright so long as he gets his own way. But the least quibble…' Her voice faltered. 'I used to be so self-confident.' She composed herself. 'Positive. Optimistic. Now I spend my entire life dancing around him, trying to anticipate his mood.' Her eyes met Maggie's in mute appeal. 'Feels like I'm slowly losing my identity.'

'Oh, Ros, I'm sure…'

'Don't tell me it will come right,' she protested. 'Because it won't. Now I've sat down and thought about it, I can see all the ways I've been trying to compensate: getting separate supermarket receipts, claiming I've mislaid them. Hiding things – in the wardrobe, under the bed. It's insane, Maggie. Even the way I cover my mouth with my hand, sometimes, when I'm speaking. I never used to do that.' She laughed, bitterly. 'It was my poor mother who picked it up.'

'Counselling?' Maggie queried. 'Did you manage to broach that with Nic?'

'I did.' Scornful face. 'Not that it got me anywhere. He won't take me seriously. Can't see that there is a problem. Correction. If there's a problem, it's entirely of my making. He even,' her voice rose in protest, 'suggested I see a mental health specialist.'

'Oh, Ros.' Maggie didn't know what to say. She was saved when the door opened and one of the older teachers entered the room.

'You two on free period?' she demanded.

Maggie felt a wash of colour rise in her neck. Why she had to have a guilt trip over sitting down for fifteen minutes she didn't know.

'Just catching up.' She offered a conciliatory smile. Classroom assistants' non-contact time was an ongoing bone of contention. She sneaked a glance at Ros. The young woman's face was buried in a tissue. Maggie leaned in towards her. 'We'll continue our conversation another time,' she whispered.

Ros nodded, mute.

Reluctantly, Maggie rose to her feet. 'Duty calls.' She looked back at Ros as she made for the door. But Ros was staring, blank-faced, at the floor.

A Major Flaw

Brian knocked on the door of Chisolm's office before sticking his head round. 'You wanted to see me, sir?'

Chisolm indicated a chair. 'Give me an update on Struthers, will you, Burnett?'

Brian sat down. 'Examination of Gordon Struthers' laptop hasn't thrown up anything salient to our investigation.'

'Hmm.' Chisolm's face darkened.

Shit! Brian's mind raced. He'd better make this good. 'Mind you,' he added, 'we've been working on a very narrow window. The solicitor wasn't at all happy, and we don't want to push our luck with Struthers, not with a guy like that. To make matters worse, the techies are snowed. They haven't been able to go into it in any depth.'

Chisolm's face darkened further.

'There is just one thing, sir,' Brian said, trying to mollify his superior officer.

'And that is?'

'There are a number of emails pertaining to Struthers' partnership.'

'In respect of?'

'Equity.'

Chisolm glowered. 'I don't follow.'

'As you're no doubt aware, sir,' Brian said, grabbing his chance to shine. 'In common with other professional firms – solicitors, architects, whoever – equity is divided proportionately between the various partners.'

'Yes,' Chisolm said acidly. 'You don't need to spell it out.'

'When a partner retires, sir, the others have to buy him out.'

'Yes, yes,' Chisolm repeated. 'But I don't see…'

'If you'll humour me, sir,' Brian interrupted. 'Some months ago,

Gordon Struthers' partner was diagnosed with a terminal illness, precipitating his early departure. Said partner is currently in a hospice. His prognosis isn't good. When he dies, Struthers will have to come up with a sizeable sum of money, and find it fast. That gives us our motive,' he added, basking in his moment in the sun.

'Oh, come on, Burnett. Struthers must be earning a bomb, he's most likely paid off his mortgage, and there's only so many meals a man can eat in one day.'

'I'm not so sure, sir. Their income must have taken a knock when the wife gave up her job, and things have been tight in Aberdeen these past few years, even for the professionals.'

Chisolm shrugged. 'You haven't convinced me.'

Brian reddened. 'Would it help if I told you there's correspondence relating to loan applications?'

Chisolm frowned. 'There could be a perfectly simple explanation.'

'Yes, but what alerted me is they've escalated in urgency over the past few months, both in frequency and size. What's more, this escalation dates back to Sheena Struthers' retention of the…' He broke off, conscious of perspiration pooling in his armpits and prickling his brow. 'Detective agency.'

'That's all well and good,' Chisolm retorted. 'But let's not lose sight of the fact the only reason we have this information is because Gordon Struthers has given it to us voluntarily.'

'Agreed, sir.'

'So.' Chisolm fixed Brian with a steely look. 'Bang goes your motive.'

'Sir.' Brian was so hot under the collar by this time he was ready to melt.

'It's back to the drugs, then. I understand Struthers denies all knowledge of any meds: what was found at the scene or any other substance.'

'Correct. Says they've never been great pill-takers, neither him nor her, and that's likely why the wife didn't let on she was using sleeping pills.'

'What about his movements on the morning of the incident?'

'Receptionist confirms he was at his desk just before 8am. There's nothing to back his statement up until then, sir, not if the wife was out of it, so he'd have had the opportunity at any time that day until the cleaner's usual starting time at nine. Or,' he hesitated, 'even during the previous night.'

'Rohypnol's way stronger than Zopiclone,' Chisolm pondered. 'It can take effect in twenty minutes and the effects can last for hours, depending on the dosage. So those two drugs combined could have put Sheena Struthers in a coma.' Chisolm frowned. 'It's unlikely, though.'

Brian scratched his head. 'I suppose.'

'Is there a chance Struthers could have ducked out of his office, nipped back out to Bieldside?'

'It's possible.'

Chisolm eyed him. 'Did either you or Dunn put the question, Sergeant?

Christ, Brian thought, *I've cocked it up again*. 'No, sir.'

Chisolm's lips compressed. 'Thought not. Make sure someone checks out any CCTV opportunities along the route.'

'Sir.'

'However,' he continued, 'that's not the only reason I asked for a meeting. There's a major flaw in our hypothesis, and I wanted to bounce it off you.'

Brian waited.

'What do you know about screening for so-called "date rape" drugs?'

'Not that much, sir, other than they're processed quickly by the body, so difficult to detect.'

'Spot on, Burnett. If my memory serves me right, Rohypnol has a plasma half-life of eleven to twenty-five hours, so it and metabolites are likely to be found in urine for quite some time. GHB, on the other hand, has a blood half-life of only about twenty minutes, so it's important to take a urine sample soonest. However, hospital samples are often taken, if at all, when only residual amounts remain in the body fluids, and it appears this was the case with Sheena Struthers. Added to which on admission…' He reached for another file. 'She'd become incontinent.'

'I see where you're going, sir.'

'And as if that weren't disappointing enough, the clinical tests done at ARI for hospital admissions are limited. For more sensitive screening they'd need samples from forensics. We're screwed on both counts. Struthers' laptop. Is it still in our possession?'

'Don't know, sir. I'll check.'

'Mmm. Pity we didn't have more time. If there has been another drug involved, one that we can't now test for, someone may have ordered it online.' Thoughtfully, he stroked his chin. 'So how did you leave things, Burnett?'

'Struthers wasn't too happy, sir, neither him nor his fancy friend. He's screaming harassment.' Brian rolled his eyes. 'The lawyer I mean. Insists his client is a kirk elder, a model of probity. Says he can't be held responsible for his wife's…'

'Ah.' Chisolm offered a wry grin. 'We're back to women's troubles now, are we?'

Brian ducked. 'Reckon so.' That was one place he didn't want to go.

Chisolm snorted. 'In summary, we have a supposedly intelligent man pleading total ignorance both of his wife's use of narcotics and of a significant injury to her arm. We have questionable email correspondence. But we still haven't established criminal activity.' He challenged Brian with a hard stare. 'What I need you to ascertain is whether there's anything else Gordon Struthers has neglected to tell us.'

Brian nodded. 'Sir.'

'As to the wife, there's only one thing we can do.'

'What's that, sir?'

'Sit on our hands until she's fully responsive.'

VII

You Couldn't Make It Up

'Christ.' Wilma's eyes were out on stalks. 'You couldn't make it up.'

'What?' Maggie demanded.

'Your pal Sheena Struthers horizontal up at ARI. And now yer wee man Brannigan's gone and joined her.'

'I know.' Maggie made a face. 'It's unfortunate, to say the least.'

'Unfortunate?' Wilma echoed. 'It's a fuckin cock-up!'

Maggie blushed scarlet. 'The way you're talking, you make it sound like I put them there deliberately.'

'Well...' Coy look.

'Wil-ma.'

'Don't get your knickers in a twist. I'm taking the piss.'

Maggie's mouth turned down. 'Well, don't.'

'Then there's your pal, Ros.' Wilma pressed on, undaunted. 'All it'll take is for that husband of hers to give her a duffing up, and the three of them will be able to throw a party.'

'Pack it in,' Maggie snapped. 'I'm not in the mood.' In her shock at hearing of Bobby Brannigan's assault, she'd forgotten about Ros.

She was loth to admit there was more than a grain of truth behind Wilma's banter. If Maggie had made a fist of Sheena Struthers' case...if she hadn't rattled Brannigan's cage...possibly none of this would have happened.

'Lighten up!' Playfully, Wilma chucked Maggie under the chin. 'All I'm saying is it's getting like Emergency Ward 10 up there. I thought last year's shenanigans in Seaton were hairy enough: thon student dead in the kirkyard, that head-banger in the high-rises. And them kids, the size of them, in the middle of it. But if Bobby pops his clogs, and your Struthers dame doesn't make it, that's another two fatalities to land at your door.' She rolled her eyes. 'Some going!'

Maggie pursed her lips. 'They're not fatalities.'

'Near as,' Wilma joshed. 'You're some woman, Maggie Laird.'

Maggie sighed. 'I wish. Truth is, though, you're right. It is a total mess.'

'You could say.'

'Let's face it, Wilma. Me with my casualties, you with your marital problems, together we've made a dog's breakfast of this private detective business.'

Crestfallen look. 'And we thought we were doing so well.'

What are we going to do now?'

'Dunno.'

Maggie sighed. 'Maybe my first instincts were right and I'm really not cut out for this sort of thing.'

'That's bollocks.' Wilma elbowed her. 'And you know it.'

'I don't agree.'

'You still obsessing about that head-case, Sheena?'

Maggie stiffened. 'That's below the belt.'

'Wasn't meant.'

'Still, it's true: there are two gravely ill patients up at ARI and both on my account.'

'Oh, come on,' Wilma began.

'Hear me out.' Maggie stopped her going further. 'Nobody can point the finger where Brannigan's concerned. That man's a bad lot. He could have been attacked for any number of reasons. But Sheena Struthers is another matter entirely. Her present circumstances are almost certainly down to my incompetence.'

'Don't beat yourself up.' Wilma stepped in. 'It could have happened to anyone.'

Maggie rounded on her. 'Wouldn't have happened to you.'

'No,' Wilma conceded.

'More than that, you warned me off, Wilma. More than once, if I recall.'

'Aye.' She nodded, grim-faced. 'But that was then. Now it's a whole new ball game.'

'One I'm determined to tackle.'

'I'll give you a hand,' Wilma volunteered.

'You will not.' Defiant look. 'You've done your bit. Now it's my turn. I've had no joy getting information out of Queen Street or Brian, so the only thing left is go up to the infirmary and find out for myself.'

'But,' Wilma protested, 'you can't just bloody swan in.'

Maggie's hackles rose. 'You did.'

'That's different. I'm a member of staff.'

'Not on ITU.'

'No, but still wearing the uniform.'

'I'll say I'm Sheena's sister.'

'Word's going around,' Wilma insisted, 'it's only the husband allowed to visit.'

'Sheena Struthers' room isn't under lock and key, is it?' Petulant voice.

'No, but she'll still be under close observation.'

'Well,' Maggie said stubbornly, 'I'll think of something.'

'There's been a detective at the bedside and all.' Wilma's face was filled with concern. 'I'm telling you, there's no way you'll get near.'

Maggie set her jaw. 'Just you watch me!'

'I'm not doubting you,' Wilma huffed. 'It's only…I don't want you to make a fool of yourself. Far less,' she pulled a scary face, 'get yourself arrested.'

'And I'm telling you, there's nothing like a determined woman. I need to get in there, Wilma Harcus. And get in there I will.'

'Well…' Hands on hips, Wilma squared up to her. 'It's your funeral!'

Whatever

Ros half turned from the sink. 'I want to take a break.'

'From teaching, do you mean?' Nic looked up from his tablet.

'From Aberdeen.' Her hands gripped the worktop. 'From us.'

'But why?' Baffled look.

'You know why.'

'I don't.'

She threw up her hands. 'Oh, come on, Nic, don't give me that. If you're to be believed, I haven't done anything right for I don't know how long. Not the house, not the job, not even our child.'

'You've been working too hard.'

'It's not work,' she retorted. 'Work's fine. In fact, if you must know, Seaton School is the only place I feel valued.'

'By that new friend of yours, I suppose,' he sneered.

'It's not that at all,' she snapped back. 'School is one of the very few places I can be myself.'

'Oh, don't be like that.'

'There you go again. Making it sound like I'm the one that's out of line and you're the voice of sweet reason.'

'Come on, sweetheart.' He rose, crossed to her side, draped an arm around her shoulders. 'We're both tired.'

'Agreed. But it's more than just tiredness, Nic. We've been here before. Way too often. It's time we did something about it. And if you won't…' She disengaged. 'I will.'

'If it's the house,' he countered. 'I know it's not ideal, but renting this place from the University is going to give us a head start in bumping up our mortgage deposit, and…'

She cut him short. 'It's not the house.'

'Though now prices have dropped, we can probably afford to buy straightaway. We could have a look together online tonight,' he rushed on. 'See if there's anything in our price bracket. Pick up some particulars at the solicitors' property centre on Saturday morning.'

'Didn't you hear me?' Her voice rose. 'I said…it's not the house.'

'There, there.' He patted her on the arm. 'No need to get worked up.'

'I'm not worked up.' She leaned back, defeated. 'Just worn out.'

'See,' he came right back. 'I knew you were depressed.'

'I'm not bloody depressed,' she shrilled. 'Well, I am. But not because I've had a child. It's because I can't get through the day without you criticising me: my job, my housekeeping, my parenting skills, my fashion sense, my family, my friends…'

'Whoa.' He held up both hands in surrender. 'Can't be that bad.'

She took a steadying breath. 'It is.'

Sheepish grin. 'Sounds like I've been a bad boy.'

Her heart tugged. 'Yes, it does.' She steeled herself. 'That's why I need a break.'

'Don't go.' He cupped her chin, tilted her face towards his. 'I'll make it up to you, I promise.'

Ros felt a stirring between her thighs. Willed it to go away.

'My intentions are good, you have to believe me, Ros. You do…' He planted a kiss on her forehead. 'Don't you, babes?'

She flinched. God, she hated when he used that word.

'If you've misunderstood, I'm sorry.'

'You're at it again,' she cried, exasperated. 'Twisting everything round. I can't hack it, Nic. It's doing my head in.'

'Please!' He grasped hold of her upper arms. Too hard. She could feel his fingers dig into the soft flesh. 'We could go out somewhere… Supper, maybe even a hotel overnight. A date night.' He flashed a boyish smile.

'But…' Ros could feel her resolve weaken. 'The baby…'

'We can get a babysitter. That cook from the halls…she managed fine that last time, didn't she?'

'Yes, but…'

'You're too hard on yourself, that's part of the problem, my precious. Not that it isn't a good thing to have standards,' he added gravely. 'In moderation, of course. Now…' He planted a kiss on her lips. 'Why don't we make a day of it on Saturday. Catch up with each other. If you're a really good girl, we might even buy you…'

A treat! Ros framed the words in her head. Wasn't that Nic's answer to everything: when he commandeered the car for some sports fixture, when he rolled in late, when he splurged on computer games? Exasperated, she wrenched free.

'So… Saturday.' Nic caught hold of her wrist, held it in a vice. 'What do you say?'

She looked into his eyes. Read challenge tempered by apprehension. 'Whatever,' she replied.

A Breakthrough

'Enter!' Allan Chisolm barked. Inwardly, he bemoaned the fact senior officers were ninety per cent deskbound. What he wouldn't give, some days, to be out in the field.

Douglas Dunn bounded in. 'I've made a breakthrough,' he announced breathlessly.

Chisolm sighed. 'Sit.'

Douglas bounced up to the desk and sat down.

Chisolm regarded the other man with a jaundiced eye. With his designer suits and Thomas Pink shirts, Douglas was the antithesis of everything Allan Chisolm stood for. With overt distaste, he eyed the baby-pink skin, the soft hands that rested confidently on the edge of the desk. The fingernails were pristine. Chisolm debated whether they were on the receiving end of a regular manicure… As for the haircut, who in hell would pay to have tufty bits sticking up like that?

'Let's have it, then.' He tried to show willing, though in truth he couldn't be arsed.

'Well,' Douglas leaned forward eagerly, 'you know how we've got Gordon Struthers' laptop?'

'Affirmative.'

'And you know how the techies only took a flier at it?'

'Yes.' Chisolm wondered where this was going.

'Well.' Douglas leaned across the desk. 'I decided it was worth another look.'

'*You* decided?' Chisolm thundered. 'On whose authority, Constable?' He laid all the emphasis on the last word.

'I – I didn't think,' Douglas stuttered.

'That's your fucking problem,' Chisolm retorted. 'You let your inflated ego lead instead of your fucking brain.'

In a show of humility, Douglas dipped his chin.

'Look at me, DC Dunn.'

Warily, Douglas looked up.

'Do I look like I suffer fools?'

'N-no.'

'Well, then,' Chisolm continued. 'Don't play silly buggers with me.'

'Sir.' The young detective's eyes slid away.

'Did you have another look?' Chisolm relented.

'I did, sir.'

'Fancy yourself as a hacker, do you?'

'No, sir. It's just…' He stopped, unsure.

'Yes?' Chisolm's voice rose.

'My degree was in computer games technology.'

Christ! Chisolm reckoned he'd heard it all. 'So,' he continued, 'let me get this right. With neither his permission, nor the say-so of a superior officer, you broke into Gordon Struthers' computer. How did you manage that?' Chisolm's mind whirred with a catalogue of chargeable offences. 'No.' He saw Douglas trying to come up with a slick answer. 'Better for both of us I don't know.'

'For someone with specialist knowledge,' Douglas responded eagerly, 'it's easy enough. The quickest way…'

'Don't tell me,' Chisolm held up a hand. 'I don't want to know.' Still, his curiosity was piqued. 'Didn't Struthers' laptop have security?'

'Yes, sir. But once you have physical access to a computer, any security measures are effectively worthless.'

Smug bastard, Chisolm thought. 'Is that right?' was all he said. Still, he'd written Douglas Dunn off as a waste of space. Maybe, if the lad buttoned his lip once in a while, he could make a contribution to the squad after all.

'I had a hunch there might be something in the search history,' Douglas continued.

'Isn't that the first place the techies would have looked?'

'Yes, sir. But they were tight for time, and they wouldn't have gone in very deep, so I decided to have a rummage around.'

'Can I take it you found something?' Chisolm asked.

'Yes, sir,' Dunn responded with enthusiasm.

'What, exactly?'

'Porn.'

'Hard porn?' Chisolm enquired.

'Not so much hard, sir, as deviant.'

'Expand.'

'Domination. Dog collars and that.'

Chisolm sighed. He was depressingly familiar with the degradation men heaped on the female of the species. 'Anything chargeable?'

'Not on that account. Though the searches were...' Dunn cleared his throat. 'In-depth.'

'A breakthrough, you said, Dunn? That's hardly...'

'There's more.'

'I take it this also relates to your...' Chisolm paused, enjoying watching his DC squirm. 'Investigative episode?'

Douglas hesitated for a moment, uncertain, then: 'Yes, sir.'

He reached into his inside pocket and drew out a folded sheet of paper. Carefully smoothing it out, he slid it across the desk.

'What's this?' Chisolm's eyes narrowed as they ran down the typed sheet.

'Struthers was still signed in to his Google account. What you have there, sir, is what I also came up with: repeated searches for...'

'Pharms?'

'Exactly. Specifically, drugs that leave no trace in the system.'

Chisolm looked down at the paper. Looked up again.

'So,' Douglas couldn't contain himself, 'Struthers could have ordered the drug online, put it in the wife's tea, and...'

'Not so fast.' Chisolm waved the sheet of paper. 'This is good work...' Grudgingly. 'But it's not enough. Anyone can surf the net. What we need now is proof that these searches led to concrete action: that drugs were actually bought.' He steepled his fingers. 'We need to pull Gordon Struthers back in here, under caution this time. And pronto. See to it, Dunn. That poor woman has suffered enough. And get hold of Strachan. We need a statement from the wife. And we need it now. Once Gordon Struthers is detained, we've only got a twelve-hour window to work with.' He broke off. 'How much longer do we have that laptop?'

Douglas checked his Apple watch. 'An hour max. Solicitor is supposed to be sending someone round to pick it up at noon.'

'Well, we've no time to lose. Get yourself back into that computer, Dunn. Chop! Chop!' Chisolm clapped his hands. 'Find me that purchase order, Constable. And fast!'

In the Wars

Ros walked into the staffroom.

'Someone's been in the wars.' One of the older teachers remarked, her lips compressed in disapproval.

'Oh.' Ros put a hand to the livid bruise on her temple. 'Doesn't look good, does it?'

'Nic been on the razzle, then?' A new voice.

'Nothing so exciting.' She felt herself flush in embarrassment as she sat down. 'Whacked myself with a broom handle.'

'How did you manage that?' Maggie had a sneaking suspicion there might be more to it.

'Stood on the brush-head. Next thing I knew the other end whipped up and caught me one.'

'Ouch,' someone said, with a shudder. 'I hope you put ice on it.'

'I wish. I was trying to blitz the housework.' Rueful smile. 'You know how it is. I'd just defrosted the fridge. Didn't even have a pack of frozen peas.'

'So, what did you do?'

'Ran the cold tap. Wrung out a tea towel. That got some of the swelling down. Then Max woke up and, well...'

'Where was Nic while all this was going on?' Maggie lapsed into private investigator mode.

'Working late.' Ros didn't meet her eyes.

'Poor you.'

'I know. Put it down to lack of sleep.'

'Pity you couldn't manage a break,' someone offered.

Her face lit up. 'As a matter of fact, I've got one planned.'

'Oh, when's that?'

'Weekend after next. Nic's giving a paper at a conference in Cambridge. I've taken the Monday off. Max and I are going down to Edinburgh for a long weekend.'

Maggie flushed with pleasure for her friend. 'That's good.'

'Better than good,' Ros beamed. 'I'll be staying with my folks. They absolutely dote on Max, so I'll be able to catch up on my sleep, maybe even meet up with some of my old school buddies.'

And get away from that controlling husband of yours! The thought ran through Maggie's head.

Ros's smile vanished. 'That's if Nic doesn't change his mind.'

'Why would he?' Maggie queried. 'Didn't you say he was going to be away?'

'Yes, but…'

'I'm sure it will turn out fine.' A third voice. 'In the meantime, what about that eye?'

Maggie seethed. She'd spent many a fretful night deliberating over the subject of Nic Prentice – that's when she wasn't worrying about Sheena Struthers or her kids. Time and again she'd told herself it was no business of hers. More, that marital problems were best left to a trained mediator. But she had a growing affinity with the young teacher, not only because they'd joined forces against the old guard in the staffroom, but because Maggie saw, in Ros, a mirror of her own isolation. They both, in their own way, ploughed a hard and lonely furrow.

'What are you saying, Maggie?' A voice broke her train of thought.

'About?' Startled look.

'Ros's black eye. Arnica or liver?'

'Oh,' she joshed. 'Give me a lump of liver every time.'

A Diamond Ring

Situated just beyond Hazlehead Park on the western outskirts of Aberdeen, Aberdeen Crematorium occupies a wooded location and is approached by a sweeping drive.

Wilma sat in her car. She clocked the straggle of mourners. They filed in and out of the East and West Chapels at frequent intervals. Although forty-five minutes was the official time allotted by the Council between services, in practice it frequently took only fifteen minutes to dispatch the dead.

It's your funeral! Her lips twitched as she recalled her parting shot to Maggie. Changed days. Time was, it was her business partner who wagged the finger, reined Wilma in. Now the boot was on the other foot.

Wilma's fingers itched as she watched a sober-suited man nip the end of his cigarette and attach himself to the end of a line filing into the squat concrete building. Funny how the stress of occasions like these heightened your dependence. Wilma busied her fingers with fishing out her phone. She'd given up smoking at the tail end of the year, but still succumbed from time to time.

She checked the mugshot on her phone one more time. The image was fuzzy, snatched on the hoof. The case was another Harlaw Insurance job: a claim flagged up as potentially fraudulent. The claimant had lost her engagement ring on holiday in Majorca, she asserted, somewhere between the swimming pool and the restaurant. Couldn't be more specific than that.

Her claims history had raised concerns.

Wilma had already checked out the subject's Facebook account. She'd pinned down her place of work and followed her around her local supermarket, but the ring in question wasn't in evidence. She'd come to the conclusion the subject only wore it on social occasions, had wasted the precious weekend waiting for one such. Was about to call it quits when she spotted the funeral announcement in the P&J. It was required reading these days for the two private investigators, for who knows what gems of information lurked in its classified columns. Wilma smacked her lips. Maggie wouldn't approve, she knew. But it's not like it was the husband had copped it. The deceased was a cousin, it transpired, and by all accounts they weren't close.

Her attention sharpened as the door of the East Chapel opened and the first of the mourners reappeared. Smartly, she exited the car and crossed the car park to join them.

Making a show of reading the cards on the wreaths that were being removed from the chapel foyer and set out on the forecourt, she sneaked a covert peek.

A knot of men in dark overcoats exited the chapel, closely followed by what she took to be their wives. Deep in conversation, their heads were bowed, their attention elsewhere. Right behind them she spotted the subject. There was no mistaking that hooked nose. Wilma edged closer, saw her opening, stuck out a hand.

'I'm sorry for your loss.' She clasped the mourner's right hand in a firm grip, her eyes all the while fixed on the left. And *bingo!* There it was, glinting on the ring finger of the other hand – the two and a half carat diamond solitaire that was the subject of the insurance claim.

The woman gave Wilma a quizzical look. 'I'm not sure I know...' she started, but Wilma had moved swiftly on, glad-handing mourners as she went.

As she reached the comparative safety of the smokers' corner, she dug in her handbag for her phone. All she needed now was photographic evidence.

She turned. The subject had moved away and was now in murmured conversation with an elderly couple. *Dammit!* Wilma palmed her phone while she waited for an opportunity. If all else failed, she could always follow the cars to the purvey. A bit dodgy, that, but it was near dinner time. Save her grabbing a sandwich later.

Edging closer, she dashed off a few shots of the wreaths, just out of respect. Then she crept up behind the subject, knees bent so as to remain as insignificant as possible.

The old geezer looked to be in the middle of a rambling story. The two women made a show of listening, but their eyes roamed the assembled company.

The subject's left hand dangled loose by her side. Wilma had just managed to fire off a couple of shots of the ring when the woman turned and caught her in the act.

The mourner's mouth yawned wide.

Anticipating an outraged yell, Wilma legged it across the car park. Thanking her lucky stars she'd left the Fiesta unlocked, she fired up the engine and shot at speed down the long winding drive.

Back Off

'Wilma?'

'Mmm?' She didn't look up.

They were sitting at opposite ends of Maggie's dining-table, their laptops open in front of them, cross-referencing their growing client list. On the sideboard, an open bottle of wine was already half-empty.

'Can I pick your brains?'

'What about?' Wilma raised her head. 'No.' Seeing Maggie's anxious face, she raised a quieting finger. 'Don't tell me. You've got yourself in another fankle over that Struthers woman.'

'I have *not*.' There was no way Maggie was going to own up to her problems in that quarter. 'It's just, there's this girl at school…'

Wilma chuckled. 'You giving the wee boys a wide berth these days?'

Maggie ignored this. 'Not girl. Woman – a teacher – she's having a bad time at home, and I'm worried about her.'

'Och, you. You're a born worrier.'

Maggie sighed. 'I know. And I wouldn't bring it up, only this girl – Ros is her name – is at such a low ebb.'

'She's got family, hasn't she?'

'Not close by. She moved up here from Edinburgh. Husband works at the university. They've a wee one at nursery.'

'Doesn't this Ros have any friends?'

'Not in Aberdeen. Except one, Fiona her name is.'

'Why hasn't your pal offloaded on Fiona, then?'

'She has, but the husband and Fiona don't hit it off, so he doesn't encourage the friendship apparently.'

'Her folks, then. Don't they come to visit? Surely they'd see if there was something not right?'

'From what I've gathered, the husband isn't that keen on having his in-laws to visit.'

Wilma grinned. 'Who is?'

'Nic uses the fact they live in rented accommodation as an excuse. Says he's too busy at work to take her down to Edinburgh to visit them, doesn't want her to go on her own. Anyhow…' Maggie's face clouded over. 'Ros turned up at school the other day with a black eye. And you know how your Darren…'

'That bastard. Don't remind me.'

'Still, you know about these things, Wilma.'

'Aye, mebbe. It could have been an accident, though.'

'That's what she said.'

'Well, then.'

'Equally, the husband's behaviour could be escalating. From what she said, he's the controlling type.'

'What age is this dame?'

'Early thirties.'

'Could have told you. Young folk these days are all the same: that self-obsessed. They live in a bubble. It's all me, me, me!' Shrugs. 'She's likely looking for attention, like your pal Sheena.'

Maggie bristled. 'You don't need to rub it in.'

'I'm not. My two are the same: got an inflated idea of their own importance. They're aye banging on about disrespect. I mean,' she rolled her eyes, 'get a life!'

'Regardless,' Maggie rushed to steer the conversation away from Sheena Struthers, 'it's obvious there are problems in the marriage.'

'Sounds pretty cushy to me,' Wilma observed. 'Them with two wages coming in.'

'You'd think so, wouldn't you? Thing is, Nic's on the demanding side. Expects her to jump to his every whim.'

'Don't they all? Talking of which, pour me another glass of red, will you pal? This record-keeping is doing my head in.'

'Be serious,' Maggie cautioned as she refilled their glasses.

'I *am* being serious. Men are big weans the lot of them, if you ask me.'

'Yes, well.' Maggie pursed her lips. 'That apart...'

'You think you can fix it for her?' Knowing look. 'Maggie Laird, you're some girl!'

Maggie jutted her lip. 'There's no need to make fun.'

'I'm not. But, as I've been trying to tell you, it's not up to you to sort.'

'Yes, but...'

'Are you listening? This Ros is not your concern. Haven't you learned your lesson from that Fatboy business? Sticking your nose in where it's not wanted damn near got you killed.'

In truth, Wilma was more concerned about their current situation. Fatboy was ancient history. What was more worrying was the time Maggie had put in on the Struthers business. And Sheena Struthers hadn't gone away. She said a secret prayer this Ros woman wasn't going to be another diversion.

Maggie's hackles rose. She knew Wilma was right. Plus, given the Struthers debacle, she'd been right twice running. Still, Maggie wanted to help her friend.

'But...' she started out.

'Back off, Maggie,' Wilma said firmly. 'Leave your Seaton job at the door. You've enough to worry about with your own bairns.'

'Accepted. But if you could just...'

Exasperated voice. 'He doesn't batter her, does he?'

'Not as far as I can make out, though I've a question mark, still, over that black eye. It's more...the guy seems to be forever putting her down. No,' Maggie corrected. 'That's not true. He does hurt her, and not just verbally. She's told me he's in the habit of pinching her, giving a jab with his elbow, that sort of thing. Some might call it playful, I suppose, but seems it's always that bit too hard.'

'You don't need to tell me!' Wilma opted to humour Maggie. 'The real bastards never hit you where it shows. When they do leave a mark, they make sure it's easily explained. My Darren was a real pro: went straight for the kidneys, either that or the groin.'

'Oh, I don't think the problem's in that league,' Maggie countered.

'According to Ros, the husband can be charming as well. It's just he's so unpredictable. One minute he's caring, the next tearing strips off her. She can never predict.'

'Domestic abuse isn't just physical. It can be psychological, too. Sounds like her man's a dead ringer.'

'Doesn't it just? I've been reading up on the Victims and Witnesses (Scotland) Act. Dire stuff. Must have led a charmed life with George.'

'Lucky you!' Wilma retorted. 'Darren wiped the floor with me, literally sometimes. Put me off men for life.' She grinned. 'Until I met Ian, that is. Speaking of sex gods, does your friend have any problems in bed?'

'Don't think so.'

'How can you tell? Sexual abuse isn't just marital rape, you know, Maggie. There's this woman I know, her man used to...'

'Let me stop you right there,' Maggie grimaced. She wished she hadn't started the conversation. 'I sense too much information coming on.'

'But,' Wilma ignored the remark, 'how did you get landed with all this?'

'Ros and I are on the same wavelength, tend to stick together in the staffroom.' Maggie pulled a face. 'Fight off the old fogies. And lately, well, I expect she felt she could confide in me. Small things: she's told me Nic keeps tabs on her spending, right down to checking her supermarket receipts. And there are other things...' She broke off.

'Classic!' Wilma jumped to her feet. 'This is all about control.'

'I suppose.'

'Never mind "suppose",' Wilma advanced across the room. 'From what you've said, this fella wants to control your friend's every move, isolate her from outside influence, on top of which he plays mind games, blows hot and cold. Take it from me.' She wagged a forefinger at Maggie. 'Guy's a fucking...' She broke off, frowning. 'Canna mind the word.'

'Narcissist?' Maggie supplied.

'That's the one. Guy's a fucking narcissist. End of.'

I Can't Explain

For the third time in as many weeks, Brian faced Gordon Struthers across a table. Only this time the table was bolted to the floor.

He ran through the formalities for the tape: date, officers present – Sharon was at the hospital, so he'd been paired with Douglas Dunn.

He served the caution. Then, in the awkward silence that followed, mentally ran through the interview plan they'd agreed beforehand. After the couple of black marks he'd earned from the boss, he'd have to run this one by the book.

'Tell me about your marriage,' he began.

'I answered that at our last meeting.' Gordon Struthers' eyes darted to his solicitor, who nodded imperceptibly. Then he looked back at Brian.

Brian smiled. 'Humour me.'

'As I already informed you,' Struthers said stiffly, 'our marriage has not been without its…' His eyes narrowed. 'Difficulties.'

'Minor difficulties, I think you described them.'

'That is correct.'

'And might these "minor difficulties" extend to the bedroom?' Brian fished.

Startled face. 'Sex, do you mean?'

'I do.'

'That's hardly relevant.'

'In your situation, Mr Struthers,' Brian replied, 'it is incumbent on me as interviewing officer to decide what is relevant and what is not.'

Struthers stole another look at his solicitor, who sat impassive. 'Our sexual interaction has always been healthy. More than that. Robust, I'd say.' He gave a satisfied smirk.

Christ. Brian wondered if their sex life was as clinical. 'So can you explain to me, please, the pornographic images we found on your computer?'

Behind the spectacles, Struthers' eyes widened. His gaze flickered from Brian to Dunn to his solicitor and back to Brian.

'Lots of men look at porn,' he said, at last, his tone defiant.

'Domination? Degradation?' Brian interjected. 'I don't think so.' He consulted his notes. 'You've told me there are no difficulties in that department. Sex, I mean.'

Gordon's lips pursed. 'That's not what I said. If I must spell it out,' he broke off, a look of distaste on his pasty face. 'Sheena – my wife – is at an age where there is a certain dryness in the vaginal walls. Discomfort on penetration. Need I elaborate?'

Brian shook his head. 'Have you looked for...' He hesitated. 'Comfort elsewhere? Other than online,' he added, for wickedness.

Gordon Struthers sat upright. 'Certainly not, Sergeant. My wife and I are devoted to one another. As you're no doubt aware, we've been married for over twenty years.'

The two detectives exchanged a glance. That would square with Dunn's report. Brian moved swiftly on. 'So, other than the "minor difficulties" you've described, you would have no grounds on which to wish your wife harm?'

'Of course not.'

'We believe otherwise,' Brian said quietly. He fixed Struthers with a steely look. 'Now is your opportunity to tell us the truth.'

From Gordon Struthers there was an obdurate silence.

'Moving on.' Douglas took over. 'Your home, am I correct in saying it's in your wife's name?'

Behind the horn-rimmed spectacles Struthers' eyes bulged. 'I...' He looked up at the camera. 'I...' He looked down again.

'Answer the question, please.'

'Yes. But that's not unusual.' Gordon Struthers looked to the lawyer for reassurance. 'Not in my profession anyhow. It's a question of tax planning.'

'Ah.' Douglas nodded sagely. 'And talking of tax planning…' He let this hang in the air. 'When our technical department examined your laptop computer, they threw up a number of loan applications.'

Behind his spectacles, Struthers blinked. 'What of it?'

'I understand you may be liable for your – sadly – late partner's equity payout.'

'I've long made provision for that,' Struthers snapped.

'My apologies, sir.' Brian assumed his fall-back expression. 'And sincere condolences.' He allowed a respectful interval, then: 'The loan applications?'

'Were made by me on behalf of…' Struthers loosed the knot of his tie. 'Another party.'

Gotcha! Brian's nerve-endings tingled.

'Would you be happy to divulge this person's identity?'

'Indeed. My godson. I'm assisting him with a business venture.' Gordon Struthers offered a knowing smirk. 'He'll happily confirm the details.'

'Right.' Brian slumped back in his seat, deflated.

'If that's all,' the solicitor intervened. 'These are spurious grounds for detaining my client. For the record,' he cast a scathing glance at the camera, 'I intend to file a complaint.'

'There is just one more thing,' Douglas jumped in. 'When we had a look at your search history, in addition to the distasteful pornographic images you,' he looked Gordon Struthers straight in the eye, 'appear to consider normal, it threw up some additional surprising results.'

He flipped open a folder, lifted the topmost sheet of paper, turned it around and slid it across the table. 'Wouldn't you agree?'

The man sitting opposite ran his eyes down the data. He looked up, first at Douglas, then at the camera, then at his solicitor and back to Douglas. He seemed to shrivel in his seat. Behind the round spectacles, the blue eyes blinked an SOS.

The words, when they came, were scarce more than a whisper. 'I can't explain.'

LoveBunny

Like Maggie's home in Mannofield, the Craigiebuckler property was a bungalow, but there the similarity ended. Detached from its neighbours, its privacy bolstered by a thicket of shrubbery, it sat on a large corner plot defined by ornate railings, the up-and-over doors of the double garage accessed over fancy block paving.

Maggie sat in the sitting room. The fireplace was marble, the drapes silk, the buttoned velvet sofa an impractical shade of pale taupe. Around her, a gaggle of women dressed in cashmere and designer jeans engaged in animated conversation.

Wilma had talked her into it.

Like a Tupperware party, she'd opined. *Only not.*

It was the 'not' that bothered Maggie.

You do it, Wilma, she'd insisted. You know more about that sort of thing than I do.

And you're used to mixing with folk like that, Wilma had come back. Posh folk.

But…

Besides, it'll be a bit of fun. Take your mind of thon Struthers business, that and your wee pal from school.

I don't need my mind taken off…

Fair enough. But I've been out three nights this week already, and you ken fine I'm needing to keep my nose clean.

In the end, she had no choice.

*

Now, the hostess – Moyra with a 'y' – drifted around the room dispensing chilled prosecco into crystal flutes.

She settled herself on an oversized pouffe. 'Right, ladies.' She tinkled a dainty cut glass bell. 'Are we sitting comfortably?'

There were nods and murmurs of assent.

'Then I'll begin.' She smiled brightly, displaying a set of expensively capped teeth. 'For those of you unfamiliar with the LoveBunny Party Plan,' her gaze took in Maggie and a rather blowsy blonde in black leather trousers. 'Our little soiree this evening offers an exclusive opportunity to browse, and even...' she did a double-take at Maggie's lazy eye, '...try out a range of saucy outfits and sex aids in the privacy and comfort of a private home. For the benefit of the new guests, I'll quickly demonstrate our best-sellers. First up...' Stage wink. 'Something the rest of you ladies have grown to love.' She dipped into a box at her feet, extracted a pink plastic object. 'Rampant Rabbit.' She brandished it in front of her face.

There was a ripple of laughter.

Dear Lord! Maggie felt the colour rise in her neck. She knew what a vibrator was but had never seen one up close, far less in someone's front room.

'Rabbit comes to you in silicone in a variety of colours and finishes,' Moira continued. 'Even platinum.' Out of the box she drew a shiny silver job.

'Got one of those last time,' piped up a mousy fifty-something from the chaise in the bay window. She grinned. 'I can recommend it.'

'Is it much better than the standard one?'

'Loads. Whole thing rotates. Done wonders for me.'

Too much information. Maggie took a careful sip of her Evian water.

'And a snip at only forty-five pounds,' the hostess beamed.

'I'll have one, then.'

A hand shot up. 'Me, too.'

Two sales and they'd hardly got started. From her research, Maggie had learned a party like this could rake in a good few hundred pounds in a couple of hours, double that at Christmastime. In her head she ran through the agency's remit: Moyra had reported an unusually high level of wastage over the past few months. The company's area manager reckoned she was under-stating sales and skimming cash. All Maggie had to do was sit through the afternoon's proceedings and make a list of what was sold.

'For those ladies whose taste isn't quite so…shall we say, exotic…' Moyra flourished a white object. 'This little number comes in a discreet finish, offers three speeds and three pulses and has the Good Housekeeping seal of approval.'

Maggie's ears burned, as the vibrator was passed around and another couple of sales registered. She'd always identified the Good Housekeeping Institute with more mundane products.

Squirming, she sat through a succession of butt plugs, cock rings and jiggle balls. When an innocuous-looking plastic object was brandished, her interest piqued, for the thing looked for all the world like the string of bobble beads her mum kept, still, in her old jewellery box. How, as a child, Maggie had loved popping and unpopping that necklace. Her buttocks clenched involuntarily as the object was described as 'anal love beads'.

Stifling a hysterical giggle, she jumped to her feet, excused herself and headed for the bathroom. Once there, she splashed her scarlet face with cold water, then, composure regained, she perched on the toilet seat and jotted down a list of the sales she'd memorised.

*

By the time she returned to the sitting room, the noise level had risen in line with the cluster of empty prosecco bottles, and Maggie had totted up four hundred and seventy pounds in sales.

The hostess moved on to what she coyly described as 'mood enhancers'. A succession of tipsy women lurched upstairs to the 'master suite', returning in various stages of undress. With ill-disguised distaste, Maggie regarded the outfits: French Maid, Naughty

Nurse, Sexy Schoolgirl. There was even a Bunny Girl. She stifled a yawn. Even she knew bunny girls were old-hat. Slack-jawed, she took in the array of underwear Moyra fished from her seemingly bottomless box: peephole and harness bras, black stockings and basques. There were crotchless, open-back and spanking knickers, wet-look thongs, even a complete bondage kit.

Fainting with embarrassment, she dipped to the carpet and fished her phone out of her bag. On the pretext of checking her messages, she clocked the time.

'Nothing take your fancy?' Moyra plonked her trim rear onto the sofa.

Maggie dropped the phone. 'Not really.' She shifted sideways. 'Not much call at the moment.' She smiled, trying to make a joke of it. Felt the smile die on her face.

'Well, you know what they say…' Moyra pressed on, relentless. 'Round every corner…'

'I know.' Brusquely, Maggie cut her short, though she had to admire the woman's persistence. Then: *Mind you buy something!* Wilma's words rang in her ears. *Otherwise they'll shop you!*

Scarlet-faced, she reached for the catalogue she'd been given and riffled through the pages.

Something small, she told herself, *just to show willing.*

Her eyes hovered over a range of salves and sprays. *G-spot Gel,* she read. *Anal Relax Spray.* In mounting desperation, she ploughed on. She was nearing the end of the catalogue when the handcuffs leapt from the page. A lurid shade of purple, they were fashioned from fake fur. Maggie shuddered. In all her life she'd never seen anything so naff. Still, needs must.

'How about a pair of these?' She turned to Moyra with a forced smile. 'Just to start me off.'

'Good choice,' her hostess said brightly, 'and a steal at eight pounds.'

Eight pounds? Maggie started in shock. You could get a pair of jeans in Primark for that. *Not to worry,* she consoled herself. That afternoon's work would earn the agency a respectable fee, plus she could always give the disgusting handcuffs to Wilma.

Then she was struck by an awful thought: Wilma probably had a pair already.

FaceTime

Maggie was halfway through collating her report for the LoveBunny organisation when her mobile pinged.

She flipped it open. Saw a FaceTime call. Pressed 'accept'.

Her daughter's face appeared on the screen.

'Kirsty.' She suffused with a warm flush of pleasure. 'What a nice surprise!'

'Right.' The small face looked pinched. 'Whatever.'

Sharp intake of breath. Since she'd brought that boy home to visit, Kirsty's calls had been thin on the ground. Maggie told herself not to worry. It was nearly a year, now, since she'd discovered Kirsty was cutting herself. That, and Colin's repeated absences from school, had given her many a sleepless night. But all that was behind them now, surely. Her thoughts ran wild.

'How are you doing, pet?' was all she said.

'Okay.'

'Just "okay"?' Maggie pressed.

There was a long silence, then: 'I've missed my period, Mum.'

Oh, no! was Maggie's immediate reaction. She had a mental picture of the girl in her class at school: her belly swelling under her uniform, the whispered asides before she was whisked away to some distant place, her parents' shame.

'How long?' Her practical side took over.

'It was due last Tuesday.'

'And you've taken nearly a week to tell me?' She couldn't mask the reproach in her voice.

'I'm telling you now,' Kirsty retorted angrily.

'I know,' Maggie's voice softened. 'And I'm pleased you have. I take it you've been...' she continued. *Sexually active* was what she'd have asked a client. *She's nineteen, for God's sake, she cursed herself for her naivety. Of course she bloody has.*

She changed tack. 'You sure?'

'One hundred per cent.'

'Right.' Pointless asking who was responsible. Maggie shuddered. Odds on it was that uncouth Shaz. On the other hand, she reasoned, Kirsty might well have multiple partners. It was a different world from the one she was brought up in. And her daughter was a student, after all.

No matter, her mind raced, all that was irrelevant now.

'Might be an idea to see a doctor. The university health centre...'

'If you're thinking of the morning after pill,' Kirsty interrupted, 'it's too late for that.'

'Yes,' she was forced to concede. 'I can see that.'

'I just thought I'd better tell you.' Small voice.

Maggie's heart lurched. At that moment, her only daughter looked so vulnerable. And she was so far away.

'Do you want to come home?' was all she could think to ask.

'No.'

'I could come down,' she offered quickly.

Kirsty shrugged. 'I'll be okay.'

'You sure?' Maggie queried for the second time.

'Positive.' Kirsty didn't at all sound convincing.

'Ring me again tomorrow, will you, pet?' Maggie wondered how she was going to get through the evening, never mind a whole day.

Kirsty nodded. 'I'll try.' In the background, a doorbell rang. She looked over her shoulder. 'Got to go.' She turned back.

'I'll say night-night, then.' Maggie mouthed the same words she'd repeated ever since her children were infants. Before they started school. Before George died.

A shiver ran down her spine. The previous year – the year her world imploded – she didn't think life could throw anything else at her. Now she knew different. Talk about life turning in an instant? If her daughter was pregnant...if she wanted to keep the baby... Maggie's mind seethed with conflicting images. And just when she was getting back on her feet…

'Night-night.' Kirsty's voice broke her train of thought.

Then the line went dead.

VIII

You Can Tell Me

As she stole into the room, Maggie's eyes took in the bank of equipment, the figure curled on the bed. At first glance, she thought Sheena Struthers was asleep, then she saw that the small body was shaking, the sound of muffled weeping percolating from beneath the swaddle of sheets.

'Sheena?' She reached out.

The figure started. 'You?'

Maggie put a finger to her lips. 'Shush!'

'What are you doing here?' Sheena whispered.

What indeed?

Earlier that day Maggie had conjured up a doctor's appointment and driven across town from her job at Seaton to Foresterhill. Getting onto the ward was another thing entirely. Lacking Wilma's silver tongue, the story Maggie had conjured up had failed even to get her past ward reception and she'd retreated, crestfallen, to the hospital cafe. There, she'd toyed with the idea of filching a staff uniform or swipe card, dismissed the notion as too dodgy.

She'd established that the ITU reception desk was unmanned outwith office hours and visitors buzzed straight through to the nurses' station. Maggie resolved to return that evening. She'd dress in an approximation of what a plainclothes policewoman would wear; nothing overly smart in case it drew attention. That way she could pass herself off as a detective, likely even benefit from a changeover in nursing staff.

Now, she leaned over the bed. 'What's the matter?'

The sobs increased in volume.

With tentative fingers, Maggie stroked the woman's hair. This seemed to have some effect, for the weeping abated somewhat. 'It's alright.' As her fingers made gentle motions, her mind raced ahead.

'You can tell me.'

'No!' With one elbow, Sheena nudged loose her bindings and rolled onto her back. 'There's nobody I can tell. Especially you.'

'What do you mean?' Maggie queried.

This was met by a renewed bout of weeping.

'What is it you can't tell anyone?' Maggie pressed.

Sheena's body shuddered as her sobs reached an ear-splitting climax.

Maggie waited for a nurse to come running, but in the corridor outside all was still. Thoughts tumbled in her head. What could have given rise to such anguished weeping? Or was it simply the product of medication and an overheated room?

For some moments she held her counsel. Finally: 'You okay?' she asked in a soft voice.

'Not really.' A hand stole across the bed to seek the comfort of her own.

'Why not?' Then, as the idiocy of the question struck her, she added, 'Apart from the obvious.'

From the bed there was a silence so prolonged Maggie held her breath, expecting at any moment to be ejected.

'It was me.' Sheena snatched her hand away.

'What was?' Maggie's PI antennae sprang to full alert.

'The stories.' Shrill voice. 'I made them up.'

Get the facts. The words screamed in Maggie's head. She drew a deep breath. 'What is it you're trying to tell me, Sheena?'

'Gordon's been a good husband to me. Never put a foot wrong. Except...'

'Yes?' she prompted.

'He's always taken the lead in everything,' Sheena hesitated, 'including our lovemaking. And I liked that, in the early years of our marriage. Thought it was masterful, romantic. That's how it was those days. For most people anyhow. Men were men, and women... well, they had their place.'

Maggie thought of her own mother, made a wry face.

'Don't get me wrong, Gordon was loving, considerate, always careful to pleasure me before he...had his way. But then, as he moved up the career ladder, his attitude seemed to shift. It's as if he wanted to belittle me. Not in company, you understand. Gordon's very correct socially. But behind the scenes.'

'Verbally, you mean?'

'No.'

'How, then?'

'In bed.'

Dear Lord! Maggie definitely hadn't seen that one coming.

'Sexually, you mean?'

'That's right.'

'Can you give me some instances?'

Coy look. 'He'd use words that made me uncomfortable.'

'Not that unusual,' Maggie came back. 'Loads of men do.'

'Yes, but he'd make me repeat them. And he'd do things to me... things I didn't like.' Her voice wobbled. 'Dirty things.'

'Like what, for instance?'

Sheena fiddled with the edge of the sheet. 'One time he wanted to urinate on me.'

Charming.

'It was bad enough at the beginning. I told myself to get on with it, that that's how marriage was. And I was younger then, stronger. I had a career to occupy me, colleagues to sustain me. It got worse when I gave up my job,' she continued plaintively. 'It's as if I'd lost something, not just my salary. Like I'd dwindled, somehow, in his eyes.'

'Mmm.' Maggie recalled her own gradual loss of confidence, how she'd argued with George over going back to work.

'It's been building for a while.' Sheena dabbed at her eyes. 'The pressure. More than a while. Years. But it's only been these last few months that it got too much. I've been feeling so dreadful: up one minute, down the next. Not sleeping. And it's not only the disturbed nights. I feel like my body's disintegrating, and my emotions are all over the place.' She paused. 'I took your advice and went to my GP. He said it was the onset of the menopause. Told me it affects people differently. Some women hardly notice, others…' She broke down once more.

Maggie pulled a tissue from the box on the metal bedside unit. 'Take your time.' She proffered it.

Noisily, Sheena blew her nose. 'Anyhow, it all got too much for me. I thought once I hit menopause Gordon wouldn't find me so attractive sexually, that he'd leave me alone. He might even look elsewhere. I wouldn't have minded, not anymore. But it's turned out just the opposite. Seems to bait him, excite him almost, me being so vulnerable. And…'

'What?' Maggie's question was drowned by the door swinging open, the squeak of rubber-soled shoes.

Despairing voice. 'I just wanted it to stop.'

A nurse bustled in. 'You still here?'

Bugger! Just when she was getting somewhere.

Maggie ignored her. Best not engage.

'Well, you'll need to wait outside. I have to change my patient's catheter bag.'

She nodded.

'Hang on.' The nurse came up close. 'Who are you?'

Maggie's heart stopped.

Roughly, the nurse took hold of her arm. 'Whoever you are, you're coming with me.' She propelled her towards the door.

'What made you choose Harcus & Laird?' Maggie called over her shoulder.

'I read about you in the paper. How your testimony got trashed in that Fatboy case.'

Sheena's eyes sought Maggie's own.

'I chose you…' Weary voice. 'Because…' Her words were drowned by the clatter of a trolley.

Home

'Comfy?'

'Mmm.' Ros snuggled under the soft fleecy throw.

'Well, relax. Max is out for the count. Your mum's just looked in on him. She's heading for bed now.' Her dad tucked a corner of the blanket under Ros's chin. 'I've put a hot water bottle in yours. Do you want to turn in, or will I leave you a while?'

'No.' She raised a wan smile. 'To both questions. Stay. If you're not too tired, that is…'

'For you, pet,' he stooped to plant a kiss on her brow, 'never.'

Her eyes welled with tears. 'Oh, Dad,' she wailed, 'I'm so glad to be home.'

'And we're glad to see you. You and Max.' He didn't mention Nic.

'We might not be able to stay that long.' Apologetic look.

'Don't fret over details like that tonight. The important thing is you get some rest. You look worn out.'

'I am.'

'Well, things will look better once you've had a good sleep.'

'You think?'

'I'm sure of it, Ros.' He perched on the edge of the sofa. 'We've all been there, you know.'

She stirred. 'You and Mum?'

He chuckled. 'You can't stay married for as long as we have and not encounter a few bumps along the way.'

'But,' she protested, 'actually leaving?'

His face darkened. 'Is that what you've done?'

'Yes… No…' she scrunched fists into her eyes. 'I don't know. Don't know much about anything anymore.'

'Oh, come on, Ros. You used to be such a strong-minded girl.'

'I used to be lots of things.' She sat up. 'And look at me now.'

'You look fine to me. A bit pale, if I'm honest. And on the thin side. Have you lost weight?'

She ignored this last question. 'I feel so inadequate, like I'm always letting people down.'

'What people? Not your parents.'

'People in Aberdeen.' She hesitated. 'Well, Nic if you must know.'

'You sure of that? Mightn't this all be down to nervous exhaustion? You've had a lot on your plate, pet, this past couple of years.' He paused for reflection. 'Maybe if you saw a doctor…'

'Don't you start.'

'I didn't mean…'

'I'm sorry. It's not your fault, it's mine.'

'In what way?'

'Oh…just…I don't live up to his expectations, is what it comes down to. And, yes, I did see our GP. And, no, I'm not suffering from depression, Dad. I'm reeling under a welter of criticism. And interference. And possessiveness.' A wave of relief overcame Ros as she spoke the words out loud. 'And if I don't do something about it…' Her words trailed off.

'Oh, Ros.' Her father's face was filled with dismay. 'Your mother and me, we had our suspicions that there was something not,' he hesitated, 'quite right. But we'd no idea it was that bad.'

'It's not,' she hastened to reassure him. 'Nic loves me, Dad, I'm sure of that. And he dotes on Max. But he's so unpredictable: he can be nice as nice one minute and fly into a rage the next. That's what I can't cope with. I have tried.' She threw a despairing look. 'Learned to be less assertive, not to contradict him. I guess that's what a good marriage is all about.' Sad smile. 'Giving up some of your own desires to please the person you love.'

'Marriage shouldn't be about giving up.'

'That's what I thought. And, to be fair, every time Nic loses it he's immediately contrite. Wants to make amends. Do stuff to make it up to me. He's good at that. He can be very persuasive, you know. And I used to enjoy it – the pampering bit, I mean – especially all those months when I was at home with Max. It was a lonely time, you see.'

'Why didn't you say? Your mother and me, we'd have come up, helped with the baby, let you get out and about.'

'Nic didn't want visitors. He was too wrapped up in the new job, and…'

'That's understandable, but it's been a while, and we did wonder…'

'Too late now. Whatever I do doesn't make the slightest difference.'

'Have you talked to anyone about this?'

'Yes. My friend Fiona.'

'What does she have to say?'

'Fi's pretty scathing. Doesn't have a lot of time for Nic. Then there's a colleague from school. Quite different from Fiona. But they both agree on one thing: they think Nic's a bit of a narcissist. I'm sure if I pressed Fiona she'd tell me to leave.'

'Have you considered that as an option?'

'Not really. When you're in that sort of situation, you get completely bogged-down. Your whole attitude to risk changes. You talk about me being strong-minded.' She sighed. 'The reality is the constant drip-drip of criticism saps your will, to the extent you feel paralysed. It's only now I'm home with you I feel myself again.'

'Oh, pet.' Her father extended a comforting hand.

'Problem is, I've more to lose leaving Nic than staying: my marriage, my job, my home. And there's Max. How can I take him away from his father?'

'No matter how badly he treats you? You have to think of yourself, Ros. You're young, pet. You've your whole life ahead of you.'

'You make it all sound so straightforward. I leave Nic…and then what? I'm thirty-two, Dad. I don't want to end up back home with a baby in tow. You and Mum have your own lives to lead now.'

'What was that?' Cath Munro came into the room. 'I couldn't sleep. Heard you talking.' Fond smile. 'Thought I'd come and join the party.'

'Dad was just telling me how I could leave Nic.'

'Leave him!' she exclaimed. 'I didn't think it had come to that.'

'It won't.' Ros raised a weary hand. 'Not without a fight. Even if I could summon the courage, it will be a messy business, I can tell you. Nic's not a nice person when he's not calling the shots.'

'So I gather. But we'll support you, you know that.'

'You might have to. I don't have the money to pay for a divorce.'

'It may not come to that. Now, enough of this talk. What you need is a good long sleep. Away to your bed. Things will look better in the morning.'

Side-tracked

Maggie had been sounding Wilma out over some Innes Crombie invoicing, when she said, 'I've been worrying about Kirsty.' She pushed the paperwork aside.

'What about her? She's not cutting again?'

'No.' She hesitated. 'At least I don't think so.'

'It's that boyfriend, isn't it? I can see it in your face.'

'Yes. No.' Nervously, Maggie wrung her hands. 'I'm not sure. She's had a pregnancy scare, that's all she told me.'

'And you think it might be him, this Shaz?'

'I've no idea, to be honest. All I know is, her period's well overdue.'

'Christ!' Wilma exclaimed. 'That's all you need!'

'It's all Kirsty needs. I wasn't going to tell you, Wilma, but I've been worried sick.'

'Why not? We're partners, aren't we?'

'You've had your own troubles this past while. Ian…' she began.

'Ach,' Wilma interrupted. 'I've told you before, Ian's a pussycat.'

'Not lately. Look at the way he…'

'He is. It's just…men, they never grow up, Maggie. You should know that. They're big kids. You need to feed their vanity now and again, give them their place.'

'Right enough,' she concurred. Though it had been so long since she'd had to humour a man she could scarcely remember.

'When did all this hit you?'

'Last week. Kirsty called me on FaceTime.'

'Last week?' Wilma shrieked. 'And she was already late? Why in hell didn't you go straight down there?'

'Until I solved the Struthers case, I didn't want to get side-tracked.'

'Side-tracked, is that what you call it? *Your own daughter?'*

Maggie hung her head in shame. For weeks on end her focus

had been channelled on Sheena Struthers, to the detriment of everything else. It was only over the past few nights she'd barely slept, torn in a tug-of-war between her only daughter and the woman who'd caused her so much grief.

'Well, you'd better do something now, or it will be too bloody late.'

'Too late for what?' Maggie demanded. Her business partner surely wasn't thinking abortion.

'The morning after pill,' Wilma clarified.

'That's no longer an option,' Maggie said stiffly.

Wilma shrugged. 'I know. But there's got to be something you can do. First off, if I was you,' she wagged a finger, 'I'd have her home.'

'She won't come.'

Wilma's brows met. 'She'll come if she's told to.'

'You don't know my Kirsty.'

Wilma glowered. 'Aye. Well.'

'I feel so helpless,' Maggie moaned.

'No bloody point in that. If that daughter of yours won't come to you.' She bustled to her feet. 'You'd better get yourself down to Dundee.'

'Sit down,' Maggie cajoled. 'I've already decided to do just that. God knows I've a full enough diary. But, if I juggle things around, I can be there and back in an afternoon.'

'Good. That's sorted.' She smiled encouragement. 'Thank Christ for sons! Your Colin okay? Haven't seen him in a while.'

'He's fine.' She broke off, uncertain whether to admit the truth. Then: 'That's another thing I meant to tell you. Colin got nicked for vandalising a car.'

'Christ Almighty!' Wilma leapt out of her seat. 'When was this?'

'A while back.'

'And you didn't tell me?' Incredulous voice. 'Is there anything else you want to share?'

'Yes,' Maggie whispered. 'There is, actually.'

'*There is, actually*,' Wilma put on a posh accent. 'And what might that be?'

Maggie took a deep breath. 'The car belonged to James Gilruth.'

'Fucking hell!' Wilma mouthed. 'I thought I'd heard it all from you, Maggie Laird, but you still manage to surprise me.' She paused. 'You said this happened a while back?'

'That's right. I contacted Brian the minute I got the call Colin was at the station. Brian and I met up that same day. He said he'd see what he could do.'

'So, what was the outcome?'

'There wasn't one.' Small shrug. 'Nothing happened.'

'Nothing at all? That's not like Gilruth. From what I've heard, he wouldn't pass up a chance to rub Police Scotland's nose in it.'

'Came as a surprise to me, I must say.'

'Surprise? It's a bleeding miracle! Maybe he took a fancy to you, Maggie,' she nudged her in the ribs. 'Thon time you called on him at Rubislaw.'

Her face froze. 'Doubt it.' She could still taste the fear.

'Maybe Gilruth just couldn't be arsed with the paperwork, got more important things on his mind. There again, maybe someone had a word.'

'Brian?' Scathing look. 'Don't be daft. He doesn't carry that sort of clout.'

'Your pal Chisholm, then?'

'Doubt it, even if...' Reddening, she broke off.

Wilma wondered – and not for the first time – if Maggie Laird was carrying a torch for the senior policeman.

'Whatever,' she retorted. 'If Gilruth's done a favour, you can be sure as shit he'll be looking for payola down the line.'

Heaven-sent

'Sheena?' Susan leaned over the bed. 'Can you hear me?'

No answer.

She brought her face up close. Her instincts told her Sheena was dissembling.

Sheena opened her eyes. 'Go away,' she snapped. 'I've told everything to the other detective.'

'What other detective?' Susan straightened, momentarily thrown.

'The *private* detective.'

'Sheena…' Adrenaline coursed through Susan's veins. 'What are you trying to tell me?'

Her mouth tightened. 'I'm not going through it all again.'

'Doesn't matter.' Susan affected a careless tone. 'I'm enjoying the peace and quiet here. I'm quite prepared to wait.'

Like hell! She never thought she'd see the day she'd miss the chaos of the station.

Several minutes passed, the only sound the hiss and bleep of the machines. Then: 'I knew if I went to the police with a made-up story they'd see through it straightaway.'

Too right. Any seasoned copper would have sent you packing.

'Those lady detectives seemed heaven-sent.'

Covertly, Susan switched on her phone, set it to record. Wouldn't do for evidence but, were she to whip out her notebook, she reckoned it would kill the conversation stone dead.

'They were heaven-sent, you said. What do you mean by that?'

'Nothing.' Muffled voice.

'You must have meant something.'

No answer.

Susan shook her gently by the shoulder.

'They were green.' Sheena's eyes narrowed. 'Just starting out. I'd ruled out the police, and I needed my husband to back off. I'd tried everything: reasoning with him, making excuses, feigning illness. None of them worked. By the time I approached the detective agency, I was in such a state. I couldn't take any more.'

'And?' Susan prompted.

'I decided the only way to change Gordon's behaviour was to give him a fright. Nothing serious,' she rushed to add. 'Just enough to, you know…' She broke off, embarrassed.

'So you hired Harcus & Laird to do what, exactly?'

'I didn't have a plan, not at first. Thought if I laid a trail. Nothing too specific, just enough to raise questions.' Shamed look. 'I spun Mrs Laird a story.'

Susan started back, aghast. 'You concocted those allegations?'

'Some of them, yes. I felt bad. But I told myself I was paying for her time, and at the end of the day there would be no harm done. Gordon would have been warned off, the detective agency would get paid, I'd get peace. And it's not as if Maggie Laird was losing anything, was it?' She looked to Susan for reassurance.

'Only her reputation.' Said with more than a hint of sarcasm.

Lost twice over. Susan thought of the trial, George Laird's disgrace. 'So you hired that decent woman.' She reckoned she'd heard everything, now. 'And told her a tissue of lies.' Thank God this wasn't a formal interview, she could have swallowed her tongue.

'Only it didn't work. Mrs Laird was so genuine. Really cared about my well-being. But she didn't believe me, I could tell. Anyhow, it's not as if I make a habit of that sort of thing.' For the first time, there was a note of defiance in Sheena's voice. 'If it wasn't me shooting her a line, it would be somebody else. I thought if suspicion fell on Gordon…' She broke off. 'If the police were to pull him in for interview, it would frighten the life out of him. The scandal…'

Susan had seen the old boy network in action. She could imagine.

'You say you wanted your husband to back off. Surely it would have been less convoluted simply to leave him.'

'And write off all those years I'd given to the marriage? No way. What sort of future would I have, tell me that? I've precious little money of my own. I haven't worked in years. And besides, outwith the marital bed, Gordon and I rub along well enough. We enjoy the good things in life. At least we did, until…' Her voice wavered. 'But when I approached Mrs Laird I wasn't thinking straight. Plus, I was so angry: that I should have been at such a low ebb, and still he'd…'

Hell hath no fury!

'So you were bent on revenge?'

'Not even that. Self-preservation would be more like it.'

'Would you care to expand on that?'

Sheena's eyes welled up. She covered her face with her hands.

'Remember what I told you. Sheena. I'm not here to upset you. I want to help.'

For long minutes Sheena Struthers remained silent. Finally, she spoke through her fingers. 'I never meant it to go this far.'

Magdalen Yard

Maggie made her way along the Perth Road and down the hill to Magdalen Yard. She'd always liked this part of Dundee, ever since the day she and George had driven Kirsty down to matriculate at university. Maggie had mixed emotions then: excitement at the world that would open up for her first child and only daughter, mingled with a deep sense of loss as she watched Kirsty prepare to fly the nest.

Now, her mind tumbled with equally conflicting thoughts. It was almost a week since Kirsty had rung with the news of a possible pregnancy. Maggie was sick with worry, especially given she'd allowed the Sheena Struthers case to overshadow concerns closer to home. Time and again, she'd scrolled through her telephone contacts, thumb hovering over her daughter's number. Time and again, she'd put the phone down. Once she'd spoken face-to-face with Sheena Struthers, she'd make the journey. Then, she'd be in a position to offer practical help, or at worst – should Kirsty prove unreceptive – moral support.

She'd skipped out of school before noon, made a bus by the skin of her teeth. In other circumstances, she'd have enjoyed the journey, savouring elevated views of the craggy coastline or the soft farmland of the Mearns. Today, though, she'd picked nervously at her cuticles, unable either to concentrate on the couple of traces she'd snatched from the table that morning or to close her eyes and switch off.

Her heart thudded in her chest as the narrow road opened out into a verdant green space. A Victorian bandstand stood in its centre, cast iron tracery looping from its supports. Beyond, the Tay Rail Bridge formed a shallow curve as it sought out the shores of Fife. Above it, the sky was dingy grey, as was the water below.

Summoning all her courage, Maggie pressed the red sandstone tenement's entry buzzer. There was no answer.

Dammit! They'd be at lectures, Kirsty and her flatmate, Sarah. Maggie should have known better than to arrive in the early afternoon.

She could check out the university. But where to start? Kirsty's lectures were in the law faculty. But she could be anywhere: the Tower, the Dalhousie Building, the library, the union. Maggie would go off and have a bash at those traces, she decided, come back later. She turned to go.

'Mum? Is that you?'

Maggie swivelled on her heel as a door banged behind her.

'What are you doing here?' Kirsty's hair was scrunched in a loose ponytail, her jeggings topped by an oversized jumper.

'I could ask you the same question,' Maggie retorted, her stomach rumbling. 'Shouldn't you be in class? It's the middle of the day.'

Instantly, she regretted her outburst. Her daughter looked about sixteen, and so vulnerable that all Maggie wanted was to take her in her arms.

'We've been coming home at lunchtime for a plate of soup. It works out cheaper.'

'Oh.' Small voice.

'I'd offer you some, only Sarah's just finished it. And I can't ask you up. She's got a friend in.'

Maggie could imagine. Her mind ran wild.

'The reason I'm here…' she broke the silence, then stopped. She sounded way too formal. 'I just wondered,' she continued lamely, 'how things were…'

Kirsty shrugged her satchel higher up her shoulder. 'Fine.'

'Honestly?'

'Yes.'

This was followed by an awkward pause.

'Any news?' Maggie enquired, trying to keep her voice casual.

'News?' Puzzled voice.

'Your period?'

'Oh, that.' Kirsty's tone was dismissive. 'It was a false alarm.'

Maggie's knees went from under her. She put out a hand to steady herself on the wall of the building, felt the rough stone prickle her palm.

Oh, George!

'And you didn't think to pick up the phone?' she asked, irritated now.

'No. Why would I?'

Because I've been worried sick, Maggie wanted to scream.

Instead: 'Wh-when did you find out?' she stuttered.

There was another long pause, then: 'Can't remember.'

Bloody kids! Not for the first time that day, Maggie's emotions churned, faint and furious in turn.

She inhaled deeply, let the breath slowly trickle out.

'That's all right, then,' was all she managed.

'Was there anything else?' Kirsty asked pointedly. 'I'll be late for my tutorial if I don't get a move on.'

'No. Just a social call.' The lie tripped off her tongue. 'But now I'm here, did you ever find that pen, the one you were chasing Colin about?'

Kirsty furrowed her brow. 'The pen Dad gave me when I got into uni?'

'That's the one.'

'Oh,' she shrugged. 'I put it to the engraver last semester and forgot all about it.' Sheepish look. 'Dad told me he'd meant to put my name on it. And the date. Only he decided to ask me first.' She smiled, sadly. 'Didn't want to do the wrong thing. I'd been meaning to do something about it. Only, what with…' She broke off.

Maggie's heart stood still. Wasn't that so like George? 'Never mind,' she managed to say. 'It's a nice thing to have.' She gathered herself. 'Right,' she said, briskly. 'I'll let you get on.'

Grudgingly: 'Thanks.'

'Before I go, I meant to ask…'

'Yes?'

'That boy, the one you brought home…'

'Shaz?'

'That's the one. How's he doing?'

'Dunno.' Bored voice. 'Haven't seen him in yonks.'

Loving Adults

Susan perched on the edge of the vinyl chair. 'How are you, Sheena?' she kicked off on a cordial note.

'Some better,' Sheena Struthers responded. 'Thank you for asking.'

'Today I'd like to take a formal statement.' Susan smiled encouragement.

Last time a nurse had sent her out of the room, she'd nipped to the toilet, taken a sneak peek at her phone. With the 'txi inhibit' button engaged on her airwave radio and her mobile switched off, she'd felt divorced from developments at HQ. But all she found was a series of text messages from Douglas. Increasing in urgency, they demanded Susan call in. There was no way she was going to respond, lest the smarmy bastard muscle in on her progress. No, she'd wrap up Sheena's statement tighter than a boiled sweet and deliver it to Chisolm on her own.

'I'd also like to record our conversation, if that's okay with you?'

'I suppose.'

Susan stood up. 'I'll give one of the nurses a shout.'

'Why?'

Corroboration. She knew she should call in a senior officer, someone not directly involved. But this was Susan's chance, maybe her only chance, to get Sheena Struthers to open up. A civilian witness would have to do.

She drew a deep breath. 'I think you know why.'

Sheena shot forward from the bank of pillows. 'No.' Shrill voice. 'I'm willing to talk to you, nobody else.'

Bugger! Susan sat down again. So much for wrapping the case up tight.

She should charge Sheena first. Protocol dictated that a voluntary statement could only be obtained from an accused person who had already been charged with a crime. But charge her with what? Wasting police time? And, besides, Sheena had already admitted culpability.

What the hell! Susan resolved to stick to her guns. She'd worry about the niceties later on. She switched her phone to record. In a steady voice, she read out the caution. Meaningless, in the circumstances, but a touch of gravitas might spur Sheena Struthers to part with the truth.

Then: 'Last time we spoke, you said you didn't mean it to go this far? Can you explain to me, Sheena, what you meant by that?'

'I wanted to send a warning.'

'So, if I'm understanding you correctly, you wanted to give your husband a fright?'

Nods.

'With a view to what?'

'To making it stop,'

'The abuse?'

'That's right.'

'I still don't understand why you didn't report it.'

'I didn't think anyone would take me seriously. I mean, would the police even consider it abuse, what goes on in the bedroom between two adults?'

Consenting adults. 'Even so...' Susan offered. 'Just because you submitted doesn't mean you gave your consent. New legislation...'

Sheena cut her short. 'By the time it began to affect my health, it had gone on for so long: years...decades.' Her voice carried a bitter note. 'Who'd have credited a mature woman – solvent, supposedly intelligent – would put up with things that long? How do you think I could explain that to some young police officer?' She worried the binding of her hospital gown. 'Someone like you?'

Susan had to admit the woman had a point.

For a few moments, Susan sat, lost in thought.

'You're thinking it's my own fault for putting up with it,' Sheena broke the silence. 'But you're from a different generation. Attitudes have changed in the twenty years I've been married. People put up with things then that would be unheard of now.'

'I suppose,' Susan said, though she couldn't imagine such a set-up as Sheena Struthers had described.

'It was after I started suffering from anxiety that I noticed there was a pattern to it: my husband's behaviour deteriorates when he has an upset at work. Gordon takes it out on me. It's a release, I expect. They've a lot of responsibility on their shoulders, men.' Said in a caring voice.

Bastard! Susan mused. And it's not as if he has money worries. Or kids. 'And this happens how often?' she asked.

'Too often.' Sheena responded bitterly.

'So the pills…' Susan brought herself back to the job in hand.

'Sleeping pills.'

'Prescribed by your GP?'

'That's right. My state of mind was affecting my sleep. Though I know, now, that I'm probably also menopausal.'

'And did you take the pills, as prescribed?'

Sheena's gaze shifted. 'I did. Except…'

'Except what?'

'I took them for several nights. Then I realised they'd only knock me out for a few hours. And Gordon, well, when I came to he'd be wide awake, waiting…'

'When your cleaner made her call to the emergency services, our officers found you deeply comatose. Can you clarify that for me, Sheena?'

Sharply, she turned away.

Susan took her time. 'Did your husband know about the pills?' It was critical she played this right.

'No.'

'Are you quite sure?'

Sheena turned back. 'Positive.'

'And have you discussed them with him at any time during his visits?'

'No. But, then, they don't let him stay long, and there have been other things to discuss.'

'Such as?'

'Domestic things, nothing important.'

'Would it surprise you to hear,' Susan asked, 'that he's been interviewed informally twice already?'

Sheena started. 'I didn't know. He hasn't mentioned it.'

'And that,' Susan said, taking a chance, 'he could be charged with your attempted murder?'

'No-o!' Sheena screamed. 'My husband is devoted to me, make no mistake. He shows his affection in so many little ways. And I love him.' Her eyes welled. 'Did love him until…'

Susan couldn't make up her mind whether Sheena Struthers was a poor soul or a practised liar. Her mind raced. She was already in trouble. She'd ignored the calls from HQ, wilfully overlooked police procedure.

Sod it! She'd better not go back without a result. 'Okay,' was all she said.

Aching with tiredness, Susan tried to plan her next move. The only thing she could come up with was to call Sheena's bluff. If it was a bluff.

'Let's take a break.' She stood and turned, as if to go.

The woman on the bed tugged at her sleeve.

'Please sit down,' she wept. 'I'll tell you everything.'

The Clock's Ticking

'Where's Strachan?' the inspector demanded.

'No idea.' George Duffy garbled the words as he swallowed the last of his morning piece.

'Didn't catch that?' Chisolm threw him a hard look.

'I've made repeated attempts to contact her,' Douglas Dunn piped up. 'But she's failed to respond.'

'She's likely still at the hospital, sir.' Brian Burnett tried to deflect Chisolm's ire.

'Well, I need her present,' Chisolm insisted. 'This is important. And time is of the essence, as you're all aware.'

'I'm sure she'll be along any minute,' Brian added, still acting peacemaker. He was rewarded with a foul look.

'Any news on Struthers?' Duffy moved to make the peace. 'Did we manage to blow holes in his loan application story?'

Chisolm sat down. 'Sadly, not. We have corroboration from the godson. However, there has been some progress.' He waved a folder. 'It transpires that Dunn, here,' he cocked his head towards Douglas, 'has some talent, after all.'

There were titters around the table.

'Talent he's been hiding from us. When all the time we thought he was a useless twat.'

Douglas looked down at his shoes.

'Don't be coy, Constable.' Chisolm was enjoying his bit of fun.

Theatrically, he waved an arm. 'DC Dunn, you have the floor.'

'Well, I...' Douglas began. He drew breath. 'Before it went back, I had a shufti at Gordon Struthers' computer.'

'Christ!' Dave Wood exclaimed. 'Get you!'

'Quite,' Chisolm concurred, his face a mask.

'I've uncovered evidence,' Douglas said, holding the floor, 'that

Gordon Struthers used a search engine to identify date rape drugs.'

Wood craned his neck. 'Is that right?'

Douglas smirked. 'Struthers has been using his search engine to check out drugs. Untraceable drugs, namely Rohypnol and GHB.'

Bingo! George Duffy raised a fist.

'Not quite. As Inspector Chisolm pointed out,' he looked to his senior officer for approbation. 'A search isn't proof.'

'Too right.' Wood again. 'And how can you prove it was Struthers? Could have been any bugger running that search.'

'Conceded.' Douglas came back. 'However…' He let the word hang in the air.

Arse-licker! Wood scowled. If Douglas had cracked the Struthers case, there would be no living with him.

'I knew we needed more: a firm order.'

'And,' Duffy jumped in, 'did you get it?'

'No,' his mouth turned down. 'There was no order.'

Around the table, shoulders slumped back into seats.

'But,' Douglas added with a camp look, 'I did find something.'

The detectives sat forward again.

'It was a race against time.' He puffed out his chest. 'But I managed to retrieve a follow-up he'd deleted from his spam folder.'

There were puzzled faces.

Chisolm spoke. 'Better explain.'

'When you place an order, companies often send a follow-up email tempting you to buy more. Sometimes a deluge of emails.'

Brian twigged. 'That's why they end up in the spam folder.'

'Precisely.'

'But,' Brian argued, 'how did you…' He paused. 'I thought you said it had been deleted.'

'Yes.' Smug look. 'But not double-deleted. He deleted it from his spam folder but not from his trash. Likely reckoned he'd covered his tracks.'

'Right,' Brian nodded, 'I get you. And that's why he was happy enough to surrender his laptop.'

'So,' Duffy stroked his chin, 'Gordon Struthers tried to top the wife right enough?'

Douglas smirked. 'Looks like it.'

'And he almost got away with it.'

'Except,' Brian qualified, 'he made a schoolboy error: not double-deleting that email.'

'Might have been in a hurry,' Duffy mused.

'Whatever,' Chisolm came back in. 'We're still in the realms of speculation here. Gordon Struthers may or may not have proceeded to order these substances, which he may or may not have used in an attempt on his wife's life.'

'What's he saying to it?' Duffy again.

'Denies all knowledge.'

Dave Wood's mouth turned down. 'Don't they all?'

'So we don't have authority to charge?' Brian queried.

'Not at this point.' Chisolm responded. 'Bottom line is we have *some* evidence, but insufficient to meet the threshold. And without a full examination of that computer...' He broke off. 'It's bad luck our timing was out on that one. If the techies hadn't been quite so pushed, and...'

'If you'll allow me,' Douglas interrupted.

Chisolm bristled. 'Did you hear what I said a minute ago?'

'I did, sir. Only...'

'As I was saying,' Chisolm looked at his watch. 'The clock's ticking. And without that order we have to let Gordon Struthers go.'

'But, sir...'

All eyes were on Dunn.

'Couldn't we ask for an extension?'

Chisolm fixed him with a thunderous look. 'On what basis?'

'I cloned the hard drive, sir.' Douglas said smugly. 'Give me a few hours more and I'll find you that order.'

No Way Back

Ros faced her parents across the dining-room table. 'I've decided to leave Nic,' she announced in a steady voice. 'But before I break the news to him, I'll need to work out a strategy. That's why I asked you both to sit down with me tonight.'

'Oh, Ros.' Cath Munro clutched a hand to her throat. 'I knew you were unhappy, but I never thought it would come to this.'

'Are you sure?' Ros's father added.

'Quite sure,' Ros answered, her chin set. 'Now I've put space between us, caught up on my sleep, I can be more objective. And looking at things from this distance, well...' She sighed. 'Doesn't look like there's any way back.'

'But,' her mother protested, 'what about Max?'

Ros pulled a face. 'I know.' She pictured her son lying asleep upstairs, not a care in the world. 'It's a dreadful thing to do: take a child away from its father. And Nic does love that wee boy, I know. But...' She broke off, her voice faltering. 'When I look back over our marriage, there's a pattern to it: the constant criticism, cutting me off from my family, my friends, wearing me down to such an extent that I'd do anything to appease him. Then, when I think I can't take any more, turning on the charm.' She put her head in her hands. 'It's a cycle that I should have recognised.' She raised her face to her parents. '*Would* have recognised, if I hadn't been blinded by love. Not even love...' Her mouth twisted. 'He was so different, Nic, from all the men I'd ever known. I let myself get carried away. Infatuated, if you like. If I'm brutally honest with myself, I think I panicked when I hit thirty, decided I wanted to get hitched, do the whole mummy thing.'

'I did wonder,' Phil Munro said.

Ros raised a small smile. 'I know you never took to him, Dad.'

'Well…'

'Oh, come on, you've never seen eye to eye.'

He held up his hands. 'I've had my doubts, I must admit. But that's mainly because of the way I've seen him treat you, pet. Nobody should have to put up with that.'

'I know. At least, I can see that now. But the way it was at home – in Aberdeen that is – seemed like it was me that was always at fault.'

'The guy's a control freak. Not only that…'

'Enough,' his wife cut in. 'We're not here to sit in judgement. The man's not here to defend himself, and who knows what goes on behind closed doors.'

'Are you defending him?' Phil demanded angrily.

'Not a bit. But there's no point indulging in character assassination. What's needed, as Ros says, is a plan of action.'

'You're right, Cath.' He reached to pat her hand. 'Practical as ever.'

With a look of forbearance, Cath Munro shook him off.

'First thing should be talk to a solicitor,' he went on. 'I can give ours a ring in the morning, if you're agreed, though he'll suggest a specialist divorce lawyer, no doubt.'

'And the first thing any divorce lawyer worth their salt will propose,' his wife added, 'is mediation.' She turned to Ros. 'Before you take such a drastic step, have you and Nic considered counselling?'

'I've brought up the subject more than once,' Ros answered wearily. 'But he won't hear of it.'

'Why not?'

'He doesn't see that there is a problem, that's why. I've tried everything, believe me. And…' Her voice faltered. 'It's no use.'

'Well, if that's the case, the best thing for now is to seek impartial advice,' her father grasped Ros by the hand. 'And the sooner the better.'

'And you don't have to worry about Max,' her mother chipped in. 'He'll be happy with us.'

'Thanks,' Ros murmured, close to tears. 'It's such a relief just to be here with you, I can't tell you.'

Good to Go

'Sir?' Brian stuck his head around Chisolm's door. 'Are we good to go?' He advanced into the room.

Frowning, Chisolm looked up from the mass of papers on his desk. 'Not yet, I'm afraid.'

'But, I thought…' Brian ventured.

'Dunn had come up with the goods?' Chisolm interrupted. Your intel on that count is correct, Burnett. But given who we're dealing with, I deemed it prudent to get the nod from upstairs.'

'Oh.' Brian's eager expression morphed into one of dejection. 'It's just, the team's getting a bit jumpy, and…'

'I know,' Chisolm cut him short. 'Upstairs are taking it to the wire.'

'You'd think those pharms searches would be damning enough. But now, with that order…'

'That's how it is,' Chisolm snapped. 'The review officer needs time to consider.'

Brian shuffled his feet. 'Sir.'

'To complicate matters further,' Chisolm continued, 'Strachan's out of radio contact and we still don't have a statement from Sheena Struthers. Without an admission of guilt from the husband, ideally backed up by incriminating evidence from Mrs Struthers, this whole question of date rape drugs was, and remains, a complete hypothesis.'

'But, sir, the porn. We'll surely find something to charge Gordon Struthers with. Guy's a total sleazebag.'

'I wish I shared your confidence, Sergeant Burnett. Added to which, Struthers' solicitor is already screaming blue murder. As I understand it, he's taken against DC Dunn. Doesn't like his attitude. Alleges he deliberately humiliated his client. I'll need you to keep a tight rein on him. If the solicitor were to file a complaint…' Chisolm could envisage the ensuing lawsuit. 'Wrongful arrest would be the least of our worries.'

Brian dropped his eyes to the carpet. 'I understand.' After a decent interval he looked up again. 'How long have we got, sir?'

Chisolm glanced at his watch. 'Ten minutes.'

Brian's shoulders slumped. It wouldn't be the first time a suspect had got off the hook because someone hadn't got their finger out. All that time and effort wasted for bugger all.

On Chisolm's desk, a telephone shrilled.

'DI Chisolm,' he answered. 'Yes.' Long pause. 'Understood.'

Chisolm replaced the handset. 'Seems you're set to go.' He fixed Brian with a level look. 'Be sure and make it good.'

A Telephone Call

Maggie was in the back garden hanging out Col's rugby kit when her mobile rang.

She dropped the pegs she was holding and ran inside. 'Hello?' she said expectantly, hoping it would be Kirsty.

Maggie's flying visit to Dundee had ended on a less than satisfactory note. On the long bus trip back north she'd felt weary and deflated. She'd told herself she should be relieved that Kirsty's pregnancy scare had been a false alarm. More, that Maggie's instincts hadn't failed her – as they had with Sheena Struthers – and that the boyfriend Shaz, whom she hadn't taken to, was a thing of the past. Instead, Maggie had felt a deep sense of loss: that her only daughter – whom she wanted nothing more than to hug close and protect – had grown away from her.

'Maggie?' A familiar voice broke her train of thought.

'Ros?' Maggie's mood lifted. 'Is that you?'

'The very same.'

'I thought you were in Edinburgh.'

For a few moments there was silence. Then Ros spoke: 'I am.'

'I'm so glad.' There was real warmth in Maggie's voice. 'You need a break. You're with your parents, I take it?'

'That's right.'

'Must be lovely,' Maggie ran on, 'to have help with the wee one. I'll bet they're spoiling him rotten.' She paused. 'You, too.'

There was another silence. 'That's just it,' Ros said, her voice grave. 'For the first time in I don't know how long, I feel free.'

'Oh, Ros.' Maggie's heart tugged. 'I knew things were bad. I never imagined they were that bad.' How Maggie wished, now, she'd sought out Ros's friend, Fiona. Had a heart-to-heart.

''Fraid so,' Ros answered. 'After that last meeting of ours, they sort of spiralled.' She gave a bitter laugh. 'A downhill spiral. But I'm home now.'

'That's good. Make the most of it. You can tell me all about it when we…'

Ros cut Maggie short. 'That's why I'm calling.'

'You're taking extra leave, is that it? Staying longer than the holiday weekend?'

'Yes. And no.' There was steel in Ros's voice that was new to Maggie. 'I'm leaving Nic. Full stop.'

Something Missing

Detective Constable Douglas Dunn faced Gordon Struthers across the interview room table. Next to Dunn sat his sergeant, Brian Burnett. As before, Struthers was accompanied by his solicitor.

Douglas ran through the preliminaries. 'Do you understand why you're still here?' he asked Struthers.

Gordon Struthers nodded. Hunched in the hard seat, he looked more compact than ever, his chest concave, his eyes blinking rapidly behind the round spectacles.

'Last time we spoke, Sergeant Burnett questioned you on the subject of your marriage. Do you remember that conversation, Gordon?' Douglas hesitated. 'Is it alright if I call you Gordon?'

A fleeting glance at the solicitor. Another slight nod.

'You stated, then, that you had no cause to wish your wife Sheena harm.'

'That is correct.' Small voice.

'Can you speak up, please, for the tape?'

'That is correct,' Struthers repeated.

'Even though you admitted to searching the internet for…' Douglas ventured a sideways glance at Brian, who sat, impassive. 'Deviant material.'

Gordon Struthers looked down at the table.

'Is this a practice you've maintained, Gordon?' Douglas was enjoying himself.

Whispered: 'No.'

'Louder, if you will.'

'No.' The word came out as almost a shout.

'Would you like to take a break?' The solicitor leaned in towards his client.

'I'm fine.' Gordon Struthers pulled a linen handkerchief from his breast pocket. He shook it out and mopped his brow.

'Turning to the other matter I raised at your last interview: the numerous searches on your computer for pharmaceutical products – have you reconsidered your position?'

Vigorously, Struthers shook his head. 'I still don't understand how they got there.'

'You maintain you have no knowledge of these searches,' Brian stepped in.

'Yes,' Gordon Struthers responded, wild-eyed. 'No. I've absolutely no idea what you're talking about.'

'Then, how do you explain this?' Douglas slid a sheet of paper across the table. 'For the benefit of the tape, I'm once again showing the suspect a list of internet searches for non-traceable drugs from a number of Canadian pharmacies.'

Struthers answered, his voice quavering, 'I can't. I told you before.'

'That's enough,' the solicitor interrupted. 'The entire world can surf the net. That piece of paper isn't evidence. It doesn't mean a thing.'

'Accepted,' Brian answered. 'But, if you'll bear with us, I think you'll find my constable has more.'

'Then it had better be good,' the solicitor snarled. 'My client has been detained for coming on twenty-four hours. Without good cause, I should add.'

Douglas suppressed a smirk. 'This,' he brandished another sheet from the file in front of him, 'is a copy order from that same computer. A computer,' he paused for effect, 'belonging to your client.' He looked Gordon Struthers in the eye.

Struthers' mouth opened and closed like a fairground goldfish.

Even the solicitor was lost for words.

'An order,' Douglas pressed on relentlessly, 'for the date rape drug GHB.'

The prolonged silence that ensued was broken by a loud rat-tat on the door.

Fuck! Douglas shot a glance at Brian.

He responded with a yank of the head.

'Will you excuse me for a moment?' Furious, Douglas scraped back his chair and rose to his feet. He stuck his head round the door.

Susan Strachan stood in the corridor, her face flushed with exertion. 'Sorry to interrupt,' she panted.

'You cunt.' Dunn's veneer of sophistication deserted him. 'You've just screwed up my interview.'

'Maybe,' she replied. 'But this is really important.'

'So fucking important it's giving Struthers the chance to regroup?' Douglas came back at her. 'I've just shown him the fucking copy order.'

'And,' Susan fixed Dunn with her brightest smile, 'has he held his hands up to it?'

'You didn't give him the opportunity,' he retorted, running his eyes up and down her body.

Inwardly, Susan shuddered. 'The reason I didn't make the briefing,' she explained, 'is I was taking a statement from Sheena Struthers.'

'Haven't we got that already?'

'Not a full statement. I'll be brief.' She threw Douglas a triumphant look. 'Mrs Struthers has admitted to fabricating the supposed murder attempts. I'll give you the background later. However, she insists that clifftop fall was no accident. She was so spooked she went into Gordon's computer, turned up those searches.'

'So?' Douglas moved to re-enter the room. 'Tell me something new. You've just screwed up a critical interview for fuck all.'

'Don't be like that,' Susan feigned concern. 'I might equally have saved your skin.'

'How?' he sneered, looking over his shoulder.

'You've no proof it was Gordon who placed that order. Sheena knew his password. She might equally well have…'

'Faked her own suicide? You reckon that's a goer, Strachan?'

'It's not beyond the realms.' The longer she'd spent in Sheena's company, the more ambivalent Susan had become.

'Whatever.' Douglas turned on his heel and slammed the door.

Such a Fool

'I feel such a fool.' Maggie sat, head in hands, in Wilma's conservatory.

'There's nowt to be said.' Wilma responded with a wry smile. 'Woman fair took a ride out of you.'

'You can say that again. I've been well and truly conned. And I've only myself to blame. Didn't you warn me from day one it would be a rerun of the Argo business?'

'That was different. Argo, she was a psychiatric case. Come to think on it, I haven't seen her up at ARI for a good while. Wouldn't surprise me if she's been sectioned.'

'You don't think Sheena Struthers is mentally ill, then?'

'No. If you ask me, the whole business was down to burnout.'

'I don't get you.'

'In a word,' Wilma replied, 'it's exhaustion. 'Only emotional rather than physical. You're that stressed out by the abuse, you completely lose the plot.'

'How do you know?'

Wilma shrugged. 'Been there.'

'Oh, Wilma.' Maggie raised her head. She looked searchingly at her friend.

'Aye. In and out of the women's refuge I don't know how often.'

'This was with Darren?'

'Aye. Bastard! But by the time I got that length, he'd reduced me to an emotional wreck. And not just emotional, I suffered physical symptoms too: headaches, irritability. I was always tired, forever getting colds and urinary infections. It was like all my defences were shattered.'

'You think it was the sexual abuse, not the menopause that tipped Sheena Struthers over the edge?'

'Who knows? The change can have a massive effect on a woman, by all accounts.' Wilma gave Maggie a nudge. 'How long, do you reckon, before it hits us?'

'Not for a long time, please God,' Maggie responded with a grimace. She'd a hard enough time reconciling the chafing and the stomach cramps and mood swings of her 'time of the month' with the demands of her home and business.

Wilma grinned. 'Watch this space. But, mentally,' she ran on, 'I reckon Sheena's as sharp as they come. How else could she have planned all that? Mind you, she's had plenty of time. That Gordon's had it coming to him since they first got married, if her account's to be believed.'

'But that's just it, Wilma. Right from our initial meeting, she came over as so authentic. So suburban, so unworldly, so… "straight" I suppose is the word.'

'Bit like you, Maggie.'

'Well, I have to admit the thought did occur to me. Sheena Struthers came across like how I used to be. Before,' she cast Wilma a sideways look, 'you corrupted me.'

'Dinna lay the blame at my door.'

'What do you think will happen to her now?'

Wilma snorted. 'Bugger all. If he sticks by her, that is.'

'You think that's on the cards?'

Wilma shrugged. 'Stranger things have happened. As I said, if he stands by her… and she gets herself a fancy solicitor. And don't forget the GP. If some smartass lawyer comes out all guns blazing, waving a medical certificate, it'll likely go no further.'

'All that time wasted for nothing!' Maggie wrung her hands in despair. 'That's what I get for being a narrow-minded, snobbish, self-regarding idiot.'

'Don't beat yourself up. We're none of us perfect.' Sly grin. 'Though some of us are more perfect than others. The way you were aye ticking me off when we first got started. Comes from working with teachers, I suppose. Still, it fair got my goat.'

'Don't rub it in. But, seriously, Wilma, I thought I had it sussed, this PI business.'

'You and me both.'

'Agreed. We've come such a long way from those first clumsy attempts at investigation. Learned such a lot. The experience has made me more savvy, that's for sure.'

Wilma pulled a comic face. 'Cynical's the word I'd use.'

'Less trusting, that's for sure. And a better judge of character. At least, I thought I was all those things until…' Her voice wavered. 'Since this thing blew up, Wilma, I haven't been sleeping. Lying in the night questioning everything. The whole point of us taking on the agency was to get justice for George. And we're not there yet. Nowhere near. I doubt we'll ever be there. If I'm honest, I don't even know if it's worth the effort, not anymore.'

'But, Maggie…'

'Don't interrupt,' she held up a hand. 'I blamed myself for the mess I was in before. Laid it on false pride – wanting to keep the kids in their private schools, keep up appearances. But now I don't know.'

'I don't follow.'

'What if it was largely down to George: his misguided loyalty in not speaking up about Brannigan's interview tape, rolling over rather than squaring up to a disciplinary hearing, shutting himself away up that close in King Street with his tin-pot agency instead of sticking out for something better.' She sighed deeply. 'I have to face up to the fact that George, nice as he was, lacked imagination. Even if he'd gone before that hearing and acquitted himself well, chances are he'd have been happy to stick at sergeant, stay on in that tatty wee house next door, settle for pipe and slippers the minute the kids moved on. Whereas I…' She drew a breath. 'I've always wanted more, ever since I was a wee girl.'

'Oh, Maggie, you can *have* more. Look how the client list is building. And they're good clients. Gilt-edged.' She grinned. 'Some of them.'

'That's what I've been telling myself. But George is dead, Wilma. Whether I succeed or fail in this crusade of mine won't make any difference to him. Sometimes, if I'm honest, I suspect I'm not doing this for George at all. I'm doing it for me. To stop the whispers and the pointed fingers and the snide asides.' Her voice wavered. 'False pride again. I'll tell you what *I* think when I lie awake in the night: what the hell is the point?'

'I'll tell you what the point is. You've two kids, Maggie Laird. Young kids with their lives still ahead of them. There's nothing will bring their father back. But you can get rid of the stigma attached to his name. So do it for them, Maggie. Your pride will recover soon enough. And you're young enough, yet,' stage wink, 'to find someone else.'

'I don't want anyone else.'

'Not now, maybe. But come the time Colin's gone and you're rattling around the house on your own…'

'Even then.'

'That's what you're saying now, but mark my words…'

'Anyway, who would want a forty-something widow with a wall eye?'

'Plenty.' Wilma stuck out her boobs. 'Look at me: a divorced wumman wi twa useless loons. I could have had my pick, let me tell you, before I settled on Ian Harcus. As for you, Maggie Laird, you're a fine-looking woman. You only have to see the way that Brian Burnett hangs on your every word.'

'Och,' Maggie pooh-poohed. 'Brian's a pushover.'

'That Chisolm, then.'

'Don't remind me.' Maggie could imagine the inspector's reaction to yet another *faux pas* from Harcus & Laird.

'I'm serious. All through that Fatboy's trial I caught him giving you sideways glances.'

'Sure. If looks could kill…'

'Might be the fella's lonely. Didn't he move up here from Glasgow? He's sure to be missing the talent.' She wiggled her hips. 'Never mind a bit of gallus humour.'

Maggie pursed her lips. 'If that's the case, he's more likely to get both from you than me.'

Wilma beamed. 'There is that. But...' She was serious again. 'I was thinking...'

Maggie's heart sank even lower. 'Go on, then.'

'The PI business is a helluva hard way to earn a crust. And I should know.' Stage wink. 'The things I've done. Now a pal of mine, he left school like I did with nothing to show for it show and went to work in an undertakers.'

'Right...' Maggie wondered where this was going.

'And didn't the old boy die. This was years later, mind you. And my mate got the lot.'

'The business, d'you mean?'

'On the nail. He's driving a Bentley now.'

'Nice story,' Maggie observed, 'but I hope you're not suggesting we go into the undertaking business.'

'Oh, I don't know. Other than the hearse, there wouldn't be a great outlay.' She pondered for a moment. 'And you can likely lease the cars.'

'Wil-ma, there's more to undertaking than carting a body from A to B. And if you think the PI business is messy, put your mind for just one minute to the embalming process – all those bodily fluids.' As she spoke, Maggie was back in that undertaker's office in George Street, her dead husband being 'processed' downstairs.

'It's no science,' Wilma scoffed. 'More like plumbing. Bit smelly, but you get used to it. And you can make a packet.' The big blue eyes were like saucers. 'And make it fast. Not like us and our "baby steps" as you call them.'

'I don't need "a packet". Just enough to see the kids through their education, pay off the mortgage and see me out.'

'Fair dos, Maggie. All I was trying to say was, now we've done our apprenticeship, we could turn our hand to anything, you and me.' She grinned. 'Not that I'd say no to the Bentley.'

A Pantomime

Brian Burnett sat in Chisolm's office. Hidden by the desk, his left knee jerked spasmodically.

Chisolm fixed him with a gimlet eye. 'As senior interviewing officer, Burnett, would you care to explain this morning's proceedings?'

Brian quailed. When Dunn had stormed back into the interview room, red-faced, he'd suspected something was awry. What he hadn't bargained for was the ensuing chaos.

'Well, sir,' he began, 'you'll have received Strachan's report.'

Chisolm inclined his head.

'So you'll know Sheena Struthers is standing by her allegations?'

'I do,' Chisolm snapped. 'In a statement given to a junior DC acting without authority.'

Brian's shirt collar felt suddenly too tight. He ran a forefinger round the inside, felt the perspiration pooling at the nape of his neck.

'Thus rendering its use in evidence against the suspect inadmissable.'

'Sir.'

'I'll deal with Strachan later. Meantime, cut to the chase, Burnett. Tell me what happened in that room.'

'Dunn was lead interviewer. Kicked off with the porn. More to unsettle the suspect than anything.'

'I was under the impression that had already been covered.' Chisolm's voice held a sharp edge.

'Affirmative.'

'So Dunn was having a bit of sport, is that what you're trying to tell me?'

Brian shifted in his seat. 'You could say that, sir.'

'I thought I told you to keep Dunn in check.' He saw Brian's face flush. 'Oh. Never mind. How did Struthers react?'

'Had the desired effect.'

'Then what?'

Brian's shirt was sticking to his back by now, sweat pricking his chest. He took a deep breath. 'Dunn shows him the pharms searches. Struthers maintains total ignorance. The solicitor starts jumping up and down, screaming there's no foundation, it's all conjecture. Dunn's just producing the copy order for the GHB when Strachan calls him out the room.'

'So,' Chisolm snarled. 'DC Strachan finally chose to honour us with her presence?'

'Yes, sir. She'd been at the hospital out of radio contact, and…'

Brusquely, Chisolm interrupted. 'I'll deal with her later. But back to Dunn. When he was outside, what happened?'

'Solicitor goes head-to-head with Struthers, whispering Christ-knows-what. Could have been framing a positional statement, given the new evidence, whatever. Then, Dunn comes crashing back in. Says the wife has given a statement standing by her allegations.'

'What was the reaction?'

'Struthers fell apart. Literally. Toppled sideways off the chair, curled up on the floor, crying like a bairn. His specs flew off and got broken in the fall, and…'

'The solicitor, what was he doing?'

'Sitting there like a spare prick giving Douglas the evils.'

'And you, Burnett? Where were you while all this was going on?'

Brian reddened. 'I have to hold my hands up, sir, there were a few moments I just sat there. Didn't know what the hell was going on. Then I went to render first aid to Mr Struthers.'

'Mmm.' Chisolm rolled his pen between finger and thumb. 'Was he faking it, would you say?'

'Hard to say, sir. I put him in the recovery position, and…'

'Why did you think it necessary to summon an ambulance?'

'I didn't, sir. That was Struthers' solicitor. Insisted upon it. He claimed his client had a panic attack. "On account of our mishandling of the interview process". Those are the exact words he used.'

Chisolm tapped the end of the pen on the desktop. 'Quite.'

He paused. 'Did they keep him in?'

'Who?'

'Struthers, you idiot.'

'Yes, sir, I checked. Detained overnight for observation.'

'Christ.' Chisolm chucked the pen the length of the room. 'We've got a full fucking cast.'

'I'm not with you, sir.'

'Up at Foresterhill. Husband. Wife. And Bobby Brannigan for good measure. All we need now is for that fucker Gilruth to meet with a mishap and we'll be able to present a full fucking pantomime.'

Brian studied the carpet.

'Get out,' Chisolm barked.

'Sir.' Brian leapt to his feet. He shot out of the room, pulling the door to behind him. With hurried steps he made for the male toilets. All of a sudden, he had a desperate urge to pee.

Maybe

Maggie stood in the big bay window. Through dirt-smeared glass, the front garden looked more uncared-for than ever. The privet hedge sprouted with new growth, the borders were choked, the lawn a patchwork of moss. She made a mental note to haul the old lawnmower out of the garage and at least cut the grass. As soon as the weather turned, she procrastinated. It was supposed to be spring, but the north-east had been battered for weeks by squalls of rain. She wouldn't have to address the grass anytime soon.

Her gaze dropped to the big chair. Time was, she'd have found it a comfort, conjuring George sitting there with his newspaper after their evening meal. For over a year, that mental image had lent Maggie strength. Now, it had begun to dissipate, her husband's burly figure dissolving, somehow, into the fabric. These days, all she felt was guilt: guilt that she'd talked him into resigning from the force, guilt that her children had been left without a father, guilt that, despite her best efforts, she was no nearer to restoring his good name.

The doorbell shattered her reverie. Maggie took one last, lingering look at the chair and walked quickly to the front door.

'Oh.' She took a step backward. 'It's you.'

'Seems to be.' Allan Chisolm was suaveness itself in his smart charcoal suit. 'Are you going to invite me in?'

'Yes.' She beckoned, blushing. There was something about the man that she found unsettling. Something dark, contained, almost dangerous.

She stepped aside, sensing the heft of him as he brushed past her, catching the faintest whiff of aftershave. 'Have a seat, won't you?' She followed him into the sitting room and indicated the settee, but remained standing. Gritting her teeth, she readied herself for what she knew was coming.

'Your client, Sheena Struthers…' he began.

'Don't tell me,' she jumped in. 'I've already heard.' She brushed a weary hand across her brow. 'I've been taken for a complete mug.'

'That's not entirely the case. It would appear this whole business emanated from your client's fragile emotional state. But then it took on a life of its own.'

'I don't understand.'

'The allegations made by your client are not entirely without foundation, the fall in particular. Added to that, we have evidence of internet searches on Gordon Struthers' computer for so-called date-rape drugs, an order subsequently placed…'

Stunned, Maggie stuttered, 'What's going to happen now?'

'Precious little, I fear. Too many imponderables. There's a question mark over who bought those drugs. Added to which…' He sighed. 'Even if we manage to bring a case against Gordon Struthers, I think, given the background, your client may not prove a reliable witness.'

Maggie had to agree. She didn't respond.

'Plus, there's always the possibility she'll refuse to press charges. in cases like these, women rarely do.'

Maggie's shoulders slumped. 'All that time and effort for nothing.' She grimaced. 'Yours and mine.'

'I'm used to it. But you mustn't take it personally.' The inspector's voice was full of concern. 'Nobody could have predicted…'

'You're wrong. I told my partner.'

'Partner?' His eyes flashed alarm bells.

'Business partner. I told Wilma – time and again I told her Sheena Struthers was crying for help. But Wilma wouldn't listen. And I dug my heels in.' She looked daggers at him. 'Too damn proud. And look where it's got me.'

'Come, now.' He rose from the settee, made to move towards her.

'Don't.' She held up her hand. 'I can do without your sympathy, especially after…'

He offered a wry smile. 'I tore you off a strip? And not just once.'

'You did,' she shrugged. 'And I deserved all I got. I was finding my feet, you have to understand and…' The tears brimmed over and streamed down her cheeks. 'We all make mistakes. Even you.' She met his eyes in mute appeal.

'I'm not some automaton, you know.' His voice softened, but he kept his distance. 'I have feelings. Strong feelings.' His steel-grey eyes sought hers. 'But in my position, I have to maintain a distance, remain objective.'

'I know. And I understand. It was the same with George.' She cast a sideways glance at the big chair. 'He internalised so much stuff. It's just, I'm always s-so tired,' she hiccupped. 'I've got such a lot on my shoulders – the house, the kids, the agency – and to tell the t-truth I can't cope.'

'Mrs Laird.' He crossed the room to stand beside her.

She raised her face to him, uncomprehending.

Then: 'Maggie.' He enfolded her in his arms. 'There.' Gently, he kissed her hair. 'There.'

Involuntarily, she stiffened.

His grip tightened. 'Don't cry.'

Despite herself, she yielded to his embrace.

It's only for a minute, she rebuked herself, *then*… Then what? Her sobs started anew.

'Trust me.' He planted a kiss on her forehead. 'Everything's going to be alright.'

A rush of happiness engulfed her. She looked up, met his earnest gaze. And for the first time in many months Maggie thought maybe – just maybe – everything really would work out.

Abruptly, he pulled away. 'I'm sorry,' he muttered. 'I shouldn't have done that.'

'No,' she replied, confused. 'It's okay.'

'It's not okay.' Allan Chisolm raised a supplicant hand. 'I overstepped the mark.'

Maggie had a wild urge to grab hold of his hand. Too late. She watched it stray to the knot of his tie, hover for a moment, then drop to his side.

The inspector backed off and resumed his place on the settee.

Coward! She seethed with frustration. Just when she'd reconciled herself to a possible future with Brian, she'd let someone else sneak into the frame. She'd had it all worked out. A gentle courtship: drinks, pictures, dinner. If they got on, Brian could move in with her. Except… Out of the corner of her eye she could see the chair. Wouldn't that sort of life set her back to where she'd left off? Brian was a decent guy but, like George, content to settle for the *status quo*. Maggie wanted more. She'd always wanted more, but the thirst was stronger, now she'd had a taste of independence.

'Whilst I'm here…' Chisolm's voice broke the silence.

Maggie pulled herself together. 'Brannigan?' she asked, eager for good news. Shattered as she was by this latest turn of events, she mustn't lose sight of her quest.

'No change there, I'm afraid.' A muscle worked in Chisolm's jaw. 'It could be a while yet before they're able to predict an outcome.' His face brightened. 'There is some slight progress, however, on the other matter.'

'Is that right?' Dismissive voice. Maggie assumed Chisolm was referring to the Struthers case.

'Sergeant Craigmyle.' He cleared his throat. 'Ex-Sergeant Craigmyle… paid us a visit yesterday.'

'Oh?' Maggie noted, with a pang of regret, that Allan Chisholm had reverted to police speak. 'He did?' Her mind took a leap, a giant leap. 'In connection with?' Her heart was thudding so hard, her breaths so short, her mouth so dry… she staggered to the big chair and sat down heavily.

'James Craigmyle has given a formal statement confirming it was he, not your husband, who switched off the tape recording that contributed to the collapse of a major trial.'

Happy Valley

'Christ.' Wilma settled herself in a conservatory chair. She reached for her glass. 'It's been some year.'

'Year?' Maggie queried. 'We're not even halfway through.'

'Feels like a feckin year,' her friend retorted. 'Seems a bloody age since we were through the house drinking champagne.'

'I'll hand you that,' Maggie conceded.

'Still,' Wilma took a greedy slurp, 'this'll do the job.'

Maggie raised her glass in a toast.

'We've fair had some turn-ups,' Wilma grinned.

Maggie ducked. And all down to her. She hoped Wilma wasn't trying to rub her nose in it.

'All the same,' Wilma rattled on, oblivious, 'we're getting there, are we not?'

Grudgingly: 'You could say that.'

'Oh, come on, Maggie.' Wilma took another swallow. 'Lighten up.'

'All I meant was,' Maggie clarified, 'it's been a mixed bag: the fraud business taking a dip, the...'

'It's no surprise insurance companies would rather settle than pay a PI.'

'No, but...'

'And the downturn only affects the small stuff. They'll still contest the big claims.'

'Maybe,' she responded dourly. 'But their business will go to the well-established agencies.'

'Still and all,' Wilma argued, 'look at the corporate clients you've signed up. We've a solid list now, bringing in steady money, month in, month out.'

'Thank God for that.' Maggie breathed a sigh of relief. 'Keeps the wolf from the door. And you've been doing a great job, Wilma, mopping up everything that's thrown at you, and never a word of complaint.'

Wilma swelled with pride. 'Well, then.'

'It's just...' Maggie's voice wobbled.

Wilma shot out of her chair. 'What's up, pal?' She bent to her friend.

'I feel so bad,' Maggie said. 'These past months, I've taken my eye off the ball.'

'Don't be daft.' Wilma patted Maggie's head as if she were a small child.

She raised a distraught face. 'I'm not being daft. I did a body-swerve,' she grimaced. 'First with Sheena...' She broke off. 'Come to think on it, I haven't heard anything more on that front. Have you?'

Wilma gave her a sideways look. 'I might have passed her door, just on the off-chance, stuck my head in.'

'And?'

'She was sitting up in bed – quite the thing – reading a cruise brochure.'

Maggie flushed scarlet. 'I don't bloody believe it. That poor man...'

Wilma cut her short. 'Gordon Struthers was the devil incarnate last time we spoke.'

'That was then. But Brian told me...'

'Hold your horses.' Wilma held up a hand. 'Thought you and Brian weren't speaking.'

'We're not. Well...' Maggie's cheeks were still tinged with pink. 'We are, but only just. Anyhow, Brian rang me up.'

'Thought he was courting. Didn't you tell me he had some wee bint...?'

'Yes.' It was Maggie's turn to interrupt. 'Megan, the civilian officer I met in the Wild Boar. They had a couple of dates, but it didn't work out. Brian said she was far too young. Couldn't talk about anything but Facebook and pop music. That's why he rang me: to apologise.'

'For going on a couple of dates? Christ, Maggie, didn't I tell you?

Fellow's mad for you.'

'He was quite upset, right enough,' Maggie said, her face a study in confusion.

'But, back to Gordon Struthers.' Wilma changed the subject. 'Did you get anything juicy on that front?'

'Only that, according to Brian, the man's suffering what is tantamount to a complete nervous breakdown. He still maintains his innocence, continues to profess his undying love for Sheena, won't hear the least criticism of her.'

'Where is he now?'

'In a private clinic at Westhill.'

Wilma hooted. 'While she's up the road planning her next holiday?'

Maggie's mouth turned down. 'Be serious.'

'I am being serious. If you hadn't convinced me Sheena Struthers has been the victim of sexual abuse, I'd have put money on she set him up.'

'Don't be ridiculous.'

Wilma squared up. 'Ridiculous, is it? If you'd seen the look I got when I appeared at her door, you wouldn't be arguing.'

'What sort of look?'

'Like she was giving me the finger.'

'Oh, come on,' Maggie reasoned. 'You're imagining things.'

'Is that right? If you ask my opinion, those "incidents" of hers were a fuckin fairy tale.' She coughed. 'Excuse my language. There's never been a shred of evidence to back them up.'

'That's not true. According to Allan…'

'Ooh,' Wilma trilled, 'it's "Allan" now.'

Maggie ignored this. 'The police have their suspicions with regard to that fall.'

'Serves Sheena right, say I. She comes to us with a load of bollocks and it comes back on her. Like a… a… what do you call it?'

'Self-fulfilling prophecy?' Maggie offered.

'That's the one.'

'Sheena may have intended to send her husband a warning,' Maggie contended. 'And she may have exaggerated some…'

'Some?' Wilma cut in. 'Woman's a total fantasist.'

'How about the drugs? They're real enough.'

'She could have ordered them.'

'Oh, come on,' Maggie groaned. 'Next thing you'll be trying to persuade me the poor woman poisoned herself.'

'She may well have done. If she knew her way around the husband's computer, she could as easy have ordered up those drugs and overdosed herself.'

'Really? And put herself in a coma?'

'You're right, Maggie.' Sly look. 'Again. Faking your own attempted murder is ludicrous, not to mention risky. Woman near died.'

'There you are, then.'

'On the other hand, she mebbe meant to top up them sleeping pills, make it look like a murder attempt gone wrong. Think on it. If Gordon Struthers were to get done for attempted murder, she'd be footloose and fancy free. Loaded an all.'

Maggie didn't respond. Sheena Struthers might well be facing life as a single woman. But it was no catwalk being on your own, solvent or not.

'Or she could have done it to scare the shite out of him and make him back off. But now you've got me thinking,' Wilma rattled on. 'Them drugs, the husband could have ordered them up right enough. Except…' Pregnant pause. 'For another purpose.'

'An affair, you mean?'

'That, or to date-rape a bunch of other women. From what I hear he's a sneaky wee bastard.'

'There's no evidence,' Maggie insisted.

'Or he may not have meant to actually kill Sheena.'

'I see where you're going. Just ramp up the abuse to maximise his dominance over her.'

Wilma grinned. 'Would you listen to the pair of us? Proper

detectives, are we no?'

'I wish,' Maggie came back. 'There are so many possibilities my head is spinning.'

'Bottom line is, it's all about control. And that will never change, not in a million years. It's just that nowadays it tends to be less physical. Some of the time, at any rate.' Winks. 'We won't mention my Darren. But think on your pal, Ros.'

'Agreed. Control has many and devious manifestations.' Maggie paused. 'Looks like we'll never know how Sheena Struthers ended up in a near-fatal coma.'

'That's the long and short of it. There's only two folk know the whole truth, Gordon and Sheena.'

Maggie pulled a face. 'Who knows what goes on in a marriage? But to get back to what I was saying, I let myself get blown off track, first with Sheena, then with Ros. I wasted so much time. Precious time that could have been spent on the business. Or on my kids.' Rueful look. 'I've neglected them. And I've taken advantage of you.'

Wilma grinned. 'As if.'

'It's true. You've been carrying the can, Wilma. Right from day one – I see that now. When we started out, it was you doing all the computer research, you bolstering me up. Then, since the turn of the year, you've been working all hours.' She broke off. 'If you hadn't been put upon, Ian and you would never have fallen out.'

'Now you're really havering,' Wilma scoffed.

'Far from it. It's made me realise you're the real star in this partnership. You're more practical than me. Faster on your feet. Quicker to identify problems. And you go straight for the solution. Seems like it's you should be running the show, not me.'

Wilma straightened. She stood, arms akimbo, feet apart. 'And what would happen, do you think, if I rolled up to a meeting with a big fancy firm of solicitors? They'd take one look and show me the door.'

Maggie eyed the big woman. With her mane of blonde hair crowning a more-than-ample bosom and wide hips, she struck a commanding pose.

'They'd love you,' she chuckled at Wilma's faux-fierce expression.

'What are we like?' Wilma chortled. 'Scrapping with one another like a pair of flyweights.'

The first bottle of wine lay empty on the floor. The second was well down.

'Speaking of which,' Maggie slurred, 'how's that coach of yours, Joe?'

'Haven't the foggiest,' Wilma giggled. 'There hasn't been time to get to the boxing gym.' She grinned. 'At least, that's my excuse.'

Maggie stuck her nose in her glass. Another thing for her to feel guilty about.

They sat for a few minutes in silence, then Wilma piped up. 'Do you mind thon time we were talking about our USP?'

'Vaguely,' Maggie replied.

'And I said we were like thon insurance company, Sheila's Wheels, only not?'

Maggie laughed. 'I remember that bit.'

'Well,' Wilma announced, 'I've been thinking and thinking…'

'And?'

'I've decided we're more like them two on the telly.'

Maggie fought to focus. 'What two?'

'Them detectives.'

'Cagney and Lacey?' Maggie guessed.

'Nah!' Wilma scoffed. 'They're ancient.'

'Scott and Bailey? They're more recent.'

'Too boring.'

Maggie pondered for a bit, then, 'How about Thelma and Louise?'

'Christ, no,' Wilma retorted. 'We haven't driven off a cliff.' She topped up their glasses. 'Not yet, anyhow.'

'Some days it feels like it,' Maggie said, with feeling.

'I know,' Wilma agreed. 'Some nights I'm that tired I could sleep on a clothesline.' She scratched her head. 'I mind, now. It was *Happy Valley*.'

'What was?' Maggie puzzled.

'Them two detectives.'

'They weren't *both* detectives,' Maggie countered. 'One was a police sergeant, I'll give you that. But the other one – the sister – she was a civilian, an alcoholic at that.'

'I *was* close,' Wilma quipped. 'We're near enough alcoholics ourselves.'

'True.' Maggie frowned, eyeing the near empty second bottle. Her alcohol intake had climbed steadily since she and Wilma went into business. Worse, it showed no sign of letting up. 'But we're not sisters.'

'Granted.' Wilma planted a wet kiss on her cheek. 'But we might as well be.'

Acknowledgments

To my publisher, Sara Hunt, for her expertise and thoughtfulness. My heartfelt thanks.

For patient and skilful editing, Russel D. McLean and Angie Harms.

For specialist input, Professor Dame Sue Black and Dr Craig McKenzie of Dundee University's Centre for Anatomy and Human Identification, Professor James Grieve, Emeritus Professor of Forensic Pathology at the University of Aberdeen, Ronald Manning of Aberdeen Public Mortuary, Sergeant Teresa Clark of Police Scotland and former Detective Sergeant Bill Ogilvie.

My appreciation goes to the reviewers, bloggers, booksellers and librarians who have brought Maggie and Wilma to a wider audience, and to the many readers who have taken this unlikely crime duo to their hearts.

To my family and friends; what can I say? There would be no Harcus & Laird without your unwavering support.

And to the good folk of Aberdeen, with whose city and Doric tongue I have taken liberties – my apologies. The events in this novel are entirely fictional and inaccuracies wholly mine.

About the author

Following a career in business, Claire MacLeary gained an MLitt with Distinction from the University of Dundee. Her short stories have been published in various magazines and anthologies. She lived for some years in Aberdeen, and subsequently in Fife, before returning to her native Glasgow. Her first novel, *Cross Purpose,* was longlisted for the McIlvanney Award for Scottish Crime Book of the Year 2017.

Harcus & Laird's next case...

When his wife goes missing and the police can find no evidence of criminality, a distraught husband turns to Harcus & Laird.

But what would it take for a young mother to abandon her children? That's the question Maggie and Wilma ask themselves.

With the clock ticking and the trail going cold, the private investigators are drawn into a world of women's refuges and rough sleepers, putting their own safety at risk.

Will Debbie be found?

And will she be found alive?